GRIT

J.M. WALKER

Cover Design: Rachel Mizer with Shoutlines Designs
Formatting: Jo-Anna Walker with Just write. Creations
Editing and Proofreading: Wendi Lynn and Katheryn
Kiden with Ready. Set. Edit
Editing: Fiona Campbell - fionalorne@gmail.com

ISBN: 978-1-329-97465-4

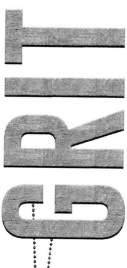

THESE VEINS ARE EMPTY
CUZ THEY CAME AND TOOK IT ALL AWAY
IT'S MY REDEMPTION
BUT I COULDN'T FIT THE MOLD
I WALKED A STRAY, I WALK AWAY
FROM THE BLOOD OF YESTERDAY
I'M NOT AFRAID...

-DEAD CELEBRITY STATUS

DEDICATION

To the woman on that beautiful
motorcycle on that hot summer day,
wearing your colors proud…

This book is for you.

ACKNOWLEDGEMENTS

First, I would like to thank the women who ride. Because of you, this series has been born and I hope I do you justice.

To my husband, the love of my life, the man who puts up with my crazy antics. I love you more as each day passes. Thank you for being you and for loving me for me.

My family and my friends. Without you none of this would be possible. None of this would be real.

Rachel Mizer with Shoutlines Designs. Thank you once again for bringing my story to life with your beautiful covers. xx

My editors: Wendi Lynn and Katheryn Kiden with Ready, Set, Edit and Fiona Campbell. You ladies helped perfect this story. My beta readers, every single one of you have helped make this story what it is.

Twinsie Talk Book Reviews: Thank you for being with me since the beginning. Before the first book and even before the first word. You ladies are my sisters and I love you to pieces.

Christine Stanley!!!!!!! My POOPY!!! Girl, you are my other half. My EVERYTHING! Thank you for all that you do. Thank you. Thank you thank you thank you. #lovemesomebutt

Tammi Plummer, my PA, I couldn't do this without you. You keep me sane. You keep me grounded. Thank you. #mysemicolon.

My Jems, my sisters. You help me stay true to myself. Your support and encouragement mean more to me than you'll ever know.

To all of the blogs and authors! Thank you. Thank you for helping me along the way. Thank you for sharing my posts, putting up with my questions, having the patience that I lack. I don't have enough words for any of you but here are two. Thank. You.

And lastly, my readers. Because of you, I keep going. Because of your messages, your shares, just saying hi, it makes me proud of what I do. I can't wait to bring you more stories like this one. Thank you to everyone who has read Grit already or who are planning to read. I took a risk with this series but without risk, there is no reward. I'm a go big or go home kind of person and this series? It will be the biggest.

J.M. Walker

XX

J.M. WALKER

ONE

—jay

AS I stared at my reflection, I wondered where I fucked up. Deep, green pools of uncertainty, not knowing whether I was coming or going. I was stuck. In time. On a shithole of a planet. With nowhere to run or turn, I went through the motions, passing each day like it was my last. Something was off. I didn't know why. I didn't know what. I couldn't explain it, but I knew that I needed...something. Anything to get me out of my head.

A deep groan rumbled through the room, the sound coming from the bed a few feet away. I waited. For it to affect me in some way. For my heart to flutter or skip a beat. My palms to sweat. My stomach to somersault like I heard so many women talking about. Nothing. Not even a wanting need pulling me toward the sound.

I knew going to bed with the guy the night before that he wasn't *the one*, but I had hoped for at least some sort of attraction. But he was just a fuck. A good lay. And he wasn't even that good. My *oh my* and *God, yes* were just to amuse him. I didn't even get an orgasm out of it. The selfish bastard he was, cared about one person: himself.

I glanced over at him again. His tanned back rose and fell with each breath, the ink on his skin becoming more pronounced in the morning sun. God, even his tattoos were lame. *Who gets armbands anymore?*

What was the guy's name? Jeff? Alex? Bob? Hell if I knew. He was supposed to be a warm body to satisfy my craving, but that turned to shit when he ignored what I wanted. What I had been *itching* for.

A soft knock sounded on the door, pulling me from my thoughts. "Yeah?" I called out, stepping into my black, leather pants.

"Jay, the girls are here," Maxine Stanton, my best friend, said as she glanced in the room. Her gaze passed between me and the guy in the bed, a small sigh leaving her mouth. She shook her head, disappearing down the hall.

"Hey, man." I kicked the guy's foot. "Wakey, wakey."

"Shit. What time is it?" he asked, rolling over onto his back.

For a moment, I allowed my gaze to travel down the length of his hard body. Muscles rippled over his bones. His morning wood jutted forth between his legs, pitching a tent under the white sheet.

"Why don't you satisfy Mr. Happy before you kick me out of your bed?" He made a point of cupping himself, gyrating his hips for added effect.

I rolled my eyes and threw his clothes on the bed. "Sorry, sweetheart. This was a one-time thing."

"Why?" He sat up and pulled on his t-shirt.

"Rules." Little did he know that he wasn't in *my* bed. No one slept in my bed except for me. And even then, it wasn't often. With the shit going on around me, who had time for sleep? I also didn't fuck a guy again who had a pet name for his dick. How old were we? Ten?

"Jay, come on. Give a little." The guy pouted. And I mean full-on, bottom lip quivering and sticking out and shit. *God. Who the hell had I spent the night with?*

"Get out."

"Oh yeah." He licked his lips. "Tell me what to do, baby. You know I like it."

"Ugh. Douche. Get the fuck out." I threw his boots at him.

"Ow. Shit." He rose from the bed and finished getting dressed. "Listen. If you ever feel the need to dominate—"

"Get *out*." I stabbed a finger toward the door. I was sick of the guys who latched on just because they got between my legs. I was not a conquest, but at times I felt like they had all teamed up, placing bets on who could get me to break first. Well guess what, losers? It wasn't going to happen.

"You know…" The guy came up to me. "You're a bitch."

"Yup. I know." So original.

"Perhaps if you warmed up a little, you wouldn't be single," he grumbled.

I opened the door just as Maxine came into view. She raised an eyebrow, her gaze darting between the guy and me.

"Maybe you should stop trying to get people to change who don't want to," I told him.

"Whatever."

I followed him out into the hallway and gave a little wave.

Before he rounded the corner, he flipped me the bird.

"Jackass," I muttered.

"You sure know how to pick 'em."

My back stiffened at the jab. "Yeah, well, a girl needs a little lovin' now and again."

Maxine, in all her feisty glory, threw her head back and laughed. "Right. Because you can't get it

12

GRIT (KING'S HARLOTS, #1)

anywhere else. Two hands don't cut it anymore, do they?"

I hooked an arm around her shoulders and kissed her cheek. "How about four hands?" I asked, waggling my eyebrows.

She elbowed me in the ribs, her laughter deepening. "*Please*. You're too fucked up for my taste. Besides, I don't have what you want."

Feigning a sigh, even though her words stung, I placed the back of my hand against my forehead. "No one does."

Max shook her head. "No. You're just too damn picky."

Maybe.

"Let's go." She clapped her hands together. "Duty calls."

I groaned. "Great."

She stopped dead in her tracks, her bright-blue gaze meeting mine. "You good?"

"Yup." I scrubbed a hand down my face, tapping my cheeks to bring life back into myself. Drinking on a weeknight was not good for the soul or mind. I swore I was losing more brain cells as I got older. *Shouldn't I be done with this shit*? I was almost thirty. I needed to get it together. Or find a man who could do it for me. I laughed.

"Are you sure you're okay?" Max's brows narrowed.

I nodded. I didn't know what was wrong, but I just wasn't feeling it. King's Harlots was my life. My world. My existence. I lived and breathed them. We were the first female motorcycle club in the country. That's right. An all-woman MC. Born and raised into the lifestyle, I grew up around bikers. Those ladies were my family. My best friends. My sisters.

"Ready?" Max asked when we reached the double set of wooden doors that opened into a large room. She had been asking me if I was okay for the past couple of weeks. Did things change? Did I show all of my feelings on my face? I bit back a scoff. No. I didn't. I never did. It was the easiest way a person could protect themselves. I should have been born a man. All of those feelings and shit were not for me. Max could see right past my hard exterior. We just never talked about it. She knew not to press or else she would end up with my fist in her face.

"I'm always ready," I told her.

"Just so you know, we *are* here for you." She squeezed my shoulder. "No matter what."

"I'm fine, Max. Promise." I took my seat at the head of the long table.

The girls—*my* girls—filed into the room. They talked amongst themselves. Max, as Vice President, sat to my left.

I cleared my throat, giving them time to settle down. It had been a couple of days since we met last. Thanksgiving had just passed, and I swore I ate a fucking cow.

"Business. What do we have?" I leaned back in the chair, crossing my ankle over the opposite knee.

"I have a showing at the art gallery on Friday night," Max's sapphire eyes twinkled. "It's supposed to be busy. Or, well…I'm hoping it is, anyways." She was our famous local artist. Growing up in our small town of Greenville, Ohio, there wasn't much to do whenever you were bored, so she started creating things.

"Are you displaying the piece you've been working on for the past couple of months?" Brogan Tapp beamed.

"I am." Max grinned. "Feels like I've been working on that shit for, like, ever."

I laughed. Max had spent a couple of summers in California and picked up their overuse of the word, 'like'. It was rather annoying, and she did it to drive me insane. That was why I loved her, though.

14

"Like, I am so *excited* for you," I added for effect. Laughter erupted around the table.

"Shut up." She pouted, her lips turning up at the corners into a smile.

"All right." I waited a beat before continuing, knowing the next topic of discussion would be heavy. "Meeka."

Our quietest member's eyes bored into mine; she sat furthest from me. Meeka Cline didn't say anything. She never did. She listened. But her big brown eyes told all. Years of pain. Heartache. We didn't know her complete story. We just knew there was one.

"How are things underground?"

"I'm getting in," she muttered. "But my connection isn't trusting."

"Understandable." We had some girls who went missing in our small town a week before and the cops weren't doing a damn thing about it. The reason: the females were on the lower end of society. No one cared about them. They came from poor families or worse. "What's your connection saying?" I asked, knowing the answer.

"Nothing. I can't get past the whole me *not* being a cop ordeal." She looked down at herself. "Do I *look* like a cop?"

Several nods and grunts resounded around the table in agreement. We wore leather, shitkickers if we saw fit, and our attitudes on our sleeves. If we *were* cops, we were fucked up ones. "Anything else?"

Meeka chewed her bottom lip. I knew right then she was hiding something. It was her tell. We all had one. Max would curl her hair in her fingers. When Brogan laughed, it became uncontrollable. And mine? Well, no one had the balls to tell me what mine was.

Being the president, I needed to know what was going down. With my town. My girls. The basic ins and outs of their daily lives. I never expected to know every single detail. It helped. There was such a thing as privacy. It wasn't like I gave them details of my own life. Not that I had much to hide. I was a pretty straightforward person. Even though I knew Max would love for me to spill every piece of information.

"I'm working through…some stuff." Meeka's cheeks reddened.

"All right." I pointed at her and let my gaze slide around the table, meeting each pair of eyes. "I won't press, Meeka." *Not yet at least.* "But I want you to know that I *will* find out what's going on."

She gripped the arms of the chair. "I know."

"I'll leave it alone for now. Second thing. Something's not sitting right with me." And it wasn't the alcohol that I had consumed the night before. I gave myself a shake. "I don't want any of you alone when you're out in public. You go to take a piss, bring one of us with you."

"What's going on?" Brogan frowned, crossing her arms under her full chest.

That was just it. I had no idea what was going on. How would I tell the girls that without sounding like a loon? "I don't know." Well, honesty would have to work. The women going missing and the law not doing a damn thing about it was rubbing me the wrong way.

"Are you worried, Prez?" Meeka sat forward, her brows narrowing.

Was I? Not for us. But the men that tried to shake up the tiny town that we lived in should have been. Being an all-woman MC had its hard times and good times. No one took us seriously because instead of having a dick, we had pussies and having a vagina made you weak. *As-fucking-if.*

"I'm concerned for the well-being of these women." Who knew what was being done to them? "Any word on the street of their ages?"

Brogan hesitated. "They range from ages twelve to eighteen."

"What the *fuck*?" I yelled, my heart pumping. "You're telling me these women are just girls? Why the hell didn't I know about this? Fuck *me*." They were just girls. Someone's daughter. Sister. Baby. God, the people who took them should be shot and pissed on.

Squeezing the bridge of my nose, I closed my eyes and took a couple of deep breaths. Images forced their way into my mind.

Her. So many years ago. Blue eyes. So bright. Shining. They twinkled. I would have given anything to see them again. To tell her that I loved her. That I had missed her—every single damn day of my life.

"Jay?" Max touched my arm. "Are you all right?"

I jumped at the soft contact, pulling my arm back. "I'm fine. Just…tell me more."

Meeka hesitated before continuing. "Well…" She took a breath. "I'm in the works with some people."

"Who?" I asked when she didn't give any more information. "Meeka."

Her back stiffened. "I… The FBI."

"Are you fucking kidding me right now?"

"Why, Meeka?"

The girls badgered her with question after question, but I didn't say anything. Our eyes locked. I knew she was waiting for me to explode. I had been known to be a bit of a hothead. Under normal circumstances, it could have been the case but I knew Meeka—she didn't make rash decisions without thinking it through. Something was getting to her. If she wouldn't say with the girls around, then I would get her to tell just me.

"Girls, stop," I barked.

They silenced, mumbling to themselves. I knew where they were coming from but I had to remain calm. Meeka had a reason for what she was doing. Whether she was in trouble or helping us find the girls on her own—whatever help she could provide—I would take it.

"Why do you feel the need to work with the FBI?" I braced myself for the response being that it had to do with a man.

She shrugged. "They approached me."

"Approached you. What the hell are you talking about, Meeka?" Although we were part of a motorcycle club, we were still human beings. Meeka was shy. If it meant spending my last breath, I would make her open up or find her a man who could do just that. It would not surprise me if she was still a virgin. *Tangent, Jay.*

"I…" Her breath caught, her shoulders slumping. "I want to help. I want to find these girls just like the rest of you, and this is the way I know how."

"Can you all give us a moment?" When the girls didn't move, I knuckle rapped the table. "*Now.* Please."

They huffed, grumbling to themselves, and left us alone.

Max hung back.

"Max." I nudged her out of her chair. "Go."

"Are you kidding me right now?"

"No. Now get. Shoo." I smacked her on the ass, trying to get her to hustle out of there, but she took her sweet ol' time.

When she reached the door, she opened her mouth to say something but sighed instead.

Once Meeka and I were alone, I moved to sit beside her and grabbed her hand. I tried pouring my strength into that small touch. It wasn't much, but I wanted her to know that whatever she was doing, whatever was going on in her world, I was there for her. The King's Harlots were there. For her. We were one, and it would always be that way no matter what.

"Jay, please don't make me say anything." Her chin quivered. "I can't. Not yet."

"Just tell me this." My heart raced. "Are you in trouble? Do I need to kill someone for you? Rip off a dick or two?"

She laughed, wiping away the single tear rolling down her cheek. "I just have some stuff going on, and I don't want to involve the club just yet. I'm not trying to keep anything from you, but for your protection, I need you to leave it alone for right now. Please."

Everything in me told me to press. That little voice inside of me told me to demand for her to give me answers. But the solemn look on her face proved she had been defeated. By what or who, I wasn't sure. "Fine. I'll let go of it for now, Meeka, but if any of us gets hurt by your lack of information, I will do more than remove your patch." I released her and headed to the large bay window overlooking the group of motorcycles we rode.

"I understand," she whispered.

"Tell the other girls they can come back in."

"Okay," she said to my back. "Are we good?"

"Yup." *Just fucking dandy.* I loved Meeka, but I loved the club more.

TWO

ANGEL

THE SKIN of the stripper glistened, drops of sweat covering her body as she moved around the stage. She was limber and agile, holding onto the pole like it was her lifeline. Like it would keep her safe from the eyes staring back at her. As if it would stop the harm from someone following her home at night. If she strips, she must put out, right? *Wrong.*

She glanced at me often, licking her lips, grazing a hand over her breasts. Trying to get a reaction from me, she moved to the end of the stage where I sat in pervert's row.

I rolled my eyes and shook my head. It was the same game we played every week. I would go out with the boys, sit in pervert's row, and ignore her advances. According to the guys, sitting at the back of the club meant we wouldn't get noticed by the ladies at all. I swore at times I was friends with children. The stripper would flirt, and I would pretend to pay attention to her when I would rather be anywhere but there. Not that I didn't find her attractive. She was beautiful, but in a plastic kind of way. If you went for that sort of thing then by all means have at it. But me? I liked my women real. Strong. Toned but curvy. Enough meat that I had something to hold onto when I was pounding into their tight body.

"Angel, my man, you gonna hit that?" My best friend for years, Dale Michaels, slurred his words, clapping a hand on my shoulder. He was hard as motherfucking nails, but get alcohol in him and he turned into a horny teenager.

It was the same shit, different day with him. The stripper would flirt. I would turn her down. And Dale would jump all over it. Same fucking thing every single damn day of my life. I needed a change. With me. With life in general. God, I needed a do-over.

I shook my head and watched him jump to his feet.

The stripper grinned when she stepped off the stage and walked right into his arms. Her gaze flashed my way like it always did, but that time, it held something different. Darkened with sadness. Disappointment? I wasn't sure. Didn't matter. I was getting too old for that shit. My dick needed something more than just a tight hole to fill. As much as I liked pussy, I was never satisfied.

Tilting back my beer, I took a swig, embracing the coolness of the carbonated liquid. It settled in the pit of my gut, sending a warmth over my skin. Two beers later and it still did nothing to mask the emptiness in my chest. The hole I needed to fix, filling it with something other than alcohol. A woman. A soft body wrapped around mine, opening to the deep thrusts—

"You alone, big guy?"

I glanced up at the smooth feminine voice. "No." Lies. All lies. Rising to my feet, I threw a twenty on the table and popped the collar of my leather jacket. Ignoring the stares of the woman who was trying to get a piece from me, I made my way to the exit. It was the same routine I had followed for the past couple of weeks. Go to the strip club, drink a little, watch my friends get shitfaced, and leave. What a fucking way to live out my days.

Heading to my black SUV, I leaned my head from side to side. A slight twinge of pain slid down the length of my spine when the tendons popped and cracked. My palms tingled. Images of a woman arching beneath me as my hands smacked her rear swam into my mind like liquid honey. I craved the heat of flesh reddening under my touch. Blood rushed to the tip of my dick, straining against my pants. Adjusting myself, I bit back a hiss. *Fuck,* I needed to get laid.

My phone rang, interrupting my thoughts as I slid into my car. "Yeah."

"We got some shit, Boss."

I squeezed the bridge of my nose, mentally counting to ten. "What kind of shit?"

Asher Donovan inhaled a sharp breath. "Uh… Well, we're at this motorcycle clubhouse, fixing the roof, and—"

"Clubhouse?" All I could picture was a fort in a tree or a box like we used to have when we were kids.

"Motorcycle club," he added. "Anyway, the roof is crap, and we don't have the supplies. But the president is adamant we get it fixed today."

"How the hell is that supposed to happen if we don't have the supplies?"

"I have no fucking idea."

"I'm on my way," I bit out through clenched teeth. I got the address from Asher and threw my phone on the seat beside me. Owning a construction company meant you were God and could get supplies just like that. Sure. Let me just pull them out of my ass. *Please.*

I punched the address into the GPS and saw I was about ten minutes away. Bracing myself for the onslaught of a miserable customer, I gripped the steering wheel tight. I was not in the mood to deal with grumpy employees or demanding—

Well, I'll be damned. Pulling into the driveway of the *clubhouse*, I saw my crew on the roof, working away.

Nothing appeared out of the ordinary. *Rod's Construction* was in full force. "What's going on?" I asked Asher when I slid out of the vehicle.

He gave a curt nod.

All of a sudden, something warm and soft smashed into my face, blinding me. Laughter erupted around me. The scent of vanilla and sugar wafted into my nostrils. I licked my lips, swallowing the sweetness. Cake. Fucking *fuckers*. "Assholes," I growled.

Asher laughed. "Here's a towel."

I grabbed the fabric from him, wiping my face.

"Happy birthday, Boss." Coby Porter clapped a hand on my shoulder. "You needed to get out."

"My birthday was a couple days ago." I had hoped they forgot. "And I was at the strip club," I said, cleaning myself up. "Why didn't you fuckers come there?"

"Yeah. Because that would have worked." Asher rolled his eyes. "You are the hardest person to celebrate a birthday with. Especially your own."

I had my reasons. Birthdays left a bad taste in my mouth. They brought back memories I never wanted to relive. My heart started pounding hard against my rib cage, a cold sweat racing down my spine. A panic attack was getting ready to hit me full-force, but I breathed through it, taking control. Inhale. Exhale. *I have this. I won't let it win.*

Asher raised an eyebrow. "You good, man?"

"Yup." I threw the towel on the table. "So, the owners of this club never had any issues with the roof? All of the supplies are here and you losers made the whole thing up?"

They nodded, wicked grins spreading across their faces.

Of course. "Well, just for that, you guys get to work until this roof is done."

That made the grins disappear.

"*What*? You can't do that."

"We were just playing."

"Asshole."

That last one was Dale. Fucker showed up in the middle of the cake toss. I bet it was his fucking idea. "Serves you all right for trying to shove my birthday down my throat."

"Such a drama queen." Dale punched my arm as he walked by me.

"So, was the stripper a ruse?" I asked, knowing the answer before he gave it.

He winked. "Just like your construction company is."

"It's not a ruse." I rolled my eyes. "It keeps me busy when I'm not in the field. You guys don't mind getting the paychecks, so stop your bitchin'."

"I'm not bitchin'. It's not often you get to smash cake into your boss's face. And the stripper wasn't an act. Besides, who can resist this?" He ran his hands down the length of his body, waggling his eyebrows.

Gag. And that was when I heard it. Laughter. Husky and melodious. Full-bellied and filled with life, not caring in the least if anyone was nearby. The laughter turned into a snort, and it was the cutest fucking thing I ever had the pleasure of listening to. It graced my ears like music to my fucking soul.

Female voices sounded, but I couldn't make out what was being said. Finding myself wanting more of her laugh, I made my way toward the chatter. Hiding behind my SUV, I leaned against the driver door and crossed my arms under my chest and listened.

"Girl, I am ready." A woman laughed.

The tiny hairs on my body vibrated. My dick hardened, jumping to attention. She was the owner of the husky laugh. *Speak. Talk more.*

"Ready for what?" another woman asked.

"To be ravished."

My back stiffened, arousal hitting me square in the nuts. *Well now, this conversation could be interesting.* I shouldn't be eavesdropping... *Fuck it.*

"Didn't that happen last night?"

A soft growl left my lips. My eyes narrowed.

"Please, girl. That was nothing. He was a pussy. A pushover. He... God, he sucked."

"And not in a good way?"

"*Ha,*" the sexy-voiced woman scoffed. "No. I want a man that has no problems telling me what they want. What they need. I want them to crave me. Why do these guys feel the need to ask me for permission before fucking me?"

"Because they're being polite?"

"That's not what I mean. I want a man to throw me up against the wall, kiss the hell out of me, and demand me to beg. I want him to fuck his way into my body like he needs me to live." She sighed, and I was becoming hard as a fucking rock.

"I think most women would love that, but this isn't a romance book. This is real life, honey."

"I know there is a man out there who would have no problems demanding me to my knees."

"Yeah, because *you* would listen," the other woman teased.

She chuckled. "If the right guy came along, I would. I'm not that scary."

The other woman laughed along with her. "If you find this guy, ask him if he has a brother."

I am *that guy. And I* do *have a brother. Three of them, to be exact.*

"Well, this guy does have brothers."

"How do you know that?"

"Because I'm making him up in my head, so he can be whatever I want him to be."

And I would be whatever she wanted. Closing my eyes, I inhaled, memorizing her voice. When I opened them, a wicked grin spread along my face. I would give her everything she wanted. I would rip her open, destroying her body and molding it into what I wanted. Before I even saw her, I wanted her. Her voice pierced straight through me, igniting a passion I had never felt.

"And how do you plan on meeting this guy?"

At that point, the two women rounded the corner, heading toward the crew.

My dick jumped in my jeans at the view before me. The woman, who I guessed was the one dreaming up the perfect man, peered over her shoulder.

Her mouth parted, her eyes darkening. She licked her full lips, giving her head a little shake, and started spouting off orders to Asher.

I couldn't focus on her words as I gazed down the length of her body. A white tank top was snug against her torso, enhancing her full breasts. But what I noticed the most was the skin-tight, black, leather pants that hugged her curves. Her round, heart-shaped ass, no doubt firm, would be perfect in my hands. Her pale skin would redden under my touch. Her flesh bruising as I impaled her body with a roughness I craved. Knee-high shitkickers adorned her feet, and fuck me if she wasn't the hottest thing I had ever seen. Her long red hair was pulled back into a tight ponytail, and I knew without a doubt she could kick my ass. I wondered how hard she trained. Images of us working out together, sweaty and spent, flowed into my mind.

When my gaze slid back up her body, our eyes locked.

Her brows narrowed.

And then she did the unexpected. She walked up to me, her hands on her hips. She was tall for a woman. Still shorter than my 6'5 but tall enough that I didn't feel like a giant.

"You got a problem, asshole?" she demanded, her lips pressing together in a firm line.

The corners of my lips twitched. *Oh yeah. This will be fun.* "Not yet I don't."

"My eyes are in my fucking head. Stop staring at my ass," she bit out, shoving a finger in my chest.

"Well, then you shouldn't wear tight as hell pants if you don't want anyone looking at your beautiful ass."

Her cheeks reddened at the compliment.

Gotcha.

"Don't compliment me. Don't even talk to me," she said between finger jabs.

I grabbed the hand that kept poking me in the chest and pulled her flush against me.

She gasped, her eyes widening at the abrupt movement.

Leaning down, I brushed my nose up the length of her neck and inhaled. Sweet perfume and a hint of something else filled my nose with a delicious scent. "You smell good, princess."

Her back stiffened. "Don't you dare call me *that*; I am *not* your princess."

"Woman, you will be whatever I want you to be," I snarled in her ear, giving it a gentle nip.

She shivered, arching her hips against mine.

"Now why don't you go run along and go shopping or some shit while us men finish fixing the roof?"

"Fuck you, dick."

I swallowed a laugh, knowing she was not the type of woman to go shopping or do any girly shit, for that matter. Pissing her off amused me more than it should. "Oh, I will."

Her breath caught in her throat. She struggled against me, trying to pull from my grip, but my hold tightened.

"I will be the man you fantasize about. I will give your body what it craves." I lowered my voice. "I *will* destroy you."

"Yeah. Right. Have fun jacking off to me tonight."

"Oh, little girl." I turned my head, brushing my mouth along the soft spot under her ear. "I will have you on your knees, begging me to fuck you, and when I do, you'll thank me."

"Please," she scoffed. "I don't thank anyone for sex."

I grinned. "That's because you've never been filled by *my* cock."

A notable shiver trembled through her, and she pushed away from me. She flipped me off and walked back to her friend, hooking her arm in the other woman's.

I watched her leave. Her cheeks were mottled pink. Her neck flushed. Oh, I would have her. And I would fucking make her break. She was the something I needed. I knew it before I saw her. She would thank me; I would make damn sure of it. The Alpha inside of me that had been dormant for so long rose to the challenge. That woman stirred a piece of me I had never felt before. Her shutting me down turned me on even more.

This is going to be one hell of a power play.

THREE

—jay

"WHAT THE hell was that about?" Max asked as we headed back into the clubhouse.

"I have no idea," I grumbled. *Holy balls on a cracker, that guy was hot.* Like, beyond hot. So hot my panties were sure to combust. When he looked at me with those sexy as hell, dark, smoldering eyes, I swore my ovaries exploded. My lady bits did a little happy dance that they were having a reaction from someone who wasn't battery operated.

"I bet he could eat you alive if you let him." Max walked around the bar and pulled two beers out of the fridge, popping the caps off. "You know you're going to go home with him, right?" She placed a bottle on the counter in front of me, waggling her eyebrows.

"And why would I do that? He clearly works with *Rod's Construction.*" I was a little pissed that Asher never told me. I had made it clear that I needed to meet everyone on his team. He never mentioned another worker.

"Just because he works with them doesn't mean you can't have a little bit of fun."

I scoffed. "Not likely." Even though I wanted to. *God, do I ever!* But I wasn't going to admit it to Max or even myself. *Okay, maybe just a little bit to myself.* Every bit? *Just the bits that mattered.* I was fucking losing it. That man had my thoughts scattered and my skin puckering with tiny goose bumps. My skin burned

29

from where he had his grip on my wrist. My ear
tingled from his bite. My belly tightened. No man had
ever made me feel so alive. So wanting with need. So
desperate that I would cut a bitch just to get him to
touch me again. Who the hell knew what he could do
once he was inside of me?

Not. Going. To. Happen.

"Because you want him, and he wants you. Him
with his tanned, smokin' body, and you and your
creamy, pale skin," she said, winking. "You two would
make hot babies."

I rolled my eyes. "In his dreams."

She laughed, shaking her head.

All of a sudden, a loud bang sounded, and an
incredible force threw me off the stool. I landed hard
on the ground, the wind leaving me on a breathless
gasp.

My ears rang, my muscles seized as I tried
reaching around me for something, anything that
would explain what the hell just happened.

Max.

I couldn't see her anywhere. One second we were
talking and laughing, the next I was on the floor. A
tightness gripped my chest whenever I inhaled. Grey
smoke clouded my vision, burning its way into my
retinas. I coughed, trying to free the ache in my lungs,
but it made things worse.

"Max," I croaked, my voice hoarse. Rolling over
onto my stomach, I lifted myself on shaky legs.
"Max," I called out again when a groan sounded from
a few feet away.

Holding onto the counter for leverage, I trudged
over to a huddled body on the floor.

"What...the..." Max wheezed.

"Anything broken?" I asked between coughs.

She shook her head.
"Everything...fucking...hurts...though."

Helping her to her feet, we both turned to the entranceway of the club. A huge-ass hole replaced the door. The whole front wall was missing.

My blood boiled, but I had to take control of the impending rage that threatened to consume me. I needed to get us out to safety and make sure that no one else was hurt.

Max and I held onto each other, making our way into the parking lot.

"Are you all right?" a deep voice asked, sending a flutter of desire racing through my body.

Sitting Max on the picnic bench, I turned to the guy who had his hands on me not long before. His brows were furrowed like he was, in fact, concerned for my well-being. *Yeah. Okay.*

"We're fine," I ground out through shaky breaths. I swallowed several times, my throat burning at the excessive movement.

"Here." He handed me a bottle of water.

I shook my head, not needing his help.

"I'll have some." Max reached out her hand.

He nodded once, keeping his gaze locked with mine, and handed her the bottle. "Do you know what happened?"

"Are your guys okay?" I asked, ignoring his question. Of course I knew what happened. It was an explosion. *Duh.* Did I know why? *No.*

"Yeah. They're fine. Coby was on the roof when it happened, but besides some minor cuts and bruises, everyone's good to go."

I breathed a sigh of relief. The club didn't need any lawsuits. Although it wasn't our fault, we didn't need to take the chance.

"My *nails*." Max's screech turned into a fit of coughing.

"Girl, your nails are fine," I said, patting her back.

"I just got them done for the gallery opening. God, this sucks." She glanced at me. "We will find out who

31

did this, right?" Her eyes darkened. Never mess with Max and her nails. Or her hair. Other than that, she was a tomboy. Having five older brothers, she had to learn to stand up for herself. She could throw a punch harder than a man more than half her size and not break a nail.

"Yes," I sat beside her. "We will."

"Was there anyone else here?" That guy... He was still there? I almost forgot about him until his smooth-as-silk voice washed over me. God, it was worse than chocolate. The deep rumble that came from his chest, oozed sex, promising a night filled with pleasure.

"No," was all I said. *Short and sweet. Right to the point. Yup. No need to give him any more information than what was required. None at all.* God, I was losing it. And now talking to myself. *Get it together, Jay.*

He cleared his throat.

"What?" I snapped, whipping my head around, and that was when I saw them. Cuts and scrapes marked his handsome face. My fingers twitched. I found myself wanting to touch him. To see if he was hurt. To rub out the pain. *Oh, dear God.* What the hell was wrong with me?

When he didn't say anything and smirked with that sexy-as-hell smile of his, I knew right then that he was trying to piss me off.

Well, have at it, big guy, 'cause this girl isn't going to break.

Sirens sounded, red and blue lights filling the front entryway of the club.

Shit. As much as we needed them, I knew the police would soon follow the fire truck, and I did not want to deal with the cops.

"I called the girls and told them to meet us here," Max said, coughing again.

I nodded once and buried my head in my hands. So many thoughts raced through my mind. *Who could have done this? Why would they even think of it? Who have we pissed off?*

"The ambulance is here."

I glanced up at another deep voice.

Eyes so blue stared back at me before he held out his hand toward Max. "Did you need the ambulance?"

"Sure." Max giggled, sliding her fingers in his, and allowed him to pull her from the table. "I'm Maxine," she told him as they walked away.

My jaw dropped. Max never told anyone her full name. It took me months to get it out of her.

Sex-on-a-stick sat beside me on the table, nudging me in the shoulder. "You should go see the medics as well."

"Why the hell would I do that?" Even though I hurt like hell, I was fine.

"Because you're in pain. You have cuts and scrapes, a bruise forming on your cheek but—" Much to my shock, he reached out and pinched my chin, tilting my head. His dark gaze bored into mine.

"But what?" I breathed, furious with myself that he was having this effect on me. My heart raced. My palms became sweaty. And if I didn't know any better, I would swear that he just purred.

"You're still beautiful," he said, his voice low and husky. He leaned in, his mouth mere inches from mine.

Kiss me. Oh, please God almighty, kiss me.

I pulled away, shaking myself. Whoever that girl was that wanted him would not be allowed to come out and play. I wouldn't allow it. He was dark and dangerous. He was no doubt every woman's fantasy. Ripped, blue jeans. Tight, white t-shirt that hugged his broad chest, tightening over his hard muscles every time he breathed. Tight abs that dipped into his pants. He no doubt had that muscle in his hip too, the one that turned grown women into hormonal teenagers.

An ache formed between my legs, and I had to fight back a groan of frustration. "You guys can go. I'll

33

pay for the damage to your equipment and the doctors' bills."

"No." He shook his head. "We're here to do construction on your place. We'll fix everything up."

"But I paid you to do the roof," I reminded him.

"So?"

"What do you want? You practically attacked me—"

"I did *not* fucking attack you," he growled, cupping the back of my nape and giving it a light squeeze. "Anything you and I do will be because *you* want it. Not because you were forced. You got me?"

My heart jumped at the underlying hint of desperation. "Yeah. I got you."

His hand loosened on my neck, his thumb brushing up and down over the smooth skin just under my ear. "Who are you, princess?"

A shiver raced down my spine. As much as I should have told him to stop touching me, I couldn't. His hold was calming; it soothed the racing nerves in my body. "What's your name?"

"What's yours?" he countered, his fingers moving to the base of my throat.

His hand was large, wrapping around my neck. He touched me. Caressed my skin. A wall I had built up so long ago broke—brick by brick, piece by piece. The longer he had his hands on me, the sooner I would fall to his undeniable desires.

"Jay," I replied, leaning into his touch. I was not a fan of how easy it was to talk to that guy. Stupid hot men and their panty-exploding smiles.

"Jay?" he asked, raising an eyebrow. "Jay what?"

"Gold."

"Nice to meet you, Miss Gold," he said, releasing me and sticking out his hand.

My skin burned with the loss of his touch. I slid my hand in his, returning the handshake.

"What's Jay short for?"

34

And that was my cue to leave. Rising from the table, I stretched, a sharp pain rippling down my spine. I winced and started coughing. Maybe seeing the medics would be a good idea after all. "Jay is just that. Jay. Nothing more. Nothing less," I told him, backing away from where he was sitting on the picnic table.

"Oh, I think it's something more." He followed me out into the middle of the parking lot, keeping his distance by a few feet.

"Tell me your name, and I'll tell you what Jay is short for," I said, circling him.

"No." He took a step toward me. "You should know, I own *Rod's Construction.*"

"Your buddy Asher never told me about you. I only deal with him." I made a point of letting my gaze roam down his body. "You're just an added bonus. So tell me, is Rod your name, then?"

"No."

"Tell me."

"I enjoy this little game." He feigned a yawn. "I'll tell you when I'm ready."

"Sorry, baby. You can't have it both ways." I licked my lips for added effect.

His nostrils flared, his hands clenching into fists at his sides.

At that point, a deep rumble sounded. It was a sound that you could hear from miles away. It let you know it was coming. By the time it was on you, it was too late. It vibrated into your heart, sliding into your soul. The engines ingrained their way into your being, becoming a part of you.

Motorcycles drove up the laneway, pulling into the parking lot. They circled us, driving around me and the beautiful man standing a few feet away.

I waited to see nervousness in his eyes at the loud dramatic effect of the bikes driving around us but he continued to stare at me. He kept his gaze locked with mine, holding me in place.

35

The girls hollered, revving their engines and circled us one more time before parking their bikes. Even though a wall was blown out of our club, they wouldn't let anything get them down. It made us strong. One. A unit. They liked to put on a show. More so when strangers were on their property. We didn't have dicks so we had to come up with ways to be intimidating. If people knew how crazy women could get, we wouldn't have that problem. I'd rather be taken hostage by a man than a woman.

Tangent, Jay. Again. Stop.

My jaw tightened. That guy. It was him. He did that to me. The air crackled and fizzled around us, washing over and through us. It still smelled of smoke, burning the hairs in my nose.

"Trying to make me nervous?" the guy asked, closing the distance between us. He stood several inches over my 5'11. It was nice to feel like a woman and not like an Amazon. He peered over my head. "Motorcycle club?"

I nodded, a wicked grin spreading on my face. "The best." Grazing a hand down his chest, I wrapped my fingers around his belt buckle. "I know you're teasing me. Trying to get me to play your little game. But, sweetheart, I *own* this fucking game."

"I'd watch what you say next, princess," he leaned down to my ear. "Because I don't care if there is a hole blown into your club. I will bend you over anywhere I see fit and fuck you so hard you'll forget your name."

Ho-ly. Shit.

Taking a deep breath, I released his belt and patted his chest. "Dream of me, big guy, and when you come, say my name."

FOUR

ANGEL

*"**DREAM OF** me, big guy, and when you come, say my name."*

Fucking hell.

Jay. I didn't know her. I didn't know a thing about the woman walking away from me but I knew by the time it was done between us, I would end up balls deep inside of her body.

The black leather hugged her every curve, every inch of her frame.

My blood stirred, the tiny hairs on my skin tingling. A cold draft washed over me at her no longer being near.

A motorcycle club. I never knew a female MC existed. Under most circumstances, I was sure that people would give them shit, telling them women could not run an MC. They would need a man for guidance. Please. Jay was beautiful but I could see a hardness behind her gaze. All of the ladies that got off their bikes weren't your typical bikers. They weren't your average badass women. One was tiny, five-foot-nothing, hundred pounds soaking wet, but she gave off an air of knowledge. Her dark gaze slid to mine while she walked up to Jay standing at the ambulance.

Something flashed in her eyes, a hint of something I couldn't quite place.

My stomach twisted.

Asher walked toward me. "You see those fucking hotties over there?" he asked, pointing at the group of women behind him.

"Yeah." I nodded, but the one I was focused on was Jay.

Her head snapped around, glaring at me over her shoulder.

I couldn't help but laugh. I was getting under her skin. It had been a couple of hours since I first saw her. I didn't know how long the teasing could go on with the raging hard on I was trying so hard to control.

"Careful with that one." Asher clapped a hand on my shoulder. "She looks like she wants to gut you."

I grunted. "I know, brother." Dale was stuck in the middle of the small group, chatting with Max. For whatever reason, they let him into their little huddle.

Asher sat beside me just as Coby joined us.

"Fuck!" Coby clenched and unclenched his hand. "I fucking hurt my arm. Do we know what the hell happened?"

I shook my head.

Coby grunted when his phone rang. "Yeah?" he barked. His eyes locked with mine, going hard and cold, his jaw tightening. "Yup."

"What's up?" I asked when he hung up.

"Boss is reeling us in."

***

Gunfire blazed around me as I crawled along the ground. Dirt and debris dug into my knees and elbows, scraping along my gear. My ears rang, my heart thumping hard against my ribcage. Adrenaline pumped through me, igniting my skin on fire. Small bursts of air left my lips as a sharp pain shot up my leg. *Oh yeah.* I had been shot. Being in the field for long periods of time, you learn to live with your injuries. That time around, we had been out for a month. Leaving Jay's club unnoticed was hard when my body was telling me to go back to her, to dive into her heat and make her mine.

We didn't know what had caused the explosion. Not like the girls would tell us anyway, but I was damn determined to find out. The Alpha male in me roared when I thought something had happened to Jay, but I breathed a sigh of relief when she and Max walked out of the club unharmed.

A shot in the distance pulled me from my thoughts. I would get out of there alive. My men would get out. To their loved ones. Their families. Their home. We would all get out. *Alive.*

"Angel. *Fuck.*"

An explosion went off twenty feet away from where I was laying. *Shit.* Any closer and I would have been blown to pieces, my body parts spread out on the ground for some scavenger to digest.

"Angel."

I winced at the barked command. "Yell any louder and we'll get fucking caught, dumbass," I whisper-yelled.

Dale glared at me and nodded in the direction we were headed.

I followed his gaze, my stomach giving a flip at the sight. A group of men huddled together in the dusk of the evening. I counted five heads, all ranging from 5'11 to 6'3 and averaging at least 200 pounds a person. I could take one, but five? I was good but not that good. As fun as it would be, I needed all of my limbs intact for when we went home.

"Angel."

I grinned. I lived for that kind of shit. Call me a masochist or a sadist or what-the-fuck-ever, but the calling to destroy those who wronged me and humanity flowed through my blood like molten lava.

Dale chuckled. "Target has been spotted," he said into his radio.

"Copy that."

My body hummed, my skin buzzing from the exertion of holding back. I was ready. I needed it. We all needed it. Being out in a world we called our own personal hell every time we ended up in the field had to shed some light at some point. There had to be a reason for why we did what we did. And there it was. Our mark. Our victim. Our *prey.*

The men standing before us were monsters. Sick and twisted of the worse kind. Their prey? Women. Some as young as twelve. Just girls. Where were their parents? Dead? Forced into selling their children to make ends meet? The oldest we knew about was twenty. Most of them were just girls, though. Not even past puberty yet. My chest tightened. It made me sick to my stomach knowing what those bastards did. Human trafficking was something that had gone on for years but not in my fucking country. But we were a small group. If we couldn't stop it in the US, we could at least put an end to the shit in our town. Although we had set out in that hellhole for other reasons, we came across the traffickers by accident. It was like we were meant to catch them. Vice-One had gone against orders and traveled through the wasteland in search of the fuckers who called themselves men. A true man wouldn't sell women. A real man didn't push his weight around just because he had a dick.

"You ready?"

I grunted in response at Dale's question. "More than fucking ever." I signaled to my right, knowing the rest of my brothers were off in the distance. Trusting that they would make their move. Deep in my gut, I knew they would respond without me having to give them the go-ahead.

"This is my favorite part," Dale said, like a kid at fucking Christmas.

I shook my head. He no doubt had some screws loose, but I loved the guy nonetheless. Having grown up in a shitty-assed part of Detroit, moving to our small town was a Godsend for him.

We watched as one of the guys in the huddle fell and then a second. The last three standing bustled out of there, frantic, and picked up the weapons from their dead counterparts.

You won't see us, fuckers, but we sure see you.

"Was that Coby?" Dale asked, his eyes twinkling with mischief. Coby was the slickest, fastest sharpshooter I had ever seen. Lethal when he struck. You wouldn't see him until it was too late.

"Prob—"

Cold metal touched the back of my neck. "You thought we didn't see you."

Fuck me.

"Stand up," the deep voice barked in my ear.

Not on your worthless piece of shit life, asshole. "I rather like it down here," I grit out. My gaze flashed Dale's way, and I noticed that I was alone. *Shit.*

"Stand. Up," the fucker repeated.

I reached for the blade in my left pocket when a pop sounded. The guy standing over me fell to the ground, huddling in a pile of groaning agony.

"Serves you right, fucker," I snarled, unloading a couple into his chest. It wasn't something I was proud of but knowing what those men were capable of, I regretted taking them out less and less.

Dale neared me, a huge smile on his tanned face. "You thought I left you alone, didn't you?"

"You *did* leave me alone," I mumbled and pushed to my full height. I did a quick scan around me. The traffickers were nowhere to be found.

41

J.M. WALKER

"I left you alone for like two seconds. I had to get headway on the asshole or else he would have popped us both."

I scoffed. I didn't believe that for a second. No one was that fast. Except for Coby. Even then, I wasn't sure just how quick that shit would go down.

"Enemy is no longer accounted for. Three down. Two got away," Dale said into the radio. "For now, anyway."

"*Copy that. Head back to base*," came the clipped response.

"We are in deep shit. I hope you know that."

I nodded. It would be worth it. Being a Navy SEAL meant you dealt with military action. Full-force shit that was thrown against your country. Well, those women? They were American. I knew that. I could feel it in my blood. They were sisters. Daughters. Nieces. They were someone. If they were mine, I would want every man out there searching for them. Bringing them back to me. I wouldn't stop until they were safe. It was etched into my soul. My very being. I couldn't stop even if I wanted to. We would head back to base. In time. Our boss was under the impression we had taken out a known terrorist. We had. We just waited to divulge the information *after* we stumbled upon the shack.

"Angel, you can't save them all." Dale clapped a hand on my shoulder before stepping in front of me.

I ignored his comment. I had to. It was not the time or the place to argue about who needed saving and who didn't. Another *pop-pop* sounded from the far right.

"Shit, Coby is full blazing tonight," Dale said in awe.

"Fall in," I commanded, signaling to my brothers. Four of us. Four men banded together. Protecting what was ours. Protecting our country and those women. Even if they didn't agree with my reasoning, they

42

would listen. It would be the same if I didn't agree with them. I would fight to the death for my men.

When we reached an old farm, my skin buzzed with anticipation. Not knowing what we would find behind those walls, we approached the broken-down building with caution. Slabs of wood once painted red were brown, the paint wearing thin. The large window at the peak of the building gave me an eerie feeling we were being watched. By whom? I wasn't sure. What I did know was that I needed to get my shit, the women, and my men out of there. Even if the women were no longer alive, I wouldn't be satisfied until I knew for sure. Until I could report it back to base and have the girls brought home to their families. They deserved a proper burial.

"Angel."

"Fall in," I said, taking a step forward when a hand grabbed my arm. "What the—"

"Mine," Dale pointed at my feet. "Stay with us."

Between Dale and I stood a near-death object that threatened to destroy me. Again. My body vibrated, a breath leaving me on a whoosh. "Thanks, man."

"No thanks needed. Now keep your head in the game."

That was my line. I was the one who was supposed to be telling my guys to keep it straight. Together. *What the hell is wrong with me?*

I cursed myself and moved around the bomb. As we neared the wooden doors of the barn, an explosion went off behind us. The heat of the fire caressed my body. I looked at Dale, raising an eyebrow.

He shrugged. "Couldn't have you almost stepping on it again."

I nodded once. I owed him big time. But of course, we had all saved each other a time or two. We had been *brothers* for years. Trained to think first, act second, but we were men. It didn't work out that way when someone was in need of our help.

When Coby and Asher showed up on scene, Dale
and I relaxed a little. Although we were in two-person
teams, the four of us were stronger as a unit.

"What if they're dead?" Asher asked, coming up
beside me.

"Then they're dead, but I won't fucking stop until
I find out," I mumbled, reaching for the door. The hair
at my nape tingled.

Coby nodded once, his emerald-green eyes
glancing back and forth, taking in his surroundings.
Knowing he had been in the field and undetected made
me feel safe. Made all of us feel safe.

"Asher is going to stay on your right," Dale
explained.

I nodded.

Asher cocked his gun. "Ready, Boss."

"Fuck me, I love this part. Almost as good as sex."
Dale crouched, getting ready to take on whoever was
behind door number one.

I took a breath and pushed open the door. A
musky scent wafted into my nostrils. I knew that smell.
Death. It was a sour taste on your tongue that made
bile rise to your throat, burning its way up your
esophagus. So much death.

Dale gasped. "Holy shit balls, batman."

We walked into the vast room. Guns drawn.
Muscles taut, our shitkickers making the only sounds
as we spread out.

Cots and sleeping bags lined the walls. Thirty or
so women filled the room. All shapes, sizes, and ages
caught our eyes.

"See if anyone's alive," I demanded, walking up
to a woman strapped to a cross against the wall. My
stomach clenched. Jagged marks covered her back, her
naked body ripped open. Blood dripped down her inner
thighs; mud and dirt matted her hair. Black and blue
bruises marred her skin.

I reached a hand out to touch her neck, checking for a pulse. I shook my head as her heart stayed silent. She was better off. Dealing with the mental aftermath of what was done to her could make her go insane or worse. Was there worse? Death would be their savior.

As my guys checked pulses of each woman, I searched for something else. Something that could lead us to the front-runner of this organization. Something that could bring that shit down and make it stop. There would always be human trafficking—I knew that—but if we could stop at least one trafficker in my time, then all of the shit would be worth it.

"Boss, we have a live one."

I turned to the sound of Asher's deep voice across the room. A girl, no more than sixteen tops, huddled in a dark corner.

"Are there others?" I asked, taking a tentative step toward the young girl.

"Three more. That's it," Dale mumbled, joining them.

Fuck. Out of thirty women, four survived. Rage pumped through my body. I would make damn sure someone would pay for their deaths.

"Try and gather them if you can. Call for backup." I watched as Asher approached the girl. The youngest survivor. He whispered to her in a soothing voice. Although he was huge, matching my 6'5 with more muscle, she didn't show any fear. She nodded every so often, taking in everything he said. With three younger sisters, he always felt the need to protect the younger females. Men were dicks. He knew, because he was one.

"Boss, base is sending backup," Dale ground out, interrupting my thoughts.

I nodded. All those women. All those females who were loved by at least one person in their lives were now gone. Most of which were a notch on someone's belt. Sex and death filled the air. Those two things

45

should in no way mix. Ever. I liked it kinky—craved it, even—but I knew when to draw the line. The so-called *men* who felt the need to push their power around would regret it in the end. After Vice-One got through with them, they would fucking *wish* they had never stepped foot in our country.

A MONTH passed since I saw the dark, brooding man who had been invading my dreams. His mocha-colored eyes pulled me in, forcing me to my knees. Night after night, I went to sleep trying hard not to think about him but his smirk with the tiny dimple in his cheek sent a flutter of desire through me. It had been four weeks since some shit head tried blowing up the clubhouse, and we were still no closer to finding out who it was. King's Harlots laid low, but being a female MC, the spotlight glowed on us whether we liked it or not. It pissed me off how many times we had people showing up at our club, egging the shit out of it or spray painting words like *cunt* and *whore* on the brick walls. It hurt but it forced us to be stronger. We had our own issues, our own demons to deal with. It brought us together.

While Max fluttered around the gallery, stressing out because the art showing needed to be perfect, I stood off to the side. Watching. Waiting. I didn't like not knowing what was going down. We had our brother club, Hell's Harlem, in New York working their shit, trying to see if they could figure out what the hell was going on. But it wasn't enough. I was twitchy. Standing around doing nothing sent an unnerving

47

feeling through my gut. Thoughts traveled to a hard male—a strong body who could make me wet with just his words. One night with the guy would help me with this anxiety gripping my spine. My mouth watered, a hot shiver racing down the length of my back. Just thinking about him made me pant with need.

My phone rang, and I breathed a sigh of relief. "Yeah?"

A deep chuckle sounded from the other end. "Always so warm with your greetings."

"Hi, Daddy," I said, my heart swelling.

"Hi, Nugget. How's my girl?"

I smiled at his nickname for me. Having the last name Gold, Nugget had stuck ever since I was born. Even his crew called me the childhood endearment. "Good."

"Don't lie to me. What's wrong? Who do I have to kill? Are the girls okay?"

I barked a laugh, moving around the large room. People milled about, huddling together to talk about each painting. "You don't have to kill anyone." *Not yet, at least.* "Everyone is fine." Leave it to my father to always be our savior. "We still can't figure out what happened to the club."

"You on a burner?"

"Yup." I made a mental note of throwing the phone out once I left the gallery. We all had phones that we could toss and phones we kept. We weren't into shady shit, not as a group, but I, on the other hand, would do anything to protect my sisters and let it be known that we were not women to be messed with.

"Good girl. You call Greyson?"

"Yes. He has his boys working on shit." Greyson Mercer was the president of Hell's Harlem. Being Brogan's stepbrother, I knew he could be trusted.

"Good. Keep me posted," my father demanded. Brian Gold was not one to be argued with.

We carried on a normal conversation for the next couple of minutes, no longer talking about MC business. I told him about Max's gallery showing and set up a time to meet him soon for coffee.

We both said our goodbyes, and I hung up the phone, continuing to make my way around the vast room. The walls were lined with all things Max Stanton. That side of art was new to me. Give me a pencil and paper, and I could sketch the shit out of it. But painting? I couldn't even paint a bowl of fruit. Everything Max painted came to life. They jumped off the canvas, gripping your soul and forcing you to see the beauty behind them. While her art covered canvas, mine covered skin.

Owning a tattoo shop across the street would allow me to see Max's art whenever I needed to. It brought a serenity to my life I hadn't felt in a long time. Each picture its own story, depicted in a different way each time it was gazed upon.

Leaning against the far wall, I watched her flow around the room. Greeting people, laughing, and shaking their hands like they had been friends for years. A twinge fluttered through my belly. Where she loved people, I would rather be by myself. I was socially inept, working much better one-on-one.

It was one thing I loved about her. Always sociable. Always friendly. I, on the other hand, hated everyone and refused to let anyone in. Reminded of that daily, it was hard not to believe it. My life revolved around the club, my sisters, everything that had nothing to do with giving up my heart. Yes, my girls had a piece of it, but it wasn't enough.

My stomach twisted with unease, memories flooding my mind. Shaking it off, I stood in front of a painting entitled "Breathe". It was black and white, two silhouettes holding each other, embracing the love they felt for the other. It screamed passion, punching you in the heart and took your breath. "Wow," I whispered, staring in awe up at the large painting.

Everything Max touched turned into a masterpiece. She would no doubt be the next Van Gogh.

The tiny hairs on the back of my neck tingled. I was being watched.

Out of nowhere, *he* appeared. The hot as hell man. Sex-on-a-stick. A sinful addiction I craved. God, he was worse than anything I ever experienced. He was… *Sin*. The nickname for him made perfect sense.

His dark gaze pierced through mine. His short, jet-black hair shone in the dim lighting of the room. Scruff had grown in on his strong jaw. It had been a couple of weeks since I first met him. A couple of weeks since his deep voice rumbled straight to the spot between my legs. My tongue tingled, itching to have a taste. To feel the scruff of his beard rubbing against my thighs as I rode… *Shit, Jay.*

He was across the room, but I could feel him. His stare stripped me, revealing every dark and dirty secret. My skin burned. My heart raced. My cheeks heated, a flush spreading up my body.

His eyes roamed down the length of me, his tongue peeking out to lick along his full bottom lip.

My core quivered, clenching, ready and willing for the man I didn't know. A man who could make me beg and leave me wanting and demanding more. What was wrong with me? No man had ever affected me that way.

Clearing my throat, I turned back around, unable to concentrate. Sin would be the death of me and my rules. On the other hand, he was everything I was hoping for. I knew it before he touched me. One word, one silent command, and I would be his ever-willing slave. To do with as he wanted, and I would enjoy every hour of it.

"Jay, that sexy as hell man is here, and I would bet my bike he wants to eat you alive," Max said, coming up beside me and hooking her arm in mine.

He wanted to eat something all right. The warmth of desire spread over my skin. I coughed. "Yeah, well, until he tells me his name, he's not eating anything." *I am a dirty girl.*

"Try telling *him* that." Max laughed. "The tension is crazy between you two. You have to rub that one out or else you'll both explode."

"I'm fine," I mumbled, shivering.

"As *if.*" She pushed me playfully. "You're fidgety, and you've been extra cranky. You need to get laid."

I glared at her. "I do not."

"Yes," she insisted, "you do."

"Please." I rolled my eyes. "He couldn't handle me."

"Is that so, princess?"

I jumped, spinning on my heel at the deep rumble of the voice caressing my ear.

Sin grinned that hot-as-hell smile and took a step toward me. "I think I can handle every inch of you."

"I'll leave you two alone," Max said, winking at me. "There's a private room in the back. Just please make sure you clean up after." She walked away, laughing and whistling to herself.

Bitch.

"Are you going to tell me your name?" I asked Sin as he stepped up beside me. The fabric of his black leather jacket brushed against my bare arm, sending a shiver down my spine. God, I loved a man in leather.

"When you're ready." He placed his hand at the small of my back, leading me around the room.

"I'm... I'm ready now." My skin burned from his touch through the thin fabric of my dress. "Tell me."

"Nope.

"What? Did you want me to beg for it?" As much as I would love to, the words would not leave my mouth until I had him in my hands. Images of me on my knees, begging, flowed into my mind. All I could picture was staring up at him, ready to take him in my mouth and—I cleared my throat. "I'm not begging." Those words didn't come out as sure as I would have liked.

He moved behind me, leaning down to my ear. His hot breath brushed along the back of my neck, the scent of mint wafting into my nostrils. "When you beg, it won't be for my name, princess."

"I'm not begging you for anything if you don't tell me your name," I raised my voice, elbowing him in the stomach.

He grunted.

I geared up to do it again when he grabbed my arm, digging his fingers into my bicep.

"You should know that I love it rough, Jay," he growled in my ear. "The more you push me, the more you hit me, the harder I get."

My body vibrated, the ache in my groin intensifying since meeting the man a month before. "What the hell do you want from me?"

"I want you to beg for it. I want you so wet that one thrust from my cock makes you explode. I know you want me, princess, just as much as I want you."

Oh. Dear. God. As much as I wanted him, I already knew that he wouldn't be just a one-night fuck. Being with him would go against my rules, and I refused to break them for him. My body battled it out with my brain. One part of me wanted him; the other part wanted to ignore him. It was a war of self-control that if he kept looking at me with those bedroom eyes and talking to me with that sex-filled voice, I was sure to lose. "Not going to happen," I squeaked. Clearing my throat, I tried again in a firmer tone. "Not happening."

I didn't like the taste of those words as they left my mouth but I had to fight it. *I. Have. To. Fight. It.* I chanted those words to myself but the pleasure growing inside of me assured I wouldn't be able to say no for long.

"Keep telling yourself that," he purred, his hand moving to my hip.

"I will." I stepped away from him and continued walking around the room. And of course, Sin followed me.

"Your friend is talented."

I stopped in my tracks, narrowing my eyes. "She is."

Sin crossed his arms under his broad chest, facing a painting on the wall. "Has she ever told you what they mean?"

"Um…no. But when I watch her paint, she's always in her head like the picture is telling her a story." Having a normal conversation with the guy was—my heart fluttered—nice. "She's private."

"I understand that. Artists are known to keep their talent to themselves."

Unless you were a tattoo artist like me; then everyone knew. "Makes sense. She didn't tell me for the longest time that she loves to paint or draw. She can sculpt, too."

He whistled. "That's some serious talent."

"She grew up in a big family so everyone knew everything about everyone. She was lucky she was able to keep her art to herself for so long."

"Why, Jay, are we having a civil conversation?" he teased.

"Jackass," I mumbled, the corners of my lips twitching.

He chuckled, brushing his fingers through his hair.

"You're not going to tell me your name, are you?" I watched his large hand mess up his hair in that sexy rocker way. His shaggy hair fell into his eyes. My fingers itched, begging to brush the strands off his forehead.

"Nope." He winked. "Don't even think about asking my boys."

"Whatever." My lips pressed into a firm line. "I'll just call you what I call you in my head then," I mumbled.

"Oh?" He raised an eyebrow. "And what's that?"

A moment of hesitation fluttered through me, not realizing I had spoken out loud. Playing into it, I licked my lips and made a point of letting my gaze roam down the length of his body. "Sin." And with that, I walked away, heading in the direction of the bathrooms.

Once I rounded the corner, I hightailed it down the hall. I could do this. I could control myself and not beg. *I won't beg.* I refused to. I broke for no one. But my body wanted him. *God, does it ever!*

Pushing my way into the bathroom, I slammed the door closed and leaned against it. My heart raced against the walls of my rib cage. I took deep breaths, trying to ease the nerves pounding through my body.

I scrubbed a hand down my face when I was suddenly pushed forward. The door was shoved open, hitting hard against the wall with a bang. My head was tugged back, igniting a cry to leave my lips. The slight pain burned through my scalp.

When a lock clicked into place, I was thrown up against the cool concrete wall. A flutter of fear twisted at my gut.

Strong fingers wrapped around my throat, tilting my head back while my lower body was restrained against the wall. "Beg for it."

Sin. "No."

His other hand slid down the side of my body to cup my rear. His hips pushed into me, the erection in his pants indicating he wanted more from me. "No? Woman, do you know what I could do to this sweet body of yours?"

A sense of pride washed over me. I was wet. He was hard. It was perfect. "Show me."

"Not until you beg," he husked, brushing his nose up the length of my neck.

He was damn determined, I would give him that. I leaned my hands against the wall, moving my rear into him. "We could be here awhile," I panted. "Because I am *not* begging."

He gripped my hips, rocking, matching the movements of my body. "Your ass is fucking perfect." His fingers gripped my flesh, kneading and bruising.

My breathing picked up.

Spinning me, he leaned his hands against the wall, caging me in. His hand wrapped around my throat, a wicked grin spreading on his face.

I glanced down at the large bulge in his pants. Licking my lips, I reached out for him.

He caught my wrist, holding my hands above my head in a firm grip. "Don't think so, princess." His mouth brushed down the line of my jaw. "I'm in control here, baby."

"You think so, do you? I can see how much you want me; I think it's you who will be begging first."

With his free hand, he grazed it under my dress, reaching my thong-clad ass. "I won't break." He lifted my leg to his hip, grinding against me.

I moaned, the heavy weight between his legs coming into contact with my heat.

"Fuck, Jay, I can feel your fire..." He circled his hips against mine.

"Oh, God," I whimpered, closing my eyes.

"Look at me," he demanded, speeding up his hips.

Pleasure coiled in my belly, a tingle brewing up my body. "*Please*," I blurted, craving the release he promised.

"I told you, you would beg." He released me and stepped away.

Arousal burned, simmering to a dull roar, but the lack of being pushed over the edge made me see red. "You bastard."

He chuckled. "I am in control. Not you."

I was seething, waiting for him to leave. Just like everyone else in my fucking life.

"Frustrated, baby?" he teased. He closed the distance between us, standing an inch away.

I could feel him. Everything about him. His heat. His touch. His *soul*.

"I never thought I'd see you in a dress."

"You've seen me once, and I'm wearing this shit for my best friend." I rubbed my hands up and down my arms, easing some of the nerves racing through my body.

"Do you always listen to what she says?" His hand inched up beneath my dress, grazing my inner thigh before reaching the tiny triangle covering my mound.

"No. I don't listen to anyone." I bit back another moan. My best friend wanted me to act like a lady and not like a biker for her gallery showing. Right then, I wished I was wearing my leather pants.

"You may not listen to anyone, but your body sure as hell is." His grip on my waist tightened while his other hand pushed the fabric of my dress to my hips.

Before I could protest—before I could shove him away—his finger pushed under my panties. His knuckle brushed over my soaked opening. His eyes locked with mine, searching, watching me. Waiting for me to break.

Heat spread over my skin, the ache between my legs growing with each stroke of his finger. "You won't break me."

Something flashed in his eyes when he released my wrists. In a quick move, he cupped my breasts, pulling the fabric lower. He licked his lips, his thumb grazing over the swell of my tits. "Fucking perfect."

I smiled at the deep rumble of his words, enjoying the fact he was losing as much control as he was trying to take from me. It was a cat and mouse game. Predator and prey. I would wait a couple more minutes before I showed him just how in control I was.

That man—that beautiful, dark man who forced his way into my life would see that I wouldn't submit to anyone. *Especially* not him.

SIX

ANGEL

THE SWELL of her breasts fit perfect in my hands. The pale skin stretched over full, ample tits. Pulling the cup of her red lace bra lower, I watched her lips part. Jay refused to break, but I knew her body was cracking. She would give in. I would make damn sure of it before I fucked her. When I ground myself against her supple hips, the heat from her pussy scorched me. She was hot, on fire, for me. She knew it. I knew it. Her bright-jade eyes begged me to push her over the edge. The moan leaving her full lips had been the breaking point.

I lowered my head, itching to have a taste, when something caught my gaze. A piercing. It sparkled in the dim lighting of the bathroom. *Holy fucking hell.*

In a rough move, I bared both of her tits and growled. Her dark pink nipples were pierced. Gold, metal barbells poked through the hard nubs.

"Something you like, Sin?" Jay purred, pushing her breasts into my hands.

My cock twitched. *God, that nickname.* Before she could get any more words out, I latched onto a nipple, sucking it hard into my mouth.

She cried out, arching against me and grabbed onto my head. Her fingers dug into my hair, pulling and tugging as she rode out the pleasure I gave her.

Swirling my tongue around the swollen nipple, I nipped at her skin. Releasing her with a pop, I pushed her other tit up to meet my mouth.

Locking eyes with her, I licked the areola, circling around the barbell before grazing my teeth over the sharp peak.

Jay hissed out a breath, her gaze darkening. Her pupils dilated, heating with lust.

I grinned, sinking my teeth into the flesh, igniting a yelp to leave her lips.

She glared, tugging my head back and pushing me back against the wall.

Fuck me, the woman could play. Wrapping a hand around her throat, I crashed my mouth to hers. Swallowing her gasp of surprise, I cupped her ass and lifted her before carrying her over to the bathroom counter. The kiss deepened. Groans sounded. She shook in my arms, spreading her legs wide.

As hard as I was, as much as I wanted her, I would not fuck her in a bathroom. But a little tease wouldn't hurt.

Her tongue slipped further into my mouth, dancing with mine, trying to regain the control she no longer had.

I slid my fingers into her hair, mussing it up from the ponytail it was in. Tugging her head back, I forced her to look up at me.

Her full lips were swollen from my mouth. Her cheeks flushed. Her eyes bright and hungry. I inched a hand between her breasts, trailing it down the center of her body. "Beg. Me."

She pushed me back, licking lips. Her chest rose and fell. The red curls of her hair fell down around her face, framing her beauty.

My gaze slid down the length of her body. Her dress was pushed to her hips, wrinkled from my touch, and I couldn't wait to give her that just-fucked glow.

Jay sat up, gripped the collar of my jacket and pulled me back down to meet her mouth. "I don't beg," she said against my lips before shoving her tongue inside.

Nipping her bottom lip, I stared down at her. "I can smell how much you fucking want me." In a quick move, I ripped off her panties.

"Those were expensive, asshole," she growled, but her eyes dilated even more. Hmm…a little roughness turned her on.

Ignoring her, I lifted her dress to her waist before lowering to my knees. "Your pretty cunt is nice and wet." I grazed a finger over her opening before inserting it deep inside her wet body.

She shook, spreading her legs wider. "Well, I bet your dick is nice and hard."

"It is." I smiled, thrusting my finger in and out of her. "If you begged, you would get to feel just how hard it is."

"No. Fucking. Way," she said between pants, rocking her hips back and forth.

"Too bad." Spreading the lips of her pussy, I covered her core with my mouth. My cock hardened to the point of pain. Her taste made my head swim. *Fucking delicious.*

Jay whimpered, trembling under my touch. "Shit."

And that just made me suck harder. Pumping my finger into her body in rough moves, I rubbed the wall of her center in come-hither motions. Releasing her with a smack, I grabbed under her knees and pushed them toward her chest. "Ready for me, baby?"

"Yes, fuck yes." Her hands grabbed my head, pushing me down to where she wanted me most. Her nails dug into my skull as her hips rocked against my face. "Oh. God."

Thrusting my tongue deep inside of her, I growled. The sweet, acidic taste of her pleasure flowed down my throat. I swallowed her essence and ate her pussy like a starved man. She was what I needed. All of that time. She didn't know it, but the heat in her eyes proved she was breaking in front of me. And I would be the one to pick up the pieces as long as it meant I could have her again and again.

"Harder!" she cried out. *"Fuck."*

I released her, pulling her off the counter. Bending her over, I wrapped a hand around her throat. "Can you smell your arousal on my lips?" I asked, brushing my mouth along her ear.

She nodded, her eyes dark and stormy, billowing with a lust so strong it took my breath.

Pulling her dress to her hips, I landed a hard swat on her ass. I was impressed when she didn't make a noise. Her pupils dilated, her tongue peeking out to lick over her bottom lip. Interesting. So I did it again.

Swat. Swat.

The crack reverberated through the room. "Tell me."

Her gaze locked with mine in the reflection of the mirror. "No."

I chuckled. "Didn't think so."

Spreading her legs, I lowered to my knees and bit the flesh of her rear.

That time, she whimpered, arching her back like a cat.

Digging my fingers into her ass cheeks, I opened her to me and dove back into her core. Lapping and sucking at her center, I fucked her with my mouth until she was crying out. But no words. No begging. No demanding me for more. Shit. She was good. But *I* was better.

I pinched her swollen clit until she bucked against me. "Tell me. Beg me to let you come."

61

"*No*," she cried out, rocking back against me. "Damn it." She shook her head. "I won't break."

"Yes, you will." I pinched the little cherry harder.

"*Fuck*. No. I refuse."

"Fine." I released her and kissed her tailbone. Grabbing a hold of her ponytail, I forced her head back. "The next time you see me, it will be when I'm fucking the shit out of your pussy. And, Jay? I will fuck you until you break. I will own every single inch of your body." I reached between us and grazed a finger over the tight hole between the cheeks of her ass. "Every. Single. Inch," I snarled in her ear.

Her eyes widened.

And with that, I let her go and left the confines of the bathroom. I couldn't help but chuckle over how pissed she would be at not having an orgasm. But the inner Alpha in me wanted her to come on my dick. I wanted to watch her eyes dilate while I fucked orgasm after orgasm out of her.

She would break.

I would make damn sure of it.

SEVEN

—jay

BY THE time I reached the clubhouse, I was a raging pile of hormones. I didn't know anything about Sin. I didn't know where he lived. I didn't know how to get a hold of the guy. The contact number I had for him was through his construction company, and there was no way I could call it. But I needed his hands on me. His mouth on my skin. His fingers inside of me. His kiss. *God, could he kiss*! Every time his tongue grazed mine, my knees grew weaker. He was a man who knew how to please a woman. I should call him. *I sound like a desperate, horny teenager.*

I hated him. I hated what he did to me. But I hated even more that my body gave in. And I still didn't know his damn *name*.

When Sin left me with my bare ass sticking up in the air, I had to hold back the urge to beg him to come back. To demand that he fuck me. To plead that he give me the orgasm I was desperate for. Never in my whole life had I experienced anything like him. I had been with a lot of guys because I was bored, but with Sin, I *needed* to be with him. My fingers clenched at my sides, itching to run them over his hard body. My tongue tingled, begging to lick over every ripple— every muscle.

My body ached from the lack of release. So fucking sore. And they say women couldn't get blue balls. *Ha.*

Walking down the hallway to my room, I pulled the elastic out of my hair and ran my fingers through it. Massaging my scalp, I sighed in frustration.

I pushed the door open with my foot, pulling my dress up and over my head. Unclasping my bra, I stretched, letting the item fall from my hands. If Sin wouldn't satisfy me—if he wouldn't curb my craving—it would be a night filled with self-induced orgasms. It wouldn't work; they never worked. They just made everything worse.

Massaging my temples, I turned to head to the bathroom when a dark, brooding man stood at my doorway.

My heart jumped in my chest, my core quivering at the sight of Sin. The light from the hall cast a shadow around him.

His nostrils flared, his gaze taking me in. "Fucking A."

This would be it. A night filled with pure, hard fucking. I ran my hands up my middle, cupping my breasts. My fingers squeezed my nipples. I moaned, a sharp shiver blazing through my body.

Sin pulled off his leather jacket, followed by the white t-shirt underneath, and threw them on the chair in the corner of the room.

My mouth watered at the sight before me. Hard muscles rippled over bones. His chest flexed with his movements. Deliriously-delicious abs twitched as he strode toward me. The heft between his legs pulsed, promising me a night filled with pleasure.

"Tell me you want me," he growled, unbuckling his belt and kicked the door closed behind him. "Tell me how wet you are for me."

"Why don't you come here and feel how wet I am?" I slid a hand down the length of my body, pushing it between the folds of my pussy. A gasp escaped my lips, my clit swelling under my touch.

"*Fuck*," he hissed, closing the distance between us. He grabbed my hand, inserting my finger into his mouth and licked my arousal off of it. "*I* will be the one to make you come."

"If you don't make me come soon, I will do it myself." I grazed my hands down his chest, a small whimper escaping me at how incredible he was.

He spun me, slamming me up against the wall and gripped my hair in one hand. "Threatening me will not make you come any faster, little girl." A zipper lowered, sending a shiver down my spine. "Can you feel how hard I am?" he bit out, resting his heavy cock against my ass. "Can you feel how much my body wants you?"

"Show me," I breathed, pushing back into him.

The sound of a foil package opening erupted through the room. Sin pulled my head back at the same time he thrust into my body.

I gasped, my body clenching down around him.

"Look at me, beautiful girl." He pulled out. It was slow and torturous before he slid back in. "Look at me when you come on my dick," he snarled, pushing further into me. His arm wrapped around my waist, holding me against him as he pumped slow and deep inside my body.

A breath left me on a whoosh, his cock reaching past the barrier of comfortable. He was huge. Larger than any man I had ever been with. He stretched me, each thrust forcing the coil of pent-up frustration to wind tighter. Tears welled in my eyes at the slight sting, but the pain soon burned into a roar of pleasure.

He gripped my throat, his hips picking up speed. "Ask me for permission to come."

"*No*," I cried out, slapping my hands against the wall. I pushed back against him, meeting him thrust for thrust. I couldn't resist the urge to hear him demand things of me. I wasn't used to it, but from him, I craved it.

"Ask, *damn it*," he demanded, pounding into me with a fervor I had never felt before.

"God, *harder*," I shouted, slamming my ass back against his pelvis. It was rough. Bruising. It was animalistic as he took the pleasure from my body.

"That's it," he breathed against my neck. "Show me how much you want me. Fuck, your cunt is greedy for me."

His words turned me on, spreading warmth through my body. "Harder!" I swallowed a gasp, stars filling my vision.

"*Beg* me, Jay," he bellowed, leaning his hand on the wall for support.

"Let me come. Please, let me come!" I screamed.

"Fucking come for me. Open your sweet body," he yelled, bending me over and digging his fingers into my hips. His balls slapped against my clit, his dick reaching that bundle of nerves that was desperate and wanted to explode. "Come. *Now!*"

At that point, I broke. The release shattered through me. It was so hard, I couldn't catch my breath. I couldn't scream. I couldn't make a sound as his cock forced a second orgasm out of me.

"Keep coming for me, Jay." His hand grazed down my spine before landing a hard swat on my ass.

My heart beat against my ribcage, the blood pounding in my ears. And then I screamed.

He grunted in satisfaction, his thrusts prolonging the orgasm. His hips slowed to a stop. Pulling me to an upright position, he held me against him. "Do you want more?" he asked, kissing my cheek and cupping my throat.

I nodded, holding his arm. He was still inside me, hard and throbbing. I breathed through the onslaught of pleasure brewing somewhere in the pit of my core.

He slid from my body and took off the rest of his clothes. "Bend over the edge of the bed."

I never gave in to demands, but at that point, he could tell me to do anything and I would have. I did as he said, gripping the blanket tight in my hands.

A hard body loomed over mine. "So beautiful," he whispered, brushing my hair off my neck. "Do you know how difficult it was for me not to fucking rip open your body at the gallery? I've had a raging hard-on for this sweet pussy since the first day I met you."

I grinned, turning onto my back. His dick stood at attention. Hard and erect. Full and *mine*. I cleared my throat. "I knew you couldn't resist me," I said, pulling myself up higher on the bed.

He grabbed my feet, spinning back onto my stomach. "I think it's the other way around." He spread my legs, crawling between my knees. "Your pussy is hungry for me. Two orgasms didn't satisfy you? What have these fuckers been doing to you all this time?"

"Nothing that two hands can't cure." I moaned when he thrust two fingers back into my body.

"Well, princess," he breathed against my neck, rubbing his thumb against the tight spot at my rear. "I'm going to show you exactly what I can do. Think this pretty little ass can handle me?"

I swallowed several times.

He replaced his thumb with his wet fingers, lubricating a piece of me that had never been touched before. "I'll be gentle, baby."

"Yeah. Right," I scoffed. "There's nothing gentle about you."

Sin wrapped his hand in my hair, rubbing the tip of him between my ass cheeks. "You don't want me to be gentle. Do you?"

"No," I blurted before I could catch myself. *Fuck.*

"Hold on, Jay." His teeth nipped at my neck, raining tiny bites along my shoulder blades. "I'm going to rip your body open."

67

***

I woke sometime during the night with a heavy arm draped over me. My body hurt in places I never knew *could* hurt. I was sore from the multiple times Sin had used me during the night. And sticky from the several releases he had given me. God, he was amazing. He was captivating. Dark and mysterious. A story hid behind his eyes and I found myself wanting to break his walls down.

He stirred beside me, rubbing his face into the crook of my neck. I had never spent the night with a man and been thankful for it. I never knew what it was like to have a man in my bed who I wanted to be there. Who I wanted to spend another night with. Who I *craved*.

Rolling onto my side, my eyes popped open. We were in *my* bed. No man had ever been in my bed. *Shit.* I was too tired to do anything about it. Already I had broken a rule because of this man. This mind-blowing, hot-as-hell man who could give me orgasms just from his words.

Sin pulled the blankets higher up my body before tightening his hold around my waist. His large hand cupped my breast, his thumb brushing back and forth over my pierced nipple. It wasn't meant to turn me on. It felt possessive, like an owning. But it wasn't possible. Not yet. Not when we didn't know each other.

I sighed, snuggling into him. My ass brushed against his semi-hard cock, my core quivering. It clenched, a slight pain erupting through me at the many times his body had filled mine. I could remember every inch of him. I could still feel the rigid length inside of me. Every single *inch* of me.

My throat burned, remembering the rough way he had fucked my mouth.

"On your knees, girl."

Fuck me. His words. Sin dominated me in ways I had fantasized about for years. He took me to new heights, new pleasures, showing me that my body enjoyed everything he could give it. He made me feel desired, like I was the most precious treasure he ever had the pleasure of gazing his eyes upon.

I lowered to my knees, licking my lips as he held his dick in his large hand.

"Open. I'm going to fuck your throat." His eyes *darkened with mischief. "Think you can handle it?"*

Oh, I knew I could.

And I did. Over and over again. He had choked me, telling me after that he would train me to deep throat him without gagging. I looked forward to it.

My stomach twisted. *Rules, Jay.*

Yeah, I was so screwed. He knew it. I knew it. But I would never admit it. One time with him and I was breaking. I became weak when he was around. My control slipped just from one of his dark stares.

"Jay." Sin shifted beside me, throwing his leg over mine. "Sleep, baby."

I was antsy, not happy with myself that I let him into my bed. Fuck the rules. I reached between us, grabbing onto his length.

"Tell me," he demanded, thrusting his hips with the movements of my hand.

"Tell me your name first," I demanded, keeping a firm hold on his cock.

He chuckled.

The deep gravel of his voice rumbled through me, vibrating through my bones. "Tell me."

"Angel." He pushed my knee up to my chest, lining his body up with mine. "My name is Angel Rodriguez." His hand wrapped around my throat. "Now scream it."

J.M. WALKER

EIGHT

ANGEL

JAY SCREAMING my name set off something inside of me. The sounds reverberated through my soul, cracking it into pieces until all I felt was her. In the beginning, when I had set out for Jay, I had every intention of making it a one-time thing. But there was something about her that made me want more. She was a drug, and I was addicted.

It had been a couple of hours since I fucked her senseless, but judging by the semi-hard erection I sported, I was good to go again. I could also rub one out. Next time, I would do it for her. Let her watch. Let her see what she did to me. I could strap her down; tie her to my bed and keep her there until she begged. Again. I never realized how much it would turn me on until the words left her mouth.

She stirred beside me, a soft sigh escaping her delicious mouth.

"Sleep, princess." I kissed her shoulder. "I'm not done with you yet."

I pulled myself from her grip and got dressed, leaving the warmth of Jay's bed and body.

Before leaving the room, I glanced back at her sleeping form. The sheets were wrapped around her waist, exposing her back. My mouth watered, itching to taste her again and kiss and suck every inch of her. My dick twitched. She would be the death of me. And I *would* be back for her.

I headed out into the vast room that held a bar, pool tables, and several tables and chairs. Coffee. That was what I needed first and foremost.

"Coffee?"

I turned at the sound of a female voice and found Max holding out a steaming mug.

"Did you take care of my girl?"

"You should ask *her* that," I said, grabbing the mug from her.

She laughed. "I'm Max."

"I know." Sitting on the stool, I took a sip of the coffee, letting the peaceful bliss wash over me.

"And you are?"

"Angel Rodriguez." Thoughts of Jay screaming my name the night before almost rendered me breathless. It brought forth the animal within. The beast who wanted to rip her apart, giving her everything she craved and fulfill all of her waking desires.

"Nice to meet you, Angel. I should say this before whatever—" Max waved a hand in front of her "—happens between you and Jay."

"I'm listening." I placed the mug on the counter and crossed my arms under my chest.

"If you hurt her, I will gut you where you sleep, letting you bleed out until you die in your own puddle of filth."

I blinked once. Twice. And then threw my head back and laughed. "Fuck, I think you're my new best friend."

Her eyes twinkled. "I aim to please."

"I could say the same about you and Dale."

"Uh…" Her cheeks reddened. "There is nothing going on there."

71

Not that she cared to admit, at least. I knew how Dale worked. He would inch his way into a woman's life, take over her mind, body, and soul. There had been one. Always one that rips your heart out and leaves you standing alone and falling to pieces.

"Besides, Dale is after a good time. Nothing else." She shrugged, running a finger around the ring of the mug.

Huh, interesting. "He's a good guy. Be patient with him."

She nodded once and grabbed some more coffee. "More?" she offered.

"No, thank you." My phone rang. "Yeah."

"Shit, man. Where the hell have you been?" Dale barked, demanding answers that he wouldn't get.

"Out."

"The boss is asking for you. He's pissed, Angel."

Fucking great. "I'm on my way."

***

"You went against orders. You and your no bullshit attitude is going to get you and your men killed."

I stood with my hands at my sides, my back rigged and straight, taking in all that my boss threw at me.

Colonel Eric Vega ripped me a new one. Yelling about morals, the safety of my men, disobeying strict orders, blah blah *fucking* blah. He also told me I should have reported to him first before fucking off and doing whatever it was that I did.

Jay. I did her good and hard. Fuck me, my dick hurt from the many times I had taken her. Her tight body squeezed me like a vice, her warm mouth sucking me dry. Her moans and pleas for more—

"Angel."

Clearing my throat, I glanced at Vega.

"Pay *attention*," he barked and continued to tear me apart.

I knew everything he was telling me. I never once forced my men to do anything they weren't inclined to do. I gave them a direct order, and they followed. Willing and ready. We worked well together. Vice-One was more than a team; we were family. Brothers. Not by blood, but by power, strength and commitment alone. I loved them like they were my own. They were a part of me.

"Are you even listening to me?"

"Yes, Colonel," I mumbled.

"Tell me what I said then." Vega leaned back in his seat, tenting his fingers and waited.

"Keep my men safe. Stop being an asshat, and think about what I do before I do it."

Vega sighed. "You are one of the best. I know this. Your team knows this, but you're going to get yourself killed."

"Those women needed to be saved."

"You were under direct orders to head back to base. You shouldn't have been in there in the first place, Angel. That was not the mission. That is not your fucking job. You know that. You did what you were set out to do, what you were sent on the mission for in the first place."

"I—"

Vega slammed his fist down on the top of the desk. "No. No fucking arguments this time. You're going on unpaid leave until I need you again."

"Excuse me?"

Dark eyes narrowed at me. "Do not question my authority. You're lucky I don't fucking send you home for good."

I bit back a smirk, knowing it would never happen. I was the best. But being on leave would be shitty as hell.

Vega waved his hand. "You're dismissed. I'm giving you a month to get your shit together. When you come back, if this I-am-an-island crap happens again, I will do everything in my power to make sure you never step onto SEAL soil again. Understood?"

I gritted my teeth and nodded.

"Leave."

I turned around and left the office, heading to the locker room. People passed me, clapping me on the back, congratulating me on saving four women. I ignored them. Not paying attention in the least at the praise. I was staying home. For a month. And didn't that just make me feel even more like a failure?

NINE

—jay

MY BODY *hurt*. My muscles tensed, rippling over my bones. I stretched and moved, rolling over onto my side to find the spot beside me empty. My heart pained. I would have been lying if I said I wasn't a little bit disappointed that Angel was no longer next to me.

Sighing, I sat up and saw a piece of paper on my nightstand. Knowing it was probably a note that said he had a good time, thanks for the lay, and so on, I braced myself. Even though I had treated men the same way, an unexpected hope that Angel wouldn't do it to me, fluttered through me.

> *Princess,*
> *I now own every single inch of you.*
> *Angel*

A shiver rippled down my spine, remembering where he had been a couple of hours before. The way he moved inside of me was like a feral beast staking claim on its mate. *Oh dear God.* The things he did to me had never crossed my mind with any other man. Angel Rodriguez was the epitome of every sinful desire I had. Every dark secret. Every fetish and fantasy. He dominated my body and took control, giving me the greatest pleasure in return.

My thumb brushed over his phone number, itching to call him. All I had was his company number but my body was desperate. To have him back inside me. To just…talk. *Shit.*

Getting dressed, I grabbed my cut and headed out into the hallway when Max rounded the corner.

"I met your man," she sang, handing me a cup of coffee.

"He is *not* my man." But I sure wished he was. *God, what the hell is wrong with me?* One sweat-soaked night with the man and I was falling in lust with him. *Kill me now.*

"Well, he's something." She winked. "But don't worry. I threatened him for you."

I laughed, shaking my head. "Thanks, lover."

"Anytime, hot stuff." She smacked me on the ass and stepped in front of me, walking backward. "The girls are here. We thought of having the meeting outside since it's a nice day. Is that cool with you?"

I nodded, knowing she had planned it to make me feel better. The subject of Angel spending the night in my bedroom went untouched but I knew she had questions. Her not asking about it grated on my nerves. Since when had she kept her thoughts to herself? "All right. Spill, Max. You're driving me fucking crazy."

"Why," she feigned a gasp, "what*ever* do you mean?"

"I know you're wondering why Angel slept in my room. I had no idea he was coming over. I came home, was about to take a shower, and then he showed up and, well, the rest is obvious." Getting the words out lifted a heavy weight off of my chest. But giving up that control, even for a couple of hours, confused the hell out of me. Angel was the first man to take any sort of control from me, and I found myself liking it. It was freeing.

"I'm not wondering anything, Jay. If Angel slept in your room and came out alive, then it's obvious he was meant to be there in the first place." She turned and headed down the hallway, motioning for me to follow her.

But all I did was stand there and stare. She was right. Of course, she was always right. That was why she was the vice president. She kept me in line and helped keep my head out of my ass. My muscles tightened at that thought.

Angel.

Fucker.

Grumbling to myself about dominating, brooding men, I stormed out of the club and made my way outside. The bright sun seared its way into my eyes, burning my retinas. All right, so maybe it wasn't that extreme but I was in a mood. I was allowed a little dramatic flair every now and again.

"Jay, girl, news around the club is you had a fuck-tastic night?" Brogan slid off her bike and pulled off her helmet.

"I have no idea what you are talking about," I mumbled, sitting on the blanket spread out on the grass.

"No need to comment," she continued. "We all heard it."

My head whipped around. "Excuse me? You bitches weren't even here."

"How do you know that?" She laughed.

I shook my head. "God, I hate you sometimes."

She blew me a kiss and sat beside me. "No, you don't."

She was right. I didn't but I was beginning to think about getting a new crew. Stupid men and their dark, possessive, man hands grabbing me and making me feel good and shit.

"Enough of this shit. Meeka." I sat up straighter. "Did you find out anything?"

"I'm working on it," she said, her voice small.

Her denial was beginning to irritate the fuck out of me. "Meeka."

"Jay…" Max grabbed my arm, shaking her head. "Leave it alone."

"How the hell can I leave it alone? We have people taking these girls, doing who knows what to them, and one of my own sisters knows shit but won't say anything." I turned back to Meeka. "Are you in trouble? Just tell me that. *Please*."

"I'm fine," was all she said.

"You can stay here. If you need to lay low for a while, this place is always open to you. You do have your own room," I reminded her, but I didn't like the sound of her words and the underlying fear hidden beneath them.

"Please be patient with me." She glanced at each of us. "I know you don't trust me right now, but please, give me time. Everything will get explained, I promise."

"Fine, but I do expect answers whenever you are ready," I said, my voice final.

She nodded.

I let out a sigh, stretching my legs out in front of me. "Any new prospects?"

"I have a client that is a hard-assed bitch. She needs a job. Husband was a douche. Left her penniless. This might be good for her; even if she doesn't join the club, she could bartend." Brogan shrugged.

"Call her up and invite her over," I told Brogan. "We need some hard women in this place."

"What's that supposed to mean?" Max pouted, inspecting her perfect manicure.

I laughed, rolling my eyes. "You spend more time getting manicures and your hair done than on your bike. That *I* bought you."

"Whatevs. I spend plenty of time on my bike." Her cheeks reddened. "Um, I mean…"

"And just who are you spending time on your bike with?" I questioned, poking her in the ribs.

She squealed, slapping my hands away. "Stop. We need to get our shit in order."

Always the vice. But I couldn't figure out anything that was going on if Meeka didn't open up. She was a vault, sealed tight, and nothing would slip out unless I forced her. I could be sadistic but I wouldn't do that to my sister.

"Do we know anything on the explosion?" Brogan asked, lighting up a smoke.

"I have our boys in New York looking in on things for us, but other than that, no one is saying shit." And I knew it was because we were women. Hard fuckers like bikers didn't talk to us because we had pussies. It was starting to get under my skin.

"It's been a month," Max huffed. "Why don't we ask *Rod's Construction*? Those guys could have seen something we haven't."

Lying down on the grass, I stretched my leg above my head, working out the kinks in my body. "Have at it, but *I'm* not talking to them."

"Aww and why not, princess?"

I frowned, my body betraying me and tingling in all the right places. "What the hell are you doing here?" I asked Angel as he hovered over me.

"Working on that big-ass hole in your club." His eyes followed my leg as I pulled it up and over my head, my foot resting beside my ear. "Fuck," he breathed. "You never told me you were flexible."

"That's because all you did was fuck me from behind." And hell if I didn't enjoy it.

He knelt at my head, wrapping his long fingers around my ankle and keeping it in place by my ear. "You say that as if it's a bad thing." He waited a couple of seconds before letting go of my ankle.

I repeated my movements with my other leg while he held it above my head for me. "Nope. Not

79

complaining. But next time you should treat a lady like a lady. What if I prefer missionary?"

He chuckled.

God, that sound. Deep and husky. It vibrated through my bones, making my girly bits squeal with undying pleasure.

"If you wanted me to fuck you like a lady, you wouldn't have let me eat your pussy in the bathroom at the gallery," he said, his voice smug.

"True." I laughed and sat up.

A throat cleared, interrupting our little banter.

My gaze landed on my sisters staring at me in awe. Their mouths parted, their eyes glancing back and forth between Angel and me.

Shit. I forgot they were still there. "Um, so, this is Angel." My cheeks heated. I never blushed. Ever. Angel did that to me. He unraveled what I had worked so hard to build. He broke down pieces of me, remolding it into what he wanted and craved. Just after one damn time together.

"It's nice to meet you," Brogan said, her brows narrowing. "If you hurt her, I'll cut you into tiny pieces and feed you to my dog."

Max giggled. "I already threatened him but that was good." They high-fived, and I couldn't help but shake my head.

Meeka didn't say anything. She stared at Angel for a brief second before heading back into the club.

I watched her go, wondering what the hell was going on with my sister.

"I didn't think I could make you blush," Angel whispered in my ear. His hand brushed along mine before wrapping around my wrist.

"Are you proud of yourself?" I asked, my breath coming out husky.

"A little bit."

Rolling my eyes, I elbowed him in the ribs—a hard laugh left his lips.

Sitting close to him, allowing him into my world with my sisters, was comfortable. It was nice. I had grown up with just my dad after my bitch of a mother left us high and dry. My family had been there for me but I found myself wanting to open up to Angel. To spend time with him. To just shoot the shit. And that *scared* me. More than anything I had ever done in my life. The fear of losing control because of one, mind-blowing, sex-filled night should have terrified me but instead it excited me in a way I needed to embrace. Angel made me feel alive. I didn't know what that said for us but for once, I didn't look at tomorrow.

TEN

ANGEL

I WATCHED her. I couldn't help it as I sat inches from her warm, slender body. I knew nothing about the woman chatting with her friends. Her voice firm, full of authority. She barked instructions, not caring in the least if she came off as a bitch. I grunted. She would get along with Vega.

Jay's gaze slid to mine, her eyebrows raising in question.

"Carry on," I said, waving my hand in front of me.

"So—" she turned back around "—as I was saying before I was rudely interrupted."

I bit back a laugh. Testing the waters, I laid down, resting my head in her lap.

"Um…what the hell do you think you're doing?" she snapped, her eyes heating with fire.

"Your meeting bores me." I feigned a yawn.

"My meeting bores you? Well, you shouldn't fucking be listening in on my meetings, Angel. This is club business. Just because we fucked—"

In a quick move, I sat up and cupped her chin. Her eyes widened, but that encouraged me further. "Listen, little girl," I growled, my words coming out smooth and deep. "Just because you feel the need to boss

82

everyone else around, doesn't mean you can do the same to me."

"I'm the president of—"

"I don't care who the *fuck* you are."

"Girls, give us a minute," Jay said quickly.

"But—"

"*Now*," she snapped.

After some shuffles and a couple of complaints later, we were alone. "Oh, Jay." I tilted her head. "It bothers you that I can make you do things you never did before. It seems to me—" I trailed a finger up her bare arm, watching the skin pucker with goose bumps "—like you're losing control. But you enjoy it, don't you? Being in control day in and day out is tiring. Let me take that from you, baby."

"Never," she breathed, her pupils dilating.

"You're lying." My hand slid to the back of her neck.

"How do you know that?"

"Your eyes tell your story, Jay. You don't know how to act around me. You open yourself up, and that scares you."

"I don't want it to," she whispered.

Ding, ding, ding!

Lying back down, I rested my head in her lap. "Tell me, Jay," I said, grabbing her hand and kissing her knuckles. "What do you want out of this?"

"I want… I want you to leave me alone."

"Nope. Not gonna happen. What else?"

She huffed, her deep-jade eyes not moving from mine. "I want to know what's going on in my club."

"We'll find out."

"We?"

"You need all the help you can get." I nipped her inner wrist. "Don't even bother arguing."

"Angel—"

"Go on a date with me," I blurted.

"Excuse me?" she asked, raising an eyebrow.

83

"One date. If you don't have a good time, I'll leave you alone."

"Why? What's in it for you?" She reached out to touch my face but stopped, pulling her hand back.

I smiled and sat up, my gaze landing on the men I called my brothers. We were working hard on fixing the hole in the club, but little did Jay know we had been trying to find out who did it since it happened. We may have been Special Operations, but we had connections.

"Why does something have to be in it for me? Can't I just want to go on a date with you?" I turned toward her, wrapping my hand around her wrist. Her gaze slid to the small touch, her cheeks reddening.

"I know how men work," she muttered.

"But you don't know how *I* work. Get used to me being around, Jay, because I'm not going anywhere."

"We fucked," Jay said, pulling out of my touch. "Nothing more."

"One date," I repeated. "I want to learn more about the woman that invades my dreams."

Her breath caught. "Fine. One date." She held up her hand when I went to speak. "But I can leave at any time."

"That won't happen, but you have a deal." I cupped her cheek, placing a soft kiss on her mouth.

Jay shivered, but she didn't pull away.

I was impressed at her control. I knew she wanted to throw a fit. Demand why I wouldn't leave her alone. She could have me thrown out. Although her sisters were smaller than me, I had no doubt they could give me a run for my money.

"I need to deal with this club shit," she muttered, her warm breath caressing my lips.

"What can I do to help?" *Besides making you feel better and keeping you stress free.* I didn't know why, but I felt the need to keep her safe. Something had sparked between us whether she wanted to admit it or not.

Jay pulled from my grasp and took the elastic out of her long red hair. "Just because I agreed to a date doesn't mean I want your help, Angel," she said, all the while running her fingers through her thick locks.

She was going to make it harder than I thought. "I'm referring to the hole in your club. I'm getting it fixed for you, and I want to help catch the person who did this."

Jay scoffed, pulling her hair back into a ponytail. "Yeah." She tapped my arm lightly. "You're cute, but don't even bother. I got this."

"Watch the attitude, woman," I snarled. "Or I'll fuck that sass out of you."

"I don't need you or anyone," she threw at me, her eyes narrowing to hard slits. "Everyone leaves me anyway," she whispered.

My breath hitched at those words. "I'm not going anywhere."

Jay shook her head and rose to her feet. "Forget what I said. It's been fun, Angel. I'll pay you, and you can leave. Don't worry about fixing the hole. I'll get someone else to do it."

Like fuck. "Jay, you are not paying me."

"Max," she said, ignoring me. "Grab the girls and meet me inside," Jay told her best friend as the tiny thing walked up to her.

"Everything okay?" Max asked, her gaze moving back and forth between us.

"Yup." Jay nodded. "I'll be there in a few."

Max gave a curt nod and whistled, rounding the rest of the sisters up before heading back into the clubhouse.

What Jay and I had, although short-lived, would not be over. She was hard assed and stubborn as hell but I knew she was attracted to me. Whether she wanted to admit to it or not, she didn't want us to be over any more than I did.

***

(Jay)

Before Angel approached me, I knew he was standing inches away from me. His spicy scent hit me hard. Leather. Sex. Male. All things I loved in a man, and it almost forced me to my knees. Whatever we had had just begun, but I had to end it before my heart got ripped out of my chest once again. I couldn't deal. The one person I could depend on was me, and that was it.

"I will prove to you that we work well together." Angel's words whispered across my skin.

"You don't know me. I don't know you. Why are you making this more difficult than it has to be?"

A deep chuckle sounded from behind me. "Oh, little girl. You want to play this game? Fine."

My eyes widened. "Excuse me?" I asked, turning around to face the man who didn't give up. So why *was* he giving up?

"I said, fine." He shrugged. "No date. I'll leave you alone. But I'm still fixing up your club."

"Angel—"

"No." He held up a hand. "It's on me. My boys would be happy to do it." And with that, he walked away, whistling to himself.

"No fight?" I called out.

"Nope." He winked, a wicked grin spread on his face.

Shit.

I watched as Angel strolled up to meet the guys as they hopped out of a black SUV. They greeted each other. Deep, rumbling laughter sounded, piercing me in the heart.

86

Angel nodded toward me, shaking his head as his brother whispered something in his ear.

My skin vibrated.

"Jay, you ready?" Max asked, approaching me.

"Yup." I linked arms with her, but my mind wandered back to the man standing a few feet away.

"Are you okay?"

"Yup," I repeated. I loved Max, but there was no way I could tell her…whatever that was. A piece of me was bothered that Angel had given up so fast. It messed with my head, and I didn't know why I cared.

"Good, cause I have some, uh…not so good news." Max fluffed her hair which I had come to know was her way of avoiding the inevitable. Her nervous gesture made my heart skip a beat.

"What now?" I snapped, pausing.

"Your dad and his boys are on their way."

ELEVEN

—jay

MOTHERFUCKING GREAT. That was all I needed. "Awesome. Why don't we invite the whole town? It's not like we have anything important to talk about. Nope. Nothing at all. Just the huge-ass hole in the wall. Or the fact that someone blew the shit out of our club when you and I were in it. But no. My dad and his crew stop by because we're just sitting on our thumbs doing nothing." What could I say? I was losing it.

"I think you need a vacation." Max linked her arm in mine, leading me to the office.

"No, what I need is for people to trust me," I muttered. I knew something was wrong. A piece of me was off. Had I had enough? The men I had to deal with day in and day out felt women had no right. If a woman had any type of authoritative bone in their body, she was considered a joke. I knew it was coming. I held the upmost respect for my father but with his boys breathing down his neck, he had to show rank. And I ended up being the victim. The back of my neck burned, the tiny hairs standing up on end. Glancing over my shoulder, my gaze locked with Angel's. His face held no emotion but much like myself, his eyes told all. Concern. Want. Need. God, the man was consuming my every waking thought.

"Do you know what they want?" I asked Max once we reached the office. I sat in my chair at the head of the table, fingering the wooden gavel in front of me.

"No, but I can't imagine it's good." Max scowled, but when the other girls strolled into the room, her expression changed from pissed off to happy in a split second. It was why I loved her. She never wanted to worry anyone. With Meeka being the timid one of our crew, Max found that she had to protect her. Meeka's dark eyes hid a story that none of us knew the words to.

"It's never good when they show up." If my dad came by himself, it was fine. But with the guys...? *Fuck my life.*

"Dante's Kings are here," Brogan pointed out, stepping away from the window she was perched at. Everyone was on edge.

My blood rippled, soaring through my body like molten lava. My heart pounded. My palms were sweaty. I didn't get nervous often but my dad's crew, although they were family, terrified even me.

A deep rumble of engines vibrated through me. The walls of the clubhouse shook from the impact of the sound. Bracing myself, I took a breath and leaned back in my seat.

Without me having to ask, Max greeted them. She was the friendly one of my sisters. She had a mouth on her like a sailor but could bring any man to his knees just by a pout from her full lips.

"Didn't feel like greeting your old man?" The deep voice caressed my ears, holding an edge of annoyance.

"You always know where to find me." I turned my chair around to face him, my breath catching at the sight before me. Four men. Large. Rough around the edges. Tattooed and scarred. They all stared down at me like I was a piece of shit they stepped in. It was a fucked up moment because I trusted these men with my life but when it came to MC business, the little ladies should be left out of it.

"Do you know why we're here?" My dad moved to the opposite end of the large table, sitting across from me. He motioned to his crew, indicating for them to sit while my girls stood behind me.

My jaw clenched, my hands curling into fists in my lap, but like always, there was nothing I could do. "To drive me fucking insane," I muttered.

A deep rumble of laughter sounded around the table.

"Now why would we want to do that?"

That voice. Tyler Bone, or T-Bone as he was known, strolled into the room. The vice president of Dante's Kings smirked, his grey eyes piercing through the heart he had shattered so long ago.

"To get under my skin," I retorted, watching the man who had destroyed my innocence years before.

His eyes twinkled. He clapped a hand on my dad's shoulder, leaning down to whisper something in his ear.

"Tell me what was so important you had to show up here unannounced," I demanded, my patience wearing thinner than a sheet of ice.

My dad looked around the table before his gaze landed on me. "You know I love you, right?"

"Of course." I crossed my arms under my chest, leaning back in my chair. "Not like you have a choice, though. I *am* fucking awesome."

An eruption of laughter exploded through the room, my racing nerves simmering a touch.

"That's my girl." My dad's face hardened. "But we have some business to deal with."

And there it was. "Every week you come in here, expecting me to change my mind and shut down my club. You were the one who convinced me to start the King's Harlots in the first place. But the last couple of months, something changed. What happened, *Daddy?*" A hot tingle raced down my spine. The more I spoke, the angrier I became. "Did you put this idea into his head, T?" I asked my ex. "Are you feeling threatened? A bunch of ladies making you feel like the pussy you are?" Bodies shifted. Gasps sounded. Glares were passed my way. Did I care? No. Would they do anything about it? No. I knew I could get away with what I said, and that made me happier than it should have.

"Jay, watch your mouth," my dad snapped, slamming his fist on the table.

I feigned a yawn. "Are we done?"

"No." Tyler placed his hands on the table, leaning on his knuckles. "We've just begun."

"Something's wrong," Max whispered.

No shit. "Fine. Talk. Tell us what's going on."

"We got news that someone else knows about the missing girls," my dad explained.

"Okay. Why is that news? I'm sure the families contacted the police about it." We needed all of the help we could get. If someone else tried to bring those fuckers down, more power to them.

"No. Someone else," Tyler added.

"I don't understand why this is a big deal." I shook my head. "We need to get these girls back."

"It's a big deal because someone is stepping on our turf trying to get the recognition for being the hero." Tyler paced back and forth.

"You're telling me right now that you would rather save the girls yourselves, risk more of them dying, than to get the extra help all because you're worried about a pissing match?" When no one responded, I laughed. "Dad, you're the president, you have nothing to prove. Why are you letting him influence you?"

My dad didn't say anything.

J.M. WALKER

"What the hell does he have on you?" I demanded, needing to know what I was getting myself into.

"Jay," Max said, grabbing my hand.

"No, Max. I'm sick of this," I told her.

"I know." She looked toward the group at the table before gazing back at me. "Just trust me on this."

I searched her face. Her eyes pleaded for me to calm down. "Fine." I rose from my spot. "I think this meeting is done. Dad, if you want to talk to me, you know where to find me. Alone."

"Nugget, we need to talk about this *now*," he insisted. "T-Bone has nothing on me."

He glanced down at his fist resting on the table before meeting my gaze.

I knew he was lying but I didn't press.

"As always, we have to clean up the streets for the fucking police. This small town would burn to the ground if it weren't for us," my dad continued.

"That's a bit dramatic, don't you think?" I asked. It wasn't like the cops didn't know about the missing girls.

"No. What's dramatic is the fact that women are disappearing and we can't do shit about it because no one cares," Max bit out.

"Jay." My dad's gaze softened. Pity.

"Don't." A lump formed in my throat. I didn't need pity. I needed fucking answers.

"We need to talk about it." My dad placed a file on the table in front of him. "But we don't have to right now." He pushed the file toward me. "On a different note, have you thought about what I said?"

"Why would I?" I asked, staring at the file like it was on fire. What was inside would no doubt burn me, leaving scars on a piece of my being that was stolen years before.

"Because this—" he waved a hand between us "— is dangerous."

"Too dangerous for women?" I snapped. "Just because we don't have dicks between our legs, it makes us weak?"

"I never said that," he ground out through clenched teeth.

"Daddy, I love you but I think you should leave." My gaze fell on each and every one of the large men surrounding the table. "All of you."

The men grumbled, attempting to argue with me, but I was having none of it. I slumped down in my chair and turned around. Facing the bay window, I stared out the tinted glass, waiting for the silence.

"Come on," Max said. "Let's go."

"We need to talk about this," my dad argued.

"You don't know your daughter. She's done talking," Max pointed out.

Grumbling.

Arguing.

I ignored it. As always, praising the silence when it came. But the quiet was louder than the noise from just a moment before.

Thought after thought bounced around in my head. I couldn't control the day-to-day nightmares that invaded my mind. They threatened to consume me even while I was awake.

I was twenty-one when she left me. My sister. My twin. My other half. The yin to my yang. I believed she was taken from me but I heard the whispers.

She ran off with a man. She eloped. She got pregnant. She needed out of our small town.

Lies. All lies.

Violet wouldn't just leave without giving some sort of explanation. My dad became a different person after that. And so had I.

A light knock sounded on the door pulling me from the thoughts pounding inside my head.

"Yeah." And then I smelled him. Leather. Man. Pure, hard male. Sex. "Angel," I breathed.

"Max said you were still in here." He stepped in front of me, leaning against the window ledge. "Rough meeting?"

I nodded. Under normal circumstances, people weren't allowed in the meeting room. But I trusted Max. And she trusted that I needed to see Angel. Which I didn't like to admit even though she was right, and it annoyed me.

"Anything I can do to help?" Angel asked, crossing his thick, tanned arms under his broad chest. His t-shirt stretched over his muscles, the veins in his biceps throbbing. My insides quivered, remembering him holding me like I was his lifeline.

"Tell me something. Anything. Something that has nothing to do with my club, your line of work, or whatever," I blurted out all in one breath.

Angel thought a moment, scratching the dark scruff on his chiseled jaw. "I have a dog. He's a Rottweiler."

"What's his name?" I asked, thankful for the distraction.

"Buck." Angel reached into the back pocket of his light-blue jeans and pulled out his wallet. "I found him as a puppy curled up on a pile of leaves under a bush in my backyard," he explained, handing me a small withered photo.

The picture showed a smiling Angel with his arm wrapped around a large dog. "He's handsome." The dog's eyes shone, happy and photogenic.

"He's my boy," Angel stated, his back straightening.

I smiled, handing him back the picture, wishing I had a friend like that. Someone who could take my mind off of everyday life. Someone who I could lay out my stresses on. When I fell apart, they would pick me up and put me back together. They would console me when I got lost inside of myself. Max was always there for me but she had her own shit going on; I couldn't expect her to drop everything whenever an issue arose.

Angel.

Yeah. Fucking. Right.

Angel pulled up a chair, sitting beside me.

We sat in silence, comfortable with the fact that neither of us spoke for what felt like hours. I was content, curling my legs under me and scrubbed a hand down my tired face. "My dad thinks I shouldn't have a motorcycle club, but he's the one who convinced me to start it in the first place." The words fell from my lips. Knowing for whatever reason they would be safe with the man sitting beside me. "I know his crew convinced him otherwise."

"But they're family."

"Yeah." I turned to Angel. "I grew up with them. My mom was my dad's old lady, but she had enough and left."

"I'm sure being raised by men wasn't easy," Angel pointed out, stretching his arms over his head. A crack sounded, causing him to shiver.

"It had its moments," I said, swallowing hard. My mouth became dry when all I could focus on were the veins protruding from his thick forearms. "Dating was hard," I added.

"I bet." Angel chuckled.

"Thank you." A slight heat crept up my neck at the outburst.

"For what?" He frowned.

When I didn't answer right away, Angel turned his chair toward me. "Jay."

"Genevieve," I corrected. "My name is Genevieve."

"Genevieve," he repeated, testing the name on his tongue. "It's nice to meet you."

My name leaving his lips forced my heart to skip a beat. "Hi."

"So why Jay?"

"It sounds rougher." I shrugged. "What person would be threatened by a Genevieve?" I joked.

"I would be." Angel laughed. "You're pretty threatening," he said, pulling my chair toward him.

"Am I?" I licked my lips, pushing my knees between his.

"Oh yeah. Especially this hot body of yours." His gaze moved to my lips, his thumb brushing over my mouth.

"Hmm. Does my body threaten you, Sin?" I purred, nipping the pad of his thumb.

With rough hands, he forced my knees apart. "Your body brings me to my knees."

"Your demands bring me to mine," I panted, leaning in for more. Grabbing onto the hem of his shirt, I inched my hands beneath the soft fabric. My fingers grazed over his hard abs, the tight muscles twitching under my touch.

"Fuck." His fingers dug into my thighs, no doubt leaving bruises in their wake.

I smirked, leaning back in my chair and pushed out of his touch. The warmth of his hands left me, and as much as I missed them, I needed to regain control before someone walked in on us. "I'm surprised you never left," I said, stretching out my legs in front of me and placing my feet in his lap.

Angel cleared his throat. "I was going to, but then I saw your dad's crew pull up."

"Aww, were you protecting me, baby?" I may have been joking with my question, but in all honesty, it warmed my heart.

"Yes."

And there you have it, folks. I think I just died and went to man-candy heaven. "Well, all right then."

"You may trust them," Angel continued. "But I don't."

"Why not?"

"I know a monster when I see one."

TWELVE

ANGEL

THEY MAY have been her family, but Dante's Kings were evil. They dealt with weapons, money laundering, drugs—anything they could get their hands on. They were lucky they left the women alone. Human trafficking and sex slavery were becoming the norm all through the world. Some places worse than others. Being in a small town, you'd think people would notice if you went missing. But people, although in everyone's business at times, stuck to themselves whenever a girl got the short end of the stick. They turned up their noses to the less fortunate. Our town was small enough that you ran into people you knew on a daily basis but big enough that you could disappear.

"Angel?"

My gaze snapped to Jay's. The frown on her face showed she had tried to get my attention. "Sorry," I mumbled.

"They aren't that bad," Jay stated, stifling a yawn.

"Do you believe that or is that what you're told to believe?" I asked, pulling off her boots one by one.

"It is what it is," she shrugged, yawning again.

"Didn't sleep well last night?"

"No," her eyes twinkled. "Someone wouldn't leave me alone."

A grin spread on my lips, remembering the warmth of her body wrapped around mine. "I think it was the other way around. You woke me up, remember?"

Her cheeks reddened. "I was hungry."

Fuck. Me. "Oh, I know." My dick twitched with thoughts of her reaching for me, begging me to make my way back inside her.

She smiled, her eyes fluttering closed. "It was worth it," she whispered, letting out a peaceful sigh. Something told me she didn't sleep much. The human trafficking shit was getting to her, but I didn't know how deep it went. Or how much she was involved.

I hadn't known her for long but every time I saw her, she became more and more beautiful. If that was even possible. Her long, red hair draped over her shoulder, her alabaster skin flushed with arousal.

My phone rang, interrupting my thoughts. "Angel."

"Where are you?" Asher asked.

"Inside the clubhouse. Why?"

"Spend as much time with her as you can, man."

He knew me well. "When?"

"Friday."

Great. That would give me three days to convince Jay to be with me. "How long?"

"I have no fucking idea, but this one will be short."

"How do you know?" I lowered my voice when Jay shifted, her eyes fluttering open.

"Vega wants us in, get what we need, and get home."

"I'm on leave." Not like that mattered. Vega didn't always play by the rules even though he expected us to. If he was pulling me in, something was wrong.

"He wants you in."

My gut twisted. "Fine."

"What gives?"

"What do you mean?" I wrapped my hand around Jay's ankle, pulling her closer.

She let out a small laugh and sat up.

"You never agree to come in so fast."

"Gotta go," I answered instead. I hung up and threw my phone on the table. Asher was right, but I would never tell him that.

"Everything okay?" Jay asked, rubbing her eyes.

No. Rising to my feet, I towered over her, blocking her in.

A small gasp escaped her lips, her mouth parting at the unexpected move.

"I have three days to show you this will work," I told her, trailing a finger over her collarbone.

"And then what?"

"I have to leave for work." I leaned down, brushing my lips over the soft spot just under her ear.

"What do you do?" she asked, tilting her head to give me better access to her neck.

"I'm a Navy SEAL."

In an abrupt move, she pushed back, her gaze snapping to mine. "You're a what?"

"Uh..." I frowned. "I'm a SEAL."

"You have *got* to be fucking kidding me."

THIRTEEN

—jay

"WELL, I wasn't expecting that kind of reaction." Angel slid his hand to the back of my neck. "What gives?"

"You're a SEAL?" It came out more as a whisper, no longer bearing the confidence I had felt a moment earlier. Why the hell was it bothering me? Oh yeah. Because it meant he would leave me just like everyone else. Angel and I hadn't known each other for long but I wanted him with me, by my side. I bit my lip to keep my face impassive, refusing to showcase any more emotions.

"We've discovered that. Jay, talk to me."

I shook my head, pushing out of his hold, and stood from the chair.

"Jay."

"I have to go. No, you should go." A million thoughts traveled through me. *We had sex. One night. That was it.* But with him being a SEAL, it sent a pang through my chest. It had been the best night of my life, and I wanted more. He wasn't stupid. He was good. Rough. Pure, hard male and I wanted to experience everything I could with the guy.

"Baby, talk to me." Angel grabbed my arm, spinning me toward him.

"I have nothing to say." I struggled to get out of his hold, but his grip tightened. My throat burned. Emotions. Fuck this. *He* did this to me. After my sister

101

left, I swore I would never let someone in again. But Angel? One night and I was already weeping like a baby over the guy.

"You sure had a lot to say last night," he reminded me, curling his fingers around the base of my throat. The hold, gentle yet strong, proved how much control he had over me.

My cheeks heated. "You need to go."

"No." He gripped my shoulders, backing me up until I hit the wall. "You need to talk to me."

"Angel." My hands clenched at my sides, itching to touch the hard body in front of me. But I couldn't. If I did, I would be done.

"I have three days." His nose brushed up the side of my neck, scenting me, breathing me in.

My mouth parted, a soft purr leaving my lips.

"Three days," he repeated, his voice oozing with sex.

"And then what?" I snapped. "Last night was a one-time thing. We fucked, and now we move on." But even I didn't believe those words leaving my mouth.

"Can you honestly stand here and tell me that's what you want?" His eyes searched my face. "You want this to be over?"

"Yes." I lifted my chin defiantly, but both of us knew I was lying. "You'll be gone for God knows how long. Why would you want to come back to this when you can have whoever you want?"

"Woman, don't you dare stand there and question what I want and don't want." His face hardened, his brows narrowing into sharp peaks. "I want you." He grabbed my hand, placing it on his crotch.

I swallowed hard, his erection growing beneath my hand. I let out a slow moan, his body tensing beneath my touch. "And why not?" I breathed.

"Because I will show you that this—" he waved his hand between us "—is worth it."

"What do you want from me?" I whispered.

"This." His mouth covered mine in a hard but slow—oh-so-agonizingly slow—kiss. His lips moved over mine, his tongue sliding into my mouth like it had done my body hours before. He kissed like he fucked. Hard. Fast. Rough and passionate. He swallowed my moans, feasting on my mouth.

My arms went around his neck on their own accord. My fingers dug into the thickness of his strong shoulders, gripping onto him like he was my lifeline. My body vibrated, my skin tingled. His pelvis pushed into mine, grinding and showing me just how much he wanted me. How much he craved me.

A groan slid between us, but I couldn't guess who made the sound.

Angel's body pressed against mine, pushing into me until all I felt was him. Every single inch. The heavy weight between his legs. The powerful, tree-trunk thighs holding me firm. His strong hands roamed down my sides until they reached my ass, grinding his hips against me.

"Angel," I breathed, breaking the kiss. The passion ensnared us, growing thick to the point of suffocating. All I could breathe was him. All I could feel was him. And I wanted more. One night was not enough. But a powerful fear closed in around me. My chest constricted.

His mouth trailed down the length of my jaw.

A warm heat spread up my body, unfurling into an inferno of desire. "Please," I panted, the ache for him growing between my legs.

He ignored my plea and continued massaging his hands over my body.

I whimpered, undulating my hips, hinting for him to take control and fuck me the way I knew he wanted.

He kissed.

I groaned.

He pushed.

I pushed back. I couldn't take it anymore. I shoved him, forcing him back into the chair.

"Not gonna happen, baby," he growled, grabbing my wrists.

"Fuck you, *this* isn't gonna happen." I straddled his lap, covering his mouth with mine. "You can't get me all hot and not do anything about it," I said against his lips, not liking the sound of the whine in my voice.

"Yes, I can. Three days." He pushed me off him.

"Why not now? You want to make me beg? Are you trying to get me to grovel at your feet, pleading for your cock?" I was getting pissed. My body vibrated, arousal and anger mixing together. "Well for your information, *baby*, I don't need you to please this ache. I know plenty of men who—" Everything next happened so fast. Angel pinned me against the wall, his hand pushing against the side of my head. My arousal for him grew. What that said about me, I didn't know, but I enjoyed when he manhandled me. When he lost self-control and took everything from me that he so desperately craved.

"Watch your next words, little girl." Angel's hold on my body strengthened, his hot breath scorching the side of my neck. "It was one night but your pussy is mine. I own it. You got me? By the time these three days are up, you will be pleading for me to take what rightfully belongs to me. Remember that when your hands slide into the depths of your heat." And with that, he released me, giving me a wicked smirk before he left the room.

As soon as the door closed, I let out a slow breath and slid down the wall. *Well, that was unexpected.*

***

(Angel)

Walking away from her was the hardest thing I had ever done. After all of the missions I had been on, getting fucking shot—leaving Jay trembling and begging for me to fuck her was the ultimate test. Who knew if I failed or not, but by the shock in her eyes, these three days would be tougher than I thought. She knew I wanted her. The erection pressing against the fly of my jeans was a clear indicator. My cock strained, begging to be set free, pleading for a warm body.

Although the exact words never left her mouth, her eyes had told me everything I needed to know. She wanted me, and she was pissed I denied her. But I was damn determined to make her see reason when the three days were up.

Three days.

It would be the longest seventy-two hours of my life.

"Hey, man," Dale stepped up beside me as I rounded the corner. "You look like shit."

"Thanks," I muttered. "And you look cute as a button."

He chuckled.

"What are you still doing here?" I asked him once we headed outside into the cool afternoon air.

"Uh…" He pushed a hand through his short, blonde hair. "Would you believe me if I said I was learning how to run an MC?"

"Nope."

"Didn't think so." Dale walked away before I could ask any more questions.

I knew he and Max had a thing, but they were more secretive than Jay and me.

Leaning against the trailer, I watched my brothers. They joked and worked, laughed and acted like they weren't about to go into the pits of hell in three days.

Everything was normal until we jumped off the plane. Everything was normal until we fell into the abyss. We would live second by second, praying and pleading that we would make it out alive. That we would get what we came for.

Jay's unexpected reaction to me being a Navy SEAL threw me off. Everyone had left her. Her words registered home. I never had anyone until I met my brothers so I could understand her worry. She had her club, her sisters, but even then, sometimes it wasn't enough. It proved right there she wanted more out of this but I could also see the fear in her eyes.

My lips tingled, remembering the impact of her mouth on mine. I could still taste her sweet scent. Hear her breathless moans and feel her slender but firm body against mine.

Three days.

"Boss," Asher called out, heading toward me. "It's time."

Fuck.

FOURTEEN

—jay

THREE DAYS.

As-fucking-if.

There was no way Angel could make me fall for him in that short amount of time. I had spent years closing myself off. Protecting my emotions and sanity against the powers of love. Love. *Puh-lease.* When Violet left me—my sister, my best friend—I realized then that the world was more corrupt than I thought. I knew it wasn't by choice. No matter what people had said. No matter what the rumors were. She was taken from me. But a part of me resented the fact she allowed herself to be taken. And then guilt took over. It was soul crushing, but I accepted the weight on my shoulders because I deserved it.

Violet was the wild one. She had no filter when it came to the words that left her mouth. She wore what she wanted. Said whatever was on her mind and had men eating out of the palm of her hand. Even though she was young. When she was taken, I took on the role so to speak. Of course, I could never take over her personality, but having some of her in me gave me peace of mind. We were twins. We could play each other perfectly, having switched places so many times: we were a part of each other.

Violet would laugh and tell me she was proud of me for standing up to our father and having a MC.

"This isn't you, Nugget. Your sister, yes. But you? Never." As soon as my father said those words, I started the MC out of spite. I needed something of my own. A sisterhood. Powerful women who could stand up to men and society in general. We would prove that we weren't the weaker sex. We were equal.

It had been two days since I last spoke with Angel. He gave me three. I knew he was talking out his ass but a part of me hoped, no, prayed, that he would be it. That I would find my one. I was almost thirty. I was ready to settle. With Angel? Who knew?

Sitting in the meeting room by myself was peaceful. I loved my girls, my sisters, but all of the different personalities crashing together grated on my nerves at times.

The room was quiet. Solemn. A serenity of hope washed over it. My thoughts traveled to the missing girls—not even women yet. Daughters. Sisters. Nieces. And *my* sister was one of them.

I knew it. Deep down in the marrow of my soul. No one believed me. Not even my father.

"Nugget, I am doing everything I can to see she comes home. But she probably ran off with some boy."

"You honestly believe that, Daddy?" I asked him, *determined to make him see that my sister would never do such a thing. She was wild but she wouldn't leave without telling me first.*

"I have to believe that. Then I can move on."

Those words stuck ever since. I loved my father but his crew, mainly Tyler, brainwashed him into thinking his daughter was a slut and hightailed it out of our Godforsaken town.

Oh, Violet. Where the hell are you?

"Jay?"

I jumped, finding Max and the girls standing in the doorway. I motioned for them to come in, not in the mood, but I knew it needed to be done. The presidency took over, and I found myself being met with anger and frustration. Those women. So young. Most just babies and hadn't even hit puberty yet. Whether my sister was one of them or not, I would avenge them. I would make it so females didn't have to be scared to leave their home or place of work. If it was a mass human trafficking job, I wasn't stupid. There was no way I could destroy them on my own but I could take them out in my town, and I would do it with or without help. I had to start somewhere, and I would take them out one by one.

Three days is what Angel gave me. Fuck that noise. The delicious brooding man could wait. I needed his skills—not the bedroom kind. But of course, if he didn't show up the next day, which I was sure he would have a good reason for, I would make him stew. A small smile crept on my face. He was adamant I would fall for him. Maybe he was right. But two could play that game. I was the creator of my own story, and no man was going to change that.

***

(Angel)

"You told us three days," I said, raising my voice at Vega. He was the captain, but at that point, he was the piece of shit on the bottom of my boot.

"You questioning a direct order?" he threw back, rising to his feet.

"I'm questioning why it's so important that we go in now. You put me on leave, remember?"

"Angel," Vega slammed a fist on the desk. "I suggest watching the attitude or I *will* put you on leave. Permanently."

Chewing my inner cheek, I mentally counted to ten and waited. I loved my job. I lived and breathed for it. But since I met Jay, I wanted a break. A vacation of sorts. I knew going in that I could get called in at any point and there was nothing I could do about it. It was why my brothers and I were single. For the most part. We weren't married. No kids. No one holding us back. No one making us feel guilty for missing birthdays and holidays. But I wasn't young anymore. Not in the physical sense of the word. I had been a SEAL for over ten years. Flying through training as fast as I could because I didn't want to go home to an empty house. My dog, Buck was all I had, but with him aging, call it selfish of me, I couldn't stand to go home to find him dead.

Those three days were supposed to be for Jay and me. I had every intention of introducing her to Buck and the guys properly. But since getting called in, I had no chance of that. And I knew she would be pissed.

"I called you in and took you off leave because you and Vice-One are my best team. *You* are Vice-One, and the team won't work without you. I am man enough to admit that," Vega confessed, leaning forward on his arms.

"What's going on?" I asked, swallowing my frustration.

"Those women you found?"

My heart sped up. "Yeah?"

"There's more."

"Are you fucking shitting me right now?" Under normal circumstances, my outburst would cost me. Extra training. Cleaning the gutters. Spending an hour in a bathtub of ice. Who the hell knew? But Vega knew I was passionate about the cause. Those women, whoever they were, were taken. Their souls stolen along with their dignity and innocence.

"A couple SEALs from another squad stumbled upon a shack smaller than our barracks," Vega explained.

"Shit." He didn't have to tell me anymore before I already knew what he was going to say.

"There were no survivors, Angel," Vega said, squeezing the bridge of his nose.

"Why the hell is this happening?" I shouted. "What do these sick fuckers want? They round up these women for what? To kill them? Do they get off on these women dying under their control?"

"This is what I need you and Vice-One to find out."

"Why us? It's not our job," I reminded him, struggling to keep it together.

"Because," Vega slumped down in his seat, "while you go in to do your regular work, I need you to keep your eyes open."

"Hush-hush?"

"Yes."

Now *that* was my kind of mission. I had been in the Navy since I was eighteen. In the beginning, I played by the rules, but I learned fast that the human race, no matter the type of authority you worked under, were evil and played by their own set of rules.

"Think you can handle it?" Something flashed in Vega's eyes, but it disappeared before I could question it.

"If you're asking me if I'll rat or if no matter what happens, will I say something, the answer is no," I reassured him.

"You know what I'm asking of you, right?"

"Go in. Find out everything we can, no matter the force, and get out." I repeated the mantra that had been drilled into our heads through training. "But why did you need to speak me alone?"

"Because," Vega sat back, brushing a hand over his buzzed head. His tanned face showed signs of defeat. "Your guys won't go in without you. As long as you have your head in the game, they will be behind you every step of the way."

"So what if I said no?"

"You wouldn't." Something flashed again. He was hiding something. Although he kept his gaze locked with mine, I could sense something was off with him. Vega had been with me every step of the way throughout my military career. But something had changed.

"Is there something going on, Sir?"

He hesitated. "Why?"

"Just asking." I shrugged. "You're stressed." He didn't appear stressed but feeding him the lie might get me some answers.

"I'm good." Vega flipped through some papers on his desk, not meeting my gaze.

"What if you couldn't find someone to replace me?" I asked, taking his silence as a hint.

"I would get someone else."

"No you wouldn't, because you have no one else. Vice-One is the squad that will do the dirty work. The one that will do anything to get the job done." We all had our own qualities, our own shit we were good at, but Vice-One got down and dirty with the bad guys. "So it's not like I have a choice. I *have* to say yes."

Vega nodded once. Reaching for the phone on his desk, he pressed a button. "Tell the rest of Vice-One to join me in my office." And that, folks, meant the conversation was over.

Ignoring the nagging feeling in the bottom of my gut, I braced myself for the bombardment of questions. The whys. The hows. It wasn't our job to know what was going on, but Vega also never went against schedule and called us in early. That was unlike him and the guys knew that.

"Angel?" Coby, the quiet one, spoke first.

"What's going on, Boss?" Asher asked me.

I looked to Vega for an answer, but his gaze hardened. *Fine*. He didn't want to assist me in making it easier—the blame would fall back on him. It wasn't like he was giving me all of the details anyway.

Taking a breath, I turned my attention to my squad. My brothers. The men I had spent the past several years with in the pits of hell and back. "More women have disappeared, leaving no traces behind." When Vega didn't say anything, I continued. "From what I have read—" I ran my fingers down the black and white photo of the young girl staring up at me from the thick file in my lap "—eight girls have gone missing within the last month. They ranged in ages from seventeen to twenty-two. We found four survivors last time, but this…" I swallowed past the bile and the anger rushing through my blood. "This time there were none."

A string of curses sounded around the room.

I waited for them to finish before allowing myself to continue. It felt like we were talking about the females as if they were objects. Bought, used, and tossed away. Those men, if they could even be called that, were the worst kind of monster. A darkness so strong the shadows consumed you. They took everything from those girls, breaking them down and building them back up to service the needs of the bastards.

"Do we know anything about these girls?" Coby asked, his dark eyes showing no hint of emotion, but after knowing him for years, I knew rage was pouring through him. Through all of us. He just hid it well. But the lack of control when it came to his anger nagged at him. I knew it was a problem for him, but I didn't know how deep that went.

"We know these girls were lost. They weren't like the others. They didn't come from prestigious families. They weren't amounting to anything." I flipped through a couple of papers, trying my hardest to ignore the faces staring up at me. "All of them were in and out of foster care, thrown into the system right from the beginning. These men made it so no one would miss

113

them. I don't believe it, though. I think some of these girls did come from good homes but no one is talking."

"We have to do something," Dale said, speaking up.

Something was up. Vega had aged in a matter of weeks. Lines had appeared at the corners of his eyes, and a furrowed brow took up residence on his forehead. Every so often he would rub a hand over his head but refused to glance my way.

"You leave for base in half an hour," Vega rose to his feet. "You'll meet Vincent Stone there."

"Who the hell is that?" I asked, my head snapping around.

"He's new to Vice-One."

"Excuse you? You added someone to my squad without consulting me?" The day just got better and better.

"I run the show here, Angel." Vega's jaw clenched. "You best remember that."

"You can't just throw an unknown into this shithole. We have no fucking idea what we're even up against. Who's to say this fucker won't fuck things up?"

"Language, Angel," Asher nudged my arm. "He signs our fucking paychecks." He winked at me, a slight grin spreading on his face.

He was right. Vega was a good man, and he was also our boss. I needed to control myself. "I don't appreciate you not coming to me first."

"I don't have to do shit." Vega walked to the window, opening the blinds to let some sun stream through onto the cloudy mood.

"What happens if we don't find what you're wanting us to find?" Dale asked, his deep voice booming through the silence of the small room.

Heads turned his way, no doubt surprised at his question. Dale was the hothead. Jump in head first and not think twice before doing it. But with the females going missing, even he had to take a step back.

"Then keep searching," Vega bit out, his voice rough.

"Captain…" Asher glanced at the file in my hand. "I don't know—"

"I don't fucking *care* what you don't know!" Vega shouted, slamming his fist against the wall. An award shook against the wall before falling to the floor with a shatter.

"Sir." I rose to my feet. "What's going on?" I had known him for years. He had a temper but his head was always in the game. But in that moment, something was off. And that was when I took in his appearance. His uniform was disheveled, the wrinkles at the corners of his eyes more pronounced. He was a lost man, hiding from whatever demons he was dealing with.

Vega leaned against the edge of the large window, gripping onto it like a lifeline. I knew him well but not enough. He had a drinking problem but no one brought it up.

"Will you give us a moment?" I asked my brothers.

They nodded in agreement but grumbled under their breath. They knew Vega wouldn't talk with a crowd. If I could get information, any at all, it would help us with our mission. That shit needed to be dealt with. We needed to move on with our lives and do our actual job.

"Watch him," Coby mumbled, clapping a hand on my shoulder. "Something's not right. He's on edge."

I nodded once, thankful my brother saw the change as well.

Coby would know since he had lived on that same edge for years.

"You need to talk, Boss," I told Vega once we were alone.

"About what?" His gaze snapped to mine, bright and shiny.

"What's going on?" I pushed, knowing it would be the one way to get him to speak.

"What's going on?" he repeated, shaking his head. A light laugh left him. "Everything is going on. These women, these girls... I've never cared about something that had nothing to do with the country we live in. We fight together. We die together. We breathe—"

"Together," I finished for him.

"Yeah." He sighed. "We do."

"So what's the problem?" My heart pounded against the walls of my ribcage. My hands became sweaty. I had a feeling, a horrible agonizing feeling, that he was closer to the mission than he let on.

"My niece." Vega swallowed hard. "She was taken during the night last night."

"*Fuck*," I blurted. "And you think it's whoever took the other girls?"

"It has to be. It makes sense. My sister is broken over this. If I don't get her back..." His eyes shone. "I don't know what will happen to her."

"We'll get your niece back," I reassured him. Something else was still bothering him. "Safe and sound," I added. Yeah, cause I was God and knew all. *Shit*.

"Don't you dare sit there and tell me that shit. I'm not stupid. That's the same line we use on civilians."

"I don't know what you want me to say," I said. "This is not our job. We protect our country. We get the bad guys who threaten it. Some of these girls aren't even from the US."

"I need you to go in because of my niece. I don't fucking care if it's against protocol. I don't care if I get fired over it. I need her back. For my sister." Vega's voice was filled with shaky desperation, his eyes moving back and forth, wild and bright. "I refuse to watch my sister lose herself because some bastards get their rocks off by preying on the weak and innocent."

I bit back a scoff. The women I knew would chew up those men and eat them for dinner. My thoughts traveled to a tall redhead with alabaster skin that I couldn't wait to feel against my own again and again. Jay and her girls were anything but weak. They each had their own story and learned to live in a world overrun by men. The Alpha inside of me wanted to protect them. Jay was the Queen of her surroundings, and I found myself wanting—no, *needing*—to be her King.

"Angel?"

My thoughts snapped back to reality. Clearing my throat, I headed to the door. "We will find your niece." Dead or alive went unsaid.

Vega nodded, slumping in his chair. "Thank you. Right now, I'm willing to do anything and give up what I've worked so hard for to see my sister happy again."

I knew how he felt. Although I had no blood relatives that I knew of, Vice-One were the brothers I never had. They were my family. We fought. We argued. We shot the shit together. We were a unit. We put our lives on the line for each other, and I wouldn't change it for anything.

"Who am I dealing with when it comes to this new guy?" I asked, remembering Vega mentioning a Victor Steve or whatever the hell his name was.

"Vincent Stone. Best in his class. Been in the military for over five years. Needed a change when he saw some shit go down and transferred to the Navy."

"Makes sense," I mumbled.

"He's strong, and he won't let you down, Angel." Vega handed me a file. "Read up on him if needed but know that he's loyal."

I nodded, leaving the office to be met by my brothers.

They threw question after question at me. *What is going on? What now? When do we leave?* But the one that stuck out the most was Dale's question of, *How long will we be gone?* I was curious to find out as well because I missed Jay. I missed her sass. Her witty humor and the sailor mouth she had on her. Knowing I needed to call her, my stomach twisted.

"Angel," Coby's baritone voice snapped me from my thoughts. "What's doing, brother?"

"We head out in ten. I don't want to think about home yet because then time will go by slower," I told the men standing around me. "We will be meeting Vincent Stone at the base."

"Ooh," Dale rubbed his hands together. "Fresh meat."

"I like 'em raw," Asher joked a long with him.

Dale sighed. "It was like we were meant to be," he swooned, batting his eyes.

Asher laughed, clapping a hand on Dale's shoulder.

"I hope Vincent knows what he's getting into," Coby said as Asher and Dale walked away.

Yeah. Me too.

FIFTEEN

ANGEL

THE MOMENT we started toward the base, the excitement in my stomach grew. It started out as a shiver, sliding up my back and gripping my spine until it took my breath away. I loved my job. I lived for it. I breathed for it. We all did.

Set up outside of town; the drive to base took three hours. That part was the worst. I would rather fly, jump, and fall, landing in the unknown until we had to find our way out.

We were all antsy.

Asher's knees bounced up and down.

Coby leaned his head against the wall of the convoy, his eyes closed. His face was calm, relaxed even, while he waited.

Dale bobbed his head up and down to the beat playing through the earbuds in his ears.

And I just sat there, watching, waiting.

We all had our own vice, our own way of dealing. We often went in blind, not knowing what we were getting into until we got to base. Even then we weren't given much information. We went in, got the bad guy, and left. Most times it went off without a hitch, but not always. We all had our scars to prove it. And Vincent Stone, the newbie, would definitely know about missions going wrong. My heart hurt for him. I wasn't a sentimental guy. But I would lay my life on the line

119

for my brothers, the men sitting around me, before I let them leave me.

"Half an hour," Asher told us, a slow grin spreading on his face. He loved that moment, going in, not knowing what would happen. I usually did too, but I was ready to go home before shit even began.

Jay.

I should call her.

"You should call her."

I glanced up at Coby. "Are you reading minds now?"

"No. I just know you," he pointed out.

And that was why I hated getting close to people. I loved my brothers but sometimes I wanted things for myself. We spent so much time together that we knew each other's dirty little secrets. Or I did, at least. Funny thing was, I hated talking, but they sure enjoyed talking to me.

Three days. It was all I wanted. Seventy-two hours to make up for the weeks away. I needed to get to know Jay. I craved her touch. Her gaze as it roamed over my body. I wanted to wrap myself in her warmth, reveal everything I had felt over the years. Fear. Happiness. Regret. Emotions I had never let anyone see before. Feelings I never considered sharing until I met her.

My phone buzzed.

Jay: Three days, huh?

Shit. I called her instead of texting her back.

"What?"

A slow grin spread on my face at Jay's sass. God, I loved the mouth on her. "Miss me?"

"Please," she scoffed.

"I will make it so every time I leave, your body aches for me." Shifting in my seat, I adjusted my pants.

The mere thought of her spread-eagle on her bed sent heat racing to my dick.

Her breath caught. "You told me three days."

"What do you want from me, Jay? I can't tell my boss that I need to stay home because I have this woman who gets under my skin."

"I hope I stay under your skin, Angel," Jay purred. "And I hope you lay awake at night, thinking of me with only your hands to satisfy you."

A loud click sounded in my ear. All of those thoughts pushed their way into my mind, giving me ideas on what I would do to her when I got home. Her attitude struck a chord with me and made me crave her even more. She was pissed, but I knew it wasn't because I had to leave for work. I was getting to her. And she hated me for it. In the short time I had known her; she had let it be clear that she would rather be alone. She loved her sisters but her trust was shattered when the people closest to her had ripped her heart out.

"Was that Jay?" Dale asked from the other side of the convoy.

"Yeah," I answered. "Did you tell Max we left?"

"Uh, yeah." His cheeks turned a light shade of pink.

Huh. It seemed my brother had a thing for the vice president of King's Harlots. Maybe more than I thought.

"Dale's in love," Asher teased, punching him in the shoulder.

"Fuck you I am," Dale snapped. "I get regular pussy with no strings. What better relationship is there?"

"Loyalty," Coby answered. "Or so I've been told."

I didn't know, either. But I knew I wanted that one person to go to bed with at night and wake up to every morning. I wanted to give her breakfast and coffee in bed. And then we would make love until we had to go to work. To see that person, knowing you are spending the rest of your life with them, would be satisfying.

I never thought I would want a committed relationship. What Jay and I had was too soon to even consider that, but my short time with her made me realize I wanted more. Marriage, kids, everything you could share with that one special person. I needed it. I craved it. And I would work damn hard to make Jay see that there would be more to us than just sex.

***

(Jay)

It was unreasonable for me to get pissed over Angel being called away earlier than expected. But a part of me wanted him to prove that I would be his in just three short days. The back and forth was enough to drive me insane. I craved the feeling of his hands on my body, his mouth brushing across my skin. His fingers kneading into the flesh of my ass as he helped me ride the beautiful essence of him.

A tingle brewed between my legs, forcing me to squeeze them together. My hands did nothing. My fingers didn't appease the torture. It hadn't been long since I saw the man, and already I was losing it.

"Jay, girl, are you all right?" Brogan approached me wearing shorts and a white tank top.

"Yeah." I shrugged. "I guess."

"Come." She hooked her arm through mine. "Let's go work out," she said, leading us down the hallway to the gym we had set up.

Brogan loved working out and being healthy. She was a couple inches shorter than me but could no doubt drop me on my ass faster than most people gave her credit for.

"Do you remember what we did last time?" she asked, stepping away from me and opening the door.

"You made me hit some things." But for the life of me, I couldn't remember all of the tips and exercises she told me.

Brogan laughed, which in turn made me smile. The sound of her laughter was full and loud. It rolled up from her stomach, letting everyone around her know that something was funny. Her dark-auburn curls bounced, brushing her shoulders with a shake of her head. She walked around the punching bag, cracking her knuckles and sizing up the item before her as if it were her victim.

"Why do you work out so much?" I asked, stretching my arms above my head. I was limber and obsessed with making my limbs move in positions that freaked most people out but lifting weights and gaining muscle wasn't important to me. I smiled to myself, remembering Angel's breathy groan when he realized how flexible I was.

"I'm single. It helps reduce my frustration." She winked, hitting the bag with a balled-up fist.

"Does it work?"

"No," she mumbled.

I laughed, grabbing hold of the bag and watching her hop from one foot to the other.

"That guy you've been seeing, he treat you good?" she asked, not breaking contact with the bag.

"Well, I don't know him that well, but yeah, I guess you could say he does," I told her, a shiver rippling down my spine at the mere mention of Angel.

"That's good." She glanced up at me through dark lashes. "I wouldn't want to have to make him disappear or anything. You think it'll become serious?"

"You think you'll start seeing someone anytime soon?" I threw back.

"*Ha*," she scoffed. "Not likely."

"Exactly." I gave her a small smile.

"You like him," she pointed out, grabbing the bag and motioning for me to start hitting.

"He's delicious and gives me what I want. What's not to like?" The man could please me with just his fingers for the rest of my life and I would be a happy girl.

"Does he give you everything you want?" Brogan started spouting off orders before I could answer her question. Smart girl, because I wouldn't have answered anyway. "Back straight. Fists up. Hit like your life depends on it."

"I think *your* life depends on it because I don't care…" My voice trailed off.

"You don't care about what?" she questioned, her brows narrowing. "About life? About *your* life?"

"That's not what I meant. Of course I care about my life. I just… Forget I said anything." I rambled. I didn't ramble. I always knew what to say, and when I did, I would say it. No questions asked. Sometimes it got me into trouble, but in most cases, people appreciated it.

"What's going on, Jay?" Brogan pressed.

I slammed my fist against the bag, a sharp pain shooting up my forearm.

"Shit, Jay, you're gonna hurt yourself." Brogan grabbed my hand, rubbing her thumb over my knuckles. She stretched out my fingers, moving my hand back and forth. "Does that hurt?"

I shook my head. I didn't know what had come over me, but I wondered if Violet felt it. Wherever she was. We had been told our whole lives that twins had a different connection than regular siblings. We would joke that it wasn't true.

"Come on, Jay. Let's switch places."

"But why?" I had asked my sister. "I'm boring."

Violet had hugged me. "You are not boring. You're my sister."

124

I was boring. She'd known it. I knew it. Everyone knew it. But for whatever reason, Violet had never said so.

We had sat on the bench in our backyard for what felt like an eternity, the silence swallowing us whole.

"Why do you want to switch places? What happened this time?" I had asked, leaning my head against her shoulder.

"Nothing."

She was lying. Every time Violet had gotten into trouble, she wanted to switch places. She told me it made her feel normal for at least a moment. She'd never told me why. But she didn't have to. We may have been twins but our personalities were different.

"Okay."

Her shoulders had relaxed, a long sigh escaping her. "Thank you."

A breath left me on a whoosh at the painful memory. It had been a beautiful day, one filled with laughter and sunshine. I wish I would have known how much Violet needed me to switch lives with her. God, I missed her. My chest ached. A cold shiver of fear rippled down my spine.

"Jay?" Brogan frowned.

"I need a moment." I knelt on the mat, taking deep, cleansing breaths. Everyone around me knew that my sister was taken. They didn't talk about it. So when the girls started going missing, I could feel the eyes on me. The questions about if I was going to snap or lose it going unsaid.

I needed an unbiased person. Someone who didn't know her. Who didn't know my relationship with her. Someone neutral.

Angel.

Usually, I would curse myself for even thinking his name, but at that moment, I needed something other than the panic attacks to keep me warm at night.

125

I needed *him*. It scared me but I would push that fear aside if it meant getting my sister back.

"If you need to talk," Brogan offered. "I'm here."

"I know." I took a deep breath. "Thank you."

"I think that's it for today," she said, helping me to my feet.

I nodded, rubbing my shaky hands down the front of my sweats. Grazing a hand down the smooth leather of the bag, I closed my eyes.

I will battle you. I will overcome you. You are my demon but I will not let you win.

SIXTEEN

ANGEL

I CALLED Jay a week into the mission. Knowing I would get the sass I was craving, a tingle of heat spread over my body.

"Hello?"

I frowned at the small voice. "Jay?"

"Hi, Angel." She sighed.

"Uh…" My stomach tensed. "Hi."

"How are you?"

"I'm…fine. How are you?" The casual conversation was throwing me off. It wasn't like her.

"I'm…" She hiccupped. "Fine."

"Have you been drinking?" I asked, catching Coby's gaze when he motioned that it was time to meet our new recruit.

"A little bit," Jay answered, a slight slur moving over her words. She was mellow, a husky tinge coating her voice.

Well, that explains it. "You should go to bed," I told her, even though I wanted to hear more of what she had to say.

"Don't want to."

"And why not?" I asked, lowering my voice.

"It's lonely. I need a big, dark, brooding man to keep me warm. Angel," she purred, "are you that man?"

Fuck me hard and call me Sally. "Yes." I would be whatever she damn well wanted me to be.

127

"Good." And with that, she hung up.

I stared at my phone, stunned by what just happened. If my semi hard-on was any indication, I needed to go home.

"Ready?" Coby asked, clapping a hand on my shoulder.

"No." I never liked new recruits. They thought they knew it all. But with Vincent Stone being in the military for a while, I had hoped that it wouldn't be so bad with him. Understanding that everyone started somewhere, you would think I would be more reasonable. Vega had taken a chance on me back in the day. I should have done the same in return. Vega had thrown Vice-One together. We were trained. Specialized. And some of us took that to heart more than others.

"Boss." Asher came up beside me. "I met Stone while working out this morning. Just wanted to say that I think he'll fit in." Asher jogged off, leaving me to my thoughts.

"He might be good for us," Coby added after the fact.

I met his dark gaze. He wasn't a man of many words, but when he did speak, I took it to heart.

"After what he's been through, I'm surprised he wants to continue on."

"Maybe he needs to," Coby suggested. "I know if it were me, I would have to do something to keep my mind off of it. I also know that you would want me to move on. You would want me to fight for what I lost."

He was right. We had a country to fight for. And we had women to save. "Does he know about the girls?"

"He's been briefed."

"Good." We just needed to figure out how to save Vega's niece. Who knew what she had already been through? I just prayed she was still alive.

"What are we going to do if we can't find Vega's niece?" Coby asked, taking the question right out of my head.

"Pray to God she doesn't suffer," I mumbled.

"Fucking A."

We left the barracks, heading out into the hot afternoon sun. We were met by the other guys and a new person who I assumed was Vincent Stone.

"I assume you are the boss," the large man said, greeting me with a nod of his head.

"You could say that," I replied, sizing him up. He was huge. Had at least twenty-five pounds on all of us. The tank of a man hid behind his wall of a shape; I could tell by the darkness in his gaze.

"Well, as soon as you need me to start, I am ready," he said, matter-of-factly.

"All right," I said slowly. "You've met everyone?"

He nodded.

Asher took his gun apart and started cleaning it. Dale and Coby sparred back and forth, nodding our way before continuing.

They were my brothers—so was Vincent now. "You're a part of us now, Vince," I told him. "Everything we do, we do it as a unit. No man goes in alone, and no man comes out alone. We are one."

"Stone."

"Excuse me?"

"Stone," he muttered. "Everyone calls me by my last name."

"All right. Stone." I clapped him in the shoulder. "Welcome to the Navy."

"I won't let you down. I've been in this for a long time but I believe no matter how long we do something, we can always learn."

I cocked my head. "I think you'll fit right in."

"My brothers come first. I may not know any of you yet, but I will lay my life on the line to make sure we all get out safely."

I liked him already.

"Tell me something I don't know," he said, crossing his thick arms under his chest.

"Asher is our newest recruit before you. I've known him since I was a kid, and I convinced him two years ago to join the military. Under normal circumstances, it takes years for someone to become special ops but as you may have guessed already, Vice-One isn't your typical squad. Coby is the quiet one but knows everything there is to know about every kind of gun out there. He also has the best times when it comes to taking a rifle apart and putting it back together. His last kill shot was the furthest on record."

"Ghost," Stone stated, staring at the solemn man a few feet away.

"Yes." Word got around about my brother. He was the best of the best, and I was thankful I had him at my back. "He doesn't go by that name, so I don't suggest calling him it."

"Understood. But he is inspiring," Stone said. "We would use him as motivation. 'Be like Ghost' was our motto for years."

"Don't tell him that," I said, nodding toward Coby.

"No doubt," Stone grunted. "I hate being the center of attention myself, so I can't imagine how he feels."

"He's told me he believes in teamwork. That he wouldn't be where he is without the rest of us." I crossed my arms under my chest. "No I in team."

"He's a good man."

"He is," I agreed. "Well, Stone. Now that you got introduced to everyone, it's time we show you how we welcome new recruits."

"I'm not new." He frowned, a slight smirk spreading on his face.

"You are to us." Asher came up beside him, clapping a hand on his shoulder.

"We want you to feel at home," Dale said, coming up on the other side of him. "And we're going to show you exactly how we do that."

"How so?" Stone challenged.

"Drinks are on you tonight," I explained. "But first, how about a little game of dress up?"

***

(Jay)

It had been three weeks since I saw Angel. We talked on the phone every now and again, but it wasn't the same. It was casual, comfortable. We didn't talk about us or what we wanted out of our time together. We told each other about our day, what latest movie we had seen or if we had read a good book. It was safe. Did we want more out of what we had? Were we ready? Was it enough? It fucking scared me to give my all to someone again when so much of me had been ripped out at the hands of another man. I had to explain that to Angel. I needed to make him understand that it wasn't him. It was me. The clichéd truth bothered me.

Music pounded through the brick walls of the clubhouse. Max had decided to throw a party, inviting half of the town over to try and get our minds off of everything. But I was having none of it. I needed to get shit done. I needed to find the taken women. I needed someone to tell me that it would be okay. It would take time but everything would work out in the end. I needed Angel, and I was woman enough to admit it.

131

The cool night air washed around me, brushing the back of my neck like a lover's touch. The dark sky was clear, the moon bright and full, surrounded by millions of stars. It was peaceful.

"Mind if I join you, princess?"

My heart skipped a beat at the deep voice. A flutter of excitement rushed through me as I met Angel's piercing gaze. I opened my mouth to answer but all I could give him was a nod of my head. God, I had missed him. I hadn't known him for long, but the mutual attraction was there. I never believed in an instant love but instant lust? *Hell yes.*

When he came into view, I gasped. Bruises and scratches covered his face. "What happened?" I asked, my voice shaky.

"There was an attack on our squad," he said, sitting beside me on the picnic table.

"Are you guys okay?" My hand reached up on its own accord, my fingers brushing along his cheek.

"We are," he said, his voice lowering. "Just a little banged up." He leaned into my hand, placing a light kiss on my palm.

My breath caught. We sat there, staring at each other. *God, this man and what he does to me.* What he did to my insides. "Everything okay now?" I asked, needing to take some sort of control before I knelt at his feet and begged like a bitch in heat.

He cleared his throat, pulling away from me. "We got in too deep. We did our job, and it backfired." He rubbed the back of his neck, letting out a heavy sigh.

"Did you find what you were looking for?" I asked, a heavy weight settling in the pit of my stomach.

"Not everything, but we have a good start." He gave me a small smile.

Bringing my knees up to my chest, I wrapped my arms around them and let out a deep sigh.

"Why aren't you inside enjoying the party?"

"Because I couldn't care less about it." I slid off the table, walking back and forth to stretch my legs. My body hurt. I was antsy. "Max throws these parties trying to get our minds off of this shitty world we live in. It used to help, but not anymore. Not for me, at least." I bent over, touching my toes.

A deep growl sounded from the table. "Jay."

"Yes?" I smiled, rising back to my full height.

"Come here," Angel demanded.

"Sorry, baby. If you want something, you're going to have to come to me," I told him, a flutter of desire soaring through my body. I had missed the cat and mouse back and forth. His Domination to my submission. I had craved the lack of control for years, and since I had found a man who could give me what I desired, I teased him. Knowing it would end with us crashing together in waves of ultimate ecstasy, I defied him.

"Is that so?"

I jumped at the rough voice in my ear. For a big guy, he moved with ease. I stood still, anticipating the touch of his hands on me. He spoke through his body. It told me how much he wanted me. How much he *needed* me.

"It's been almost a month, princess," he whispered, his hot breath scorching my neck.

"I haven't noticed," I lied. Of course I noticed. I missed him more than I wanted to admit. It was easy to be around him, to talk to him. I couldn't get enough.

"Well, I noticed. Every time I touched myself, I noticed," he purred, wrapping his thick arms around my waist and pulling me back against his hard body. The heavy weight between his legs pushed into the curves of my ass.

All I could picture was his large hand gripping his length as if it were a lifeline. As if with one touch and he would explode, waiting for the next release. "How often?" I asked, pushing back against him.

133

"Every damn day." Angel spun me, pushing me up against the wall. "But I'm going to show you exactly how much I missed you, princess. How much I missed your mouth. How much I missed you giving in to me."

"You're bossy," I said, gripping the fabric of his hoodie.

"You enjoy it. And I enjoy when you submit to me, giving me what I want and what I know you are so desperate for." His mouth moved along the shell of my ear. "I can feel the heat coming off of you."

"And I can feel how hard you are," I panted, arching into him.

"For you, baby. How hard I am for *you*." He pushed his knees between mine, roughly spreading my legs. His calloused hands roamed down the side of my body, reaching under my tank top until they covered my breasts. "I'm going to spend the night devouring your sweetness."

"Please," I pleaded, fisting the fabric of his hoodie in my hands. Being with Angel would take my mind off of things. Not a damn party. I wanted to dive into his body and spread myself thin. The wakening of emotions and desire, pleasure, and bliss wrapped around me. They ensnared us in beautiful passion. Our hips moved together, rubbing and building a friction so great, my skin burned.

"Fuck, Jay." His hand reached between my legs, cupping my mound. "Did you miss me, princess?" His tongue peeked out, licking up the side of my neck.

I moaned, leaning into his touch, silently begging for him to destroy me. To make me *feel* him. "Yes," I whispered. "I missed you."

"Fucking right you did." His thick fingers unbuttoned my pants and lowered the zipper before diving inside to where I wanted him most. "Tell me you dreamt I would please all of your fantasies. Tell me it's because of me you feel this way. Tell me how wet you are for me."

"I'm...I'm soaked." I gripped his collar, pulling him down to meet my mouth. "For you."

He growled at the same time his fingers delved inside my panties. Not teasing me in any way, he pushed them into me without a warning.

I cried out, shaking against him. Pleasure swam through me like waves of molten lava. He consumed my senses. Everything about that man took over until I gave him all of me.

"That's it, baby." He cupped my throat, tilting my head back. "Coat my fingers with your delicious essence."

"Oh, God." I spread my legs wider, hinting, needing him to take things further.

His fingers pumped in and out of me. Hard. Fast. Rough. It was everything I had craved over the past few weeks. Everything I had needed since the last time I saw him. I couldn't understand how someone could have that much effect over another person. With Angel, it had been everything I had imagined.

"You're going to come, and then I'm going to fuck the shit out of your hot body until all you feel is me." His hold on my throat tightened. "Look at me when you let go. I want to watch you break."

I whimpered, gripping his arms and moving my hips against his fingers. A nagging notion forced me to succumb to his controlling wrath. As much as I had promised myself I would never give in to another man's domination, with Angel, I desired it.

"Move those hips like I know you can," he demanded, rubbing his thumb over my swollen clit. "Your sweet little nub is hard for me, baby. Does it turn you on knowing your body submits to me before you do?"

"Angel," I breathed, begging for him to give me the release my body craved. The fight of Domination versus submission battled between us. He wanted to break me. He craved it. And I couldn't help but give in. It was all in the name of sex, right? Nothing more. Even though I didn't believe that.

"You're going to come until I tell you to stop," he said, pushing his fingers into me as far as my body would allow.

"Oh, dear *God*," I cried out, a fast release hitting me hard. His name left my lips on a guttural scream.

"That's it," he coaxed, crashing his mouth to mine and swallowed the rest of my cries. "So fucking beautiful."

"Please," I begged, riding out the release.

"What do you want, baby?"

"More." God, I needed him inside of me.

Angel turned me in his arms, pushing me face first against the brick wall. He brushed the hair off the back of my neck, sinking his teeth into the skin. "What else do you want, little girl?"

I moaned, the slight burning pain making the desire I had for him grow into an inferno. "You."

His fingers remained, his body holding me against the side of the building, his hot, minty breath washing over my exposed skin.

My body vibrated. I needed more. I was about to combust with lust for the man holding me, and if I wasn't careful, I would fuck him out in the open, not caring in the least if anyone walked in on us.

"Jay, you have a moment?"

I jumped at the unexpected voice coming from the doorway.

Angel chuckled, shifting his body to shield me from Max. "Give us a few."

"Don't hurry on my account," she laughed, closing the door behind her.

"A few?" I asked Angel, pulling his hand from inside my pants.

He winked, sticking his fingers in his mouth, and sucked the juices from my body off of them. He groaned, a wicked smirk spreading on his handsome face. "This is going to be fast, baby. Later tonight I'll take my time, but right now, I need you hard."

My breath left me on a whoosh. Never before had a man told me that he needed me in a way it pained him to go without.

Angel grabbed my hand, pulling me toward his SUV. "I hope you don't mind me fucking you in my vehicle."

"The way I'm feeling right now, you could bend me over the picnic table, and I wouldn't object."

He stopped once we reached the rear passenger door. "And how do you feel?"

I opened the door, crawling into the back seat, and pulled down my pants. "I ache for you. I want you so bad it hurts." Hooking my thumbs in the sides of my panties, I pushed them down to my ankles. "I want you to destroy my body, leaving me spent and sore, covered in your marks." When those words left my mouth, I thought it had been too much when Angel didn't say anything. His dark piercing gaze stared at me. Just when I was about to backtrack what I had confessed, his next words stopped me.

"Fuck. Me. That is the hottest thing a woman has ever said to me." Angel joined me on the backseat, closing the door behind him, and pulled me into his lap. "You want my fingerprints on your pale skin?"

"Yes," I said, my breath leaving me on a whoosh. "Hurt me, baby." I kissed him hard, nipping his lip and sucking his tongue into my mouth. The closer it got to fucking him, the more my body vibrated, aware of what was to come in a moment.

Rising to my knees, I waited for Angel to slide the condom down his beautiful length.

"Are you ready?" he asked with a growl.

Showing him I was, I slammed my body down the thickness of him causing us both to yell out. Not giving either of us a chance to get used to the connection, I rode him hard and fast. I took from him what I

137

needed—what I craved. What I had so desperately
wanted since the moment I met him. We had already
spent a night together but that time it was different. We
knew more about each other. We had opened up. We
had bared feelings, stripping each layer until there was
nothing left.

Angel closed his eyes, leaned his head back
against the seat, and dug his fingers into the flesh of
my ass.

I leaned down, brushing my mouth along his thick
neck. Nipping and sucking, leaving my own mark on
him. A possessive need to cover him in my touch took
over. My hips sped up. Our pelvises connected in ways
I had never felt before. Angel did that to me. He was
bossy and brooding. Dark and mysterious. And he was
mine. No matter what happened, I knew it. For that
moment, there was no one else. It was just him and me
in our fucked up world.

"Harder," he demanded, his dark eyes boring into
mine. "Come on, baby. Fuck the shit out of my dick
like I know you can."

My heart sped up, my breathing quickened, and a
tingle shot straight down my back. "Please."

"What do you want, little girl?" he asked, a
darkness taking over his words.

I loved when he spoke this way and I knew there
were more commands and desires in his darkest of
cravings. "Come for me," I whispered in his ear.

"I'm going to come hard for you, baby. So fucking
hard you feel it in your soul." His hips reared up,
pumping into me with so much strength, I came fast. It
was so hard it took my breath.

Angel grunted, his fingers digging into the flesh of
my rear. His length twitched, growing harder and
thicker by the second. "Come again. Scream my
name."

"Angel!" I yelled out, digging my nails into his
shoulders.

"*Fuck*," he roared, gearing up for that final blow of ecstasy that took him over the edge. "Jay." He shivered. "Shit, woman, you're going to fucking kill me."

I laughed, kissing him hard on the mouth. "Best way to die, baby."

"Fucking A." He kissed me back, hard and deep before releasing me with a wet smack. "So beautiful."

My cheeks heated, and I slid off his lap, missing the connection we had just shared.

Angel pulled off the condom, tied the end into a knot and dropped it into a plastic garbage bag on the floor. "Thank you," he said, righting his pants.

"I wish we could just drive away," I confessed, getting dressed.

"Not in the mood to deal with them?" he asked, opening the door once I was covered.

"I love the girls but sometimes I feel like I have to put on a show." I was surprised by the truth leaving my lips. I had never opened up like that to anyone. Not even my sister.

"I feel you." He reached for my hand, giving me a soft smile.

"Are you staying?" I asked, a moment of trepidation coursing through me.

"Do you want me to?"

"You know I do." I patted him on the chest. "You promised me a night of pleasure," I reminded him, the remnants of the delicious sex we just had tingling on my skin.

He chuckled. "I sure did." He kissed the top of my head. "And I will keep my promise, baby. You just let me know when you're ready to leave."

Now. But I knew it couldn't happen.

Angel wrapped his arm around my shoulder, leading me into my club. My home. But right then, I felt out of place. Whatever was going on with me, I didn't like it. I wasn't used to it. Was it Angel? Was it the fact that all of those girls were disappearing and it brought up memories of my sister? I had no idea but I knew I needed a change.

"Jay," Max called out, rushing to my side once we entered the building.

"What's wrong?" I asked her, searching her face.

Her gaze moved back and forth between Angel and me, a hint of curiosity flashing in her light-blue eyes. She shook her head and gripped my shoulders. "The Kings are here."

Fuck my life with a rusty chainsaw.

"I'll be at the table with the guys," Angel whispered in my ear. "Come get me whenever you are ready." He kissed my cheek and walked toward the large table at the front of the club. The men had already claimed their spot, sitting in the same booth every time they made an appearance. The guys waved. I smiled, nodding in their direction.

"I am so sorry to take you away from him," Max said, stepping in front of me.

"What's going on?" I frowned, ignoring her questioning gaze.

"Dante's Kings need to talk," she explained.

"No. I mean besides that. You usually make some sort of smartass comment," I pointed out. "What gives?"

She shrugged. "I need you happy. If he makes you happy, that's all I care about."

I didn't get a chance to respond when the other girls approached us and I got bombarded by questions.

"Something's going on. What are we going to do?"

"What's happening?"

"I can't stand these fuckers." That was Max.

I sighed. "Let's get this done and over with." So I could spend the night with someone who would take all of my frustration away even just for a little bit.

I headed into the meeting room. A room I had called my own since the beginning. But at that very moment, I felt like a stranger.

Loud chatter sounded behind me, following me into the room. I braced myself for the unknown. Dealing with my father would be one thing. I loved the rest of his crew like they were family, but Tyler put a darkness on that group. I should have known from the first time he hit me. Oh God. What would Angel think? I wasn't broken because of it. I was stronger. But would he see that? Would he feel sorry for me and want to fix me?

"Nugget."

I turned to the sound of my father's voice. "Are you talking to me or is he?" I asked, nodding toward Tyler.

"We both are," Tyler answered for him.

"*He* is the president," I snapped. "Why don't you let him fucking speak for once?"

Tyler smirked, rubbing his jaw.

"Come, Jay. Let's sit down." Max gently grabbed hold of my arm and pulled me to my chair at the head of the table.

I had the urge to tell her to mind her own business but she was right. I needed to calm down for fear of losing it completely. "Fine. Talk. Tell me what's so important that you have to ruin our Friday night—"

"Do you ever get sick of listening to the sound of your own voice?" Tyler glared at me.

"Listen, asshole. You don't get to talk to me that way anymore. You got me? I don't care who you are or who you know." My blood vibrated, my heart pounding hard against the walls of my ribcage.

"You talked to my daughter that way?" My dad smacked Tyler across the head. "You're lucky I don't take your fucking cut." Because taking his cut would be way worse than hurting him. Sometimes I didn't understand the MC lifestyle.

141

"Fuck you." Tyler pushed him, causing the guys to circle around them.

Shit. I didn't need this. Not now. "All right." I stepped between them, forcing myself to wedge them apart. "Stop this now or I'll kick all of you out."

"Jay." Fetch, the youngest and newest member of Dante's Kings stepped forward. "We received this in the mail." He handed me a manila envelope. He was the calm one of the group, not being in it long enough to allow the lifestyle to take over and blacken his soul.

I sighed, taking it from him, and slouched onto the couch not caring in the least that everyone was watching me. Opening up the envelope, I bit back a gasp when my gaze landed on a picture of Angel and the guys. Photo after photo of Vice-One stared back at me. "What is this?"

"That's the man you're spending time with," my dad pointed out.

Max crouched beside me, grabbing a picture of Dale out of my hands. "What are you trying to tell us? And stop beating around the fucking bush," she demanded.

My father, Tyler, and Fetch stood around the four of us. We outnumbered them, but we still felt small. At that moment, I decided we needed another girl. A new prospect who had a good head on her shoulders and would bring any of those men to their knees. And not in the sexual way.

"Your man knows more about the missing girls than he lets on," Tyler stated, implying I found myself another asshole. But no one could be like him. I had the scars to prove it.

"He's doing his job," I corrected him. "It's none of my business what Vice-One does on their missions. Don't you watch movies? All of that shit is classified."

"Not when it comes to the fact that it isn't their job to find these girls. They're Navy SEALs, Jay. They deal with terrorists and people trying to threaten our country. Not human trafficking." My dad placed his hand on mine, giving it a light squeeze. "I know we haven't seen eye-to-eye for a while, but trust me when I tell you something bigger is going on. Be careful."

"I don't get why you're making a big deal out of this," Max said. "Vice-One is doing their job and more. Why does it matter if they're going out of their way to find these girls?"

"It matters when they use girls as bait," Tyler pointed out.

"Excuse me?" My head whipped around. "How the hell do you know that?"

"I have my connections." He shrugged, a slight smirk spreading on his face.

I stared at him. To other women, he would be considered gorgeous. Model material. He was blond, blue-eyed, built like a tank. But his personality ruined it for me. And so did his fists.

"If Vice-One is going in this using girls as bait to bring this organization down, I can't argue with that." I personally wouldn't have used them as bait, but I didn't even know how true that was. Could I bring it up to the guys? I would have to. But not when Dante's Kings were around. I didn't trust them. I grew up with them but the members had come and gone over the years. When my grandfather recruited my dad, he was my role model. But once my grandpa had passed and with the disappearance of my sister, I lost that connection.

"Nugget," my dad said gently.

"What, Daddy?" I snapped. "You can't come into my club, threaten to take what I've worked so hard at building, and accuse my new friends of shitty activity." I pointed at him. "You of all people shouldn't judge." Drugs, weapons—whatever Dante's Kings could get their hands on, they would move it. They would do anything to make money and get their name out there.

"We're not judging," Tyler said, crossing his arms under his chest.

"No? So what, you feeling a little righteous because Vice-One will do anything to protect these girls? Do you feel threatened? I'm surprised you even care, Tyler."

"Of course I care." His brows narrowed. "Don't accuse me of different, woman."

"Fuck you!" I took a step toward him.

"Leave us," he demanded, his voice booming around the small room.

My sisters objected, but I reassured them I would be fine. Tyler wouldn't hurt me again. I was no longer scared of him, especially after I got up the courage to take a knife to his balls. I smiled to myself at the memory.

"I'll be in the hall," Max whispered in my ear. "One scream, and I'll get Angel in here."

I nodded. But it wouldn't happen. Tyler and I had done the same song and dance for years. After the first time he hit me, I became a different person. When Violet disappeared, I changed. Tyler and I had a toxic relationship. In another life, I had loved him. But I realized after I got away from him that it wasn't love. I just didn't want to be alone.

"You have become sassier, Jenny," Tyler said once we were alone. He sat on the couch, watching me.

My stomach twisted at the use of his nickname for me. No one else called me *Jenny,* and he made sure of it. It was a part of me he would own forever. "You did that to me, T."

He grunted with satisfaction.

Dick. "What do you want?"

"I have a proposition for you."

"Oh geeze. Of course you do," I rolled my eyes. "Don't you think you've gotten enough from me over the years?"

"No. If I did, you would still be mine," he said, his voice rough.

I swallowed hard. I wasn't scared of him, even when we were together but sometimes a darkness washed over him. His club knew to back away when that happened.

"I want you to back off. We will find these women. You don't need to mess up your hair and dirty your fingernails over this shit."

"You chauvinistic bastard. Don't you dare—"

"Listen to me, Jay," he snapped, his voice eerily calm. "You keep searching out these girls, I promise you it will make things worse."

"Are you threatening me?"

"Take it as you will." He shrugged.

"My sister disappeared because of these sick fucks. There is no way I'm dropping this search." Not like I had any leads anyway, but he didn't need to know that.

"It's been years. She probably ran off with a man."

"No. Don't you dare sit there and say that to me. You were there when she left. You should have been there for *me*," I cried, gripping my shirt. "But you weren't. You were too caught up in becoming my dad's bitch."

"Watch your mouth." Tyler rose to his feet and strode toward me, forcing me to take a step back. "I gave you everything. I helped you start this club. If it weren't for me convincing your father, King's Harlots wouldn't even be alive today. He's the one who said women shouldn't have motorcycle clubs. He's the one who said his daughter was too much of a princess."

His words hurt, but I knew they were true. My dad had told me time and time again that I was too much of a girly girl to have my own MC. Violet was the risk taker and when she disappeared, I took over that role, surprising everyone.

145

"It's as if Violet never left," my father had told me once. It made me sick to my stomach that she would be a part of me no matter what when I wanted her physically around. I knew it broke his heart that both of his daughters had left him. One involuntarily. One by sheer will. I would never be the same until Violet came back into our lives. And even then, I would never get the old me back. Genevieve was no longer alive.

"You did nothing for me, Tyler. You broke me and laughed in my face after," I reminded him. He destroyed a piece of me beyond repair, the piece that would never truly love again.

Tyler shoved his hands in his pockets, standing a foot away from me. "You loved me."

"I don't know anymore." I let out a deep sigh. "If you weren't the vice president of Dante's Kings, I would have nothing to do with you."

"But you have no choice." A slight smirk spread on his lips. "And you hate me for it."

"I've hated you for less," I mumbled, turning and headed toward the door.

"Jenny." He grabbed my arm. "You need to stop searching. If you know what's good for you, you will quit while you're ahead."

"What the hell is that supposed to mean?" When he didn't say anything, I continued. "I'm sick of your shit. Because of your influence over my father, he has been keeping secrets from me. I am an equal in this world. I have just as much of a right to be in it as you."

"*Ha*," Tyler scoffed. "You're a woman. You have no rights."

"You fucking chauvinistic *pig*," I screamed, my fist landing against his face. Before I knew what was happening, I lunged for him, beating my small fists against him.

He only laughed, and that made me hit him harder.

146

"I hate you. I hate what you've done to me. I hate how you control my father. *I hate you*," I shouted over and over.

Tyler pushed me off of him, flipped me onto my back, and wrapped a hand around my throat. "Little girl, I am the darkness in your fucking nightmares. I made it so you will never forget me. When you're with Angel, all you will feel is me." He crashed his lips to mine, shoving his tongue into my mouth.

Bile rose to my throat. Biting down hard, I tore into his lip until a metallic taste wafted through my senses.

He yelped, breaking the contact. "I almost forgot how dirty you liked to play."

"*Fuck* you," I said roughly.

"Aww. You see, Jenny, we've done that. Many painful and delicious times, I might add."

"What the *fuck* is going on in here?"

I jumped at the deep voice coming from the doorway.

"I'm teaching your woman a lesson," Tyler sneered, releasing me.

I pushed to my feet. "Go to hell, Tyler."

"Did he hurt you?" Angel searched my face. "There's blood on your lip. What the actual fuck?"

"I'm fine. I bit him."

Angel's eyes brightened, a grunt leaving his lips.

"Piece of advice. She likes it rough." Tyler leaned his head from side to side, a loud crack sounding in the room.

"You fucking bastard." Angel charged his way and before Tyler knew it, he was thrown up against the wall.

He grinned.

"Angel," I cried, attempting to pry him off Tyler.

"You touch my girl again, I'll feed you to my fucking dog."

J.M. WALKER

"He's not worth it," I wedged myself between
them, putting my hands against Angel's chest to stop
him from what I could only imagine would be painful
for Tyler. As much as I wanted to see him writhing in
pain, it wasn't worth it. "Angel is more of a man than
you will ever be. He's not a selfish asshole like you."

"Remember what I said," Tyler smirked, crossing
his arms under his chest.

"You do not get to tell me what to do anymore.
Until I find my sister, no matter the outcome, I will not
stop. You and my dad will just have to get used to
that." I grabbed Angel's hand and stomped out of the
room. My body vibrated. My heart pounded hard, the
blood pumping through my veins.

Loud voices and music pierced my ears,
screaming for me to enjoy the party, but I couldn't. I
needed out. I needed away. My feet led us to the table
surrounded by Angel's brothers. The men of Vice-One
looked up at us.

"Angel," I said once I reached their table. The
burn of his gaze seared through me. He could make me
forget. He could help me get my mind off of
everything even if it was just for a moment.

He squeezed my hand. "I'm calling it a night," he
told his brothers, not leaving my side.

They grunted in response, not asking any
questions.

Angel wrapped his arm around my shoulders,
guiding us outside.

"Jay," Max called out.

"I'll call you in the morning," I told her.

She nodded, giving me a quick hug. "Be safe. We
need to talk about Tyler."

"Tomorrow."

"Okay." She hugged me again. "Love you."

"Love you too," I said, hugging her back.

Angel and I headed outside, the cool air whipping around us. He didn't say anything as I led us to my bike. He reached a hand out, waiting.

Not even hesitating, I dropped my keys into his open palm. As much as I enjoyed feeling the wind in my hair, that night I wasn't in the mood. Giving up control, I allowed Angel the freedom to take me wherever he saw fit.

He slid onto the bike, turned it on, and looked back at me, but he didn't say anything. He didn't look at me with pity. He didn't ask where I wanted to go or why I wanted to leave. He just waited.

Taking a breath, I stepped onto the peg and swung my leg over the other side.

"Hold on to me, baby. I won't let you fall." His deep voice traveled through me.

Knowing his words meant more than what he said, I pushed my hands up under his hoodie and t-shirt until I touched bare skin. Letting my fingers travel to his hard stomach, I leaned my head against his back. I could feel his length grow where my elbow rested in his lap but he didn't comment. No dirty talk. No demands. No telling me what to do or what he wanted. It would come. I knew that. And I was ready. Always. But for right then, I reveled in the warmth of his skin burning beneath my touch.

Angel pulled the bike out of the parking lot, driving at the speed limit until we reached the outskirts of town. Once we hit the open road, he sped up, forcing me to hold onto him tighter. I smiled, knowing it was intentional.

My hands moved to his chest, grazing over the bumpy ridges of old scars. The times we had been together, I never paid attention to them. But they told a story. A memory of what happened.

I held onto him like he was only thing that mattered. The one thing that existed in my world. It was just him and me in our journey. Those thoughts surprised me. We had gone into it for the sex. It was amazing and delicious. I had tried to disperse my feelings but I wasn't stupid. Even I was woman enough to admit that I was attracted to the guy. Who wouldn't be? He was all Spanish, hard male. A sex god who could make me weak in the knees from just his words. I never believed in that instalove shit; it wasn't realistic. Of course there was such a thing as instant attraction. We were human. It happened. But it would be a long while before I allowed myself to fall in love again. And even then, I would never say those words unless I was absolutely sure that was it.

A half an hour later, Angel pulled onto a long gravel driveway until we reached a large farmhouse. It was surrounded by trees, hidden from the world by nature.

He shut off the bike, letting me get off first before he put the kickstand down. "This was my parents' place," he told me, breaking the silence. "Once I became old enough, I contacted a lawyer and did everything I could to find out as much about them as possible. This house came on the market, and I bought it. Buck and I have been here ever since."

"I like how it's not near anything," I told him, hanging onto his every word. "It's quiet."

"It is, but the silence can be loud sometimes."

I watched him head up the steps and sit on the porch swing. He patted the empty spot beside him.

"Does the silence ever get too loud for you?" I asked, joining him. I curled my feet under me, leaning into his side, and breathed in the spicy scent of his cologne.

"It can." He kissed my forehead, letting his lips linger. "Want to tell me what happened?"

"I wish I could, but even I don't know what's going on." I sighed, rising to my feet. "The Kings are saying shit, accusing Vice-One of using girls as bait."

"Well, that's not exactly true."

"I didn't think it was." I paced back and forth. "I don't expect to know everything. I know it's classified information." I met his gaze. "But I need to know that you will do anything to get these girls home."

"I won't lie and say we will get them home, but I will tell you that we will do everything in our power to put an end to this. No matter how long it takes."

A sigh of relief washed over me. "I'll take whatever I can get."

"You have to do what you can, Jay," Angel said, unlocking the door to his house. "Buck," he whistled. "Come here, boy." He flipped on the hallway light.

"I have help," I reminded him. But he was right; I needed patience. I wasn't God and even then, I wondered if God could save these girls.

"I know you do but you need to remember that these people are evil. They will do everything they can to not get caught." He whistled again. "Buck," he repeated. "Lazy fucker."

I gasped when a large Rottweiler came barreling toward me. "Hi, Buck." I crouched down, smothering Buck with hugs and pets. He licked my face, causing me to laugh. "Oh, you are a handsome boy. Yes, you are." He panted and snuffed, giving me all the kisses he could.

Angel chuckled. "Hey, stop kissing my woman."

I giggled, rising to my feet. "Jealous, baby?"

"You know it." Angel grabbed my hand, pulling me against him and smacked a hard peck on my mouth. He swatted my ass, rubbing the slight burn.

I yelped, laughing even harder. "Thank you."

He cupped my nape, gently tugging my head back. "No thanks needed, princess."

My heart skipped a beat at the heat in his eyes. Standing on tiptoes, I placed a soft kiss on his mouth.

"Hmm…" His hand moved down my spine to the small of my back, holding me firmly against his hard body. "Your mouth is fucking delicious."

I smiled, kissing him again, and stepped out of his embrace.

Angel winked at me, heading to the kitchen, and whistled along the way.

I caught the large bulge in his jeans before he had a chance to turn away. That was one thing I liked about him. No matter how turned on he was, he made a point of letting me know exactly how hard I made him. A shiver of desire slid over my skin.

"Beer?" he asked, handing me a bottle.

I took it, brought it to my lips, and sighed once the brew hit my tongue.

He grabbed my hand, sitting on the couch and pulled me onto his lap. "Feel better?"

"I do." But something was still missing. An idea came to mind. Sliding off his lap, I placed the beer on the table and started stripping.

Surprisingly enough, Angel didn't say anything, but I could feel his eyes burning their way into my skin.

"Can I wear your shirt?" I asked him, my cheeks heating at the odd question.

"Of course." He pulled off his hoodie and white t-shirt, handing me the thin cotton.

My mouth watered at the half-naked sight before me. I slid the soft material over my head, savoring the feel of it brushing against my bare skin. The scent of him tickled my nose, my core clenched.

He grabbed the hem of the shirt, pulling me onto his lap and laid us back on the couch. His body curled around mine, his hands softly rubbing up and down my side. The touch was so gentle, so sweet—it made my eyes well up with tears.

Angel pushed his hand beneath the fabric, cupping my breast and kissed my neck. "I enjoy when you smell like me."

"I enjoy it too," I whispered, playing with a hem on the cushion.

"Do you feel it?"

I turned onto my back, staring up into his beautiful dark eyes. "I don't know what *it* is, but yes, I feel it."

"*It* is something new." He cupped my cheek, brushing his thumb over my bottom lip. "It's something between you and me."

"Why?" I breathed, kissing his palm.

"Because neither of us have felt it before. It's new for us. A new journey. A new mission."

"It scares me," I confessed. Not even what I had with Tyler scared me so much.

"As it should." He replaced his thumb with his mouth, brushing his lips over mine.

I breathed him in, taking his scent deep down into my lungs until all I could taste was him.

His mouth moved fluidly over mine—slow, passionate. It was everything I needed and everything I craved. But I wasn't sure if whatever it was that I had with Angel would be enough.

SEVENTEEN

ANGEL

I WANTED to dive deep into her soul, taking away the hurt and pain. Take away everything that had harmed her in her life. Destroy the monsters. Protect her from the evils of the men she trusted. She was a woman, and she was looked down on because of that. I would show her she was strong. She was everything that I was not. She was soft where I was hard. She was pure where I was tainted.

She slid her slender but firm body beneath mine, wrapping her legs around my waist.

We kissed. For minutes. Hours. Who knew? I didn't care. I became hard as a rock but I didn't want to ruin the moment, the connection, just yet. It was more than sex. It was more than lust. It was passion. It was raw. It was real. And it was *ours*.

I swallowed her moans every now and again. Heat soared between us, igniting our bodies in a raging inferno of desire.

"Angel," she purred into my mouth.

"Yeah, baby?" My lips brushed down her jawline, kissing and sucking until the taste of her skin was ingrained in my mind. I no doubt would dream of her. Her touch. Her sounds. Her taste. Everything that was Genevieve Gold would be in my thoughts.

"Your kisses make my knees weak." Her fingers brushed through the hair at my nape.

"Your taste makes me delusional," I responded, smiling.

Her eyes flashed, growing bright with lust. "I was told to stop looking for the girls," she said, her brows narrowing.

I kissed her swollen mouth, rolling us over until she was on top of me. "By who?"

"Tyler." She sighed. "We have a history. But we're over. It's over."

"Are you reassuring me I have no asshole to compete with?" I asked, forcing the bile of jealousy down.

"Yeah. I am." Her eyes darkened. "Are there any other women I have to deal with?"

"Ha. No," I scoffed, running my hands up her inner thighs. "My relationships don't last because of my job." I flipped us over, covering her body with mine and brushed my mouth along the shell of her ear. "Don't worry, baby. I am all yours."

She shivered. "Good."

As much as I wanted to continue teasing her, I found that I needed to know why she had changed the subject. "You're hurting." I brushed a strand of hair off her forehead.

She shrugged, squirming beneath me. She tried moving out from under me, but I was having none of that. "Angel, I'm fine."

"No, you're not. If you were, you wouldn't blurt out what you said while making out with me."

"I didn't mean to blurt it out," she insisted, pushing against my chest.

"You can push me all you want, princess, but I am not going anywhere." That was true for the moment and for the future. I could feel her tugging, pulling me in, and when I did, she shoved me away.

"Angel," she huffed, crossing her arms under her full chest.

I chuckled, kissing her bottom lip. "Talk to me, beautiful. What's doing?"

"Tyler threatened me, telling me to watch my back if I continue searching for these girls. I told him that I wouldn't stop until my sister was found. I also told him that he couldn't boss me around anymore," she said all in one breath.

"Wait." I shook my head. "Your sister is missing?"

"Uh, yeah. She disappeared a couple years ago." She swallowed hard. "People have tried convincing me that she ran off with a man or moved to the city because she was sick of our small town, but I refuse to believe it. My dad won't even talk about her."

"I'm so sorry."

"Thank you." She frowned. "The guys said your squad is in this when you shouldn't be."

"Our boss sent us on a personal mission. A couple of months ago, we stumbled upon a warehouse..." My gut twisted at the memories. The scent of death.

"Not a good outcome?" she finished for me.

I shook my head.

"I don't know how you guys do what you do. It makes me proud to be your woman." Her cheeks reddened. "If you want me to be your woman, that is."

Something passed between us. The feelings I had for her changed from lust to more. I couldn't quite explain it, but it was a possessive need to make sure every man knew who she belonged to. And yes, she *was* my woman. The fact she admitted it made my inner-Alpha roar and come to life. The caveman inside of me wanted to beat against my chest and grunt.

"Angel," she panted, her breathing picking up.

Was it the look on my face? Was it the erection between my legs that sparked her arousal? Was it her confession that she wanted to be mine? Whatever it was, the drive to push her over the edge of submission burned its way into my body. A powerful force took over and I flipped her onto her stomach. "Tell me who you belong to," I demanded. My voice, deep and guttural, didn't even sound like mine. I knew men could become dark with a possessive need to claim their women completely, but I had thought it was a joke. The guys and I joked that it would never happen to us. Well, I would be the first to admit that I wanted it to happen to me and since it had, I would accept it with open arms.

She gasped, her long slender fingers gripping the arm of the couch but she didn't say anything. She didn't object. She didn't ask what I was doing. She knew. She was smart. And she craved everything I had to give her.

"Tell me," I repeated, sinking my teeth into the flesh of her neck.

"I'm yours," she said on a hard moan.

It was surreal to me how she knew that I needed to make her see that she would be mine and not just then but forever. That thought struck me as odd. I never went into it with the intention of making it a forever relationship, and I knew Jay felt the same way. But fuck, I was *addicted*.

Pushing her hair off her nape, I kissed her neck. "You have no idea what you do to me," I said, grinding my hips into the flesh of her ass.

"I can feel it." She licked her lips. "God, I can feel all of you."

"Can you?" My teeth sunk into the soft skin behind her ear. "Can you feel my cock growing for you?"

"You're so hard, baby."

"For you," I corrected her. Reaching between us, I lifted the shirt to her hips. "Tell me."

"Fuck me, please…but…"

"What?" I asked, unbuttoning my jeans.

"I want to feel *you*." She looked back at me over her shoulder. "No condom."

A growl of satisfaction escaped me. "You will feel me." Ripping open my jeans, I wrapped my hand around my dick, beating the heavy weight against her ass.

Jay arched her hips, spreading her legs for me.

I couldn't wait any longer and forced myself into the flesh of her body.

She cried out, throwing her head back.

I took that as my hint and circled a hand around the base of her throat. "I'm going to fuck you so hard, everyone will know it was my cock that made you feel good."

"Oh, God yes," she whimpered. "Please," she begged. "Make me feel good."

"I will. Fuck, Jay. You're shaking." I held her trembling body against me, covering her with mine and pumped into her heat.

"I—" A cry left her lips.

Her core gripped me tight. *Holy fucking hell.*

"Oh," Jay moaned, shaking her head back and forth until she screamed.

A wicked smirk spread on my face at the fast orgasm I had so proudly given her. "That's it, baby. Come for me. Come all over my dick. Make me smell like you." Planting my foot on the floor, I gripped the arm of the couch and pounded into her with so much strength, spots danced in my vision.

She called out my name, her voice becoming hoarse.

"That's it. Louder, baby. Make my ears fucking bleed," I demanded, taking from her what I knew she could give me.

"Harder, Angel. Please," she begged between gasps.

I gripped her ass, digging my fingers into her flesh. "Milk my cock." I wrapped my arm around her shoulders, pulling her upright against me.

She moaned, pushing back against me and met me thrust for thrust.

"That's right." Reaching for the hem of her shirt, I lifted the fabric up and over her head, needing to feel her dewy skin against mine.

"Come inside me," she breathed.

My balls tightened, a hot tingle shooting straight down my spine. I groaned, her name leaving my lips on a hard cry. My release shot straight into her warmth. My hips pulsed. Once. Twice. Three times before I fell over, covering her with the weight of my body.

"I can never get enough of that," she said, stifling a yawn and stretching out beneath me.

I kissed her cheek. "I'm proud of you, baby."

"I didn't do anything." Her eyes fluttered closed.

"You gave yourself to me," I said between soft pecks on her neck.

"Mmm... I think I've done that multiple times already."

"This time was different." Wrapping my hand in her hair, I pulled her head back and continued kissing her exposed throat.

"How so?" Her body clenched around me, pulsing with each touch of my mouth against her flesh.

"You allowed me to take what I want and give it back to you in return." My hips started moving again. "I told you I would make you fall for me."

***

(Jay)

The sex was amazing. *He* was amazing. But the words that left Angel's mouth didn't sit well. I didn't want to fall for him. I didn't want to allow myself to become vulnerable and to be ripped apart again. He could hurt me worse than Tyler did. Those scars healed. But with Angel, he would be the ultimate destroyer. But he didn't know it, and I would never tell him for fear that he would take advantage. How I could think those things about the man still inside my body was beyond me. Something had switched between us in the last little while. We became comfortable. The attraction was instant, but the feelings grew slowly as each day passed. There had been a spark in the beginning. That little tingle of lust that promised you a night filled with pleasure. With Angel, it had been more. The pleasure was so great it took my breath away. He knew everything there was to know about my body. He had fucked me so hard I forgot my name. He was the Dominant to my submissive.

"Jay," his rough voice washed over me.

I cleared my throat, hiding my face in the crook of my bent elbow.

"Baby."

"What, Angel? What do you want me to say? Do you want me to tell you that I'm falling for you? Do you want me to say that I can't think of anything else but you? That I go to sleep at night missing you so much it hurts? That every time you go on a mission, my stomach sinks because I worry I'll never see you again just like I won't see my sister? Is that what you want to hear?" My chest rose and fell with ragged breaths.

"Is all of that true?" he asked, releasing himself from my body and turning me onto my back. "Is that how you feel?"

"Is that how you *want* me to feel?" I threw back at him.

"Of course it is, but only if *you* want to feel that way. I can't force you to fall for me but I know you feel this connection between us. You can't lie about that."

"Obviously there's a connection, Angel, or else I wouldn't be here beneath you."

His eyes darkened to the point of black. "Let me make something clear, woman." He pinched my chin. "You are beneath me because I put you there. Not because it's how I feel. We are equal in this relationship. You feel me? Whatever this shit is between us, is because you want it and I want it."

"I know," I said quickly, not liking the darkness in his voice.

"Do you? Because somehow I feel you don't know."

"What have you been told?" I asked, trepidation coursing through me.

"People talk." Angel pulled the blanket off the back of the couch, covering us both before he continued. "I know what you had with Tyler was dangerous."

"It was what it was." At least I learned from it. I learned not to allow myself to fall in love. I refused to give someone the chance to break me—again.

"It was toxic, Jay." He turned my head to face him. "No relationship should be like that."

"I didn't know any better. I was young and stupid."

"But now you're not."

"What are you trying to tell me, Angel? That you won't hurt me like him? That whatever this is between us could get serious? You want to spend your life with me?" I wasn't trying to be a bitch, but I didn't want him to fall for me, and I knew I couldn't resist him. His touch. His words. *Him*. Angel was my new addiction.

"Where is this coming from? I don't know the answer to any of those questions. I can't predict the future but I know I want *this*." He waved a hand between us. "I'm having fun. *We* are having fun."

I nodded, scrubbing a hand down my face and turned onto my side. "I'm sorry," I whispered.

"Me too, baby." He kissed my cheek, wrapping his arm around my waist, and pulled me tight against his warm body. "I won't hurt you. I know you don't trust me yet, but I will prove to you that I want nothing but your happiness. I will show you that you can have more in life. If that means not being with me, then that's fine. I just want you to be happy."

A lonely tear escaped. I believed him. Every word he had said. But I couldn't control this urge inside me that begged me to run away. To protect myself. To hole up somewhere and just be alone. "Why do you care if I'm happy?"

"Why wouldn't I?" he asked, thrown aback at my question.

"We haven't known each other for that long, Angel," I reminded him.

"And you think that matters? My parents died when I was a child. I was in the system until I turned eighteen and joined the military instantly. I've never loved anyone. I don't even remember loving my mom and dad. Do I love my brothers? I care for them and would lay my life on the line for them but I have no fucking idea if I love them. You want to know why? Because I don't know how to. Is that what you wanted to hear, Jay? You want to hear that I'm fucked up? My feelings are a mess and even more so now that I've met you." He rose from the couch and righted his pants.

"Angel." I sat up, wrapping the blanket around me. "I don't know what you want from me."

"Well, I don't know what you want from me, either," he shouted, spinning to face me.

"So what are we doing then?" I cried. "Just fucking? Because I don't know about you but I'm cool with that."

"Well, I'm not," he admitted. "I don't want anyone else touching you. Your fucking pussy is mine. You got me?"

162

"Yeah, well, the same could be said for you." Crossing my arms under my chest, I lifted my chin defiantly. "Your cock is mine, baby."

"And it will stay yours because no woman can do to me what you can."

Well, doesn't that make me feel all sorts of special? "What do you want out of this?"

He sighed, grabbing the blanket from my hands. "I want you." He pulled me to my feet, letting the fabric drop to the ground. "That's it." He kissed me softly on the mouth. "We'll worry about the rest later."

EIGHTEEN

—jay

ANGEL HAD spent the night reminding me exactly what I did to him. How his length became hard at the mere sound of my moans. How his breathing deepened at my touch. How his eyes brightened with lust and desire at the mention of how wet my core was.

His words rang true in my mind. I was falling for him. Hard and fast. But I couldn't let him know. I couldn't let him see the affection I had for him in my eyes. I knew he wasn't stupid, though. What he did for a living would prove that it would be hard to keep my feelings from him. He was trained to read people. I had seen enough movies to know that.

Angel wasn't Tyler. He wasn't a monster. He wasn't the bastard I had fallen in love with.

"I don't know how to love." Angel's words broke my heart.

I sighed. I sure knew how to pick them.

He was beautiful in the way he had expressed his feelings through the use of his body. I felt the same. God, did I ever feel the same. Maybe more. Thoughts of him were constant. I felt him when I wasn't with him. I craved him in ways I never knew was possible.

Angel stirred beside me. His brows furrowed, his face grim and pained.

"Baby," I said gently, touching his cheek.

He jumped, his eyes snapping open.

"You're fine," I told him, coaxing the fear of the nightmare out of him.

"Jay," he whispered, hugging me against him.

"You're fine," I repeated, rubbing his back.

"*Shit*." With a shaky hand, he pushed it through his hair. "I haven't had a nightmare in a while."

"Knocks the breath out of you, doesn't it?" I cupped his cheek, brushing my thumb over his full bottom lip.

"Yeah. It fucking does." He didn't ask how I understood. He just rested his head in the crook of my neck and fell back asleep.

That. That was what I needed. What I had been craving my whole life. I was in a rut. Going through the motions of day-to-day life when I knew it wasn't enough.

"What are we doing, Angel?" I asked, kissing his forehead. What if I couldn't love him? What if Tyler had fucked me up so bad that I didn't know how to love again? Tears welled in my eyes. Life was unfair. The one time I wanted to fall in love, the one time I had met a man who cared more about me than himself, I was scared to open up. I was terrified to give him all of me.

Maybe he wouldn't like what he saw. I rolled out from under Angel, laying on my stomach and stretched my arms out under the pillow.

His arm wrapped around my waist, his hand rubbing up and down my back in small circles. Warm lips caressed my skin, placing light pecks here and there.

My heart sped up, a lump burning in my throat at the sweet contact. "What time is it?" I asked, trying to play it cool.

"Time to just feel." The deep vibrato of his voice pushed its way into my soul. It was like silky chocolate, smooth and vibrant with its taste.

"Feelings hurt," I told him. I slid out of his grip, rising from the bed, and got dressed. The clothes helped against the vulnerability I felt since meeting him weeks ago.

"What are you doing?" Angel asked, sitting up in bed.

"I should go." I turned back toward him, regretting it instantly.

The early morning light shone between the curtains, casting a soft glow on Angel's tanned skin. His muscles rippled with each breath. Scars marred his torso, begging for me to brush my fingertips against each and every mark.

"Baby, you know you don't want to leave."

"No. I don't. But I have to go back to the club. I have shit to do. I'm not letting Tyler stop me from finding those girls or my sister. I need some sort of closure." I was surprised at myself. Confessing my feelings to him threw me off. I didn't like it. One dark stare and I revealed all.

"If you need any help, any at all, Vice-One is here for you. *I* am here for you." He inched to the edge of the bed, reaching his hands out for me.

Placing my hands in his, I sighed at the contact. "Thank you."

"I mean it, Jay. I know what these bastards are capable of." He kissed my knuckles.

"I need all the help I can get," I said, stepping between his knees.

"Can I see you again?"

"Yes," I said without any hesitation at all.

"Good." A wicked grin spread on his face. "Now let me give you a goodbye kiss."

And he did. For the next hour.

***

(Angel)

"There has to be something we can do," I told Vega, wrapping tape around my wrist.

"You couldn't find shit about my niece," he grumbled. "What makes you think you can find out something about your girl's sister?"

"We need more time." I rose to my feet. "It's not our fucking fault they attacked us. They knew we were there."

"That's impossible." He shook his head.

"Nothing's impossible when it comes to this job." I pointed at him. "You of all people should know that. Someone knew we were going to be there." I didn't know how. Even before all of that shit went down, a sickening feeling had taken up permanent residence in my stomach. None of it made sense.

"We can't save everyone, Angel," he muttered.

"But you want us to do everything we can to save your niece," I added, rising to my full height.

"Yes." He looked away. "I will do whatever it takes to get her back."

"What about my girl's sister? *I* will do everything I can to get her back. Dead or alive. Doesn't fucking matter," I insisted. Jay needed closure, and I would do everything in my power to give that to her. She may have been pushing me away. She may have been trying to convince herself that she wasn't falling for me. It didn't matter, either way, I wanted her happy.

"If you go against orders, this time you will be put on leave and not come back," he ground out, meeting me with his dark stare.

"You have got to be fucking kidding me." My fists clenched at my sides. "What would you do if it was your wife's sister? Your daughter? Huh? Would you choose someone more important? How can you decide that? No one person is more important than the other. Put me on leave. Fire me. I'll fucking resign my commission if I have to. I don't give a shit. But I will find her."

167

He nodded once. "Good."

I shook my head. "Excuse me?"

"That's good," he repeated, turning on his heel.

"Wait. What the hell just happened?" I asked, stopping him.

"I wanted to make sure you were passionate about this."

"I'm not following."

Vega clapped a hand on my shoulder. "I know you've had a hard upbringing, Angel. I wanted to make sure you were choosing to do something for someone else and not just yourself. Now, piece of advice."

"Uh..." I stuttered like a dumbass.

"Go tell her you love her before it's too late."

Fucking A.

***

(Jay)

The moment I arrived at the clubhouse, I had assumed the girls would be on me. Demanding where I went the night before. Needing to know how I was. How I felt. What I was fucking thinking. I loved them. My sisters were my life but they were women. They loved to talk. But I couldn't talk to them. I couldn't tell them that there was a darkness inside of me that became light since meeting Angel. I couldn't tell them I had changed since my sister left. Max noticed but she never said anything. A part of me wished she would.

"We're in here, boss," Max said, peeking her head out of the office.

I nodded, making my way toward her. The time had come. Would I tell them everything I had wanted to? No. Because I was a little bitch and I was fucking scared.

"Hi," I said softly, closing the door behind me.

A round of greetings circled the table.

"Now, before we begin, I have a couple rules. No asking about Angel and me. Vice-One is here to fix up our club and hang out. I'm sure you've met them already. I consider them friends, but what goes on behind closed doors, I can't talk about yet." There, I said it. Sort of. "We will talk about Dante's Kings." I pushed away from the door. "Give me your thoughts."

"I think there's a mole," Brogan answered first.

"Excuse me?" My gaze snapped to hers. "How do you figure?"

"Something seems off. I have no idea," she shrugged.

"Why do you think there's a mole, Brogan?" She had me wondering if maybe she was correct. Especially when Meeka hadn't commented at all. She just sat there solemnly, her gaze on her lap.

"How else would the Kings know anything about Vice-One? I know they have connections but we hardly know them ourselves," Brogan explained. "Someone has to be telling them something."

That was true except for the fact that I knew Angel. *God, do I ever know him!* His body. His scent. His taste. A burning heat spread between my legs, causing me to squirm in my chair.

Fucking Angel.

I cleared my throat. "Vice-One is looking for the same thing we are: the men and women who are taking these girls. I know some of them are junkies, some of them people won't miss, but it doesn't matter. It's not cleaning the streets when murder is involved." My heart sped up, my voice rising. "Meeka, can you talk to your FBI contact and see if they can pull some strings to set up a curfew?"

"I mentioned that already, and they said that more girls have to disappear before they'll consider it," she said quickly.

"Are you fucking kidding me?"

"More girls have to die?"

169

Max and Brogan went back and forth with their outbursts, but I just sat there, staring at nothing. More girls had to disappear. *Who came up with this shit?*

"What else did they say?" I asked Meeka, interrupting the ranting.

"They said we have no grounds to search out the girls ourselves. If we take this into our own hands and an accident happens, we are held accountable." She sighed. "Basically, we won't have any protection."

"This isn't right," Max snapped, slamming her small fist on the table.

"No." I sat back in the chair. "It's not. But there's nothing we can do. So, we'll just have to deal with this on our own and make sure no one finds out."

Max and Brogan agreed.

Meeka nodded slowly. A twinkle flashed in her gaze, the corners of her lips twitching.

Interesting.

But I knew if we did have a mole, that information would get out and if it did, it would be from one of the three women sitting in front of me. I trusted Max with everything in me. Brogan went with the flow. And Meeka? She was desperate. I didn't know for what, but something told me that she was the mole. I just prayed she had just cause.

I didn't want to have to kill my sister.

NINETEEN

—jay

THE OPEN road was my absolute solace. It gave me the room to think. To stew over life. To wonder where I had gone wrong. *Would everything still be the same if Violet were around? What would she think of me now?*

The fresh air whipped around me. My fingers gripped the handlebars in a vice-like grip, wishing I could drive straight into the ground.

While I continued to drive, a blur caught my attention. A deep rumble pounded through me, sliding down my spine. My gaze landed on a large group of bikers I had never seen before. Five bikes led the pack in a V-formation. They wore leather cuts, dark sunglasses hid their eyes, and bandanas covered their faces. They gave off an air of authority. The large group of bikers, who I assumed were men, drove past me. The leader of the group nodded my way before disappearing behind me. My heart jumped. I had no idea who they were, never seeing them before in my life. Five bikers, followed by ten more. Another motorcycle club. And even *I* was scared of them.

I shook it off, ignoring the unease they had caused.

After the meeting with my sisters, nothing changed. I still didn't trust Meeka, and a part of me felt guilty over it. The question of why I kept her in our club bounced in my mind. She was good at what she did. She was the calm one of our little group, and even though we didn't see eye to eye on certain things, she

171

kept us grounded. I wished I could trust her. I just prayed that there was a reason for her secrets. Max and Brogan were still upset. And I just sat there. Like a lump.

What the hell was wrong with me that I couldn't put my foot down and demand answers like I used to? If it were a year before, Meeka would have been long gone. Even if she had valid reasons, I wouldn't have put up with that shit.

"God, help me," I said to no one. Not like anyone would listen anyway. I was alone in the world, as selfish as that sounded. I needed my sister. She would understand. She would force me to smarten up, shaking some sense into me.

"Jay, girl, you are beautiful. You got this. You have a gorgeous man at your beck and call. You are the president of a motorcycle club. You have people who love you," Violet's voice slid into my mind.

Tears burned my eyes, sliding down my cheeks, and rolled off my chin. "Fuck." I pulled over by the base of a cliff. Propping up my bike, I fell to my knees before the panic attack set in. I took deep, cleansing breaths, waiting it out.

"Help…me…"

My head snapped up at the soft sound.

"Help," the voice said again, stronger this time.

It was a woman's voice. "Hello?" I called out, but there was no one in sight.

"Please." A cough. "Help."

"Can you keep talking?" I asked, following the sound of the voice. "I can't find you." My palms became sweaty. My heart raced.

"Please. Help."

"I'm coming." I circled around the cliff, my gaze zeroing in on a limp body lying on the ground. I rushed to her side. The woman's eyes were closed. Her clothes torn, blood marring her pale skin. Dirt and debris matted her hair. "I'm here," I told her, touching her cheek.

Her eyes popped open. "I knew you would come. You couldn't resist."

"Excuse me?" Her voice. So strong and sure. Not weak like a moment before. I went to ask what the hell was going on when a sharp pain erupted at the back of my head. My vision faded, but not before I saw the evil sneer on the woman's face.

TWENTY

—jay

HOLY HELL, my head hurt. An intense shooting pain forced my eyes open. I gasped, swallowing some dust, and coughed. Rolling over onto my stomach, I realized I was still by the cliff but by that time I was alone.

That woman. Her eyes. Bright blue, but they showcased an unexplainable amount of evil I had never seen before. The satisfaction that adorned her face when someone hit me made me sick to my stomach. Why knock me out and leave? Were they making a point? Was it the same bastards who had been taking the girls?

I needed to get home. Pushing to my feet, I slowly made my way around the cliff to find my bike— missing. My stomach sunk. It had been a gift from my grandfather. Oh, that meant fucking *war*.

Pulling out my phone, I sent up a silent thank you that I remembered to put it in my pocket. I called Max. No answer. I frowned, knowing she had her phone attached to her hip. I called Brogan and then Meeka. Again, no answer. *What the hell?*

My head spun, the bright sun making me squint. *Fuck. Me.* Sitting on the ground, I placed my head in my hands, breathing through the sudden pain. My sisters were supposed to answer their phone. It was a rule, in case of an emergency. We had made sure to set up a special ring tone, and it usually worked. Not that we had to use it often, but right then, I could have used them.

Bracing myself against the rocky cliff, I dialed Angel's number.

"Hey, princess," he answered a moment later.

"Angel," I groaned, rubbing my temple. When I pulled my hand away, blood appeared on my fingertips. "Shit."

"What's wrong?" he barked, his voice hardening.

"I need you." I told him where I was and that my bike was stolen.

"I'm on my way."

I sighed when he hung up the phone, knowing I would be safe in a matter of minutes. I tried wrapping my mind around what had happened. It was a set-up. The woman's eyes stuck in my mind. Wild. Raging. Dark with an evil so powerful it took my breath away.

"Jay."

My eyes snapped open at the abrupt use of my name, landing on Angel standing over me.

"What the hell happened to you?" he asked, helping me to my feet.

"I got hit in the head," I said, wavering on my feet.

"You're bleeding." Angel picked me up, cradling me to his chest.

At that moment, I felt safe. Truly safe. "I hurt too."

"I want every detail. From the beginning," he demanded. "Tell me." He placed me in his SUV, buckling the seatbelt around my waist. He kissed my forehead, letting his lips linger before he shut the door.

I let out a heavy sigh, wishing I had just called him first. I didn't want to call my sisters out. I didn't want to make them feel guilty or be mad at them. I didn't want any of it. But when I couldn't rely on the three women who I had spent every day with for the past several years, especially when I was lying on the side of the road, what good were they?

"Now, tell me what happened." Angel grabbed my hand, holding it tight in his.

"I needed to clear my head so I went for a ride." I curled on my side, leaning my head against his shoulder to stop the painful pressure behind my eyes. "I started thinking of my sister and pulled over. A woman called out for help." My stomach twisted, remembering the evil smirk on her face. "She was on the ground behind the cliff. She said that she knew I would go to her. And then everything went dark."

"Fuck. You didn't see anything else?"

"No." I shook my head. "She was in on it. Whatever it was, she set me up. Someone hit me, Angel. Someone is trying to make a point."

"They're trying to scare you." He brought our joined hands up to his mouth, kissing the back of my knuckles. "It sounds to me like they want you to stop doing what the police *should* be doing."

"I think so too," I grumbled. "Please, take me back to the clubhouse. I have some shit to deal with, and then I am going to bed."

"You need to go to the hospital." He held my hand tight in his. "I'm taking you there."

"I'm fine," I insisted.

"No, you are not." His gaze darkened. "You're fucking bleeding, and it will be over my dead body before I let you fall asleep without knowing if you have a concussion or not."

"Angel."

"Woman, I am taking you to the hospital, and then after, I will take you home," he said, his voice final.

"Fine."

***

When we arrived at the clubhouse, the anger in my belly simmered. I shouldn't be mad at my sisters. They probably had a good reason for not answering the emergency line. I bit back a scoff. Yeah-fucking-right.

Angel had taken me to the hospital much to my dismay. Thankfully, I didn't have a concussion, just a huge-ass headache.

"How are you doing?" he asked, squeezing my hand.

"My head hurts. I'm so fucking confused. And my sisters weren't there when I needed them most." *There. I said it.* But the truth leaving my mouth didn't sit well with me.

"I'm sure they had good excuses." Angel shrugged, shutting off his SUV.

"Tell me something, Angel." I turned to him. "What would you have done if something happened to you and your brothers weren't there for you?"

"We're trained to be a unit. A team. We fight together. We die together," he said without hesitation. "But..." he thought a moment, cupping my cheek. "I will be honest with you. If one of us got hurt and we couldn't be there for each other, if we had some excuse, what would be the point? They would need to have a good reason as to why they weren't there."

"I know Vice-One is different than King's Harlots. I get that," I told him. "But Vice-One is a brotherhood just like King's Harlots is a sisterhood. If I can't have the people I trust the most at my back, then how can I count on them being at my front?"

He nodded. "Do you trust them?"

My jaw clenched. "I trust Max. I trust Brogan, but I know she would do anything to save her own ass first. Meeka? Something is going on. She won't tell me what. No one will tell me. But I know I can count on her. All of them. Or I thought I did."

"Would you like me to tell you what I would do?"
"Yes."

Angel gripped the steering wheel, his knuckles going white. "My brothers mean everything to me.

Vice-One is my life. I will be a part of it until the day I die and they lower my cold body into the ground. But if one of them stepped out, after all of the shit we have to deal with on a daily basis, I would call them on it."

"In the motorcycle club life, we would be killed first and asked questions later. I don't want my club to be like that. I don't want to be a part of the life my father's club is and the others. I've seen what it does to them." I was rambling. *God, this is odd for me.* To find that person I could talk to. Besides Violet, I had never been able to talk to anyone. "I'm sorry. I'm chatting your ear off."

He smiled and placed a soft kiss on my mouth. "I enjoy when you talk to me but you need rest. Talk to your girls, and then you're going to get your beautiful ass to bed."

"Yes, Sir," I saluted him.

Something flashed in his gaze. His mouth pressed firm against mine.

I sighed, leaning into him. "Thank you."

"No thanks needed, princess." He kissed me again before leaving the vehicle.

Taking a couple of deep, cleansing breaths, I waited. For what, I wasn't sure. My head hurt. My body ached. I knew I needed to go to bed, but the urge to find out what the hell happened took over.

"Jay, what's going on?" Max called out, rushing to my side when I slowly slid from the vehicle.

Angel kept a firm hold on my arm, stopping me from stumbling.

"If you would have answered your phone, you would already know," I bit out through clenched teeth.

"What are you talking about?" Max asked, frowning.

"I was in trouble. I called you," I cried.

"No." She shook her head. "You didn't."

"Yes, I did. I called all of you," I said, my voice raising.

"Let's get you inside, beautiful," Angel whispered in my ear.

"Jay, I'm sorry." Max's voice was small. She quickly headed back inside the clubhouse.

"I called them," I insisted, holding onto Angel's arm for support.

"I believe you." He whistled, rounding up the rest of Vice-One and we made our way into the meeting room. Why the guys were there was beyond me. "We'll be here until you no longer need us," Angel told me, pulling the thought from my mind.

"We like having you around," I said, answering for my sisters. "It's nice to have some testosterone up in this place."

"We like being here." Angel nodded. "And I know someone else feels the same way."

I followed his gaze. Dale was quietly speaking to Max. His hand reached out to cup her face. She leaned in, her lips parting. When her gaze moved back to his, I could see the love in her eyes. Had I been so oblivious the past couple of weeks to not even notice my best friend had fallen in love? Was I so selfish that I didn't even know my sisters anymore?

Dale kissed her softly on the mouth and held her hand, leading her into the meeting room. The rest of Vice-One joined us, followed by a man I hadn't seen before. He was large. Built like a tank. Hollywood movie star good looks but a dark shadow hid behind his eyes. His gaze met mine, no emotion showed on his face. He nodded once and walked away.

"Who is that?" I asked Angel softly.

"Vincent Stone. He's our newest squad member," he kissed my head. "I'll introduce you properly at a more appropriate time."

I nodded, taking a deep breath. Knowing I had to get the meeting done and over with, I squeezed the bridge of my nose and took my spot at the head of the table. Angel stood behind me, leaning against the window ledge, and crossed his arms under his chest.

"Tell us what happened," Max pleaded. "Please."

"I was stranded at the side of the road," I explained. "I called you. Each of you."

"My phone never rang," Brogan placed her phone on the table in front of her. "Please believe me."

"I don't understand." I pulled out my phone, checked the activity and saw the attempts of calling out.

"None of us got your calls," Meeka placed her phone on the table as well. "What happened?"

"There has to be an explanation," Dale said, squeezing Max's shoulder.

"It doesn't make sense. I know I called you, each of you, but your phones are saying I didn't?" I looked at Angel. "Is that possible?"

He rubbed his chin. "Yes. I'll have a guy I know find out how."

"Tell us what happened, at least." Max grabbed my hand. "You have a bandage on your head."

I touched the spot and brought my hand down, expecting to see blood on my fingertips like before. But when I didn't, a part of me thought I was hallucinating. That I imagined the whole thing.

"Tell them," Angel said, his voice firm.

"I went for a ride to clear my head," I explained. I told them about the woman, the evil in her eyes and the blow to the back of my head.

"Someone is trying to leave a message," Stone said, his deep voice booming around the small room. "They're warning you to stay away or they're trying to make a point."

"How do you know that?" I asked him, invested in every word he had to say.

"These girls that are going missing, whoever is running it clearly doesn't want their organization to stop. Whatever this shit is, whether it be just girls, sex

180

slavery, weapons, drugs… Either way, they're making it known that they mean business. They're trying to scare you." He took a step toward me. "I also know about your sister."

J.M. WALKER

TWENTY-
ONE
ANGEL

WHEN I got the call from Jay that she had been
stranded on the side of the road, my stomach sunk to
my feet. I refused to lose her over some bastards that
got their rocks off on hurting women. But those girls
were not the weaker sex like some thought. They were
the minority in a world run by men, but I bet my life
they would do anything to protect what belonged to
them. I didn't come across a lot of women who could
kick my ass but Jay's sister, Brogan, could put me flat
on my back. I bet there wasn't an ounce of fat on her.
She was ripped in a healthy way. Not having the
masculinity that most women thought would happen if
you lifted weights. No. She was strong. Powerful.

Holding Jay's hand tight in mine, I braced for the
news Stone had to give her. Before I got her call, he
had met with me to tell me that he knew of her sister
disappearing. I didn't know how. He made it clear that
he needed to tell her first, but I refused to allow him to
do it alone. Especially since she got attacked by God
knew who.

"You… You know my sister?" Jay asked, her
voice small.

"No." Stone pulled up a chair in front of her. "Not
personally."

182

"What do you mean?" Her chin trembled, haunted by memories that no longer existed.

"I…" He looked at me before continuing. "Before my squad got attacked, we were searching for the missing girls but came across nothing until we stumbled upon a shed."

"Is that a normal thing for you guys?" Max asked, sitting forward.

"No, it's not," I answered. "But these fuckers have multiple compounds all over so anyone can come across them."

"I need to know why me. Why was I targeted? The woman knew I would be there." Jay scrubbed a hand down her face. "But I didn't tell anyone. I just left."

That was when I caught Meeka reaching into her pocket for her phone. I saw the shadow of guilt pass over her face. She knew something. She caught my gaze, her eyebrow raising, challenging me.

Oh, little girl, if you are the reason Jay ended up stranded on the side of the road, I will end you without her knowing. Rubbing my chin, I gave her a curt nod.

Meeka glanced down at her lap.

Something was up, but being a nice guy and all, I wouldn't call her out on it until we were alone.

"Jay," Stone said, his voice firm. "I knew I recognized you. I thought I had seen a ghost." He pulled a picture out of his leather jacket and paused before giving it to her.

Jay gasped, clapping a hand to her mouth.

I knew beforehand what I would see. An image of a woman who mirrored Jay stared up at her. At a quick glance you'd think it was the same person, but taking a closer look, you could see her eyes were further apart than Jay's. Her nose smaller. And a light freckle sat just above her lip. Where her skin had many marks, Jay's was pure. Untouched. Except for the marks I adorned her body with.

183

"Violet," Jay whispered, grazing her fingers down the black and white image of her sister. "Where did you get this? How did... Have you seen her?"

Stone hesitated.

"Please," Jay pressed. "I'm sick of secrets. These people are my family."

My heart swelled at that.

"Fine." Stone squared his shoulders, rolling his head on his neck much like I did when I was about to hit something. "I've seen your sister with some people. Men. My squad was working on finding out exactly who they were before we got attacked. I don't know if your sister is working with them or if she's a victim."

"Excuse me?" Jay shook her head. "Violet would have nothing to do with this. These men—she's there against her will. Doing whatever shit they make her do."

"Jay," I cupped her shoulder. "You need rest."

"Angel," her eyes met mine. "I can't believe she would be in on this. I can't. There's no fucking way."

I nodded, giving her the reassurance I knew she needed even though I felt like a liar. It made sense. I had seen the pictures. Why else would Violet still be alive?

***

(Jay)

I sat there. Alone. My heart broken. My mind shattered into a million pieces because I had no idea what was going on. I appreciated Stone's honesty but there was no way I could even begin to fathom that Violet would be working with these bastards. I was so confused. My thoughts were jumbled, breaking apart like a jigsaw puzzle. The wrong pieces didn't fit, but I tried so desperately to force them.

Oh, Violet. What have you done to yourself?

There had to be an explanation.

With my arms crossed on the table in front of me, I leaned my forehead against them. Taking deep breaths to calm my racing nerves, I tried so hard to fight the pain. Angel had insisted I rest but I needed some time alone. Some time to gather whatever thoughts I had left. Whatever hope I had regarding my sister.

"Nugget?"

Tears welled in my eyes. My head slowly lifted, finding my father standing in the doorway to my office. "Daddy."

"Come here, baby girl." He held his arms out for me and needing the moment of protection, I ran into his arms. "Talk to me," he said, rubbing my back in small, soothing circles.

"I'm so confused. I don't know what's going on," I sobbed, my voice muffled by the cut of his leather. "I feel so alone."

"Hey." He cupped my cheeks, kissing my forehead. "You are not alone." My old man led me to the couch, pulling me into his arms. "Now talk to me."

I told him everything I could. Everything I knew about Violet and what Stone had told me. How I thought someone was leaking information. How I got left at the side of the road...

"Why the hell didn't you call me?" he demanded, his voice booming.

"You have enough shit going on, Daddy," I told him, wiping the tears from under my eyes. "You have Tyler to worry about, remember?"

"Fuck him. *You* are my daughter. I'm not the one who wants your club to end."

"Wait." I shook my head. "What?"

"Listen." My father sighed, holding my hands in his. "Be careful. That's all I can say. I know you have a good head on your shoulders and I trust that you will use it."

185

"What about Violet?" I continued when I saw the grimace on his old, weathered face, "I know you don't want to talk about her."

"It's not that I don't want to. It's that I can't. It hurts too much," he explained, his voice cracking. "I don't want to think that she left because she was unhappy. That one of my daughters was so depressed that she had to get up and leave without a goodbye. But then a part of me wishes that were the case because if I find out she has been—" He swallowed hard. "It'll kill me."

"I will do everything in my power to bring her home, Daddy." We needed closure. We needed some sort of solace. I couldn't stand the vice president of Dante's Kings but Tyler and I had a history. There was a time where we did love each other. He had to understand that no matter what, he couldn't shut down King's Harlots. I just prayed my dad wouldn't get shit on because of it. "You need to be careful too."

"If you're referring to T, I'm not scared of him." But something flashed in his gaze. It was so fast I almost missed it, but I knew something was there.

I didn't press. "Are you here alone?"

"No. Scab and Trace are outside."

"Good." I was thankful that T wasn't around, even though being the VP, he should be by my father's side at all times. I knew they were having problems. Tyler went by his own rules but had the other guys so wrapped around his fingers that my dad couldn't get his patch taken away. He would have to kill him first. Dante's Kings lived on the brink of the law. Teetering on that edge of good versus evil. If it came down to it, my father would do what he had to, but even I knew that he couldn't take Tyler on by himself.

"You need to get some rest," my dad said, interrupting my thoughts.

We left the office where we were greeted by Angel.

"Hey," I said to Angel, ignoring the way my heart fluttered at the closeness of him. My nose betrayed me, inhaling the spicy scent of his cologne. Leather and sex. God, he smelled good.

"Hey yourself." He reached out for my hand, slowly sliding his fingers between mine.

A throat cleared, making me jump.

"Daddy." I coughed. "This is Angel Rodriguez. Angel, this is my father, Brian Gold."

"President of Dante's Kings," my father added, puffing out his chest.

"He knows who you are, old man," I said, rolling my eyes.

"Yeah, well." He popped his collar. "Don't fucking forget it, either."

"It's nice to meet you," Angel said, a slight smirk twitching at the corners of his mouth.

"Jay, call me if you need anything." My dad kissed my head. "And just to warn you, Tyler wants to set up another meeting. I'm the fucking president and he's pissing down my throat with these orders and demands and shit. Fucking A." My dad trudged off, continuing to mumble and curse under his breath.

"You good?" Angel asked me once we were alone.

"I..." My gaze wandered to the table occupied by my sisters. Their heads were down, quietly speaking amongst themselves. They felt guilty even though it wasn't their fault. "I have to go do something, and then I'll go to bed," I added when Angel went to protest.

He nodded. "I'll be in your room. You better not make me have to come and find you."

"I'll be a few minutes," I promised him, patting him on the chest and kissing his chin.

"Fine." He kissed me hard on the mouth before letting me go.

I sighed, spinning on my heel, and slowly walked toward my sisters. Their heads lifted when I approached. "Hi."

"Hi," they all said in unison.

"Listen, I want to apologize for how I acted earlier. I assumed you didn't answer your phones because you were ignoring me or were too busy, and I shouldn't have done that. I never would have imagined that someone could have hacked into the phones. We'll find out how that happened and get this shit underway." I wrung my hands in front of me, an unsettling feeling swimming in the pit of my gut. We had to get to the bottom of everything before I lost my damn mind.

"You don't need to apologize," Max said. She grabbed my hand and pulled me down beside her. "We should have been there for you no matter what."

"Yes," Brogan added. "I am just glad that Angel was there to help you."

"Me too," I muttered, glancing at Meeka.

She didn't say anything.

"Can you girls give us a moment?" I asked Max and Brogan.

They nodded, sliding out of the booth.

Meeka's gaze snapped up, her eyes darting back and forth before landing on me. "I'm sorry," she said once we were alone. "I would have been there for you if I could but I wasn't allowed. I'm never allowed. Don't make me say anything. Please. I can't tell you yet," she said quickly.

My heart stopped. "What are you talking about?"

"I can't. I've said too much."

"Meeka," I reached out for her, stopping her from leaving the table. "Talk to me."

"I can't. Not yet. Just trust me. Please trust me. That's all I can ask."

"How can you expect me to trust you if you don't talk to me?" I pressed. "You haven't given me much to go on, Meeka. You're quiet. Withdrawn. I don't know if you're coming or going. Do you want out? Is that it?"

Her eyes widened. "No. Of course not. I just have some things going on, and I don't know how to deal with them."

"Let me help you," I insisted. "Let *us* help you. That's what we're here for."

"I wish I could ask for your help."

"Why can't you?"

"It's not time," she whispered.

I went to ask her what she meant, but a throat clearing stopped me.

"Jay," Angel's deep voice caressed me. "You need to rest."

"But—"

"I said, you need your rest," he said, his voice final, daring me to challenge him.

"Fine." I gave Meeka a tight hug. "This conversation isn't over."

"I know," she said, hugging me back. "I'm glad you're okay."

"Me too." I sighed. "Keep the girls in line. If shit gets out of hand, Max can deal with it."

"You got it, Prez." Meeka squeezed my hand before making her way toward the bar.

"Come," Angel demanded.

"You're so damn bossy," I mumbled, crossing my arms under my chest.

"You love it." He gave my butt a light swat. "And after what you went through today, you need sleep."

I nodded, silently giving in. Wishing it were that simple, I prayed sleep could take away the pain. Take away the fear that had been ingrained in my soul. The woman's eyes pierced into my brain, digging their way into the recesses of my thoughts. "Angel." My voice came out weak, shaky.

"Jay?"

"I…" Hugging my arms around my middle, I hunched over. My breathing became shallow, spots dancing in my vision.

"Breathe, baby," Angel sat me on my bed, holding my hands tight in his. "Let it out."

Tears burned my eyes, a hard lump lodging its way in my throat. "I-I can't."

"Yes, you can." He kissed my forehead.

And that was when I broke. Sobs tore through me. My body racked with cries. Fear took up residence inside of me.

"That's it." He wrapped me in his arms, rubbing small circles on my back. "You're fine. You're safe. As long as you are with me, you are safe. I won't let anything happen to you, beautiful girl."

"Oh, Angel." I continued to cry, gripping his shirt in my fingers. Tugging on him like he was my lifeline. He was safe. Protective. Everything I needed to feel normal. After what happened, I couldn't go on without him. I put up a façade that I was strong when I was weak. So damn weak.

"Shhh…" he said soothingly.

"I was so scared," I cried, my voice muffled by his shirt.

"I was too."

I pulled back, wiping the tears from under my eyes. "You were?"

"Of course." He gave me a small smile. "I just found you, Jay. I don't want to lose you."

His words took my breath away. So much so that I didn't know how to respond. *What does he want from me? Are we just fucking? Is this more? Did I want it to be more? God, yes!* I wanted everything he had to offer. I wanted to go to sleep with him every night and wake up next to him every morning. I wanted to give him every piece of me, the pieces no one had ever seen before.

"Jay," Angel whispered, brushing his mouth along mine.

"Spend the night with me," I told him, not wanting any words at the moment. I didn't want to know how he felt for fear that he didn't feel the same as I did. I knew something was there. I could feel it, but I didn't know if it was enough.

"You couldn't make me leave even if you tried." He kissed my forehead and helped me get undressed. He removed his own clothing before tucking me in safe beside him.

With our naked bodies touching, the solace and serenity that it wasn't about sex made my body relax.

Angel wrapped his body around mine, holding me against him. Never in my life had I felt like I truly belonged. Until then. I fit perfectly in his arms. I felt safe, and because of him I felt strong.

TWENTY-TWO

ANGEL

WHILE I watched Jay sleep soundly beside me, I thought about how I never knew what it truly felt like to have that one person you could share everything with. I never knew what it was like to love or be in love. I had no guidance—no instruction. No father figure telling me everything he knew about women. No mother to tell me how to treat a lady. *Should I buy flowers? Chocolate? Does Jay even like chocolate?* I didn't know much about her. Not the little things, anyway. But I knew that we were one in the same. Yes, she may have had a father. She may have experienced love but there was still something missing. She blamed it on the disappearance of her sister, but I knew it was long before that. Jay lived in a world that was dominated by men. She was raised by them and tried to overcome the fear of always being that little girl. I knew because I felt the same way. The little boy who lost his parents at such a young age. The little boy who would sit in the corner of his bedroom, waiting for the next hand to strike. Jay and I weren't that different.

When she called me, telling me she was stranded on the side of the road, I thought my world had ended. Even though it had just begun. And I knew. Right then and there. It all made sense. But I couldn't tell her yet.

Not when every time she looked at me, there was doubt in her jade-green eyes. She was scared. Well, so was I.

"Are you sleeping?" she muttered, her voice rough from lack of sleep.

"Not anymore," I kissed her neck. "How are you feeling?"

She rolled over onto her side and cupped my cheek. "Better." Her eyes heated, burning into mine. "Much better."

"What do you want, baby?" I asked, placing a soft peck on her lips.

"You," she breathed, leaning her head back. "Always you."

"For how long?" I knew I shouldn't have asked that question, especially when her body stiffened. *Shit.* "Jay, I'm sorry. I didn't—"

Her mouth crashed to mine, silencing me. "I want you for however long you'll have me."

Forever. But that word never left my mouth.

***

(Jay)

"Jay? Princess."

My body stirred, my eyes fluttering open to find Angel standing over me. I frowned, sitting up. I was in one of the large booths by the bar of the clubhouse.

"What are you doing?" he asked, sitting beside me.

"I..." I stifled a yawn, rubbing the grit out of my eyes. "I must have fallen asleep." Sometime through the night after Angel had used my body for both of our pleasure, I woke up antsy. Angel had been sound asleep, and not wanting to disturb him, I took my laptop and left my room. The sun had just been coming up at that point, the birds chirping like their little bodies depended on it.

"What are you researching?" he asked, nodding toward my laptop.

Tab after tab of news articles filled my browser. What *was* I researching? "I got a thought."

"Want to talk about it?" He pulled me against him, circling his arm around my waist.

"I'm not sure, but I woke up when a thought crossed my mind." I clicked on each of the tabs. "All of these articles have one thing in common. The missing girls. We already know that. I've read these over and over again. But it's been weeks, so I figured I would come back with a fresh perspective."

"Makes sense." He nodded. "Go on."

"Well this time, I found something odd. Before yesterday, I never thought that a woman would be in on this. I'm sure the police never thought that, either. Why would they? Why would a woman want to kidnap and sell other women? To make her more powerful? To throw authorities off her trail? It all makes sense. No one would expect this. It's the ultimate move. Well, look at this." I brought up an article, waited for him to read it, then brought up another one, and so on.

"These all mention a woman, the same woman, at every crime scene." Angel frowned. "Why haven't the police contacted her?"

"Because they can't find her." I tapped the screen. "It has to be the woman from yesterday."

"But you don't know that."

"No. I don't. But I have this feeling, Angel. I would bet everything I own that a woman is running this. Or she's running it with another person, but I wouldn't be surprised if she thinks she's the front runner."

"How can you be sure?" he asked. "I don't mean to be a dick, but this isn't a movie, Jay. This is real life. These are real people we are dealing with."

194

"I know that," I snapped, pulling away from him. "Right now, I'm willing to believe anything to get my sister back and these girls safe."

"I know." He cupped my jaw. "I get that. But I don't want you doing anything irrational or something that will get you hurt."

"Why?"

"What do you mean why? Because. I don't need to explain why." His brows narrowed, a dark shadow passing over his face.

"Tell me why you care so much," I pressed. It was the wrong time. I knew that, but I couldn't stop the words from leaving my mouth.

"Jay, you would be smart not to push me right now," he bit out through clenched teeth, his grip on my chin tightening.

His underlying threat sent a flutter racing through me.

I pulled my head from his grip and slid out the other side of the booth. Needing to use the ladies room and clear my head for a moment, I left the table without saying anything to him. My body burned, no doubt, from being stared at by the dark and brooding man.

A woman leading the human trafficking amused me in a way. Maybe she had men controlling her life. Maybe she needed to prove a point that she should not be messed with. I almost felt sorry for her if that were the case. I would never know. We had something in common, and it should have scared me, but it didn't. I knew how it felt to live under someone else's shadow. Even when Violet was around, I was always left in the dark. She was the light in my darkness. She was the sunshine where I was the rain. Everyone loved her. She was the perfect daughter and since she disappeared, I had tried so hard to take her place.

When I came back from the bathroom, I took a deep breath, ready to take Angel on headfirst. But when I saw him sitting there, hunched over the table, his head in his hands, my heart broke. God, I was turning into a pussy because of this guy. A small smile tugged at my lips.

"Name, Violet Mary Gold. Age, twenty-seven. Born on October 5th, 1988. Twin sister to Genevieve Elizabeth Gold. Daughter to Brian and Jenna Gold. Last known location, Greeneville, Ohio. Missing since June 19th, 2000."

My heart stopped beating, all of the blood rushing through my body now pooling in the soles of my feet.

"I need this information fast, man," Angel said, moving the cell to his other ear. "Yeah. She is important to me."

My stomach somersaulted. "Angel?" I slid into the booth across from him, his eyes watching me and following my movements.

"Thank you," he told the person on the phone.

"Who are you talking to?" I asked, not caring in the least that it was rude of me.

"Call me when you get something," Angel said, hanging up his cell. "I'm trying to help you."

"I don't need your help."

"Say that again, Jay," he demanded, leaning forward. "Tell me you don't need me. Tell me you can handle this all on your own. Tell me you won't get caught off-guard and attacked. *Again.*"

"That was not my fucking fault. I thought the woman needed help. What was I supposed to do?"

"You are way too close to this."

"I am not," I said, raising my voice. "You do not get to sit there and tell me what to do. I can't deal with this from you. Not you, Angel. Anyone else I expect it. From Tyler. My father. Even my sisters. But not you."

"I'm trying to look out for you," he said, his gaze softening.

"I don't need you to look out for me," I shouted. "I need you to be at my side. Not in front of me or behind me. At my fucking side. If you can't do that, then you can leave."

"Is that what you want?" he challenged and crossed his arms under his chest.

I mirrored his pose, not having any idea what I wanted. "I want you to be there for me."

"I will always be there for you. If you fall, I'll be there to catch you. If you cry, I'll be there to dry your tears. If you break, I'll be there to pick up the pieces." He tapped his knuckles on the table. "But I refuse to allow you to put yourself in danger. Not even for your sister."

"You can't stop me." He could, I knew he could, but I needed to show him that I wasn't backing down. His words meant so much to me. They were exactly what I needed to hear and what I had been craving my whole entire life. To have that person who would stand by you no matter what. But that was different.

"Yes, I can. If I have to tie you to my bed, I will."

Now didn't that leave a yummy image in my mind? "Angel," I said softly. *Where did this weak girl come from?* After everything that had happened, was I too tired?

"Jay." Angel moved from his spot and sat beside me. "We can keep going back and forth or just move forward. I want to help you. Please. Just let me do that. Everything else will fall into place."

"But I—"

"Stop with this I-am-an-island bullshit!" His fist landed on top of the table, rattling the wood. "I will tell you this once." In a rough move, he cupped my throat, forcing me to look into his beautiful dark eyes. "I am falling for you. All right? I don't know exactly what that means, so don't expect me to elaborate. Just know that when I fall, I fall hard, and I will fall to the pits of the Earth for you."

I swallowed loudly, not quite sure what to say to that. I searched his face, looking for any sign that he was lying, but his gaze stayed on mine, his mouth set firm and grim. He was falling for me. Everything I had hoped for had come true. It was a start. For us. For *me*.

"I don't expect you to tell me you feel the same," he said, loosening his hold on my throat and rubbing his thumb back and forth over my collarbone. "But I do know you feel something. I can sense it."

"I do." I nodded. "There is no way I can deny that." I gripped his arms, rubbing my hands up and down the thick muscles. "I'm not trying to do everything by myself. It's just how I'm wired. Please understand that." And I was making excuses. I was delaying the inevitable. *Tell him, Jay.* God, I was so dumb. "Angel." I inched closer to him, my mouth a hair's breadth away.

"Yeah?"

"I…I'm…" My heart started racing.

"Jay, girl, there you are," Max said a little too loudly and headed behind the counter to the coffee machine. Dale followed her, wrapping his arms around her waist.

"Another time, princess," Angel whispered, his lips caressing the shell of my ear.

"Yeah," I mumbled.

He pulled me in front of him, switching spots with me, and sat me in his lap.

"Boss," Dale called out. "You good?"

"Yup," Angel grunted. "You?"

Dale kissed Max hard on the mouth. "Definitely." She giggled, smacking him playfully on the arm. "Jay, how are you feeling?"

"I'm fine," I said, relaxing into Angel's hard body.

"Good," Max slid into the booth across from us. "Did you still want to have the meeting today?"

"She needs some rest, baby," Dale suggested, sitting beside her.

"No," I shook my head. "I've had enough rest."

"Okay," Max took a sip of her coffee. "You do know that Hell's Harlem is stopping by, right?"

I know now. Shit. "I forgot."

"Who's Hell's Harlem?" Dale and Angel asked in unison.

"Brogan's step-brother's MC," I told them.

"They're the good guys," Max said when Dale shifted in his seat.

"Are they?" Angel whispered.

"Yes." I patted his knee reassuringly. "It's just an inconvenient time." I would rather go back to bed but not to rest. I also had to stop by my shop.

"You're burning the candle at both ends, Nugget."

My father's words bounced around in my mind. So true. Always damn true.

A rumble of engines interrupted my thoughts. It would be good to see the guys again.

"They're here! They're here!" Brogan appeared out of nowhere, clapping her hands together, and threw open the doors. "Hurry up and get off your damn bike. I want a hug, asshole."

Angel chuckled. "Family love."

I smiled. "They're best friends. It's pretty amazing."

"Yeah and he's hot," Max swooned, fanning herself.

"Excuse me?" Dale bit out.

"Oh, whatever, baby. Just because I'm tied to the fence doesn't mean I can't bark at cars." she kissed him on the cheek. "And so can you."

"Woof woof." He rolled his eyes, but when they landed on her again, they were filled with warmth.

She gave him a smile, one that was meant for him.

Do I smile at Angel like that? Do I give him a look that is just for him? I liked to think so, but I honestly had no idea.

"Where are my favorite bitches?" Greyson Mercer called out.

"Who the fuck is he calling a bitch?" Angel growled.

"Hey." I cupped his cheek. "He doesn't mean it. We're family, baby."

"I'm not used to this," he muttered.

My chest tightened at the pain in his eyes. "That includes you," I whispered in his ear and rose to my feet. Kissing his cheek, I slid my fingers between his.

"Fucking A," he said, puffing out his chest and smacking me lightly on the butt.

I laughed, shaking my head. "Now, let me introduce you. What's mine is yours, Angel." It wasn't everything I felt, but it was a start. And I knew he accepted that when he kissed me hard on the mouth. So hard it took my breath. It took everything in me not to push him down on the bench and show him how I felt. Show him that he meant more to me as each day passed. That *he* was enough.

TWENTY-THREE

ANGEL

"HAVE YOU told her you love her yet?"

I stared across the table at Greyson and took a swig of my beer.

He smirked when I didn't answer. "What do you want with her?"

"I want to make her happy," I answered. "That's it."

"Good," he nodded. "She needs a strong man at her side. Not a fucker like Tyler."

I scoffed, rolling my eyes. "I don't know the whole story but I know there's bad blood there. I haven't officially met him."

"He's a fucking bastard. Only good thing he's ever done is keep that MC in line when Brian can't." Greyson rested his arm on the back of the booth. "I'm guessing you don't need the whole *don't hurt her or I'll kill you* speech."

"Nah. Max and Brogan took care of that already." I chuckled to myself, remembering their idle threats.

"They could probably do more damage than I can anyway." He leaned forward. "These girls are my sisters. My family."

"I get that." He didn't have to tell me twice. I nodded toward Vice-One. Dale and Asher played a

201

round of pool with Coby and Vince watching. "*They* are my family. I would lay my life on the line for those men. We have been through shit—some of us more than others." I glanced back at Greyson. "I don't have to tell you that if anything happened to them, I will fucking kill you."

"Touché." He scratched his jaw. "I promise you, Hell's Harlem is not out for blood. We do what we need to to get by."

"Understood."

"Well, I guess we're all family now." Greyson winked.

My eyes scanned the room until they landed on the back of Jay's head. She was in the middle of a conversation with Max, but as I allowed my gaze to roam down her curvy body, her back stiffened. She looked at me over her shoulder, catching me staring at her. She excused herself from Max and headed my way. Her hips swayed side to side, teasing me. Her long, curly, red hair brushed her arms with each step.

"Greyson, can you meet me in the office?" she asked him, not taking her eyes off me.

"Yup. I'll round everyone up. It was nice meeting you, Angel." He tapped the table once and left us alone.

As soon as Jay stepped between my legs, her mouth crashed to mine. Forcing her tongue between my lips, she took my breath and swallowed it deep into her lungs, forcing the moment of submission. Her fingers ran through my hair, tugging my head back. Allowing her the control, I kept my hands to myself. As much as I wanted to take over, I needed to give her that. A hot shiver ran down my spine, piercing me straight in the dick. My pants tightened to the point of painful, the offensive material cutting off the blood supply to the part of my body that craved Jay's touch.

I growled, wrapping my arms around her waist. "Harder," I demanded.

Opening her mouth wider, she licked her tongue against mine. Dancing. Tasting. Taking from me what rightfully belonged to her. Everything about me belonged to her. My skin. My body. My fucking soul. It was hers. I realized it then. I was in love with this woman but it was more. So much more. She was everything I needed. She was the air I breathed. The sustenance I tasted. The light in the shadows that haunted my dreams.

"Jay," I breathed, swallowing her purrs of pleasure.

"Later," she said as if she knew what I was going to say. Her mouth pressed to mine in a firm kiss. She cupped my cheek, staring intently into my eyes. "Definitely later."

"No." I pulled away.

"Yes." She kissed me one last time before stepping away from me. "Later," she repeated and spun on her heel.

My fingers reached up to touch my swollen lips. The tingle reminded me of where she had been. Where she would always be.

***

(Jay)

That kiss told Angel everything my words couldn't. What I felt for him. What I wanted from him. Instant attraction was common, but instant love? It wasn't normal in my part of the world. It may have happened for some, but not me. Weeks later and I had realized that I wanted to spend time with Angel. More time. For how long? I couldn't be sure, but as I sat there in the meeting room, listening to the demands and questions of my friends and confidants, all I could think about was staking a claim on what rightfully belonged to me.

"Why didn't you call me when this happened?" Greyson boomed, pacing back and forth.

"It was taken care of," I told him. "Angel picked me up and took me to the hospital."

He paused in his steps, his hard gaze meeting mine. I knew he wanted to say that Angel wasn't family and I should have called him instead, but he was smart enough not to. Angel had been the one person the last couple of weeks who gave an unbiased opinion about…everything. He knew me in ways no one else did. Not even Violet. She was my twin and would always be a piece of me, but Angel, he owned every inch. Every fiber ingrained in my soul.

"I didn't know when you would be in town anyway," I explained. "It didn't make sense for me to call you."

"I know." He gripped the edge of the table, leaning on his knuckles. "What do we have?"

I explained to him and everyone what I had come across when going through the articles and news clippings again. There were grumbles, curses, raised voices, but we were all in agreement that the woman who attacked me had something to do with the disappearances. How much she was involved, we had no idea.

"I'll get my guy on this. He'll have an unbiased view, so he'll be able to see something that we haven't." Greyson motioned to his VP, Carter Jones. "Write this down." He nodded toward me.

I repeated the description of the woman I saw the day before. "And I also need my bike back." *In one piece, preferably.* I sighed, closing my eyes, and leaned my head against the back of the chair. I listened to the voices surrounding me. Greyson continued to chat with Carter. Max and Brogan spoke with the other guys about possible ways to maim the people who hurt me. Meeka carried on a conversation with Smoke, the newest prospect for Hell's Harlem. All of the voices had one thing in common. The women who disappeared. The police weren't doing shit. The FBI had their own way of doing things. The military? I had no idea what they were capable of but I knew that Angel's team was doing the best they could even if they had to go against orders.

My eyes grew heavy. Taking a break, I leaned my head against the back of the booth. A moment later, a warm mouth caressed mine, making me jump. My eyes popped open.

"You fell asleep." Angel chuckled. "Everyone is in the bar having a drink."

"Oh." I scrubbed my hands down my face. "I guess I needed more rest than I thought." I yawned.

"I guess so." He lifted me and sat in my chair, placing me in his lap. "How did the meeting go?"

"All right." I snuggled into him, savouring the warmth his body created every time I touched him. "Greyson is getting someone to look into the articles a little more." I shrugged. "I feel like nothing is moving forward. We're stuck in this time loop. A girl goes missing. We freak out. We search. Nothing. Same thing. Different day."

"The disappearances are happening more frequently."

My back stiffened. "They are?"

He nodded. "I'll show you on your laptop, but now they're running a month apart."

"Oh God." Bile rose to my throat. "This can't be happening."

"We'll stop this."

"We have to, Angel," I cried, desperation coating my voice. "I feel like I'm losing my fucking mind."

"Jay, look at me." He grabbed my hands, turning my head.

I still couldn't meet his eyes. I couldn't see the expression of pity in his gaze. The wonder of what he was getting himself into.

205

"Look at me," he repeated, his voice firm.

I did as I was told, meeting his gaze.

"You are not losing your mind." His eyes burned into mine.

I scoffed.

"Hey." He pinched my chin. "You are *not* losing your mind. Do you understand me? You're stressed. Your sister has been missing for years. You live in a world dominated by men and you're trying to fit in. You're trying to make it easier for your sisters. For other like-minded women. You're also trying to save these girls that are disappearing. I'd say you have every reason to be stressed, Jay."

"I just want this over." My chin quivered. "I want these people stopped. I—"

A soft knock sounded on the door, Max appearing a moment later. "Hi, guys. Sorry to interrupt, but, Jay? This package came for you."

I thanked her and placed it on the table, frowning.

"What's wrong?" Angel asked, coming up beside me.

"I never get mail," I told him.

"Don't open it." Angel pulled open the door abruptly and whistled. All of Vice-One appeared within seconds, surrounding me and the small box.

"What's going on?" I asked, my heart racing.

"Jay, I want you to take a step back," Asher said gently, placing his hands on my shoulders.

"No. If you're concerned about what's in it, I'll open it slowly." I didn't know why I was arguing, but I refused to let those fuckers win. Whoever they were.

"Jay," Angel barked.

"Fine," I stepped back. "But I'm not leaving," I said, crossing my arms under my chest.

Dale chuckled, earning a glare from Angel.

Coby came up on my left, standing as close to me as possible without touching my skin. For some it would be uncomfortable, but for me, I realized it made

206

me feel safe. The hard man glanced down at me, giving me a curt nod. A muscle in his jaw ticked every so often, but other than that, he didn't show any hint of emotion. My heart panged for the guy.

"It's impolite to stare, Genevieve," Coby muttered under his breath.

I let out a small gasp. "You are the first person to call me that in years."

"It's your name, isn't it?" he asked, his eyes twinkling.

"Yes. It is." I enjoyed hearing the sound of my full name. It was a different part of me. A part I had hidden so long ago. A part I was desperate to get back but I didn't know how. It was the light to my dark, much like my relationship with Violet. She was wild where I was tame. *If she could see me now...* "Thank you."

He nodded.

"Do you know who delivered this?" Angel asked Max, who stood at the door.

"No. I'm sorry, I don't," she answered, her voice shaking.

"Come here." I reached out for her.

She ran to my side, hugging her arm around me, mumbling how sorry she was.

"Fuck me," Angel growled, moving in front of me.

"What's wrong?" I asked, trying to see over his shoulder.

"Stay here," Asher took a step toward us, shielding Max and me from the view of the box.

"You have got to be fucking kidding me," Dale bit out through clenched teeth.

Coby and Vince didn't say anything. They just looked at each other, a knowing glance passing between them.

"Please tell me what it is," I demanded, but no one budged. They continued talking amongst themselves. *Well, as-fucking-if.* It was my club. My house. My rules. I may not like what I saw, but what my brain conjured up was way worse. "Angel." He didn't move. Not one word. Not one acknowledgement. "Excuse me." Nothing. I released myself from Max, patting her hand and stood my ground. "I said, *excuse me*," I shouted.

All heads turned toward me.

"If you don't let me see what is in the package, I will call every biker I fucking know and get them to force you to show me." Hey, it was worth a shot. I was a Daddy's girl through, and through and I could be a whiny brat when I didn't get my way. This was one of those times, and I had every right to know when I was being threatened.

"Is that so?" Asher asked, raising an eyebrow.

Angel didn't respond, but a slight smirk tugged at his lips.

"I like her," Dale said in awe.

Vince shook his head and Coby kept his back to me. *Smart man.*

"You know I will call them," I told Angel.

"I thought you could handle things on your own."

"You guys are all bigger than me. I know when to pick my fights. One of you I could take, but not all five." I crossed my arms under my chest, lifting my chin defiantly.

"Wow." Dale whistled. "Where did you find her?"

"She is the president of some bad ass bitches," Greyson answered for him, coming up behind us. "I would listen to her."

"You're not going to like it," Angel mumbled, reaching out for my hand.

My heart skipped a beat when our fingers touched. I knew I wouldn't like what I saw. But I was prepared. "Can't be any worse then what's in my head," I muttered.

My mind ran wild with thoughts of what it could be. I had seen enough movies to know that if a package came from an unknown source, it was probably something I wouldn't want.

Blood pounded in my ears. It was so loud I was surprised no one could hear it. Palms sweaty. Stomach twisted into knots. I knew I shouldn't look in the box, but I had to. No matter what it was, I knew I needed to see it before I drove myself crazy with what it could actually be.

"Take a breath, princess," Angel said gently, pulling me in front of him. "I'm here."

Those words didn't register until my gaze landed on the contents of the box. "Oh…" I gasped, clapping a hand over my mouth. My heart raced against the walls of my ribcage, my stomach twisting and turning. My body numb. A bloody finger stared up at me, the nail painted black. The edge of the finger was jagged, the bone sticking out like it had been chewed off the hand by a savage animal.

"Breathe, baby," Angel whispered in my ear, placing his hands on my shoulders.

I didn't know who the package came from. I didn't know what they were trying to tell me. *Are they trying to scare me? Warn me? Make me stay away? Demand that I stop looking for these girls? Will I get more packages like this one until all that is left of the victim is nothing but dust in the wind?* All of those questions, all of those thoughts, bounced around in my mind. They nagged and dug at the recesses of my soul. I was lost. I had no idea where to go, but I knew I needed to get away. From everyone. From the box. From *me*.

Spinning on my heels, I tore out of there and ran outside. The fresh night air cut at my skin, biting and gnawing until all I felt was the wind.

Voices sounded from behind me, but I couldn't make them out. They were strong but unsure. Pity hid behind their words.

Oh, poor Jay. She's losing her ever-loving mind.

209

I wasn't but I couldn't concentrate with them around. I couldn't focus. I was driven to the point where I would search for Violet on my own. It wasn't smart. It was downright stupid of me to even consider it, but with the lack of help I had been getting from all sides, it was my last resort.

The image of the finger forced its way into my mind. My gaze glanced down at my hands splayed on the cement beneath me. When had I knelt? Tears burned my eyes, the vision of my fingers becoming blurry.

Oh, dear God. My finger. Although it had no nail polish on it, it was the twin to the one ripped from its owner.

"Violet!"

TWENTY-FOUR

—jay

MY BODY shook as bone crushing sobs racking through my soul. It had been the first hint of her existence in over five years. Everyone told me she had died but I could feel her breath within my being. If I could just reach her. If I could hear her voice, it would give me the strength I needed to move on. We were twins. If one died, the other would feel it. I knew that. We may have had different personalities but we were one. I accepted her for who she was. I understood her.

Heavy arms wrapped around me, holding me close against a hard body. The gentleness of the touch forced the cries to leave me in agonizing bouts of air. My throat dried up, going raw like I had swallowed shards of broken glass.

"Let it out, Jay," Angel coaxed, hugging me to him.

"I can't-I can't do this," I choked between sobs.

"Yes, you can," he soothed, rocking me back and forth.

"No," I shook my head, gripping him tighter. If I could have, I would have burrowed under his skin, hiding in his soul where I would be safe. From harm. From pain. I had trained myself for so many years not to let things bother me. To be cold and heartless. To

211

show no emotion for fear of getting hurt. But the emotions I struggled to hold back that time were different. They were real. They were excruciating, and I couldn't control them.

"Listen to me." Angel cupped my cheeks, staring intently into my eyes. His thumbs brushed away the tears, his lips curling into a small smile. "You are the strongest person I know. Even stronger than the men I go to hell and back with. Yes, the finger probably belongs to your sister and that fucking sucks. I will kill the bastards who are doing this if you don't get to them first."

That part made me smile. He knew me well.

"But I refuse to watch you break because of this. That's what they want. It's what they crave. They want to see you crumble. They want to see you give up because that means they won. But, Jay," he kissed my mouth, "no matter what happens, *I* will be the one to make you break, and it will be because you want it to happen. I'm not Tyler. I'm not a biker. But I am a fucking man, and I am only strong with you by my side."

"I…" My mouth opened and closed. I had no idea what to say to that but I took his words to heart. He was right. He was always fucking right. He was the King to my Queen. My smile grew, knowing Violet would love that. I made a mental note to tell her everything when I found her. And I *would* find her. No matter what happened. Even if it ended badly, I would still tell her. Some way. Somehow.

"Take me home," I blurted.

"You are home," Angel frowned.

I shook my head and rose to my feet. Wiping the tears from under my eyes, I took a breath. "No. I'm not." I spun on my heel, walking down the parking lot toward the main street of our town. My home. A piece of me no one knew about. Not even my sisters. Guilt settled in the pit of my stomach.

I couldn't tell them about it. Not yet. Although I had a home somewhere else for years, I couldn't muster up the courage to tell people about it. Until that moment. Something inside of me told me to bring Angel to that place. My safe haven. It was as if I was getting a nudge from Violet. She had never been to my apartment but she knew about it. Before she disappeared, I had mentioned it to her. I explained I wanted it close by but I didn't want anyone to know. She had liked the idea and understood all the same.

"Jay, where are we going?" Angel asked, walking beside me. He didn't reach for my hand, but every so often, he would brush a strand of hair off my cheek and push it behind my ear. I would smile up at him, appreciating the small touch.

A block later, we stopped in front of my tattoo shop. The lights were off, the open sign no longer flashing with invitation. I sighed, needing to get my head back in the game. It would be what Violet would have wanted. She would also kick my ass for allowing all of my unreasonable feelings to surface over her. But they made sense. She would feel the same if the roles were reversed. I prayed over and over that we could switch places. I would sacrifice myself to make sure she was safe.

"Jay," Angel pressed, grabbing hold of my hand. "Talk to me. Tell me what's going on."

His thumb rubbed over my knuckles, his tanned skin dark in comparison to mine. My heart fluttered, a breath leaving me on a whoosh. "Every time you touch me, I can feel it in my soul." I glanced up at him through my lashes, my cheeks heating at the confession.

His eyes twinkled in the dim moonlight. He took a step closer, reaching out to brush another strand of red hair behind my ear. "No matter what I do, my body reacts to you before I even see you. My skin becomes flushed. My heart picks up speed." His voice lowered.

213

"My dick lengthens, twitching like a beacon as it waits for you."

I licked my lips but stepped out of his grasp. I needed to keep some distance between us, even if it were only a foot. Control was something I longed for, but with Angel, it was something I needed to give him. "I bought this place a month after Violet disappeared. She knew I had always wanted to own a tattoo shop, and she helped me but I was scared. Her being taken from me gave me that extra push because I knew if I didn't buy it, I never would."

Angel cleared his throat. "How come you never mentioned this place before?"

Meaning how come I never brought him there. "I wasn't sure if I could trust you. No one knows about this place."

"And now?"

"Now what?" I asked, heading down the alley beside the shop.

"Do you trust me?"

I stopped in my tracks, glancing up at him. "If I didn't, we wouldn't be here." And I wouldn't still be sleeping with him.

"Say it," he demanded. Closing the distance between us, he cupped my nape. "Tell me you trust me."

"I trust you." It felt good to say that. To tell the man touching me that I trusted him when I had never trusted anyone I had been with. Not even Tyler when we were happy together.

Angel's shoulders relaxed. He had nothing to worry about. Although whatever it was between us scared me, I trusted him with everything I had to give. With everything I was. Genevieve Gold. Not Jay. Not the person who put on an act to appear strong. Not the bitch. Genevieve came out when Angel and I made love. I wasn't sure if he noticed the different sides to me. If he did, he never mentioned them.

A shiver rippled down my spine.

"Come on," Angel said, wrapping his arm around my shoulders. "Show me your home, baby."

I led the way toward the door at the end of the alley and punched the security code into the keypad.

Angel whistled. "That's some high-tech security system."

"Yeah. I thought it would be best after everything that has happened." I pushed open the door.

"Makes sense…" His voice trailed off when he saw the second door. "Did your father set this up for you?"

"No." I barked a laugh. "I know it doesn't make sense that I've kept this place private with me being a tattoo artist and all but I needed this for myself. Just for a little bit. Everyone will know about this place eventually, so I figured I'd get everything set up beforehand. I don't need the lectures."

"Understood." Angel grabbed my key from my hand and unlocked the second door for me. "After you, princess."

It had been awhile since I had been at my place, which was sad. Every time I stepped over the threshold I felt guilty. But being there with Angel made all of those feelings go away and be replaced with new ones.

It was *my* home. No one else had slept in my bed besides me. No one had eaten at the dining room table. No one else had watered my plants. The plants I had named after my favorite movie characters. Plants that were wilting because I couldn't get away from the MC to water them. A lump burned the back of my throat. I was sad because those things were dying. *What the hell was wrong with me?*

"Tell me what it's like to be here by yourself, Jay. What do you do?" Angel asked, shutting the door behind him. The deep rumble of his voice slid over my skin, hinting, promising pleasure.

215

He was distracting me in the best way possible. Was it wrong to use sex as an out? Was it so bad that after the shitty day I had, I just wanted to lose myself in the man standing a few feet away from me? To taste his skin. To feel his muscles ripple beneath my fingers as my nails dug into his back. My body wet. Hot. Ripe. Just for him. My core swollen and sore from the rough pounding of his thick cock. I wanted him to use me. To throw me up against the wall. To demand that I please him before he allows me the greatest pleasure I craved.

"What are you thinking about?" His voice, dark and rough, hinting at an ecstasy so great it would bring me to my knees.

"You," I said, backing up until I reached the arm of my couch.

"No," he shook his head. "I want to know exactly what you're thinking about. Give me your words."

I swallowed hard. I had always been one to say what I wanted when it came to sex, but with Angel, it was difficult. Every time I was with him I felt like a virgin learning the ropes. Learning what he wanted and liked. What made him hard? What made him salivate? "I want to devour every inch of you," I whispered.

"Say that again." He took off his leather jacket, throwing it over the back of a chair. "Louder this time."

Desire soared through me at the bossy tone. "I want to devour you. Every inch," I repeated. "I want to lick the waves of your muscles. I want to feel the ripples of pleasure I bring you."

His eyes darkened, roaming down my body that was still fully clothed. "Undress." His eyes popped back to mine. "*Now.*"

With fumbling fingers, I took off my leather cut, followed by my tank top. When I reached for the button on my pants, rough hands stopped me.

"Too fucking slow." Angel pushed me onto my back. "You need distracting." He pulled my ass to the arm of the couch. "You need me, don't you?"

"Yes," I panted. "Please."

Angel grunted, ripping open my pants and pulled them down my legs to my ankles. "Only I can make you feel good, isn't that right, Jay?"

"Yes." I nodded. "Only you."

He leaned over me, kissing my belly. "You're mine."

"Please, Angel." I shook, aching for him in a way I had never felt before. My nerves were frazzled from the day I'd had. I just wanted to forget. I didn't want to remember that my sister was missing or that those women needed to be found. I wanted to forget that my club thought I was losing my mind. I was being selfish. Just for a moment.

With rough hands, Angel ripped my panties in half, his gaze darkening even more. "Your pussy is glistening. Fuck, Jay, I haven't even touched you yet."

"I can't..." I threw my head back, arching beneath him. "It hurts. Please. I need you."

"And you have me. Every time you need a good fucking, I am here, baby. Know that." Some would think he meant it as a joke, but I knew he was serious. I had times where I needed to get out of my head and feeling his body move against mine cleared my mind.

Angel pulled my ankles—still bound with my pants—over his head, crouching between my knees. His fingers massaged my thighs, spreading me wider for him. He knelt at the spot I wanted him most and he blew on the area that was about to explode.

As soon as he touched me, I would break. As soon as he kissed me, I would crash. And as soon as he loved me, I would shatter.

His hot breath slid across my mound, and I moaned, arching my back. "Please," I begged, spreading my legs wider, inviting him in. Hinting for him to take from me what I knew he wanted. What he craved.

"Your pussy is swollen, baby." Angel made a point of grazing a finger from my clit to the opening.

"*Fuck*," I cried out, frustration settling in. A hot sheen of sweat coated my skin, my chest heaving with each ragged breath. Just one touch. A little kiss from his full mouth would send me over the edge.

Before I could process what was happening, his hot mouth crashed to my core, covering me completely.

I gasped, my eyes widening at the rough but delicious impact.

He growled, thrusting his tongue inside of my body in one smooth stroke. His arms wrapped around my waist, holding me as I trembled against him.

The pleasure was so great, no sounds left my lips. All I could do was stare. It was as if he were a beautiful artist owning his canvas. Like a stroke of a brush, he rubbed his tongue against me. Inside of me. All over me.

My fingers dug into the couch cushion, my hips rocking upward to meet the thrusts of his tongue. "Oh…" Dots danced in my vision. A hot tingle spread from my toes to my head. "Harder," I pleaded. I wanted him to devour my soul. I wanted him to take away all of my pain with a stroke of his tongue.

"Shit, Jay." He released me with a smack, licking the juices off his lips.

"Don't stop," I begged, reaching out for him.

"I'm not, but I want you to come on my cock." He pulled my pants off my ankles and removed his clothing.

I followed suit by taking off my bra, my body vibrating and shaking with need for him. I slid up the couch, reaching out to him. "Angel."

"Show me what you want, baby," he said, kneeling between my legs.

218

Lifting my hips, I rubbed my slick center over his hard tip. "Fuck me. God, please. Fuck me hard."

He brushed a hand over my head before wrapping it around my throat. "Show me."

Wiggling my hips, I lined up our bodies and dug my heels into the flesh of his ass. "*Now.*"

In one smooth thrust, he filled me.

I broke, his name leaving my lips on a hard cry. The release rocked me to the core, but it wasn't enough. I needed more. "Harder."

A wicked grin spread on his face. He pulled me further beneath him, resting most of his weight on my body. I was pinned between him and the couch. His hips sped up, pumping hard and deep. Fast and powerful.

Another tingle. Another gasp. A second scream.

"That's it, baby. Dig those heels into my ass. Take me deep," he demanded, his voice taking on a rough edge.

God, this man and what he does to me.

"Eyes on me," he said, his voice firm.

My gaze met his, my fingers dug deeper into the muscles of his shoulders.

"Do you feel that?" he asked, pushing into me as far as my body would allow. "Do you feel the ridges of my cock inside your pussy? Do you feel how your cunt squeezes me, begging for another release?"

"Yes!" I nodded vigorously. "Oh God, yes!"

"Good." He released me, pulling out of my aching body and sat back on the couch. "Come here and kneel between my legs. I want your mouth."

My body vibrated at his demand, my tongue tingling with the need for his taste. I did as I was told and before I could get any more commands from him, I took him in my mouth. Swallowing the acidic taste of my body, I licked and sucked. Nibbled and swallowed. No inch of him went untouched. His moans and grunts, the use of my name, all slid into my ears. They

219

controlled my actions. They hinted for me to go faster. Slower. Rough then soft. Hard yet gentle.

When Angel had had enough, he pushed me onto the ground and found his way back inside my body without so much as a warning.

I cried out, hugging myself around him and took him all in. Arching beneath him, I lifted my legs. Angel grabbed my ankles, pushing my legs above my head.

"Oh my…" My body opened to him, giving him better access from the flexed position.

He grinned, crashing his lips to mine.

I couldn't move. I was stuck beneath him. Around him. All I could feel was him. All I could taste was his essence on my tongue, our pleasure mixing together as he kissed me like he fucked me. The thrusts of his tongue matched the movements of his cock. In. Out. Hard. Rough. Deep. There wasn't a soft bone in his body as he took what he wanted from me on the floor of my apartment. It was rough. Bordering on violent as he powered into me with so much strength, I was surprised I didn't get pushed into the floor. But it was needed. I could feel my attraction to him grow. The reason hit me and I gasped into his mouth.

He growled, shoving his tongue further between my lips.

Running my fingers through the back of his hair, I pulled, deepening the kiss. I took from him what *I* wanted. What I craved. And in return, I gave him my heart. I just prayed he wouldn't break it.

TWENTY-FIVE

ANGEL

WHEN JAY took me to her apartment to show me the piece of her she hadn't shown anyone, I didn't have any intentions of fucking her. Not until later when she was lying beside me wrapped in my arms. But her body shaking with her hands rubbing her arms, set me off. I knew I had to do something. At first I felt like I might have been taking advantage of her. Thinking with my dick first instead of my head. But when she played on it and told me in detail what she wanted, I knew there was a reason behind it. She wanted to forget. Even just for a moment. She was filled with the same darkness I was. For different reasons, it consumed us both. The billowy shadows of our past threatened to swallow us whole if we didn't do something about it. Sex. It was the cure-all. With Jay and me, it helped us focus on the here and now. It had never been something I craved. I was a man. I loved sex. But with Jay, I *needed* it.

She lay beside me, and I took full advantage of her nakedness. I caressed her skin with a touch of my finger, watching her shiver. She sighed, pushing her beautiful ass into my pelvis. My dick lengthened, twitching against her rear with a mind of its own. It begged for her to wake up and give it the attention it felt it deserved. But even *I* was tired.

After taking her hard and spending the next several hours showing her how I felt through the use of my body, we were both spent. But I couldn't sleep. I could never sleep. Not soundly. The silence in my head screamed at me. The noises were no longer loud but fierce and in control.

"I love you, Jay." I brushed my lips over the shell of her ear. With everything in me, I begged for her to wake up and tell me she felt the same. She stirred, her eyes fluttering, but much to my dismay, she remained asleep.

"I am so in love with you." I slid my hand down the length of her arm, watching the skin pucker with tiny little bumps. I kissed her neck, noticing for the first time a tiny tattoo. A semi-colon. My heart thumped hard, my chest swelling with pride. I knew the tattoo signified self-harm, but it could also be to show support for anyone with a mental illness. PTSD had been a mental battle for me over the years. Knowing I had someone else to care for, Buck kept me sane. Animals were a form of therapy, and if any of my guys showed any sign of breaking down, I would show them how a puppy could help.

With Jay, it was like everything was meant to be. *We* were meant to be. I kissed the spot behind her ear, wondering who the tattoo was for.

"My sister," Jay said, as if she could read my thoughts.

"Excuse me?"

She turned over, peering up at me through dark lashes and grazed a finger over my nipple. "The tattoo is for my sister," she repeated. "She was the happiest person I knew. A little abrupt and rough around the edges but she lived life every day to its fullest. I know that's a tad cliché but it was true. But I knew the real Violet, though. She wasn't happy. I didn't know why.

And I don't think she did either. If she did, she never told me, and I was fine with that. I'm still fine with that. She never knew I got the tattoo either. I…" Jay swallowed hard. "I never got a chance to show her."

"You *will* get to show her." I didn't know how I knew that. I couldn't promise Jay anything but I could promise my love for her. That I would be there for her.

Jay curled on her side, pulling the blankets up and around her further. "If I don't get to, maybe I was never meant to show her in the first place."

"Jay."

"No." She sat up abruptly, letting the covers pool around her lap.

The moon cast a dim glow around her, shining onto her pale skin. Her long red curls were haphazard and wild. They were a contradiction; Jay was anything but.

"Maybe she's…" Jay swallowed hard. "She's dead and I won't get to save her. I won't get to say goodbye or see her again. That one last time. That final time."

"You can't think like that." I grabbed her hand, attempting to pull her toward me, but she shoved out of my hold.

"Why can't I? Angel, I need to do something because this is driving me crazy. What if she left on her own? I should be mad at her but I can't. When I get mad I feel guilty because what if she was forced?" Jay brought her knees to her chest, hugging them.

"Stop this. You'll drive yourself crazy." I kissed her shoulder, my lips lingering so I could smell her a little longer. Her skin gave off the scent of sex and my cologne. If I had it my way, she would smell like me forever.

"Are you smelling me, Angel?"

"I sure am." I kissed her mouth. "You smell like me, baby."

Jay sighed. "You can't always distract me."

223

"I know." I shrugged. "It was worth a shot."

We sat there, comfortable in each other's silence.

"Did you mean what you said?" Her cheeks reddened.

"Depends on what you think I said." She heard my confession. Although I had wanted her to know what I had said, a part of me was scared she wouldn't feel the same.

"I didn't want to tell you how I feel because it scares me. I can't get hurt again, Angel. I refuse to allow that to happen." She cupped my cheek. "Please don't hurt me."

Leaning into her touch, I kissed her palm. "Never."

"Say it," she breathed, glancing down at my mouth.

"I am falling in love with you," I told her, inching closer.

"Oh, Angel." Her mouth crushed to mine. "I am falling in love with you too."

Fucking A.

***

(Jay)

He loved me.

I loved him.

All was right in the world. Until realization dawned on me and the fantasy popped in my face. Our love was true but our world was still shitty.

While Angel slept soundlessly beside me, I slid out of bed. Stretching my arms over my head, my whole body cracked.

I smiled to myself, knowing Angel was the reason I was stiff and sore but elated. A part of me still couldn't believe he loved me. Me. Genevieve Gold. My throat burned. If only I could tell Violet. If only I could show her how happy Angel made me. We had shit to work through, every relationship did, but it… It was real. It wasn't what I had with Tyler. I didn't fear that every time I spoke to Angel, he would yell at me. I wasn't walking around our relationship worried he wasn't happy. He was rough and dark but he never showed me that side of him. But I knew it was there because I could feel it. When his Dominance came out, I held onto the fact that he would never hurt me. He would never try and break me down. If he did, it would be to benefit me.

Pulling on shorts and a t-shirt, I grabbed my laptop and turned on my small lamp. The light cast an eerie glow around the room, shadows dancing in its wake.

Making sure Angel was still asleep, I kissed his forehead. When he didn't stir, I reached into my end table and grabbed the folder that had been my life for the past several years. Since Violet went missing. Since the first girl was stolen from her home or the street. It didn't matter. A victim was a victim no matter what lifestyle they lived. I had collected everything from newspaper clippings to pictures to files that my source was able to get access to. Thankfully, I knew a person or two. It was a give and take sort of world. I scratch your back. You scratch mine. Greyson had helped me gather everything I needed. He never argued even though I had seen the doubt in his eyes. Brogan's stepbrother wanted those girls found just as much as the next person.

In the MC world—even though I wanted my club to be straight and narrow—every now and again a girl had to do what she could to get accepted. My sisters didn't know. They had no idea what I had done to make a name for our club. But they weren't stupid. They knew how this world was run. I had told Angel before we both fell asleep. He never judged.

"I've done some bad things, Angel. Horrible things to get my club acceptance," I had told him,

225

*wringing my hands in my lap. "I've never hurt anyone,
not directly, but I've stolen things, made deals with
bad people." I took a breath. "I understand if you
judge me."*

*"I would never judge you," Angel had yawned. "I
have no right to. I've done some shitty things in my
own line of work. Even though I'm fighting for my
country, it doesn't make me feel any better."*

*"How do you get through it?" I'd asked, curling
on my side to face him.*

*"That's just it. I haven't. Buck is not just my dog. I
have PTSD, Jay."*

*I'd nodded. "I expect that in what you do. Do your
brothers know this?"*

*"No." He had rolled over onto his back, crossing
his arms behind his head. "I will tell them eventually
but I can't yet. I have to work some things out first."*

"Does your boss know?"

"If he does, he hasn't mentioned anything."

*"I won't tell." And I wouldn't. It wasn't my place.
I didn't know a lot about the military, but I knew that if
they deemed you unfit to work even if it was because of
something small, they would discharge you. It was sad
because I knew Angel loved what he did.*

*"I know." His eyes had searched my face. "It's
hard making money the legal way."*

*I'd scoffed, lying down beside him and wrapping
my arm around his waist. "It is. I do well with my shop
but it's not enough. And putting ink on bikers doesn't
get me any more acceptance than if I were to kill
someone. They're hard to please."*

*"Have you ever thought of not trying to please
them?"*

*"Every damn day." I'd huffed. Why I cared what
these clubs thought was beyond me. These men who
thought they were God's gift to women. Who treated
them as whores if they acted or dressed a certain way.
Even if the woman felt like wearing cut-off shorts, they*

were thrown in the ring like meat. It disgusted me and made me almost wish I never started this club.

"Tell me about your sister," Angel had demanded softly, his eyes closed.

"She was the life of the party," I'd traced my finger around his nipple. "Most people didn't like her because she was in-your-face honest. They took it as her being obnoxious. She told the truth and people didn't like that. Especially in a young woman. They thought it was impolite for a girl to say what was on her mind."

"Mmmhmm..." Angel had sighed, his breathing becoming deep and even.

I'd smiled, pulling the blankets up and around us. I'd closed my eyes, following him into a dreamless sleep.

It was a sleep I had wanted to spend every night in. Comfortable. Silent. Peaceful. But I knew as soon as I woke up, my thoughts would be loud again. They would take over everything I was and drown out the calm I had tried so hard to muster over the years.

Opening the folder, my fingers brushed over the images of the girls I had saved. Not that it was overly hard. Put up some fliers, bat your eyes and big burly men would fall all over themselves to save these little girls.

A black and white photo fell from the pile. Dropping the others, I picked up the picture I forgot I had. Violet stared up at me. Her dark hair blowing in the wind behind her. Her full lips turned into a wide smile. The mischievous way her eyes twinkled. For the life of me, I couldn't remember what she had planned that day and why she was ready to tackle the world. She was headstrong and passionate about everything, where I was timid and shy. But no more.

Turning on my laptop, I checked my emails; some more articles but otherwise nothing. Mustering up the courage to go on all of the social media outlets Violet

had joined, I read message after message from people. Her friends. Coworkers. Anyone who knew her or had an idea of her. They were nice messages. Wishing her well. Praying for her. Most had nothing to do with her disappearance and everything to do with her moving on to bigger and better things. Even the public believed she left on her own but I knew they were wrong.

Going back to the emails, I prayed something new had come up. When the inbox showed empty, I cursed under my breath. About to give up, a pop up appeared with a new message from someone who wasn't on Violet's friends list.

Unknown: Hi.

I never answered the random hellos as they creeped me out but this one, something about it stuck out at me.

Me: Hello.

I responded under Violet's profile, thinking it would get me somewhere.

Unknown: I missed you this morning.

My stomach dropped. This wasn't possible but I decided to play along anyway.

Me: I'm sorry. I had plans.

Unknown: You're sorry? How the fuck can you be sorry? You don't get to be sorry. That's a choice. Remember, I took that from you when I bought you.

Oh, dear God. Bile rose to my throat.

Me: I have every right to be sorry. I feel bad.

Unknown: Every right? Who the hell is this?

Shit. Did I just get Violet in trouble? Who was she sold to? My heart started racing, my sweaty fingers sliding over the keyboard.

Me: This is someone who is trying to find Violet. Please tell me you know where she is and that she's safe.

The message was read but no reply came. Tears burned my eyes. *No, please reply.* "Please reply," I repeated. "Please."

"Jay? What are you doing?" Angel asked from behind me.

"Reply, damn it!" I cried.

Me: Please. I'm sorry. Just tell me. I need to know that she's okay.

Still no reply.

"Who are you talking to?" Angel demanded. "Shit. What the hell? Who is that?"

"I don't know. I have no fucking idea. He knows Violet." My head spun around. "He knows her. He has her, Angel. He bought her. How can someone be bought? Tell me, *please*. God, we have to find her. What if I got her in trouble?" I was rambling, my heart racing hard against my rib cage. I was losing it. "Angel, please. Please tell me what to do." A ding from the computer caught my attention.

Unknown: Who is this?

Me: Someone who loves Violet. Please. I need to know my sister is okay.

Unknown: Sister? You mean there are two of you? That just made my fucking day.

TWENTY-SIX

—jay

WHAT HAD I done to deserve this? What had my sister done? Did she make a deal with the Devil, sell her soul and end up at the feet of a sadistic bastard? Not that I knew anything about the unknown person I was chatting with but his words dripped with evil. Pure hatred and venom hidden in the darkest part of nightmares.

"We need to have a meeting," Angel demanded, barking orders and directions into his cell. He paced back and forth in front of where I was sitting on the floor. "We're at Jay's apartment. Yes, her apartment. We'll explain later. Just write down the address and get your asses over here." I wrote down the address for him and he repeated it, hanging up the phone before kneeling in front of me. "I know you wanted to keep this place private but we need to tell everyone what's going on. This has become a lot more serious."

I nodded. "I know," I whispered, my voice shaky.

"Get dressed." He helped me to my feet. "Do you have any liquor?"

"I do. There's a pantry in the kitchen stocked with everything." I pulled on sweatpants and a black tank top, followed by an oversized sweater that I wish I could get lost in.

231

"Good." Angel slid his fingers between mine, leading us down the stairs to my living room. "Sit on the couch. I'm going to make you a drink and then deal with everyone."

"You don't have to."

"Yes, I do. They're going to bombard you with questions, Jay. You don't need that right now." He kissed me hard on the mouth, sealing the deal.

I didn't bother arguing and sat on the couch like he instructed.

Angel moved around in the kitchen. Glasses clanked together. Ice cubes fell from their trays. And all I did was curl up on the couch with my legs under me and dreaded the company that was about to come over. The girls would be mad. The guys wouldn't care about the apartment situation but they would be pissed over the unknown source I'd chatted with.

Dropping my head in my hands, all I could think about were his words. He *bought* Violet. How the hell could someone do that? Either way, it didn't matter. I just needed to know if she was okay. I wasn't stupid. If she was into…whatever this was…I couldn't force her to come home but I could make her see me. All I wanted was to know that she was safe and well. I needed to talk to that guy again. I shook my head, gripping my hair. No. I couldn't. It would get her in trouble.

"Here you go, princess," Angel handed me a tumbler filled with red liquid. "This is my own personal recipe. It helps with relaxing and sleep."

"So you mean it will knock me on my ass." I took the drink from him and brought it to my nose. A sweet, cherry scent wafted into my sinuses.

"No, not unless you have several. I'll make you another before you go to bed." He kissed my head.

"Thank you." I took a sip, swallowing the sweetness.

"Anything for you." His eyes shone.

A beep sounded in the air, indicating someone had arrived at the first door. I gave Angel the security code so he could allow the others in. When a heavy knock sounded on the main door, my heart jumped.

"I don't want to do this," I whispered. I was usually stronger. I could take on the world. I stood up to men twice my size, fought them when I needed to, and never even thought twice about it. But…after everything, I felt defeated. My soul crushed. I was tired. Oh, so very tired.

"We'll get this done and over with fast, Jay." He kissed me again. "I promise you." A shadow passed over his face, his eyes growing dark.

"I love you," I muttered, curling into myself.

He stopped in his steps, glancing at me over his shoulder. "And I love you," he said, standing a little taller.

I smiled, pulling my sweater tighter around me. That was the moment I knew would come but didn't want to deal with. My apartment was mine and mine alone. It had everything I had saved since I was a child. Collectibles, old books, pictures…things that made me…*me*. My girls wouldn't understand why I needed this apartment. Why I didn't tell them. Why I felt the need to keep it to myself when they insisted that I should stop this I-Am-An-Island bullshit. Sometimes being an island was needed. I could go in, get out, and not have to worry about anyone else. If I got hurt it was one thing but if anything happened to my sisters, it would destroy me. I couldn't deal knowing I put them in this situation.

"Where the hell is Jay?" Max demanded from the doorway. "And why the fuck were we not told about this place? Jay, tell us."

"You need to calm down," Angel told her.

"No. You need to get out of my way so I can find out why my best friend has been keeping secrets from me."

"You are not the only one she's been keeping secrets from, Max," Brogan reminded her.

"Angel, get out of my way!" Max shouted. I could almost picture her standing there, tapping her foot with her hands on her hips.

Angel blocked the way, not letting her through. When he allowed his brothers to walk past him, she huffed.

"You have got to be fucking kidding me," Max cried. "You let them go but you won't budge for me? Get out of my way, asshole."

That was it. Embracing the rage bubbling inside of me, I shoved to my feet and stomped toward Angel, who was surrounded by King's Harlots. My sisters. But right then, Max was just another woman who needed to get her shit together before I shoved my fist down her throat.

"Say that again, Max," I demanded, stepping in front of Angel.

Her eyes widened, taken aback by my sudden appearance.

"I-I'm..." she stammered. "I'm sorry. I just—"

"You just what? You see this man behind me?"

She nodded.

"Do all of you see him?" I asked, making a point to meet all of their eyes.

Meeka nodded, chewing her bottom lip.

Brogan brushed a hand through her dark, curly hair and Max gave an exaggerated sigh.

"Listen to me. I'm sick of your attitude, Max. Call my boyfriend an asshole again and I'll ram my foot so far up your ass, you'll be puking leather for weeks. You got me?" I patted Angel on the chest. "I can handle this."

He nodded once and joined his brothers in the living room.

"Now," I continued after he left. "I'm sorry. I should have told you about this place. I get that. And I will always feel guilty over it. But sometimes a girl needs something of her own. I intended to buy this place with my sister but bought it on my own instead. I wasn't ready to share that with anyone else. But now you're here because some sick fuck is messing with my head."

"What's going on?" Meeka asked, her brows furrowing.

"I'll explain, but first I need to know that we're okay." I didn't want to hurt them, but I especially didn't want to hurt Max. She had been there for me when I needed her most.

"We still love you, baby," Brogan kissed my cheek. "Don't worry your pretty self."

I gave a small laugh. "Thank you."

"I understand why you did what you did." Meeka hugged me gently.

"I'm glad." I hugged her back. "Join the guys. We'll be there in a minute."

They both gave me another light squeeze before leaving me alone with Max.

"I *am* sorry," I told her. "I wish I could have told you."

"Why didn't you?" she sniffed, her eyes welling. "We're best friends, Jay. You can be a bitch sometimes but I love you and accept you no matter what. We're in this together, but lately…"

"What?" I asked, my throat closing.

"I feel like you've been shutting me out. The girls… We've been talking about it. You don't come to us anymore for things. And this isn't because of Angel. It's been going on way before him. If you're not okay, we get it, we just want you to tell us. That's all." A lonely tear rolled down her cheek, and she roughly wiped it away.

"I'm not okay," I whispered. "I'm not. I don't know what's been going on. I feel normal when I'm with Angel. It's like he has an unbiased view of me

and I can be whatever I want with him. He gets the real
Jay. Genevieve. And I love to give it to him. He…”

“You’re in love with him,” she gasped, her eyes
widening.

“Yeah.” My cheeks heated. “I am.”

She sighed. “I’m sorry you haven’t felt like you
can come to us.”

“I miss my sister.” A sob escaped me.

“Oh, Jay,” Max threw her arms around my neck,
hugging me tight. “Thank you. Thank you for saying
that.”

“What do you mean?” I wiped the tears from
under my eyes.

“We’ve been best friends since we were kids.
After Violet disappeared, you became withdrawn and
you never expressed your feelings. I didn’t even see
you cry, Jay.” She held me at arm’s length, her gaze
searching my face.

She was right. I cried when I was by myself. I felt
the need to show that I was strong when I should have
shown that I was destroyed. My sister disappearing
fucked me up. “I’m sorry,” I whispered.

“I love you and I forgive you.” She hugged me
again. “Now let’s get this over with so you can spend
the rest of the night with your man.”

***

(Angel)

Seeing Jay walk arm in arm with Max, a small smile
on her face and the blush in her cheeks made my heart
swell. Her long, crimson hair was messy from my
earlier touch and I couldn’t be prouder. Knowing she
needed me in ways I never knew I could provide but
would die trying, made the Alpha inside of me roar
with life.

"You have a keeper, boss," Dale said, clapping a hand on my shoulder.

"I do." And I planned on keeping her for as long as she would have me. "How are you and Max doing?"

He shrugged. "It is what it is," he said casually, but his eyes heated when they landed on her.

"Right. And I'm a fucking virgin." Asher chuckled.

"Leave it alone, man," Dale cracked his knuckles, his jaw clenching. "We're through."

"What the actual fuck?" He could fool everyone else but he definitely wasn't fooling me. He was in love with Max but when she sat on the other side of the living room, as far away from him as possible, it made me second-guess that.

"We are," he mumbled, shaking his head.

I dropped it. I knew how he worked and I didn't need a fist to the face. "Jay." I reached out for her. "We need to tell them what happened."

She slid onto the couch beside me, curling against my side.

"I was dreading you coming over but now that you all are here, I'm glad." She took a breath, letting it out slowly before she continued. "I don't know what's going on, and I have no idea what to say so I'm just going to tell you." Jay mentioned doing research, the chat, the sick bastard who claimed to have bought her sister. Hearing her repeat what happened all over again caused bile to rise in my throat.

My gut churned. I was all for kink. Consensual kink. Between consenting adults. But when someone is bought, it usually meant they were sold by a desperate family. A broken father who wanted to see nothing more than his daughter get the best she deserved, thinking that in the hands of another man, it would happen. Those girls weren't even women yet. They were young. Helpless when it came to the hands of evil. Maybe they thought it would be fun—a new adventure. But when they realized they were being held against their will, the excitement diminished. It brought forth a terror even I couldn't imagine.

As Jay talked, I couldn't help but think of all the girls. The death. The horror that these families wouldn't get their baby girls back. It wasn't my fault but I felt the weight of it on my shoulders. No matter what I did.

"Boss." Coby stood at my side.

"I'm fine," I lied, pinching the bridge of my nose.

"Touch her," he suggested. "I'm going for a walk." Meaning he was going to scope out the place, making sure we were safe.

I slid my hand up Jay's back, leaning my head on her shoulder and took a couple deep breaths.

"Hey, what's wrong?" she asked, her body shifting closer to me.

"We'll talk later," I mumbled, breathing in her scent.

"Oh…" She frowned. "'Kay…so…"

"Is there any way we can get Greyson to check the IP address and see if we can find out who this fucker is?" Asher asked, pacing back and forth in front of us.

"I don't care who he is," Jay snapped. "I just want my sister back."

"We need to find out who he is as well," I explained. "Just in case he has more of these girls."

"What did he mean that he bought her?" Brogan asked, her gaze moving to the door every so often.

"Exactly how it sounds. These women, or girls in this case, get taken from their homes, the streets, wherever they may be and sold into slavery to become sex slaves. It happens all over the world. No matter what we do, we'll never stop it completely but we can sure put a dent into it if we're lucky." I sat back, scrubbing a hand down my face and crossed my ankle over my opposite knee.

"That…" Brogan swallowed hard. "I feel the need to murder someone."

We all chuckled.

"You're not the only one," I told her.

"I'll get Greyson on finding out what he can about this guy. It might take a little bit but hopefully we can get some answers." Max rose from her spot, pulling her phone from her purse. "Hi, Grey. Listen, we have a problem," she said, heading into the kitchen.

"Boss," Stone came up beside me. "I got word on the contents of the package."

"Go ahead," I squeezed Jay's hand in reassurance.

"I know who it belongs to," Jay interrupted.

"How?" I asked her, frowning.

"My fingers." She held her hand up between us. "Notice anything?"

"There's no way," Meeka insisted, shaking her head, not keeping her gaze off Jay's hand.

"It makes sense though, Angel." She grabbed my hand. "The finger belonged to Violet."

TWENTY-SEVEN

—jay

"AND YOU didn't tell me this earlier because…" Angel's voice trailed off, a deep frown furrowing on his handsome face.

"Because I wasn't sure but it makes sense." I couldn't help but stare at my hands. I didn't want the finger to belong to Violet. But if she was missing a piece of her, I would take it if she were still alive.

"Well, Jay," Stone handed me a piece of paper. "You're correct. I'm sorry to tell you but that finger does belong to your sister."

"Fuckin' hell," Angel bit out. "What else you got?"

"Just that it was a fresh wound. Meaning the injury is recent."

My head whipped around. "Are you telling me that she is still alive? That all of this time, she's been held somewhere but alive?"

"Well," Stone scratched his buzzed head. "I don't know about being held somewhere and I'm no doctor, but from what I understand, yes, she's still alive."

Cheering sounded around me.

"What did I miss?" Max asked, coming back into the room.

"Violet's alive," I told her but a part of me wouldn't believe it until I could see her. Until I could touch her and see for myself that she was alive and well.

Max squealed, crushing me into a hard hug. I returned the embrace but my stomach felt queasy. Something was wrong. Still very wrong.

"I have Grey cracking into the IP address to see if we can get the owner." Max sat beside me.

"Now all we do is wait," Asher stated. "Which fucking sucks."

I agreed with him. "Do you guys want a beer?" I rose to my feet and headed to the kitchen, not waiting for them to respond.

"Jay." Coby closed the front door and nodded toward the security panel on the wall. "You need to set your alarm."

"Okay." I nodded; I'd forgotten to do that when Angel and I had arrived hours before. I set the alarm and headed back to the kitchen.

"Need any help?" Coby asked, following me.

"Sure." I opened the fridge and handed him some bottles.

"Don't get too drunk tonight," he said, taking the beer from me. "Alcohol and depression do not mix, especially when something happens to trigger your mood."

"I don't have depression." I frowned.

"You don't have to be diagnosed with it to have it, darlin'. But that is what the tattoo on your ear is for, isn't it?" he asked, raising an eyebrow.

"How did you know about that?" I asked the quiet man.

"I notice everything." He shrugged, a huge move for him when I never saw him express any sort of emotion.

"I like you for him," he added, nodding toward Angel. "He's not the man he once was but with you,

241

he'll be the best man he can be." And with that he walked away.

Coby was a different person. Angel had told me he had been in Vice-One with him since the beginning. He had led a hard life but other than that, I knew nothing about him.

While everyone talked, I made my way up the stairs to my bedroom. I was drawn by the force of my computer. The need to know if the unknown source left me any more messages drove me toward it. I grabbed my laptop and shut myself inside the bathroom, locking the door behind me. It was stupid of me. I knew it. But finding out everything I could about my sister was more important.

I opened the browser, the chat instantly coming up. It flashed with new messages, blinking repeatedly. My heart raced. Why I did this to myself I couldn't be sure. I was desperate, driven mad with the need to find out anything that could bring me closer to the whereabouts of Violet.

Unknown: Tell me about yourself. I heard you are twins. Two pets. Two for the price of one.

Oh, dear God. The message had been sent a couple hours before.

Unknown: Where are you? I know you're dying to find out where your sister is.

Unknown: Listen, if you don't reply, I'll send you every fucking piece of her until there's nothing left. You got me?

I gasped, a cold shiver of fear scratching down my spine.

Unknown: How did you like my present?

242

I read the last message over and over. The time stamp: seven hours ago.

"Jay?" Angel called through the closed door. "What are you doing?"

I couldn't answer him. All I could do was read over and over how this guy was going to send me every piece of my sister. Every body part. I should have stayed chatting with him. I should have checked the inbox daily. Because of me, my sister was missing a finger. Because of me, she would be tortured until there was nothing left of her.

"Jay, damn it!" the doorknob shook. "Open the door."

"It's all my fault," I sobbed. "She's hurt because of me."

"Open this fucking door," Angel bellowed, banging into it.

"I can't. God," I rocked back and forth. "I can't do this anymore." My fingers moved along the keyboard of their own accord.

Me: Please. Let me see her.

Unknown: Ah. There you are. I guess you're just going to have to continue talking to me.

Me: I can't. You know I can't. Please. I need to see her.

Unknown: Yes. You can. If I don't get a reply next time I message you, I'll send her fucking head.

I screamed, picked up the laptop and threw it against the wall. It shattered into pieces but I kept at it. Rage powered through me, controlling my movements until all I could see was red.

The door slammed open, and I continued screaming.

My throat became raw. Tears streamed down my face. Everything I had felt over the past couple of months poured out of me, through my fingertips, and into the debris of the machine laying in pieces on the floor in front of me.

"Jay, calm down." Angel grabbed my hands.

I shoved out of his grip, picking up a piece of the laptop. "No. I can't. I need to message him. I need to find out where she is. She's going to die because of me. I can't. It'll hurt her. He'll hurt her."

"You're not making sense. Please, princess," Angel pleaded, wrapping his arms around me.

"No, let me go." I struggled against him but his hold tightened.

"No. Not until you calm the fuck down and tell me what's going on."

Sobs took over. They were so hard I couldn't catch my breath.

"Geeze, baby. Breathe." He cupped my cheeks. "Breathe, damn it."

"I-I...can't...do...this..." After all of this time I broke. I fell apart in front of the man I loved. I was distraught with grief, enraged with helplessness.

"Breathe." He kissed my mouth. "Breathe." He held me against him, caressing my back and continued to tell me to breathe.

I gripped his shirt, holding onto him for dear life. Taking deep breaths, I eased my racing heart that threatened to explode if I didn't control these cries.

"Talk to me." He shut the door, giving us some privacy.

"I needed to find out more. To see if there were more messages." I roughly wiped my face. "I know it was stupid, but I couldn't help it." I told him about the messages, the threats.

244

"Shit, Jay." He pulled me to my feet. "I'm sick of this. He's trying to fucking destroy you. No one has been able to break you, not even me, but this fucker gets an in because he has your sister?"

"I'm not trying to let him. But I can't help it, Angel," I cried, pushing him. "What if he had one of your brothers? What if he had me?" I yelled.

"Don't fucking say that!" he shouted, slamming his fist against the wall.

"It's true. It could happen. He wants me too." I gripped my hair, pulling and tugging until a sharp tingle exploded through my scalp. "God, what did we do to deserve this?"

"Bad things always happen to good people," he muttered, cupping my nape.

"I can't keep doing this. Crying over shit. It's not me." I didn't know who I was anymore. I had tried for years to be like Violet. To be strong. Brave. Confident. But the real me was quiet—introverted. The real world didn't accept people like me. They would devour me before I even had a chance to defend myself.

"This *is* you, Jay." He pinched my chin. "I know you're not like the person you claim to be. You may be the president of King's Harlots but you're loud and outspoken because you have to be. Not because you want to."

"I don't even know who I am anymore."

"We'll find you. I promise."

***

(Angel)

After Jay's breakdown, I made her another drink and let her sleep. She pleaded and begged for me to stay, but I promised I would be back in the morning. She fell asleep mid-argument. As much as I wanted to stay with her, she needed her rest and *I* needed to sort some shit out.

I made everyone leave, promising I would explain when I could. For the time being, the best thing for Jay would be for her to be alone. Even away from me. Coby offered to keep watch over night, standing in the dark shadows of the alleyway. I almost objected, not wanting to take advantage of him but knowing he would be honored to watch out for Jay, I accepted his offer.

The music in the speakers of my SUV shut off, indicating an incoming call. When I realized it was coming from Max, my gaze slid to Dale sitting in the passenger seat.

"I'll be quiet," he grumbled.

"Hey, Max," I greeted, wondering just what happened between them.

"How's our girl?"

"She's sleeping. I made her a drink, checked to be sure she was safe, and now I'm heading home." In a little bit, at least. We had some stops to make first.

"Good," she cleared her throat. "Is Dale with you?"

Dale shook his head.

"No," I sighed. "He's not."

"Listen, take care of him please."

"I don't want to get caught up in your shit," I told her. "If he needs time, give him time."

"It's not that. He just doesn't want to settle down. According to him, I'm good enough for sex but not a relationship."

I elbowed Dale, giving him a glare. "I'll bash his head in for you."

"No," she laughed. "It's fine. I already did that."

Dale smirked, rubbing the scruff on his jaw.

Asshole.

"If it comes up, I'll say something but I'm not one to press when it comes to my brothers' relationships."

"I know. I just…" she stammered. "Anyway, thank you for taking care of Jay." A click sounded, the music turning up in its place.

"Care to explain that?" I asked Dale.

"Nope." He crossed his arms under his chest, staring out the window.

"I don't want to pry but Max is my woman's best friend. If she's not happy, then Jay isn't happy, and that makes me very unhappy," I said, venom coating my voice.

"Listen, man." Dale brushed a hand over his head. "Max wants what I can't give her."

"And why not?" It was easy for me. I had never loved like this, if at all. I would be the first to admit that I thought I would never find that person. That one I could be myself around. That I could give my all too. What Jay and I had was new and we would continue learning more about each other as each day passed.

"I'm not you, Angel. I'm twenty-five. I don't want to settle down."

"So you'd rather fuck around?" I wasn't much older than him but he had a point.

"God, no. I just don't want…" He waved a hand in front of him. "I guess to put a label on it. But she wants more. She wants it to be called something and I can't. Not yet. So she freaked and kicked me out. That was a week ago."

"Man, I'm sorry." I knew he liked Max. They were perfect for each other. With him being obnoxious and her saying exactly what was on her mind, they fit well.

"It fucking sucks. The sex was fantastic. She could suck a golf ball through a garden hose." He groaned.

"Okay. I did not need to know that."

"And she fucks like—"

"Dale, man, shut the fuck up." I slapped him on the shoulder.

"Sorry," he muttered, a slow grin spreading on his face. "Where are we headed?"

"You know where we're headed. We're meeting the guys, doing our shit, and leaving." I wanted to head back to Jay's even though I told her I would leave her alone for the night.

"Do you know why Vega wants to meet us?"

"Yeah." I held back a string of curse words. "He said he thinks he found some information on his niece. I have a feeling we're getting assigned a new mission, and I think this one is going to be a long one."

"Are you fucking kidding me?" Dale's head whipped around.

"It's our job."

"I know, but I still don't have to like it," he whined. He actually whined. Like a five-year old. Full bottom lip sticking out and all.

I chuckled, shaking my head. "Thank you."

"Anytime, Boss." He sat up, stretched his arms over his head until a crack sounded. "Fuck, that felt good."

"That means you're getting old," I teased, needing the light back and forth jab.

"Nah." Dale brushed his shoulder, a cocky grin spreading on his face. "Nothing old in this body."

I laughed, scratching the scruff on my jaw.

"Did you tell Jay you're leaving?" he asked, changing the subject.

My gut twisted. "Not yet, because I wasn't sure if we were or not."

"Gotta tell her soon, man."

"I know."

***

(Jay)

I woke to warm lips caressing a path up my neck. Hands roamed under my shirt until they reached the curve of my breasts. "Mmm…"

"Wake up, baby," Angel coaxed, pinching my nipple into a sharp peak. "I don't have much time."

My eyes popped open, landing on a very naked Angel with a very hard body. Ready and waiting for me. "What do you mean you don't have much time?"

He kissed me on the mouth, the peck soft as a feather. "Work calls."

"Another mission?" I asked, sitting up.

"Yeah," he pulled the blankets off of me and helped me out of my clothes. "I don't know how long we'll be gone for." His gaze met mine. "It could be awhile."

My chest tightened. "Okay. I'll… I'll miss you."

"I'll miss you too," he smiled. "But I'll call you every chance I get."

"Okay. I'd like that." My eyes welled but I forced back the tears. I was crying over a man. I bit back a scoff. Before I met Angel, I would have been the first to throw a man out of my bed, not caring if he ever came back. But since I had Angel, the dark delicious man kneeling in front of me, I never wanted him to leave. I didn't want him to go away on his missions even though I knew it was an unreasonable request. It was his job. He fought for our country, and I couldn't be prouder. But I wasn't sure if I could live with it. The fact he laid his life on the line every single day. No matter if he was on a mission or not, he was always working. They all were.

"Where did you go, princess?" Angel asked, cupping my cheek and pushed me back on the bed.

"Make love to me," I said, ignoring his question.

"Jay." He frowned.

"Please, Angel. Do to me everything you want to do. Leave here satisfied and happy, knowing you'll come back to me. You'll always come back to me. You have to."

"Of course," he said against my mouth.

"Please, promise me." I wasn't sure why I was pleading.

"I promise."

And for the next hour, he expressed those promises all over my body. Inside and out, he poured his love for me. With each thrust, it grew. With each peck of a kiss, feathery touch of a finger, our affection for the other grew. It was fast and hard. It took my breath. The passion consumed us, ensnaring us in a safe net of comfort.

When he left, the darkness took over. Although, I still had his black hoodie with me and I could smell him on the soft fabric, not knowing when he would be back drove my mind wild. That was why I never wanted to fall in love again. That was why I had refused to give my heart away. The pain of not knowing if he'll return to me fell on my shoulders like a ton of bricks.

My phone rang, but I ignored it. My stomach grumbled but I didn't feel the need to satisfy the hunger when all I wanted was a warm body next to me.

The anxiety racked through me like a hurricane, billowing inside of me. The feeling was familiar. It had hit me hard the first time after my sister disappeared and again when I was able to get out of Tyler's sadistic grip. I realized now that I never loved Tyler. I never gave him my all. He didn't see me in sweats or my hair pulled back into a messy bun. He always called me Jenny because he wanted to be different from everyone else. He was different in the fact he laid his hands on me, making it clear no other man could touch me. I was his prized possession, his object that he liked to play with whenever he saw fit.

In my pity of slumber, I laughed, curling myself around Angel's sweater. If my sister could see me, I had hoped that she would think I picked well when it came to him. I had just started to date Tyler when she disappeared. I could just imagine how she would react if I was ever able to tell her what he did to me. What *I* did to *him*. We were both to blame. It helped me feel superior. Confident. He egged me on, begged me to hit him. It was fucked up, but a part of me thanked him for it. It helped me grow into a stronger person. Call it sick and twisted, but I didn't regret anything.

The depression and anxiety came on strong. Thoughts hit me every so often. Nightmares took over my sleep. What ifs constantly came up, and I couldn't control the thought that maybe Angel just left. Left me like Violet did. Like everyone did.

TWENTY-
EIGHT
ANGEL

HELL.

That was where we were.

Gunshots sounded. Flares flew into the sky. Screams, both male and female, burned into my ears. They were sounds I would never get out of my head. Noises that crept along my bones: fingers of fear. They gripped me until all I could focus on were the cries of agony, the moans of pain, and the bubbling groans of death.

"Fucking shit storm," Dale said beside me, his voice shaking with each ragged breath. He had been shot in the left calf and his right arm was broken—the bone to his elbow protruding out of the flesh. He had fallen down a cliff when a hand grenade was thrown at his feet. He was lucky and acted fast. The explosion missed him but the fall did some serious damage.

"They knew we were coming." Coby pulled the pin out of his own grenade. He winked at me before throwing it over his head, the explosion sounding seconds later.

Yells sounded from our attackers but the grenade didn't slow them down. There were too many of them.

Stone was ten feet away, on the other side of a large rock, holding his own. I couldn't imagine what he was going through with his squad being attacked just a couple months ago. He should have been on leave, but somehow got out of it. I never asked but I was grateful to have him at our sides. We were broken and bloody but at least we were breathing.

Asher leaned against a tree a foot away from me, trying to get the radio transmitter working. He cursed up a storm, banging the shit out of the device until it crackled.

My eyes snapped to his. "Keep trying. We have to get out of here." I wasn't one to give up but we were outnumbered and I refused to risk the lives of my brothers.

He nodded. "Vice-One to base. Emergency evacuation. Mission has been tampered with. Repeat. Vice-One…" he kept repeating over and over again, trying to get anyone to listen. He tried different radio frequencies, even something a trucker could hear. "Fuck. This doesn't make sense."

We had been gone for what felt like a lifetime, living and eating through hell. We couldn't find anything to do with Vega's niece. It was like she never even existed. No trace. No hair from her fucking head. But we did find three storage units holding girls. They were crammed into the small spaces like sardines, victimized like they were worthless pieces of shit. We got them out to safety and once they were gone, shit went down.

"Boss." Coby pointed up. "The shots have stopped."

Dale groaned beside me, grumbling about how he hated getting shot.

"It's not something you're supposed to enjoy, ass," I told him. "Keep that leg wrapped. How long?" I asked Coby.

He checked his watch. "Three minutes."

"I think someone is messing with us." I cocked my rifle. "Watch my back." I rose to my knees, slowly crawling up the cliff Dale had fallen down.

None of it made sense. We were careful, not letting anyone know our whereabouts. Even Vega had no idea. He told us to go in, find his niece, and get out. But we never gave him our coordinates until that morning. Something poked at my gut. It gripped my heart and squeezed until I had to force out my next breath. All of it was a setup. It began to make sense. We were outed, and I had no idea how or why. Did Vega's niece even exist? That thought crossed my mind unexpectedly. He would pay. If we were thrown into this shit for no reason at all, when saving those girls was not our responsibility, I would make him fucking suffer.

When I reached the top of the hill, I stayed low to the ground and listened.

Silence.

Quiet. Deadly.

It was louder than the noise in my head. It took control, begging me to fall victim to the pureness of it.

And then I heard them. Voices. Not loud but muffled by the wind whipping around me through the trees. Back and forth like it had a mind of its own.

I couldn't hear what they were saying but I could see them. A group of men stood outside a large warehouse, much like the one we found months ago. This was the building we were trying to gain access to. And we would have succeeded if someone hadn't warned these men we were there. I didn't know who they were but I did recognize the one. I had seen his ugly-ass mug in pictures. Files Vega gave us so we would be ready. I went through everything I knew about him in my mind. I had memorized his information the first time I opened his file.

Charles Brian.

Thirty-two.

Single.

And a motherfucking monster.

But he wasn't the ringleader of this organization. No. He was the bitch—but we could never pinpoint who he spoke with. Who his boss was. These men were good. Never showing what they did with the girls, when they touched them, or when they first took them from wherever they were. No. They were better than that. They had others do it for them. Those men got caught or killed if we got to them first. But it wasn't satisfying. It wasn't enough. We needed the source. The leader. The master behind it all. Call us sick, twisted, or just plain desperate but we even used girls as bait. Dante's Kings tried telling Jay. I knew that. I wasn't fucking stupid. I was there when they confronted her about the man she was fucking. Acting all concerned when really they wanted to control her and bring down her MC.

Yes, we used the girls as bait. But not all. One or two and they survived every time. They were trained, going in undercover. In. Out. Be done with it.

Out of a hundred or so missing girls, we had found at least forty. The numbers sucked. They were downright disgusting. We couldn't save them all. We couldn't stop every human trafficking and sex slave ring but we would bring this one down. They hit too close to home. They took my woman's sister and I'd be damned if I was going to let it go.

"Boss," Asher's voice boomed through my earpiece. "See anything?"

"Five men," I said, my voice low. "They're standing by the warehouse we were trying to get in. Charles Brian is with them."

"That fucker won't stay dead," Asher grumbled.

We had shot him once—the bullet coming from Asher's rifle. But Charles had disappeared soon after and we hoped— no, prayed— the bastard was gone for good. Not that it would have done any good when he could be replaced but it would have been a start.

"I got the radio working," Asher stated. "Get down here."

I cursed under my breath but knowing I couldn't take on the five men by myself, I crawled back down to safety.

***

(Jay)

It felt like a lifetime since I had seen Angel. No matter how long I went without seeing him, I could still picture him in my mind. Every inch. Every curve. Every ripple of hard muscle. He had been active his whole life, working out daily and I craved the feeling of his strength wrapped around me. His taste tingled on my tongue, a permanent reminder of where he had been. It would always be etched into my mind, burned into my skin until I had more of him. I knew it. He knew it. And he loved every second of it.

Angel Rodriguez became an obsession. The ultimate desire. We Skyped. We texted. We chatted on the phone—but it wasn't enough. He would come home soon and it still wouldn't be enough. I had to fight the urge to bury myself in the recesses of his soul. He would protect me. He would love me. He would use me. And I gave him everything I had and more. But it still wasn't enough.

No matter how hard I tried, this emptiness still simmered inside of me. It needed to be filled and Angel was the person who could. After being alone for so long, having people ripped from my life, I couldn't give him everything he needed. I wanted to. God did I ever. But I didn't know how. I didn't know if he even wanted it. He loved me. I knew that. I accepted it with open arms in hopes he would be patient. I loved him with every fiber of my being. Every inch of my skin. Every breath that left my lungs. He was the food for my soul, the sustenance I needed to move on. Every time I thought about how much I loved him, a twinge of fear coated my skin. My skin danced with goose bumps, the blood flowing through my veins like molten lava.

I didn't know where he was. I prayed that he and his brothers were safe. But how could they be with the job they did? Were they ever safe? Did they ever feel like their lives weren't on the line? They dealt with protecting their country but for some reason they were given the task to find these girls. With all the movies and books I had dived into, I knew it wasn't the norm. Some of my father's brothers in Dante's Kings were ex-military. They even said it wasn't often that SEALs dealt with human trafficking issues. They went to these countries to get people out. People of higher power. Doctors. Politicians. Anyone the US needed to come home. I saw *Tears of the Sun*. Even though it was a movie, I knew how hard it was to go in and bring these people home to safety.

My phone rang, vibrating on my end table. I let out a heavy sigh, not in the mood to talk to anyone but I knew if it was Max, she would keep calling or show up until I got my shit together. I loved her, but sometimes I would prefer to be left alone. She meant well. She honestly did. But my shit wanted to be a mess sometimes.

"Hello," I muttered, rolling over onto my back.

"Good morning, Miss Sunshine," Max teased, a slight tremor filling her voice.

"What's wrong?" I sat up, my heart racing.

"The guys are home," she sighed. "They were attacked, Jay. They're banged up pretty bad."

Oh God. *Angel.* "Are they okay?"

"Dale…" her voice shook. "He got shot twice, had surgery and he's recovering well. Coby and Asher have some bumps and bruises, cuts, the usual. Vince broke his arm."

"A-and Angel? Please tell me he's okay," I pleaded.

"He is. We need to go see them."

"I'm on my way."

***

We made our way to the hospital in silence. Max sat in the passenger seat, staring out the window chewing her bottom lip.

I drove. And drove. And drove. The closer we got to the hospital the more it felt like we got further away. My fingers ached from the tight grip they had on the steering wheel. I was anxious. Nervous. Anticipation flowed through me, unsure of what to expect when I saw Angel. I didn't know why but I was scared. To see him? To show him how terrified I was that his job would take away his life? It was selfish of me to wish he could retire. To wish he could stay home with me all of the time. For him to get a day job and work behind a desk. I was not the type of partner who could live months and months on end without seeing their other half. They were somewhere unknown fighting forces conjured up in our nightmares. How these other people did it, I couldn't imagine. I couldn't go to sleep each night wondering if Angel was safe. If he was hidden somewhere, scared out of his mind that he wouldn't make it home. It was unreasonable of me to worry so much. Wasn't it? Vice-One knew what they were doing. They had been to hell and back.

"I told Dale I love him," Max blurted, interrupting my thoughts.

"You did?" I wasn't surprised. Her eyes shone every time she saw him. Her cheeks reddened and I knew she fell for the man hard. "But?"

258

"He doesn't feel the same way." Her chin trembled. "He doesn't want a relationship. He doesn't want to put a label on—" she waved a hand in front of her "—us. But no, my heart is stupid and fell in love with the bastard. He blew me off. Made a joke of it." Her eyes snapped to mine. "He fucking laughed in my face."

"Maybe he was nervous," I suggested, focusing back on the road in front of me.

"No. He's a fucking pussy, and I hope he's in pain," she mumbled, crossing her arms under her chest.

"You don't mean that." But I could understand how she felt. She was hurt. Confused.

"I don't." Her eyes welled. "I'm happy he's okay. God, I would die if something happened to him. He makes me feel...alive."

I smiled, nudging her shoulder. "I know what you mean."

"You do, don't you?" Max wiped at the lonely tear that rolled down her cheek.

"Oh yes." I sighed. But it still didn't make me feel any better or understand why I was so scared. Why I couldn't give him my all even though I tried.

Why have we both fallen in love with men who lay their lives on the line every damn day?

"Because our hearts want what they want," Max mumbled.

My head whipped around, not realizing I had spoken out loud. "Yeah, I guess."

"What are we going to do?" she whispered, more to herself.

I shrugged, unsure, and that pissed me off even more.

***

259

When I stood outside Angel's hospital room, I froze. Unable to move from my spot at the door, I counted to ten. Twenty. One hundred before I could muster up the courage to step over the threshold. He was sleeping. My heart hurt when my eyes landed on the bandage on his head. His ribs were wrapped, his shoulder in a sling. Bruises and cuts marred his tanned skin. My fingers itched, tingled with the need to run them over his body. To make him feel better. To take away whatever pain he was in.

My mouth became thick with cotton. My heart raced. My muscles slid over my bones.

His big body stirred, his eyes opening slowly. They landed on mine, holding me in my place. No hint of emotion in his dark stare.

At that point I wished I could read his thoughts. Find out if he was as scared as I was. What were we doing? We were in love, yes, but was it enough? Could I live through the fact that he had to leave every couple of weeks for months on end? Could he live with the club I ran, the sometimes illegal ways I had to bring us together? What we had was dangerous. Our worlds were different but our feelings the same.

"Come here." His firm demand sent a shiver down my spine but I was stuck. My feet glued to the floor. They wouldn't move. They wouldn't budge even though I tried. God did I try. I needed to go to him but a part of me didn't want to. I didn't want to prove to myself how I felt. My heart lay in my hands for him, waiting for him to truly accept it. He said he loved me, but did he love all of me? Does a person really know everything about another human being? Was it even possible?

"Jay." Angel sat up, grimacing. "Come here. Please."

I shook my head, ignoring his plea. His begging set me off. Tears escaped, rolling down my cheeks and dripped off my chin. "I'm sorry."

"No," he said, his voice raising. "Don't you fucking dare. You will not leave me."

"I can't do this. I can't keep worrying about you," I told him, more for myself than for him. I needed to get the words out. To say them out loud to prove that I wasn't losing my ever-loving mind.

"Damn it, Jay. Get your ass over here!" he shouted this time.

"I'm sorry." I backed up. "I'm so sorry."

"No, baby. God, don't do this. Don't end this when it's just begun." His eyes shone, his chest heaving. "Please," he rasped.

"I'm sorry."

TWENTY-NINE

ANGEL

SHE WAS backing up.

I let her go.

Why the fuck I let Jay leave was beyond me. But I was strapped to the bed by tubes and needles. Scorching hot pain consumed me.

She left.

My nose burned, impending tears threatening to escape. A growl left my mouth, rumbling from my chest before I punched the bed. It didn't do anything. It didn't satisfy the rage pumping through me. It started with a flame and with each step Jay took away from me it grew into an inferno. It was a volcano, waiting to explode at the right moment.

Jay couldn't meet me in the eyes as she left but before she disappeared out of my room, I could see the shadow of fear. There was a glimmer of hope that I wouldn't be mad, that I would forgive her.

"Fuck, *Jay*," I shouted, my voice bouncing around the room when she disappeared around the corner.

"Sir?"

I ignored the nurse standing at the entrance to my private room that was set up by the military. I didn't need a private room. I needed Jay. I needed to get to her, to find out why she was scared. *What had*

262

happened in the weeks I was gone? Did someone say something to her? Did her ex put stories in her head? Did she get more information about her sister? Something set her off. She was terrified. I got that. So was I. But there was more.

"Are you okay?" The nurse took a step into my room.

I shoved from the bed, my legs shaking under my weight. Falling to my knees, I gasped for air at the onslaught of pain erupting through my bones.

"Sir, you need to get back into bed," the nurse demanded, reaching for me.

"I don't fucking suggest you touch me right now," I snarled, meeting her wide eyes.

She nodded vigorously, backing up.

I didn't care. I could feel the rage, the anger, the fucking fury bubbling through me. It was so fierce it controlled my actions. It consumed me and I let it. I embraced it. It had been so long since I felt this…this need to destroy everything in my path. If I could just channel this feeling while on a mission, then we could find these girls.

Rising to my feet, the beeping of the heart monitor machine pounded into my skull. It was loud, taking over my thoughts. I roared, ripping the machine from the wall, tearing the needle out of my hand.

"Security!" someone shouted.

Call security, I don't fucking care. The thing I cared about was Jay leaving me. My woman actually fucking left me when I needed her most. Her warmth would help me get better. It would get me through the fact I almost died. That my brothers almost died. Dale had fought for his life in my arms. And I almost lost him. But she left. She didn't let me cry in her arms. She didn't let me break in her hold, begging for her to make me feel better.

She didn't let me tell her I loved her over and over until my voice gave out. She didn't let me plead,

263

demanding for her to stay with me. She never gave me the option. She made up my mind for me, never giving me the choice to let her go.

***

(Jay)

For days I cried. I didn't know how many had passed. They were all a blur. I didn't care. I didn't care about anything. I was so stupid. How could I walk away from Angel like that? Especially when he needed me most. What kind of person did that make me? I was no better than the men I tried to impress. I cried myself to sleep. I would wake up, think about what I did and cry all over again. I never knew a person could shed so many tears. Just when I thought they were dried up, the flood would come again. It was pointless when the whole thing was my fault. How could I just leave him? When I ran out of the hospital, I could hear him yelling, begging for me to go back to him, but my legs wouldn't allow me. They ran in the opposite direction. I was terrified I would fall harder and something would happen to take him away from me.

I ended up crashing at the club because I couldn't stand to be in a place where I spent so much time with Angel. Even though I spent time with him at the club, the apartment hurt worse. Although we had only been there once, I could smell him everywhere. His scent was on my bed, on my clothes, on my fucking skin. I showered more than I needed to, trying to wash him off of me.

It hurt. It hurt so damn much. My chest constricted with the lack of air. My palms became sweaty. My body vibrated. "Angel," I gasped out. I pulled at his hoodie that I had stupidly decided to wear. "Oh, baby." My big, dark man. How could I do this to him? To us? What the hell was I thinking?

A heavy knock sounded on my door, followed by some whispers.

I curled in and around myself, shutting out the world. Depression had set in fast. At first it was the same feeling I had when my sister disappeared, when the unknown person started contacting me but then it grew into something that gripped my throat. It choked me, forcing me to gasp for the very breath I didn't want. I didn't want anything. Not until I knew Angel and I were okay. I would beg. I would plead for him to forgive me. I would explain how stupid I was. There would be no excuses. Just apologies. But how could I expect him to let me back in?

Everything happened so fast. Meeting Angel. Falling in love. Finding out my sister was still alive but I couldn't see her. No more packages came. The man was fucking with my head. Bile rose to my throat, my stomach churned. A set of dry heaves wracked through my body.

Several dings sounded from the computer Greyson had left me after I destroyed my own. Shit. Taking several deep breaths before I opened it, I prayed to whoever would listen that my sister was okay.

Unknown: How does it feel not knowing when another package will come? Does it fuck with your head?

Biting my lip, I mustered up the anger and frustration from deep within myself.

Me: I'm waiting for you. No matter what happens, I will avenge my sister.

Slamming the laptop closed, I threw it on the floor.

"Jay." Max peeked her head into my room. "You need to get your ass out of bed."

Ignoring her, I rolled back onto my side.

A hard smack landed on my rear, forcing a yelp to leave my lips.

"What the hell?" I glared up at her.

"You look like shit." She frowned. "You've been in here for three days. I haven't seen you eat or drink anything. You're going to wither away."

"I don't fucking care." I rolled back over, ignoring her protests.

"Jay," a deep voice boomed. "Get your fucking ass out of bed."

My body stiffened. *Oh God. Angel. No.* This was not how I wanted to see him. The tears threatened to escape again. I was never one to cry. Even though there were times where I should have, I closed up like a vault, not letting any emotion show through at all. But now, I had no control over them.

"Angel," I whispered, choking back a sob.

"Max, I got this," Angel bit out through clenched teeth.

"Be gentle with her," Max said, her voice low, probably thinking I wouldn't hear her. Or maybe she hoped I would. "But she needs you to be straight and to the point. Don't beat around the bush, Angel."

He didn't say anything but closed the door behind him. "Look at me."

I sat up, not meeting his gaze and let my knotty hair fall in my face.

"I said, look at me!" he bellowed. "It's the least I fucking deserve."

"No," I shook my head. "You deserve more," I added on a whisper.

"You will look at me or I will fuck you until you do."

My back stiffened, my gaze snapping to his. I bit back a gasp. Bruises and cuts marred his face. His dark eyes showed he had seen shit. Nightmares I could only dream about.

"Ah," he smirked. "That got your attention. Is that the way to get through to you? Sex, baby? Cause I can fuck you anytime. Who needs feelings? Is that what you want? You want to be treated like a whore? Cause I can pay you, too."

"Fuck you, Angel." I knew he was furious with me but he didn't need to be an asshole. I didn't need the constant reminder that I deserved everything he had to throw at me.

"Oh we've done that, baby. Many delicious times, I might add. It's all you want, isn't it? Even though I happen to remember you telling me you love me. Was that a lie? Do you not love me?"

"Of course I love you," I cried. "How can you even question that?"

"Because you don't fucking know how to show it!" he yelled, slamming his fist against the wall. "You told me you love me. I told you I love you. But it clearly isn't enough."

"Love is never enough." My mouth snapped shut as soon as the words left my lips. But it was the truth.

"Explain that to me, Jay." He leaned against the door. "Tell me why our love can't be enough?"

Shaking my head, I rose from the bed.

A soft growl sounded from behind me causing a slight flush to spread up my body. I forgot I was only wearing a tank top and panties but at that point I didn't care. I didn't care that I made his body react to me. I didn't care about anything because I knew he would leave me. Just like everyone else.

"What are you doing to me, Jay?" he asked, softer that time.

"I don't know. I have no fucking idea. I don't know what I'm doing to myself. I don't know what's going on anymore." I rambled on and on, not sure when to stop, not sure if I was even making sense anymore. No control. Never any control.

"Where is this coming from?" He took a few powerful steps toward me.

"I…I don't know," I shook my head, ignoring the thoughts of how much I wanted him between my legs. "I…"

"Jay." His voice lowered. He took another step until he reached me, standing a few inches away, but he didn't touch me. He didn't have to. I could feel the heat coming off of him. I could see the heft in his sweatpants, semi-hard like he always was. I could smell his spicy scent.

A breath left me on a whoosh, my head spinning from the lack of contact. A contact I had craved since before meeting him. And now that he was there, in front of me, after so many weeks, I was terrified. He could destroy me. One powerful move and he could break my soul.

"I missed you," he reached out, brushing a strand of hair behind my ear. "I needed you and you weren't there."

Tears welled in my eyes. "I am so sorry. I am. I can't explain it. But I can try. Please let me try." I gripped his shirt, leaning my forehead against his chest and inhaled. The scent of leather, man, and sex wafted into my nose. "Please let me try."

"Why should I?" he asked, his voice pained. He didn't touch me but he didn't push me away either. It was all I could ask for.

"My sister left me. My mom never wanted us. Tyler broke me. But if something happened to you," I looked up at him through my tear-soaked lashes, "you could destroy me. You could ruin everything I worked so hard to gain. I love you so much. Too much."

"No such thing." His jaw clenched.

"Don't leave me," I begged.

"You left *me*," he snapped, shoving out of my grip.

I fell to my knees at the abrupt move, digging my fingers into the carpet. "I'm sorry."

"You're sorry," he scoffed. "Jay, I fucking love you. Do you understand that? Do you know what that even means? Do you know how hard it is for me to love someone? I don't even know if I love my brothers. I can't know. I never knew how to love until I met you. Can you get that through your stubborn-as-hell head? *Can you?*"

"Angel, I said I was sorry. I didn't want to leave but seeing you in that bed, I can't…I'm not strong enough to be without you."

A heavy hand wrapped in my hair, pulling my head back.

I gasped at the sudden movement, staring up into Angel's dark eyes. They were black, enraged with fury.

"Don't you fucking say that to me again," his voice was rough, laced with a darkness I had never heard before. "You got me?"

"I…"

"I said, do you got me?"

I nodded, swallowing hard.

"No woman should ever feel they are weak without a man. You don't need me to survive. We need each other. We make each other strong together and alone. You do not *need* me. Not in the way you think."

"I do. I do need you," I pleaded, gripping his wrist.

"No!" he yelled. "Listen to me good, little girl. You are strong. You are the strongest woman…no…the strongest *person* I know. You can take on men twice your size. You can take on a group of them. You think you need your sisters, me, these men you are trying so hard to impress but all you need is yourself. You need to love yourself first before you can let anyone in. I get that. I need to as well. But the difference between you and me is I know that I don't need anyone else to build me up. Fuck everyone, Jay. Fuck Vice-One. Fuck Dante's Kings. And fuck King's Harlots. *You* are all that matters. *We* are all that matter. You and I."

"I don't know how to be alone," I confessed, shocked at my outburst.

Angel sat back on his haunches, cupping my cheek. "Yes you do. What did you do before me? Before Violet left?"

"She was always around. I was the only one who understood her. We're twins, Angel. She's a part of me, and no matter what, I'll never be alone."

"You can't depend on that. I don't know Violet, but I have a feeling she wouldn't want you to do this to yourself."

I sat back, pulling my head out of his grip. "No. You're right. You don't know her."

A shadow passed over his face. "If you're going to keep fighting with me, I'm done. I can't play these games with you. I'm too old for this shit." He pushed to his feet.

"No!" I grabbed his leg. "Please. God, I'm sorry. I don't know…" Tears streamed down my face. Shame and anger bubbled up from that deep part of myself that I could no longer control. I knelt at his feet, wrapping my arms around his waist. "I'm sorry. I love you. I'm confused. I'm so fucking confused."

"What the hell is so confusing?" He tried pulling out of my hold but my grip tightened. "Jay, let go of me. You walked away last time. Now, *I* am walking away. I won't let you rip my heart out again."

"I didn't…I…"

"What, Jay? What didn't you do? You didn't rip out my heart? You didn't mean to? You're *sorry*?"

"Please." I couldn't…I couldn't do this anymore.

"Please what? Tell me, Jay," he demanded. "Tell me what has you so scared."

"I can't." The words wouldn't leave my mouth.

"Tell me!" he bellowed, forcing me back on my ass. "Tell me."

"I'm scared you'll leave and not come back, all right? I'm terrified I'll get the call that you're dead and...and...I know I shouldn't worry. I know that. But I can't help it. I can't live like this. I can't go day to day, scared you won't come home to me. I—"

Warm lips crushed to mine, a tongue forcing its way into my mouth. Angel growled, wrapping his hand around my throat and deepening the kiss. He controlled what I gave him. He took what he needed, giving me back everything he could.

The kiss was hard, rough, but it was called-for. We snapped, giving into our desires for the other. It was wrong. On so many levels. Sex didn't solve anything. It only put a mask over our true feelings.

"Fuck, Jay. I need your mouth. I need your body. I need everything about you." He stared intently into my eyes, licking his kiss-swollen lips. "But most of all, I need your heart. Please don't hold that back from me."

My body trembled against him, desire for him unfurling deep in the pits of my belly. "I..."

"I'm giving you my heart, baby. Everything about me is yours. Everything I am is yours. I accept you. All of you. I don't care what you've done in your past. I don't care who you've been with. I don't care about your club. *You*," he poked me gently in the chest, "you are all I care about. Your happiness. Your safety. Your love. Please let me have your heart."

"I...I want that. I want all of that." I took a breath, wrapping my arms around his thick neck and straddled his lap. "Please forgive me for walking out on you. I can't move on if I don't know that we're okay. I am sorry."

"We're strong, baby. I am your fucking King, and I will stand at your side and be by you every step of the way. I'll go to hell and back for you. I'll destroy

271

everything in my path to get to you. This will be hard. Every relationship is. But I'm not giving up."

"I know," I whispered, allowing myself to get lost in his dark eyes.

A small smile spread on his face. "Let me love you."

I wrapped my body around him, a thin barrier of clothing keeping us apart. I missed him. I needed him. But I loved him most. "Yes. Love me. Love me with all of you. Every inch. Every breath."

"Then do the same to me." He kissed me hard on the mouth, running his hands up my back. "Love me hard, baby. Love me with every fiber of your being. Love me with every inch of your beautiful body."

"Yes," I circled my hips against him, feeling the weight of his erection pressing into my core. "Angel."

His hands roamed down to my thighs. Digging his fingers into my flesh, he spread me wide.

"Angel," I said louder. My body shook, my core quivering with need for the man I loved. The man in my arms. The man holding me, moving against me like he couldn't get enough.

"Quiet." He fisted my hair, pulling my head back and caught my mouth in a hard, bruising kiss. With his other hand, it grazed to the small of my back, holding me against him. His hips thrust into mine.

I gasped into his mouth, missing the feel of him taking control. "Please."

"I said, quiet." He nipped my lip.

I shook my head, moving my pelvis against his. Hinting.

"I'm in control now, baby." His lips brushed down my jaw to my ear. "You owe me that much."

***

(Angel)

Attempting to rein in my feelings of control and rage, I tried hard to push them out of my mind. But our fight forced them to the forefront of my thoughts. Jay had pleaded with me not to leave her. She begged for me to forgive her. But right now I would show her what happens to a man when they go without their woman for several weeks.

My tongue pushed its way into Jay's mouth, licking along the curve of her lips. Her hips rocked against mine, demanding for me to take control and take what rightfully belonged to me. Call me a dick, but I wanted to make her wait. To build up the anticipation when she had put my heart through so much. I thought I lost her. Everything wasn't forgotten and I was no longer mad at her but the thought of her fear still nudged at my mind. I refused to let her see that we weren't meant to be together. However long this lasted, it was ours.

"Angel."

Jay's breathy moan sent a shiver down my back. I tugged her head further, forcing her mouth open wide. I kissed her hard. Devoured her like a starving man. It had been weeks since I tasted her, and fuck me if the wait wasn't worth it.

I hooked a finger into her panties, brushing my knuckle over her soaked pussy. A growl escaped me. Pulling her toward me, I reached for the knife that I always kept in my pocket and cut the fabric off of her.

She shivered, the cool metal of the blade grazing her mound.

I smiled against her lips and reached into my pants. She swallowed my hiss when my hand came into contact with my cock.

Jay rose to her knees, waiting, and ran her fingers through my hair. Her nails dug into my scalp. A slight burn spread over my skin, forcing me to kiss her harder.

Lifting her, I dropped her in one smooth move onto my dick.

She cried out, throwing her head back.

"Fucking A," I snarled, pulling her tank top free from her breast and covered the pierced nipple.

"Oh..." She shivered, slamming her hips against mine.

The walls of her pussy tightened around me. I held onto her shoulders, thrusting upwards until she gasped. I fucked her hard. I took from her everything she had to offer. Her love. Her frustration. Her pain. Her fear. I took it all and gave her my heart in return. It was rough. But she held on. It was everything I had to give her. The confusion of never loving anyone. Of not knowing what it was like to be loved.

"Give me all of you," I breathed, trailing kisses down her jaw to her neck. "Please."

"Yes. I do." Jay wrapped her arms around my shoulders, holding me, pouring everything she felt into that touch. Words we had said a moment before disappeared as our lovemaking turned desperate.

"I love you, Genevieve," I whispered, holding onto her for dear life. I couldn't take her leaving me again. I couldn't deal with the loss. I told her not to need me when in fact, I needed her.

"I love you, Angel."

And we showed each other for the rest of the night just how much we loved the other. Over and over. Until we were both spent and exhausted, sticky from our pleasure and relaxed from the arousal floating around us.

Jay slept soundly, half her body on top of mine with me rubbing small circles on her back. We laid on top of the bed, wrapped in each other. No blankets. No barriers. Just skin against skin. I never knew how much I needed another person or how much I needed the contact of another human being. Jay let out a heavy sigh, wrapping her leg further around my pelvis. My dick twitched, beating against her thigh.

What I would do for her. I loved her. I was still a little pissed about her leaving me at the hospital but I had to get over it. A part of me understood. When everyone she had loved left her, it made it hard for her to see that I wouldn't do the same.

I wouldn't. There was nothing about her that would make me leave. Everything she was would make me stay, would make me fall in love with her more.

Vibration jarred in my head. What the hell? I groaned, rolling over and grabbed my cell off the end table careful not to disturb Jay. Not realizing I had fallen asleep, I scrubbed life back into my face before I hit the green button on my phone.

Jay sighed, wrapping herself tighter around me.

"Yeah?" I barked into the phone.

"I need you and Jay to come to my gallery," Max demanded without so much as a hello.

"What's wrong?" I asked.

"Nothing." Max hung up the phone.

"Who was that?" Jay asked, yawning.

"Max. She wants us to come to her gallery." I sat up but not before I placed a hard kiss on Jay's mouth.

She sighed, leaning into me. "I don't want to leave this bed."

"Neither do I, princess." I cupped her cheek, brushing my thumb over her bottom lip.

"Are we good?"

"Yes." I pinched her chin, forcing her to meet my stare. "We are. Now let's go see what your best friend wants before I get sucked into your sweetness."

"Mmm…I love giving you my sweetness."

"Fuck me," I snarled into her neck.

She giggled. An actual fucking giggle. For *me*. And I welcomed it with open arms.

THIRTY

—jay

WE WERE fine. Angel and I were…fine. Every so often he would glance my way, his eyes lingering a little too long, almost as if he were concerned I would run again. We had apologized for things we said. We had shown each other that fights happen and relationships were hard but we would make it work. We would live each day for each other.

A tremor of fear still sat deep in the pits of my belly but I wasn't sure what caused it. Yes, I was scared of Angel's job taking him away from me. Yes, I was terrified that all this work to find these girls would be for nothing.

"Baby, stop thinking so much." Angel stepped in front of me and cupped my cheeks. His thumb rubbed the frown between my eyebrows, a small smile splaying on his handsome face.

"Something has changed in me, Angel," I blurted, a slight flush spreading up the back of my neck.

"How so?" He wrapped an arm around my shoulders, guiding us back down the street toward Max's gallery.

"I'm…" I rubbed the back of my neck. "Before you, I never had any issues saying what was on my mind. But now I stumble."

"And I will catch you every damn time." He winked at me. "You haven't changed. You just know that you don't have to be a bitch to get what you want. You don't need to impress anyone."

Didn't I? It was the one way I could get my club moving forward. I sighed. We needed another member but I honestly had no idea how to even begin searching one out. My sisters and I all started out at the same time. It had been my idea along with the help of Violet but after she disappeared, it gave me the nudge I needed.

"Hi guys." Max gave us a wave as she headed back inside her gallery carrying a large box.

"I'm going to go help her." Angel kissed my forehead.

I nodded, watching him walk away. My belly fluttered, that familiar desire for the man burning through me.

"Hey, girl," Max greeted me, embracing me in a tight hug.

"Hi," I hugged her back. "What's all this?" I motioned toward the deliverymen carrying large boxes into the building.

"I'm giving the place a little makeover. I ordered a shit-ton of stuff off the Internet and our home supply store here. Have you ever been in the thrift shop on the other side of town? That place is amazing," she rambled, placing her hands on her hips and letting out a heavy sigh.

"What's going on?" Max was not the type of woman to shop unless it was necessary. She saved her money but when something drastic happened, she shopped. And shopped.

Her jaw clenched. "I guess there's no point beating around the bush, is there?"

"Not really," I smiled, nudging her playfully in the shoulder.

"Jay." Her eyes welled.

"What's wrong?" My heart jumped.

"I'm pregnant," she whispered, pushing a stone around with her shoe.

"Oh, Max." I wrapped an arm around her, holding her tight against me. "Does Dale know?"

Pinching her nose, she closed her eyes, letting the tears fall freely down her cheeks. "Yeah."

"I assume he didn't take it well."

She shook her head, her shoulders trembling.

Angel looked our way, his eyebrow raising. I shook my head. I was sure Dale would tell him anyway.

"He snapped, Jay," Max said, her voice small. "I've never seen him so mad."

"He's mad?" I exclaimed. "How the hell can he be mad?"

"He accused me of trapping him." Her sobs hardened. "We were careful, Jay, but shit happens. We were doing well after the last time. We were trying to make it work. And now...now..." She stood up taller, roughly wiping the tears from under her eyes. "Fuck it. Fuck him. Fuck everyone. Fuck this." She turned to me abruptly. "I'm done."

I shook my head. What the hell just happened? One moment she was sobbing over the guy and the next she was brushing it off like it was nothing? "Max."

"I'm done," she repeated, her voice firm.

My eyes searched her face. Determination set deep in her soft features. Her body stiffened, her chin lifted defiantly.

"Are you sure?" I asked, tentatively.

"Yes." She clapped her hands together. "Now let's head inside." She winked at me. "I have a surprise for both of you." She whistled, walking away barking orders at the deliverymen.

"What was that about?" Angel asked, coming up beside me.

"I have no idea," I muttered, unsure of what the hell I just witnessed. It was one thing for me to act all cool when shit went down but Max wore her emotions on her sleeve. Whatever Dale said or did to her hardened her. My blood rushed into my ears. My sister bear roared inside of me, wanting to protect my family.

"Jay?" Angel tugged my hand. "What's wrong?"

"Tell Dale he better get his shit together or he'll be spitting gravel," I threatened and walked into the gallery. Not that it was any of my business and I would leave it alone for Max's sake but a little threat—a promise, so to speak—never hurt.

***

"What is so important that you had to get us out of bed this morning?" I asked Max once we were seated in her studio. Angel and I sat on a couch covered by a black satin sheet.

"This," Max said, turning her easel toward us.

"Holy shit," Angel said in awe.

My eyes widened, landing on the picture before me. The canvas held a drawing of Angel and me. It was done in pencil, minor details left out but it was enough that you could tell it was us. Angel's thick arms wrapped around me. His hand fisted in my curly hair. My face turned up toward him, my lips parted slightly.

"Max, you…" I cleared my throat, squirming in my seat. The drawing oozed passion.

"I've had a lot of requests to paint people." She shrugged. "So I hope you don't mind, but I chose you two to be my first models."

"I-I-" I stammered, unable to take my gaze away from the canvas.

"I think she's honored," Angel laughed.

279

"There's a reason I chose you, Jay," Max smiled. "You're inspiring. Look at what you've done."

I shifted uncomfortably, my cheeks heating. Not a fan of praise, I didn't do any of this to get recognition. I did it because I was sick of women being treated as the weaker sex.

"I did it because I was told I couldn't." I shrugged. "It's no big deal."

"Yes." Max turned on her stool, facing me directly. "It's a huge fucking deal. *You* started King's Harlots. You are passionate about getting these girls home safely. Without you, who knows how long it would take for them to be found?"

"But I haven't found many."

"Yet." Max pointed her paintbrush at me. "You will. We will. But it's because of you."

"She's right, princess," Angel said, brushing a strand of hair behind my ear. "We do what we can because it's our job and we're told to do it. But you do it because it's your passion. You're driven to save these girls."

"I'm only one person." As much as I wanted to save them, even I knew it wasn't possible to do it alone.

"It is possible," Angel insisted.

My cheeks burned, not realizing I had spoken out loud.

"Look at all the research you've done for your sister. Look at the shit you've been dealing with because of that fucker," Angel pointed out, his eyes darkening.

A tremor of fear rippled down my spine. Not that I forgot about the unknown guy or woman for that matter, but a part of me had hoped it was all a bad dream. A nightmare. The person hadn't tried contacting me again but I made sure to keep checking the social media app on my phone. It burned in my hands as I gripped my cell tight.

280

"Has he contacted you again?" Max asked, her voice shaking.

"No." I should have been thankful but not knowing anything increased the anxiety flowing through me.

"Good. Now let me draw you." She cleared her throat. "I need it."

Angel and I agreed even though we had no idea what we were doing. Max had insisted I take off my shirt, allowing Angel to cover me with his body.

"Now press your chest against his. Hold each other tight. I want the love to ooze off of you." Her barked commands would have made me laugh under normal circumstances but when I stared up into Angel's eyes, I fell. Hard.

He kissed my forehead before leaning his head into the crook of my neck. "I love you, princess. More than anything I've ever known. Love was taken away from me as a child but you've given it to me as an adult. Thank you for giving me your heart."

His sweet words and confession of love for me made my stomach flip. Max had insisted I not talk so she could get the curve of my mouth but I didn't need to tell Angel how I felt. He knew. I poured everything I felt for him into that hug. Even though Max was there with us, I went to that place. That place in my mind where it was just me and now Angel. I closed my eyes, breathing in the spicy scent of the man in my arms. His heart beat hard against my chest. His arms wrapped around me in a vice-like grip, promising to never let me go.

He consumed me. I was utterly and irrevocably his. Every breath, every inch of my skin, had belonged to the man holding me. Every waking thought. Every sleepless night. My mind. My flesh. My soul.

I cupped his cheek, forgetting that I needed to stay still.

Angel's eyebrow rose in question. The dark pools of his gaze swallowed me whole. Specks of gold simmered in the chocolate hue.

"I love you," I whispered. "More than my next breath. I never thought I would need someone. My sister taught me to be my own person, not giving into the clutches of a man. But you…" My thumb brushed over his mouth. "You're bossy. Militant. And you command every inch of my skin. I know I can be difficult but thank you, thank you for loving me." My voice wavered. "For me."

"I…" Max stood up from her spot on the stool. "I'm going to give you guys a moment." She rushed out of the room but not before I caught her wiping under her eyes.

My stomach twisted and I looked down at my lap.

"Hey." Angel pinched my chin, meeting my gaze. "What was that?"

"Max and Dale…they're not doing well."

"And you feel guilty because you're happy when your best friend got pregnant by an asshole."

"How did you know that?" I asked, taken aback.

"I put two and two together," Angel shrugged. "Dale can be hard to get along with. He's young and wants to explore the world before settling down. But I think he's actually in love with Max and is just scared."

"I hope so." My heart panged. "I just hope they can find a way back to each other before it's too late."

"I agree, princess." He kissed my mouth. "Now, did you mean everything you said?"

"Yes." My cheeks heated. Again. I had never blushed so damn much before meeting Angel. I huffed. It was frustrating as hell.

"What's wrong?" He chuckled, grazing the back of his knuckle down the center of my body.

My nipples peaked, tingling, hinting for his hand to move a little further to the left or right. But my arm moved of its own accord, attempting to shield my semi-nakedness from him.

"Don't." He pulled my arm away from my body. "Don't ever hide yourself from me. You're beautiful. You're soft where I am hard. You're stubborn. And I will always love you for you."

"I don't even know who I am anymore," I whispered. I slipped my tank top over my head, needing some sort of control in the way he looked at me. But he made me feel beautiful. He made me feel like I was the only woman who mattered. The only person for him. The only person in this world. It was the just the two of us. Together we could take on anything and everyone.

"You are Genevieve Gold," his grin grew. "You are my Queen, and I am your motherfucking King."

"God, I love you." I kissed him hard on the mouth.

"I love you, baby," he breathed against my lips.

"Mind if I interrupt?" Max asked, opening the door slightly.

"Not at all." I smiled at her. "You good?" I asked, my stomach tightening.

"Of course," she said, waving her hand in front of her. "I am wonderful." But those words never reached her eyes. They were red-rimmed. If she would just talk to Dale. But she was even more stubborn than I was. "Now let's finish so I can open up the gallery."

"Don't you have decorating to do?" I raised an eyebrow.

"It's an art gallery," she picked up her paintbrush, chewing her bottom lip. "People like messy. It shows character."

"I'll never understand artists," I mumbled.

"You're an artist," Angel reminded me.

"I draw and tattoo willing participants who like the feel of my needle," I corrected.

"Well, when you put it like that," he teased, gently nudging me in the shoulder.

I laughed, letting out a contented sigh. I caught Max staring at us. A glimmer of hope flashed in her eyes but she shook her head, the hint of something there quickly disappearing.

Max shook herself before bringing the paintbrush up to the canvas before her.

"Don't feel guilty about what you have, Jay," Angel whispered in my ear. "She'll get through this. She wants you to be happy. Dale is a dick."

"But that's no excuse for how he's treating her," I said a little too loud.

Max cleared her throat.

"Sorry," I said, wringing my hands in my lap. "I just worry for you."

"I'm fine." Max's voice was firm and to the point. "You can tell your friend that I want nothing to do with him," she told Angel. "Enough about him." She turned the canvas toward us. "What do you think?"

My eyes widened.

Angel whistled. "You have some serious fucking talent, Max."

The painting of Angel and I popped off the canvas. Curves outlined our bodies. Every freckle. Every muscle. Every hint of passion we had for each other screamed in the painting Max had done.

"I don't generally paint people," Max explained. "But I really like this one."

"Like?" I asked in awe. "This...wow." I had no words for how beautiful the image was. Max was able to capture every emotion.

"It's not done but you at least get the idea." She stroked a finger down the side, staring longingly at the painting.

My heart jumped. I didn't pray often but I prayed at that moment for my best friend. Not for myself. Not for Angel. For her. She had a good life. The only thing missing was the man she fell in love with. You couldn't control what the heart wants. Even if it was an obnoxious player like Dale. I didn't know him well but out of Vice-One, he was the one that went through women faster than half the men I knew. Bikers had a thing for women who were easy. But if you acted like a lady, they treated you like one. Act like a slut, and you would be bent over the nearest hard surface in a matter of minutes.

"Angel, can you give us a moment?" I asked, not taking my gaze away from my best friend.

"Of course," he kissed my head. "I have some calls to make anyway. Thank you, Max." He gave her a quick hug, whispering something in her ear.

She nodded, hugging him back, a shaky breath leaving her.

"I'll be outside," he told me, shutting the door quietly behind him.

"I want you to take some time off. I'll have Brogan in your place while you get some rest."

"No," Max shook her head. "I need to be out and about. I can't sit at home, thinking over this shit and how much I hate Dale right now. It'll drive me crazy."

"Are you sure? Because I understand—"

"No," she snapped. "I'm sorry." She took a deep breath, running her hand through her shoulder length hair. "I don't want any time off. Not right now."

"Okay," I nodded. "Is there anything I can do?"
Besides ripping the balls off of the man who hurt you.

"No…well…" She thought a moment. "I want to tell the girls but not for a couple of days. I don't want any of you going after Dale. I need to deal with it on my own."

"Angel knows. He figured it out on his own," I added before she could accuse me of blabbing her business.

"What did he say?" Max asked, continuing with the painting.

"That he's young, he's an asshole. He doesn't know what he's missing."

285

"You added that last part in yourself didn't you?"

"Maybe."

"I'm not going to force him to be with me or to want this baby. He can go fuck himself." Her voice wavered, tears rolling down her cheeks. "God, I'm sick of crying over him."

"He doesn't deserve you." I stood from my spot and closed the distance between us. "You deserve someone who loves you back, who feels for you what you feel for them. Who would move the world to make sure you're happy."

"Does Angel do that? Do you feel he loves you that way?" she asked, hopeful.

"Yeah. I think he does." What we had was so new that I didn't know how long we would be together but who went into a relationship thinking that? I loved him. He loved me. We were stuck with each other, and it worked for us.

THIRTY-ONE

—jay

UNKNOWN: I know you wait for my messages. You wait to see what I'll say. If I'll talk about your sister. If I'll tell you where she is. If she's happy. Alive. Trust me. She is indeed all of those things. She loves being with me. You'll never get her back.

Me: I just want to see her.

When there was no reply, I fought back the urge to throw my phone against the wall. But having broken my laptop already, I decided against it.

"We'll find her." Angel rubbed my back.

"We'll do more than that," Greyson boomed, his deep voice coming through loud and clear on speakerphone. "I told you we should have stayed."

"And do what, Grey? Drive me fucking crazy with the back and forth pacing you like to do?" I huffed, leaning my head in my hands.

"We could protect you," Grey argued.

"I like you, man," Angel said. "But I got that covered."

"Of course you do." Grey huffed. "Listen, you call us if anything changes. No matter the fucking time. You got me?"

"Yes, boss." I nodded toward Brogan.

She picked up the cell, turning off the speakerphone, and continued talking to her stepbrother. She headed out into the hall but not before I caught a look between her and Coby. His gaze followed her. Her cheeks reddened. Huh. Interesting.

"What are we doing?" Dale glanced around the table. "We need to stop this. We need to put an end to this shit that keeps piling up on our table. We need to find these girls."

"How, Dale?" Angel sat forward. "We had clearance to go in once. We couldn't find Vega's niece. Someone knew we were there, remember?"

"But something needs to be *done*," Dale shouted, slamming a fist on the table in front of him.

"Remember who you are talking to," Angel bit out through clenched teeth. "You don't think I want these girls found? You don't think I want to get Violet home to Jay and her dad? To her fucking family? You don't think I want to find out who attacked my woman and who keeps harassing her every damn day? You don't think I want any of that?" Angel yelled, shoving abruptly to his feet.

"Then why are we just sitting here? We should be out there searching or, fuck, I don't know, but I'm getting antsy." Dale rose from his chair. "I need to hit something."

"Oh!" Meeka exclaimed. "Follow me. I know exactly who can help with that." She walked past Max, giving her shoulder a light squeeze.

Dale glanced down at her, a shadow passing over his face before he was led out of the room.

Max's body stiffened, her cheeks turning a light shade of pink. Was she jealous? Did she wish she could help him relieve the tension he no doubt felt? I would put everything I owned on it.

"Go talk to him," I suggested.

"No." She shook her head. "I've tried already. He wants nothing to do with me. No matter what, don't lose what you have. You're both strong apart, but together you can take on the world. Between the two of you, these girls will be saved. I have no doubt about that. I…I need some time."

I nodded. "Take all the time you want."

Her lips tightened into a thin line. "Thank you."

"I worry about her," I muttered when she left the room.

"I worry about Dale," Angel confessed. "He's going to rebel like he always does."

"Everyone is stressed." I stretched my arms over my head, the tendons in my back cracking and popping. A slight sting erupted through my bones.

"I'll make you feel better," Angel whispered in my ear, his hot breath scorching my skin.

A warm shiver slid up my spine. "We'll help each other."

***

"Girl, you got some kickass talent," Creena Chan whistled, walking around the tattoo shop and glanced up at the drawings I had hung on the dark red walls. "I wish I was half as good as you."

"Please." I laughed. Creena had come into the shop a couple days before, looking for a job. I didn't know much about her but I knew she was a nurse. There was a twinkle of mischief in her eyes when she had told me her dad would be so proud. Apparently she was rebelling. "All of my clients keep telling me they'll trade me in for you."

"Yeah, right," she scoffed, her light-blue eyes twinkling. Her olive skin tone glowed in the bright lighting of the shop. She was beautiful. Freckles

289

adorned her nose and cheeks, kissing her face in a subtle way.

The doorbell chimed, interrupting my perusal of my new friend.

"Jay, darlin'," Stone stepped into the shop, holding a package. "This was on the doorstep for you."

"Thanks." I ran to him. "It's my new ink."

"Let's hope. Angel asked me to open it for you though…" His voice trailed off, his gaze landing on Creena, who was now standing beside me. "Hi."

"Hello," she said, her cheeks reddening.

"Uh…Creena, this is Vince Stone. Vince, Creena Chan," I introduced them, fighting back a giggle over them staring at each other.

"It's nice to meet you." Stone held out his hand. "Very nice to meet you."

"You too," Creena answered, returning his handshake.

"Well, I'm just going to open my mail," I told them, backing away slowly. "You guys have fun."

"Wait," Stone called out. "Angel said—"

"It's fine. You guys have fun." I laughed to myself, heading to the back of the shop before making my way into my apartment. Opening the package, I kicked the door closed, humming to myself. It had been a long time since I was in this good of a mood. Angel had helped with that over the past couple of nights. My skin hummed with memories of his touch.

I rummaged through the papers in the small box, placing it on the coffee table in the middle of my living room. I frowned when my fingers grazed a small velvet box. My heart jumped. Something told me to go back to Stone. To show him that this wasn't what I had ordered. That something was wrong. I snapped open the box and stifled a cry. Throwing the box to the ground, I shoved to my feet, getting away from the package as if it were on fire. I was naïve to think this was over. To think that the unknown person had stopped contacting me. God, I was so fucking stupid. I got wrapped up in my happiness, not considering that this wasn't over.

Images played over and over in my mind. An orange and white cat lay on the carpet, staring up at me with lifeless eyes. The collar around its neck read, 'Piggy'. How…I couldn't process what I was looking at. Violet and I kept the cat a secret. We had hidden it as little girls from our father for fear he would be mad and get rid of it. But he wouldn't hurt it. No. He would send it somewhere safe as we couldn't afford to feed another mouth. As I got older, I realized that if I had just told him about the cat, he probably would have been fine with it. Especially after Violet left. This cat, though, staring up at me, was dirty, its hair matted like it had been raised from the dead. A corpse. I prayed that it wasn't harmed in the process of trying to scare me. Who the hell knew about Piggy? We had tried so hard to tell my father about the cat and then one day, we found our animal lying on the side of the road after getting hit by a vehicle.

How could someone do this? How could they even consider sending a dead animal to a person? Suddenly, my phone rang, making me jump. "H-Hello?"

"Hello, Genevieve." A deep voice rumbled into my ear, vibrating down my spine.

"Who is this?" I asked, gripping the phone tight in my hand.

"Who the fuck do you think it is?"

My body wavered, spots dancing in my vision. "What do you want?"

"You, of course."

I spun on my heel at the voice coming from behind me. Tripping over my feet, I landed hard on my ass.

A tall man loomed over me, his mouth twisting up into a snarl. "You are more beautiful than I imagined. I can't wait to have both you and your sister at once."

The man straddled me, shoving my arms above my head. "You see, your sister wanted this, but you, you're a fighter." He brushed his nose up the side of my neck, inhaling deep. "And that turns me on."

"You won't get away with this." I squirmed in his grip, attempting to push out of his hold.

"Oh, pet, I already have." Holding my wrists with one hand, he pulled a syringe out of his jacket pocket with the other.

"Please, don't!" I cried, my chest rising and falling. I whimpered when the prick of the needle poked me in the side of the neck. My vision faded in and out, whatever the drug was, hitting me fast.

"You'll enjoy this. Just like your sister did." His hand wrapped around my throat. "But unfortunately, she's used up." He kissed my cheek. "Now it's your turn."

THIRTY-TWO

ANGEL

MY FIST landed against my victim, knocking him onto the mat.

Dale groaned, glaring up at me. "What the hell was that for?"

"Just training, my man," I told him, helping him to his feet.

He rubbed his jaw, moving it back and forth. "Fuck, that hurt."

I laughed. "Yeah, well, you're lucky I don't hit you harder."

"I'm guessing you know," he said, walking to a bench on the other side of the gym.

"Yeah." I followed him. "What the hell are you thinking?"

"I'm not ready to be a fucking father, Angel," he snapped. "I can't even take care of myself, let alone a baby."

"Well, it's a little late for that, isn't it?" I smacked him across the shoulder when he didn't answer. "Listen to me." I cupped his nape, leaning my forehead against his. "I love you, you know that, right?" It had taken me a long time to figure that out.

"'Bout time you say it," Dale muttered.

293

"Fuck off." I chuckled. "Listen, you have a good woman there, Dale. She needs a man at her side. Not some kid who fucks around because he feels he's too young to settle down. She needs you. And so does your baby."

"I'm scared. What if I screw up?"

"Every parent screws up. How do you think I feel? It's taken me a long time to say those words."

Dale punched me in the shoulder. "Yeah, fucker. I've been telling you it for years but," he sniffed, "you never said it back."

"You're a dick."

"Yup, but you love me."

I rolled my eyes. "You need to talk to Max before she shuts you out completely."

"I don't want to talk about this anymore," Dale said, his voice final.

"I'm not kidding." I crossed my arms under my chest, raising an eyebrow.

"Neither am I." His threat went unspoken.

If I pressed, he would kick my ass. Or try to.

He huffed. "Listen, I have some shit to work out in my head but I will...I'll try to talk to her."

I nodded. It was all I could ask for.

Dale nodded toward the entrance to the gym. "Stone must be excited to work out."

I followed his gaze, seeing Stone barreling full speed up the parking lot with a woman I didn't recognize, running beside him. "What's going on?" I asked, meeting him at the door.

"Shit!" he gasped, clutching his chest.

My heart thumped. The guy was in excellent shape so for him to be out of breath from running, depending on how long he actually ran for, was not the norm. "Where did you just come from?"

"Jay's tattoo shop," the woman answered. "I'm Creena. I work with her."

"Right." I had heard of her but never met her until now. "Angel."

"Good." Her brows furrowed. "We need to talk."

***

(Jay)

Everything from my head to my toes ached. My muscles were tight from the uncomfortable cement I was laying on. I didn't know where I was or even what day it was. The last thing I remembered was his disturbing words. A flutter of fear simmered in my soul, not for me but for Angel and my sisters. I knew what it was like to go day to day not knowing what happened to a person you loved. Where did they go? Did they run away? Did something happen? Were they mad at you? Did they hate you so much they couldn't even fathom telling you they were leaving in the first place? All of these unanswered questions had gone through my head for years after Violet left. A part of me knew she didn't leave because she wanted to and had no choice. But then another part, that dark part that nagged at me every damn day, tried convincing me she left because she wanted to. She didn't care about anyone else's feelings but her own. Or so I had been told. Whether it was true or not, I would never know.

I rolled onto my back, a clink sounding a few feet away. I moved my foot; the clinking sound happened again. A chain. Great. The darkness simmered some— my eyes getting used to the shadows surrounding me. Light streamed into the room through the small hole in the door. The musty scent of a dungeon surrounded me. If Violet volunteered for this, then there was more about my sister that I didn't know than I cared to admit.

Either way, we had to get out of there. If she was being held in the same place as I was, I would force her to leave with me. Whether she wanted to admit it or not, this place was dangerous. This lifestyle toxic. I had heard about girls being taken from their homes, sold into sex slavery and falling victim to the wrath of the men who bought them. They would pull wool over their eyes. Act charming. The girls would fall for it eventually, not knowing any better. It was Stockholm syndrome at its finest. I had also researched that the girls would become drug addicts, some dying because they couldn't get the sustenance to curb their addictions.

"Hello?" I called out, my throat parched, my lips dry and cracked. No answer. Of course there wouldn't be an answer. Why would there be one? I rose to my feet on shaky legs, seeing how far I could make it to the door before the chain stopped me. But when I reached the door and the chain still had some give, I questioned what the point of the chain actually was. So I wouldn't run? So I wouldn't have anywhere to go? I brushed my hands over the solid door until I found the doorknob and twisted it, surprised when it turned all the way in my hand. What the hell kind of dungeon was this?

I pulled open the door, peaking my head out into a dark hallway. Red carpet lined the floor, a slight lavender scent filling my nose. None of this made sense. It was too easy.

"Ah, I see you're awake." A large man came out of the shadows, the same man who took me from my apartment.

My eyes widened, and I stepped back, fumbling over the chain cuffed around my ankle. A strong hand reached out, catching my wrist before I fell on my ass.

"Let me help you with this." He leaned down, unlocking the cuff around my ankle. "There you go. Better?" He glanced up at me through dark eyelashes.

Lashes that reminded me of Angel. My chest tightened.

"Where am I?" I whispered, not liking how weak my voice sounded.

"I know you're confused," the man rose to his feet. "Come with me and I'll explain."

"Why should I trust you when you took me from my home?"

"I did just unlock the cuff." He waved a hand out in front of him. "Feel free to run. You can leave any time but you'll leave here with more questions than answers."

"You would let me go?"

His dark gaze held no hint of emotion. "Yes but I should warn you, I do enjoy the chase. Playing with my meal has always been a hobby of mine."

I swallowed hard. "I'll walk with you but on one condition." I nodded toward the gun at the small of his back. "You let me hold the gun."

He smirked, reaching behind him and handed me the pistol.

I held it in my left hand, keeping my finger on the trigger. A girl needed to be protected at all times. Having the gun at my side made me feel less stupid for agreeing to go with the man. Wherever that would be.

"Feel better?" he asked, a teasing lilt to his voice.

"I'm still waiting on the answers to my questions you have yet to provide," I rubbed my bare arm, my skin raising in goose bumps as a cold draft enveloped me.

"Here." The man took off his jacket and placed it on my shoulders. "Follow me." He started walking down the hall, not waiting for me. "I'm sorry for the room I put you in," he added a moment later.

I ran to catch up to him.

"I had to make it look real." He clasped his hands behind his back.

"Real?"

"People were watching. In my line of work, people are always watching." He shrugged. "It sucks but it's a living."

"I think I'm even more confused," I mumbled.

He laughed. "Your questions will be answered momentarily but I have to warn you, you won't like what you have to hear."

"Can't be any worse than the last couple of weeks I've had."

He nodded. "All right then." He pushed open a double set of doors at the end of the hallway. "Let's get those questions answered for you."

***

(Angel)

"Where the hell are we? Where the fuck is my woman? I swear I will kill anyone who has laid a finger on her. I don't care who they are." My voice was not my own as it bounced from wall to wall. I was enraged, fury bubbling in me like a volcano. It burst forth when I was brought to this mother fucking mansion that still didn't give me any damn answers. When Stone had told me that he couldn't find Jay and she had disappeared from her apartment, the world was ripped out from under me. The hand of evil wrapped around my soul, yanking it free from its safety. He mentioned the cat he saw on the floor and how it came in a package and I lost it. I demanded to know why he let her open it. How he could do that after everything she had been through. How she already got a package that he was there for. My fist had ended up connecting with his face at some point but I couldn't remember when that had happened. Coby had pulled me off of him but the guy just stood there, stock still, taking what I had to give him. I was impressed.

298

And now we waited at this mansion. King's Harlots and Vice-One. All together in a room and if any of us knew what was going on, they weren't talking.

"This is driving me insane," Max said, breaking the silence. "Where are we?"

"I feel like we're in one of those movies where people wake up and don't remember anything or how they got there," Brogan said, leaning her head back on the couch.

"Yeah, but we do remember how we got here." It was in a van. Much to my dismay, Stone had brought us to this place but he wouldn't give us any more information.

"Stone," Max bit out. "I swear to God if someone has hurt her—"

"No one has hurt her," Meeka said softly.

I learned that she was not one to talk, but hell if she didn't listen. There was something off about her. She didn't say much but she was always watching. When she looked at you, she saw into your soul, seeing your deepest secrets.

"How do you know that?" Max sat forward.

"Because," Meeka hesitated, "I'm the reason we're here."

All heads turned toward her, question after question flew at her but she raised her hand.

"I know you have questions, and I'll answer them when Jay arrives." Meeka looked toward the door, then down at her phone, before back at the door.

My heart sped up each time she frowned. "What gives, Meeka?"

"Tell them," Asher told her, moving to the spot beside her on the couch.

"Now? Shouldn't we wait?" Meeka asked, looking at everyone but at me.

"Ash," I bit out. "I order you to tell me what the hell is going on."

"Meeka and I have been working together undercover," Asher explained. "We've known each other since we were kids, went to school together all through our childhood, and again at the police academy. We've been best friends ever since. I joined the Navy and Meeka moved."

"Police academy?" Max cried, her eyes widening. "Meeka, you're a fucking cop?"

"No, I didn't pass," Meeka answered quickly. "I had to move, and when Ash said that he was moving here, I joined him."

I shook my head. "This doesn't make sense. I don't care that you two know each other. I just want my girl back."

"I care," Max and Brogan mumbled at the same time.

"I want to know why we are here," I repeated. "What is this place, and where is Jay?"

Asher brushed a hand over his buzzed head. "Jay was used as bait."

"What the actual fuck?" I shouted, charging for him. "You used my girlfriend as fucking bait? How could you even consider doing that?" Coby and Dale both had to hold me back for fear I would rip Asher's head off.

When Asher didn't budge and crossed his arms under his chest, it pissed me off even more.

"We had no choice," Meeka moved in front of him. "It would help us get her sister back. We couldn't say anything because we didn't want to break our cover."

"Why now? Why are you telling us this now? And where the hell is Violet, then?" All of those questions bounced in my mind and I couldn't control the urge to murder the man who had stood by my side for years. I realized then that I knew nothing about him. And that was why I didn't allow myself to love. Family or not. SEAL or not. "If Jay doesn't come out of this alive, you will be dead to me, and I will make it so you fear for your life every damn day for the rest of your time above ground."

THIRTY-THREE

—jay

"HOW IS this answering my questions?" I asked, stepping into a large, empty room.

"I know there are more questions burning in that beautiful brain of yours than what you are saying." The man flicked a switch on the wall, turning on light after light adorning a high ceiling.

"I don't know what you're talking about." I gasped when curtains lifted, revealing rooms lining the far wall. They were dark except for a small red light in the corner of each room. I didn't know what they were for but something told me not to ask. "I want to know where my sister is and what you've done with her."

"Oh, little girl. I haven't done anything with her. Everything that's happened, she's agreed to." He winked at me. "I'm sadistic, but I'm not a monster."

"Are you sure, because I happen to remember you bringing me here against my will."

"I had to keep you safe. They would have hurt you. They would have put lies in your head that would make you question everything you know."

"What are you talking about?" I asked, confusion coursing through me.

"Vice-One. Those men are going to get you killed." He shook his head, clapping his hands together. "And don't even get me started on King's Harlots. You really should learn to choose your friends better."

"I...I don't know what you're talking about." I watched him move around the room like a predator stalking its prey. "Please tell me where my sister is."

"Your sister." He laughed. "Your sister. Why, your sister isn't here, sweet girl."

"Excuse me? But you...I thought you had her." What the hell was going on? None of this made sense.

"I did. For a while." He feigned a yawn. "But I got bored so I got rid of her." He snapped his fingers and each of the rooms lit up, revealing makeshift bedrooms. "Wake up, wake up, my little pets."

I watched as girls sat up in each of the beds. "Oh my...oh God," bile rose to my throat. "What are you—? How could you?"

"These girls came of their own free will," the man said, his voice hardening. "They had no one. I found them on the street, picking their food out of garbage cans. Doing anything for their next meal. These girls had no one until they met me. Don't you understand that, Genevieve? I am their Master. Their father, of sorts."

"But you're holding them against their will," I cried, thrusting my hands out in front of me. "Have you asked them if they want to be here?"

"Of course. Look at the first room." The man slapped a hand against the wall, speaking into the intercom. "One, you want to be here, right?"

The girl in the room marked number one nodded quickly, her head bobbing up and down like a bobble head doll.

"These girls wouldn't be here if they weren't afraid." I spun on him. "You probably scared her into agreeing."

"I would never do such a thing," he said, his voice calm and even. He didn't show any emotion. He actually believed what he was saying.

"What do you do with these girls?" I didn't want to know but I needed to know who I was dealing with. I needed to know so if I did get out of there safely, I could report it to the authorities or the people in my life who would actually do something about it.

"Why, Genevieve, they're my pets, of course," the man said nonchalantly. "And I want you to help me take care of them."

"Me?" My head whipped around. "Why?"

"How about we leave that as a secret for now." He winked. "Now to answer your question. These girls need help. They need a motherly figure. Someone who can take care of them. They need a role model."

"So you're going to keep me here against my will then? How does any of this make sense? These girls should be in school. They should be with their families. They should be free to grow and live and have families of their own."

"No!" the man snapped, punching the wall closest to him. A bone snapped in his knuckle, forcing bile to my throat, but he didn't even flinch. He didn't even look at the blood seeping from the cut in his hand. "These girls are *mine!*" he screamed. "Do you understand me?"

"Why? What could you possibly want with them?"

"I want to protect them. Keep them safe from the horrors of the world." His voice became even again. "I am God to them."

This guy was sick in the head. "You can't honestly believe they would want this over freedom."

"They are free. They are free with me." To my horror, he brought his hand up to his mouth, licking the blood off of his knuckle. He didn't even wince when his tongue slid over the bone protruding from his skin.

"Then let them leave those rooms. Let them wander the house. Let them be free," I insisted.

"If you agree, I will let them do whatever they want within the walls of this house."

My heart raced. "What are you saying?"

He slapped the intercom again. "Five. Stand. When I say, pull the trigger."

My gaze landed on the small girl standing five rooms away. "What...no." He couldn't honestly...

"Now," he barked.

A shot sounded through the large room, the girl falling to the floor in a crumbled heap. A voice rang out, bouncing inside my head. It was mine. The horror of what I just saw ingrained itself into the recesses of my soul. It burned its way into my eyes. I screamed, lunging at the man.

He laughed, pushing me off of him with strength I wasn't expecting. "Now, now. Tsk, tsk, Genevieve. I was showing you what would happen if you don't agree."

"So you kill the girls? You're fucking—" A hard slap landed against my cheek, forcing my head to the side.

"Watch your mouth," He grabbed my cheeks, digging his fingers into my flesh. "I want you at my side but you will still answer to me and be respectful."

"Why?" Tears burned my eyes at the rough hold he had on my face.

"Because I've watched how you are with your sisters. With King's Harlots. And besides," he released me, pushing me away. "My last partner died."

"How?" I asked on a shaky breath.

"I got bored of her."

***

(Angel)

305

"You need to stop checking your phone," I told Meeka when she did it for the hundredth time.

"I just don't understand." She looked at Asher. "She should be here by now."

"Who should be here? Talk to me, to us, please," I pleaded, needing some answers before I ripped my hair out of my head.

"We had set it up so Jay would talk to the man who took Violet, thinking it would lead us right to him," Asher explained.

"I put a bug in Jay's phone a couple of days ago," Meeka added. "But she fell off the radar as soon as we got here. That's why I've been checking my phone. Angel, I am so sorry."

"So you went off a hunch in hopes that if you threw Jay into the pits of hell, her sister would be saved?" My blood boiled, my heart pounding hard in my ears.

"It wasn't a hunch, Boss," Asher insisted.

"You shut the fuck up," I shouted, pointing at him. "I can hit you but I can't hit her. If you know what's good for you, you'll keep your mouth closed and sit there wondering what I'm going to do to you if I don't get my woman back. Meeka, continue."

"Um…" Her mouth opened and closed. "I…" She cleared her throat. "We had word that one of the higher ups of the organization was in this town and that he lived here. But we don't know who he is."

"Then how the hell do you expect to find him?" Dale demanded, pacing back and forth behind me. "None of this makes sense at all. Angel, we need to just go in there and blow the motherfucker up."

"We don't even know where they are," Coby said, his voice calm but firm. "Angel."

I met his gaze, bracing myself. I needed to find Jay. My girlfriend. My fucking *Queen*.

"We'll find her, brother." Coby cupped my nape, leaning his forehead against mine. "No matter what, we will."

"This doesn't make sense," I told him.

"She was supposed to be here." Meeka rose to her feet, holding her phone up to her ear. "Shit." She threw her phone on the couch. "Something's wrong."

A heavy knock on the door sounded around the room, jarring my thoughts.

"It's about damn time." Meeka ran to the door.

We followed behind her, not caring in the least if we were blocking the entrance.

"Jay, where have…" Meeka's voice trailed off.

My gaze landed on a slender frail woman standing before me. She was blonde, doe-eyed and was vaguely familiar. "Violet?"

She nodded, wavering on her feet. "Where's my sister?"

"She's supposed to be with you," Meeka said, pulling her into a gentle hug.

"Where is she?" Max asked, giving her a warm embrace.

"I don't know." Violet shook her head. "She was never with me."

"What are you talking about?" Meeka demanded. "She was brought to you an hour ago."

"No, she wasn't. I've been here the whole time. I just woke up. I…" Violet started shaking. "I…oh, God. What if…"

"Boss," Coby called from behind me. He handed me his phone.

Unknown: Give this message to your brother. How much are you willing to pay for the love of your life?

***

307

What the fuck was going on? I couldn't understand why Violet was there and Jay wasn't. The whole point of this operation—according to Ash and Meeka—was to save Violet but Jay should have been right behind her. I was losing my ever-loving mind not knowing where she was or if she was okay. We had searched the house we were in, finding out that it had actually belonged to Violet.

"I didn't run away. I got mixed up with some bad people and had to get out. I didn't want my father and his club to go after everyone, knowing their lives would be put on the line if they did," Violet explained. "I should have called my sister but I had to wait for the heat to die down. Unfortunately, it took longer than I had hoped."

"How is this even possible? Where did you get the money?" I demanded even though it was none of my business, but when it came to Jay, I would make it so I found out everything I could.

"I…"

"And how the hell didn't we find any tax records?" My eyes snapped to Brogan's. "Wouldn't your step-brother be all over that? What the fuck is going on?"

"You're not paying your taxes, are you?" Max interjected. "Who are you involved with?"

Violet's gaze passed back and forth between all of us before finally landing on mine. "You love my sister."

"Of course I do. Now tell me why we haven't been able to find you."

"Like I said, I got involved with some horrible people. Everything was wiped clean so I could have a new life. I've been here under protection, waiting for the changes when you found me."

"This doesn't make sense. Jay thought she did something that made you want to leave," I told her.

"What?" Violet gasped, clapping a hand over her mouth. "Never. I could never do that. I stayed away to protect her. Oh God." Her eyes welled. "What have I done? And now she's missing." She sat forward, placing her head in her hands and rocked back and forth. "This can't be happening."

"You've been under protection and no one knew about it. You basically died on paper but your father and sister didn't know. That is what I'm not understanding." I noted the scars on her forearms, how skinny she was and how lifeless her eyes were. "What are you addicted to?"

Gasps from the girls sounded around me. If they had been paying attention, they would have caught it when she first let herself be known.

"I'm..." Violet sighed. "Everything. This is why I'm here. Besides being a safe house, it's rehab for me. I have a team of workers that show up twice a week. Jay's going to be so disappointed in me."

"She wants you safe. That's all she cares about. How did you two know she was here?" I asked Asher and Meeka. "Did you know she lived here?"

"We didn't know she lived here. I'm..." Meeka took a deep breath. "I've been working undercover with the FBI, trying to bring down this human trafficking ring. Through my resources I found Violet."

Fuck me. This shit was messed up, and it just kept getting worse. The more answers I got, the more questions I had. "Jay is going to rip your face off."

"I know." Meeka rubbed the back of her neck. "I don't care about that as long as she's safe. And now we have to move Violet."

"We'll worry about that later." I turned to Coby. "Anything?"

"No. But that doesn't mean we aren't being watched. If Violet's under protection, these people won't want us seeing them. Trust me," he winked. "I know."

Touché.

"Well, who knows where the fuck she is?" My phone dinged and I braced myself for the incoming text. After the last one from the unknown person, I lost my shit. I had never reacted that way toward anyone. Ever. Even in the line of work I did. Jay's safety brought out this Alpha in me that needed to protect her in an uncontrollable way. She could take care of herself, I knew that, but I needed to help. I needed to see that she was happy.

Unknown: How much do you want to see your girl?

Another ding came through, indicating a photo message.

The image was of Jay sitting on a bed, her knees to her chest, her head curled in her arms. A second image came through of her looking at the camera, giving it the finger. I barked a laugh, my throat burning. She was sassy no matter the situation. Fuck, I loved her and I would kill the person who took her from me.

A heavy hand clapped on the back of my neck, taking the phone from my trembling hands. "We'll get her back, boss," Coby whispered in my ear. "You know I've done some shit I'm not proud of. Angel, I'd do it all over again if it meant saving your woman."

I nodded, my tongue thickening. I didn't respond for fear that I would blubber like a baby.

My phone dinged again. This time my stomach sunk to the core of the earth. An image of Jay stared back at me with a man's hand wrapped around her throat. Her eyes wide, showing fear and anger. A possessive roar left me. I picked up the nearest thing I could find. My knuckles whitened as I gripped the lamp. I threw it until it landed against the wall, shattering to the floor in a million pieces.

THIRTY-FOUR

—jay

MY KNEE lifted, connecting with the man's balls.

He yelled, rolling off of me and cupped his crotch. "You fucking bitch! I'll kill you."

"You can't do to me what hasn't been done already!" I screamed, running for the gun.

When he started taking pictures of me, he told me he was sending them to Angel. Something broke inside me. I knew Angel would have snapped. He would have lost his mind. He would tear through anything to get to me. To get me back to him and to make sure I was safe.

"You can't hold me here. You can't keep killing these girls. You can't keep taking them out of their home or wherever you got them from. It's not right." I reached for the gun when a heavy body landed on top of me, pinning me to the ground.

"There is no way you will stop this. You're not strong enough. You can't focus on anything other than saving these girls. You didn't even know that your sister has been living under your nose this whole time."

"What are you talking about?" I wheezed when he covered me with his whole weight.

"I've followed you everywhere, Genevieve. You have a routine. And I've done my research." He straddled my waist. "Half an hour left and the next girl dies."

"No!" With all of my weight, I turned on my back, shoving him off of me. Holding the gun, I aimed it at his head and pulled the trigger. A click and nothing happened. *Fuck me.*

"You think I would actually give you a loaded gun. How stupid do you think I am?" The man pushed to his feet.

"Very stupid." I mustered up everything inside of me, focusing on what I had been taught by my father and uncles. Time seemed to slow down when I pulled my arm back and swung the butt of the gun against his head as hard as I could.

He let out a yelp and fell to my feet, gasping for breath.

I hit him again. And again. I hit him hard until blood splattered my clothes. My hands. My face. I could taste the warm metallic liquid on my tongue. I sneered and hit him again.

***

(Angel)

The moment my phone rang, I sent up a silent prayer for Jay and for me. "You listen you motherfucker. If I—"

"Angel?"

"Jay!" My heart raced at the sweet sound of her beautiful voice gracing my ear. "Baby."

All eyes landed on me, my friends, my family, surrounding me.

"Hi." She sniffed.

"Hi." I cleared my throat. "Where are you?"

"I don't…I don't know." Her voice started shaking, her words jumbling together.

"It's okay, baby. We'll find you." I snapped my fingers, motioning to the guys to get on the phone to start tracking where Jay was. "Stay on the phone with me. Tell me anything. What do you see?"

"It's a big mansion. Angel, there are girls here. Five that I've seen. Three… Three are alive. Oh God, he killed them, Angel. Because of me." She sobbed. "It's all my fault."

"None of this is your fault. You hear me? He'll pay for this. Do you know who he is?" I asked, channeling my military background for fear I would lose it.

"No. I knocked him out. I don't…I don't know if he's alive, Angel."

"Don't worry about that," I told her. "Try and find something with the address on it."

"Okay. I'm looking."

I could hear her shuffling around, a heavy clinking filling the earpiece. "What are you doing?"

"He had me chained. I'm cuffing him to the bed just in case."

"That's my girl," I said, praise puffing out my chest.

"We got her," Asher said, holding up his phone.

"Jay, we know where you are," I shoved to my feet. "We're calling the police, and we're on our way. Stay on the phone with me, baby."

"Oh God. Angel, he's awake. *Shit*." The phone disconnected.

I heard a scream, and then I realized it was coming from me.

***

(Jay)

313

"You won't get away with this," I wheezed, my back arching off the floor.

The man stood over me, his boot pressing into my chest, forcing me against the ground.

"You thought you could get rid of me? I don't break that easy, little girl," he snarled, spittle flying out of his mouth. Blood had rolled down the side of his face from where I had hit him. If I had hit him harder... If none of this had happened.

"Maybe not but you will die at the hands of someone more powerful than you." It might not have been me but once Angel got there, he would destroy the fucker.

"Ha!" he scoffed, throwing his head back. "I've been doing this for years and have never been caught. Now since you are here and decided to use my phone, all of the girls will die and so will you. I will make you suffer. I will make it so you never see the light of day again. You will wish you were dead. Die on me and I'll bring you back to life to make you suffer all over again."

"This isn't a paranormal show," I told him, attempting to push his foot off of my chest.

"No, but I have medical training, pet. Or should I say...*slave*." He released me but not before he fisted my hair, pulling me roughly to my feet.

"How about we go say goodbye to our friends? I will make you pay for this."

"They're little girls you are holding captive in your home and who knows what else you do with them."

He pushed me. "I don't do anything with them. I prepare them for the next part of their life. I make them strong, viable women who men would love to have with them. They learn everything there is to know about a man and his desires."

"So you turn them into sex slaves? Little girls? You force them. Do you drug them? Is that how you get them to stay here? Is that how you get them to not put up a fight? Because they're practically in a coma?" I screamed, charging for him.

He laughed, wrapping his arms around my waist and threw me over his shoulder. "You sure are a feisty one. I wish I could keep you."

Sirens sounded outside. They were still a ways away but I could hear them. Music to my fucking ears.

The man didn't notice. "We would do so well together."

"How many girls have you sold?" I asked, closing my eyes.

"The good ones," he smacked my ass, rubbing the spot soon after.

Bile rose to my throat at the feel of his hands on me. "What-what did you do with the other girls?"

"We got rid of them of course," he said it like he was talking about the weather.

"We?"

"Oh, Genevieve. You think I'm the one running this show? That's kind of you but not true at all. You can't even begin to understand how many people work in this organization. How many levels you have to go through to reach the top." He pulled me off of him and grabbed my wrists, tying a thin strap of leather around them until my skin burned.

I let out a yelp when I was forced onto my back.

He did the same to my ankles before pulling me upright and hooked me to a cross. His hand grazed down the center of my body. "You make a man want to sin." His fingers pushed beneath the hem of my shirt, sliding up my stomach before reaching my breasts. "Fuck, your tits are perfect and…" He gave my nipple a sharp twist. "Pierced."

I cried out, my eyes welling at the sharp bite of pain. "Please. Let me go. Let us go." I could feel eyes on me. I looked across the room, my gaze landing on the only rooms occupied by girls now.

No emotion showed on their face but their eyes told all. There was still some life behind them as they watched the man fondle me. They were probably thankful that it wasn't them he was touching. They were girls. Teenagers. The man may have thought he was treating them well, giving them what he thought they deserved. Maybe they were living on the streets. Maybe they had nowhere to go but being held captive was not a better life for them. Being trained into what these men or even women wanted was not safe when most of these girls were underage.

The sirens became louder, interrupting my thoughts.

"What the hell?" the man sneered, glaring at me. "You called the fucking police?"

"No," I spat. "I called my fucking boyfriend."

The man let out a yell, his fist landing against my jaw.

Hot pain shot up the side of my face, my lip splitting at the sudden contact. My tongue peaked out, licking the metallic taste and laughed. "They're coming for you, you bastard. I hope you rot in jail."

"Doesn't matter where the fuck I am, little girl, there will always be someone a step ahead of you. These girls?" he waved at the rooms in front of us. "They will be found by the men who want them."

"Not if I have anything to do with it," I growled, struggling in my binds.

"You think so, do you?" He gripped my throat, leaning his face into mine. "We are always watching. You won't end this organization."

"Why are you doing this? These girls have done nothing to deserve this. You're fucked in the head if you think you're going to get away with this." My chest heaved. The longer I kept him talking, the safer the girls were. He knew he was caught but he didn't try to run. Whatever the reason for that was, I didn't know.

"We're doing this because we can. It's exciting knowing you can have something you're not allowed."

"That doesn't even make sense."

"It will when you realize that there is nothing you can do. These girls want this life. Some are even given to us as long as we pay their families." He smirked. "Desperate times. Some of these girls come from families so poor, they'll do anything to get a buck."

"That's…" I would be naïve to think it wasn't true. I watched the news. I read the paper. I knew of these older men who traveled to places to get a piece of these kids when back home they wouldn't be allowed. It was disgusting. The world was evil but it would be over my dead body before I let this shit continue in my small town. I may be one person but I would do everything I could.

"Every person has a dominant bone in their body whether they care to admit it or not. Just think of what you can do to a person far less superior than you."

"You're sick."

"Oh no, little girl, I am completely healthy and with it. My mind has never been so clear." His eyes roamed down the length of my body. "Now let's give that man of yours something to remember me by."

"No," I pleaded, my heart pumping hard and fast. "Please."

His hands moved over my torso, my ass, the flesh of my skin. His fingers kneaded, bruising every part they touched.

I whimpered, tears welling in my eyes. "Stop," I whispered.

A loud bang sounded through the room but the fear racing through my body kept my gaze locked on the girls across the room from me.

"Hands in the air!" someone shouted.

The man grabbed my jaw, forcing me to look at him. "I will haunt your fucking dreams." He kissed me hard on the mouth. "Remember that every time you go

317

to sleep." He lifted a gun to his head and pulled the trigger.

A scream sounded around me, bouncing off the walls. I could taste his blood, the remains of what was left of him.

He shot himself.

In front of me.

And he was right.

I would never get the image out of my head. The image of him taking his own life, of him crumpling to the floor at my feet. I tried to get away but my binds held me. How dare he? How dare he have the control and take what rightfully belonged to these girls? These victims who never had a chance.

"Ma'am. Miss. Are you all right?"

Someone was talking to me. Voices sounded in my head. My vision faded in and out. I would never get over this. And it was what he wanted. Control. It was always about that, wasn't it?

"Ma'am, we're going to get you down from there now." A soft, feminine voice whispered across my skin but I couldn't focus. I couldn't understand if I was dreaming or if this was real. Where was I? This had to be some fucked-up nightmare.

My body felt heavy until I was lifted into the air and placed on a soft bed.

"You're fine, Miss. Everything will be all right."

I shook my head. "Please." Nothing would ever be all right. "The girls."

"They're fine." A smiling face appeared in front of my field of vision. "You're fine."

"Max," I whispered, my throat burning.

"All five girls have been reported alive and well," she continued, holding my hand tight in hers.

"Five? No. Three." I shook my head. "Three survived."

"No," she frowned. "They're all alive, Jay. Every girl in this room is. You saved them."

Did I? Did I really? I was confused, my mind throwing image after image of the girls shooting themselves. Of the man shooting himself. I couldn't take it. I needed to get them out. I needed to get away from the onslaught of my nightmares.

"Jay?" Max's brows furrowed. "They're fine. I promise you."

Sobs wracked my shoulders, my body breaking with the weight of the mind fuck I had been thrown in.

THIRTY- FIVE

—jay

"WHERE THE *fuck* is my woman? Don't touch me. If you don't bring me to her, I will destroy this fucking hospital until you tell me where she is."

I groaned, the yelling pounding its way into my head. "Angel," I whispered, bringing my hand up to the bridge of my nose. A sharp pain shot into my skull.

"You're awake," a woman said, lifting my eyelids and shining a light into both.

"Where the hell is she?" the yelling continued.

"Is he yours?" the nurse asked, raising an eyebrow.

I nodded but even that hurt. God, this sucked.

"She's in here, Sir," the nurse called out. "I'll give you a moment but you need to take it easy."

I thanked her and waited.

"Jay."

My gaze locked with Angel's. He paused in the doorway, his eyes roaming down the length of me. My mind went back in time to when he was in the hospital and I left him. He had called out for me and I ignored him. I ran away. I was scared, terrified even at the feelings coursing through me. I loved him. I had known that but for some reason that love made me believe that I had to depend on him. That I couldn't live without him. That he couldn't live without me. It wasn't true. None of it was true. We lived for each other. We would survive together.

"Angel," I sobbed, reaching out to him.

His eyes shone and before I knew it, he charged at me. Wrapping his arms around me, he held me against him as tight as possible without hurting me. His pushed his face into the crook of my neck, his body shaking. "I should have protected you," he said, his voice thick. "I should have been there to stop him. I should have known."

"Stop." I pulled him against me, holding onto him for dear life. He was my lifeline, the reason I survived. "You couldn't have known. There was no way to know, baby."

"Fuck, Jay," he continued shaking but his shoulders slumped with relief. "What he did…"

"Don't," I pleaded, the tears streaming down my face, soaking into his hoodie. "Just hold me. Make me forget everything."

"I thought I lost you. I just found you and I thought I lost you. I love you. So fucking much. I promise to protect you. I won't take this for granted ever again."

"Angel." I leaned back, cupping his face. "Stop. You have no reason to feel guilty. It wasn't your fault."

"I should have been there with you!" he snapped, attempting to shove his head out of my grip but I held on. "I should have," he said, his voice softer. His eyes were bright but they showed a darkness I never wanted him to feel again. He had been alone for so many years. Never knowing what true love was. I would never allow him to feel that emptiness again.

"You can't protect me all of the time, Angel."

He cupped my hand that was against his cheek and kissed my wrist. "Maybe not, but I can damn well try."

"How? What are you going to do that's different?"

J.M. WALKER

"Retire."

***
(Angel)

The word left my mouth automatically. I had been thinking about it for a while but Jay being taken from me confirmed my decision. I almost lost her. I took life for granted even in my job. I went in knowing I might not make it but every time I made it home, that fear lessened. It shouldn't be that way. Yes, I loved my job but I realized that I loved Jay more. I was ready to settle down. To have a wife. To start a family. I was ready to be home for longer than a couple days at a time.

"You want to retire?" Jay asked, keeping her hands on my face.

"Yes. Sooner than later preferably." I kissed her mouth, holding back a growl of possessive need when my lips touched the split in her lip. "I'm ready to settle down. To start a family. To spend time with my dog. To read a book." I was babbling but I didn't fucking care. Jay needed to know how I felt. She needed to know that I wanted to spend the rest of my life with her. To start a family with her if it was what she wanted. If she didn't want kids, it wouldn't matter as long as I was with her.

"I like books," she smiled, tears rolling down her cheeks.

"I like books too." I kissed her again. "What do you say, Jay?"

"About what?"

"Will you settle down with me?" I cupped her chin, staring intently into her eyes.

"Are you proposing to me?" she breathed, gripping my shirt tight in her hands.

322

"Unofficially, yes. I'll get you a ring and do it better next—"

"No!" she cried, shaking her head. "I mean, yes. I want to settle down with you, but no, I don't want another proposal."

"You don't?" I raised an eyebrow.

"No!" She threw her arms around my neck. "This is perfect."

Holding her in my arms, I hugged her tight, pouring everything I felt into that touch. Every fiber of my being vibrated with love for this woman. This woman I almost lost at the hands of a sadistic fuck. Questions went unanswered but I knew the answer to this one: I loved her and she loved me.

"Excuse me?" a voice came from the doorway.

A police officer and two men dressed in suits stood a few feet away from us.

"Sorry to interrupt," the officer said. "I'm Officer Peck and this is Agent James and Agent Cole." The officer looked to Jay. "How are you feeling?"

She shrugged, glancing up at me. "I was held captive for God knows how long, I saw two girls and a man blow their brains out in front of me. Other than that, I'm fucking peachy." Although the sass left her mouth, Jay's eyes welled. It would take a while for her to get those images out of her head.

"We understand." The officer smiled, his eyes softening. "Now—"

"Do you know the man who held you captive?" Agent Cole asked, stepping forward.

"No. Should I?" Jay kept my hand tight in hers.

"How about you?" the agent asked me. "Do you know this man?" He pulled a picture out of a photo and placed it on the bed.

The blood drained from my face, spots dancing in my vision. "Wha...this..." It wasn't possible. Vega's dark eyes stared up at me from the black and white photograph.

J.M. WALKER

"That's the man," Jay confirmed, shaking beside me. "He wouldn't tell me his name."

"Colonel Eric Vega," I answered, dropping to the chair behind me.

"What?" Jay cried. "How do you know him?"

"He… He's my boss."

THIRTY– SIX

—jay

SOMETIMES LIFE throws things at you, expecting you to be able to deal with it. It thinks you're strong enough to handle the battles, the war raging inside of your head. The battle I won was the walls I had to break down in order to give my heart to Angel.

"How could this happen?" I asked, utterly horrified at what I was hearing.

"Eric Vega had apparently been in the sex slave industry for years," Agent Cole explained. "Although he was a decorated member of the military, he had a dark craving we hadn't been able to pinpoint until now. Mr. Rodriguez, we understand that you were friends with him, but we have to tell you he wasn't the man you thought you knew. We are sorry you had to find out this way."

"Call the rest of my squad in here," Angel demanded, his voice rough.

"Sir, we understand—"

"Call them in here," Angel ordered. "I need my brothers, and they need to hear this as well."

Agent Cole left the room and came back a moment later with the rest of Vice-One, my girls following behind them.

325

Max rushed to my side, Brogan and Meeka right behind her. To my surprise, Creena Chan stuck her head around the corner.

"Mind if I come give you a hug?" she asked me.

I nodded my head.

"Creena and Stone came to me when they realized you were missing," Angel told me.

"Thank you." I hugged her.

"I am so sorry," she sniffed. "I should have been with you."

"No," I snapped. "Stop this, all of you, before anymore of you say anything. None of this is your fault. You hear me?"

Grunts. Nods. Even some curses. I was sick of them blaming themselves. If anyone was going to be blamed, it would be me.

"Tell them," Angel told the agents, probably needing to hear it again for fear that it wasn't actually true and that it was some sick joke.

"Eric Vega was the one to hold Genevieve captive," Agent James said.

"What the actual fuck?"

"You're joking, right? This is some sick game that you want us to fall for."

"This can't be happening."

Vice-One lost their shit, rightfully so, at the unexpected news of what their boss did behind closed doors. If Angel's brothers were anything like him, I knew they were blaming themselves. It wasn't their fault. None of it was.

"We had been watching him for a while," Agent Peck told them. "Genevieve is lucky to be alive."

I shook my head. "Those girls, they are the lucky ones."

"Jay," Angel tugged my hand. "Baby, you saved them. All of them."

"I didn't. Two girls shot themselves." My body shook, trembling with the terrible images of the girls crumpling to the floor.

"They didn't shoot themselves," Agent Cole said. "It was a sick joke. It was a setup to make you think they did, but they didn't. They're safe. Because of you."

"I don't understand," I whispered.

"The girls told us that Vega ordered them to do it. He wanted to make you think you couldn't go on without saving the girls. Every door and window was unlocked but yet you chose to stay." Peck pulled a tablet out of the inside pocket of his suit jacket. "He was fucking with your head, trying to make you believe that you had to stay in order to save them." The display turned on, revealing five girls.

My eyes widened, my throat burning.

"We just wanted to thank you," the one girl said. The one I saw take her life in front of me. "I'm sorry for what we had to put you through."

"We had no choice," another girl said. "But that's not an excuse. We hope we can meet someday. We wouldn't be alive if it weren't for you and we'll never forget it."

All of the girls waved into the camera and blew kisses before the screen shut off.

"Can I see them?" I asked through my tears.

"Not right now," Peck said gently. "They're under protection until we can dig into this further and get a control on things."

I nodded, understanding their reasoning. The girls. They were alive and well. They had been forced to live somewhere else, again, but at least this time they were safe. They had each other.

"Ash, did you know Vega was in on this shit?" Dale asked him. "Did you, Meeka?"

They both shook their heads.

327

"We knew it was someone close. Someone in this town but we couldn't figure out who. These people are good. They know what they're doing and won't let you know who they are until they want you to or until it's too late," Meeka said, her light-blue eyes holding a confidence I had never seen before.

"What's going on?" I asked, sitting up in the bed. "How would Asher and Meeka know anything about this?"

"Asher and Meeka have known each other for years it seems," he said, glaring at his brother before turning back to me. "They're undercover."

"Excuse me?" My eyes widened, not understanding what I was hearing. Angel went on to explain that Asher and Meeka had been in the police academy together and that she was now undercover with the FBI. They had also known each other since they were kids.

"I was right," I said, keeping my gaze locked with hers. "You were hiding something from me. From all of us. Your sisters."

"I couldn't tell you," she said, holding my stare.

"Why are you telling me now? Isn't your cover blown? This isn't making sense." I shook my head, a slight pain burning up the back of my neck.

"Maybe I can explain."

My eyes snapped to the woman standing in the doorway. A person I hadn't seen in years. A reflection of myself stared back at me. An image I never thought I'd see again. "Violet."

THIRTY-SEVEN

—jay

EVERYTHING HAPPENED for a reason. Life. Death. So on and so forth. Blah, blah, blah. But seeing my sister standing in front of me, her lips moving but no sound coming out, I couldn't process what I was hearing. I just kept hearing, *"I had to"*, over and over again. She had to. To protect me. To protect herself. She got caught up with the wrong people. She had to leave. She could have called. She could have fucking called. Or written a letter. I would have known it was her. I would have been able to live with myself, knowing she hadn't left because of me. "You could have called," I whispered.

Everyone had filed out of the room but not before Meeka apologized to me for all of the secrets. I hugged her back because I knew it was the right thing to do and I didn't want to make a scene in front of everyone—but I was pissed. Beyond mad. Fury and betrayal battled each other inside of me. She had something to do with Violet's disappearance but I didn't know what.

"How, Jay?" she asked, sitting on the edge of my bed and reached for my hand. A bandage had been wrapped around the hand with the missing finger. Bile rose to my throat as memories surfaced of the package I had received.

"How?" I snatched my hand away. "By picking up the damn phone. I would have been fine with a letter."

"None of that was possible." She folded and unfolded her hands in her lap. "You can't imagine what I went through not being able to contact you."

"You?" I screamed. "What *you* went through? I thought you left because of me, Vi. I was told over and over how you left because you found a man or you ran off because you couldn't stand our home. People even told me you died."

Tears streamed down her face. "I'm sorry. It was selfish of me. I know that now. I should have told you. I should have come to you first. I know. God, I know."

"I could have helped you. We could have disappeared together." That time I was the one to reach for her hand.

She slid her fingers between mine, cupping our joined hands with the other. "I couldn't do that to you."

"Why the hell not? You could have saved me from Tyler."

Her eyes snapped to mine. "I...oh God."

"Yeah, exactly," I mumbled.

"But you were able to get away from him. You're in love."

"Don't change the subject." I pulled from her grip and removed the covers. My gaze slid to my legs. I gasped, stifling a sob. Bruises and scratches marred my pale skin.

A growl sounded from the doorway.

My gaze snapped up, seeing Angel's large frame filling the small space. "I'm fine."

"Are you? Because I sure as hell am not, knowing another man laid his hands on your body. That another man hurt you. That he tried to fucking break you." Angel shook, his hands clenching into fists at his sides.

"I should go," Violet mumbled.

"No," I told her. "I haven't seen you in years. You are not leaving." I looked back at Angel. "She's not leaving."

"That's fine," he took a step forward. "But neither am I."

I sighed, patting the spot beside me. I loved him in all of his Alpha glory and I understood where he was coming from. Having a man who was possessive of me was not the norm. Tyler never gave a shit about who touched me. He found it hilarious, the bastard.

Angel sat on the bed, pulling me forward and wrapping his arms around me.

"I assume you two have met each other already," I mumbled.

***

(Angel)

I had to fight back the urge to run my hands over Jay's body where Vega had touched her. Where he bruised and marked her. Bile had risen in my throat, taking up permanent residence from the moment his name had left the Agent's mouth. How the man I had respected for years—the person I called my friend—had done all of this, I would never understand. I wasn't even sure I wanted to understand. He was a sick bastard, forcing Jay to watch him kill himself in front of her. She was strong, hiding within herself. She would break and I would be there to pick up the pieces.

The possessive hold I had on her, and her hand cupping my inner thigh, gave me a peace I hadn't felt since she was taken out of her home almost three days ago.

Jay and Violet talked and talked. Catching up, crying, laughing, revealing parts of their lives they hadn't shared with each other in years. Although Jay joked and cried along with her sister, her tone was clipped. Her heart was hard to get a piece of and now that her sister had hurt her, Jay wouldn't let her back in for a while. I understood why Violet had stayed away, wanting to protect her family, but making Jay go through that pain of not knowing bordered on unforgivable.

They may have been twins but once I saw them both together, Jay was more beautiful. Call me biased and maybe it was the fact that Violet had led a harder life, but Jay was vibrant. Where Violet was thin and frail, Jay's eyes held a strength stretched beyond imagination. A hint of something hid behind them. The person who cracked through that wall would never be the same on the other side.

"You can stay at my place," Jay told her between visits from the nurse.

"I can't do that," Violet shook her head. "It's your home."

"After everything… I don't know if I can go back." Jay gripped my thigh. "I-I need time away."

"I understand that but what about your tattoo shop?" Violet asked. "And besides, I don't know when I can pay you back."

"You're my sister. I would never ask you to pay me back. You can be my receptionist if you want to help but you don't have to. I need someone to live in the apartment anyway," Jay insisted. "Do you mind having a roomie?" she asked me.

"Not at all." I kissed her forehead, my heart swelling with the fact that something good was able to come out of this shit. We both knew it would be more than her being my roommate. She would live with me and I would make it so she never wanted to leave.

"What do you say, Violet?" Jay asked her sister. "You owe me this much."

"I…okay." She nodded. "I just pray you can find it in your heart to forgive me someday." She rose to her feet and gave Jay a hug before leaving the room.

"Do you think you can?" I asked Jay once we were alone. "I want to. But right now I'm so pissed at her, Angel. Is that wrong of me?"

"No," I told her, my voice firm.

She sighed. "How are you doing?"

I scoffed. "I found out my boss kidnapped my girlfriend and blew his head off in front of her. I'm fucking great." And this was why I never trusted anyone. Why I had refused to love for so long. "I wish I would have known."

"We're not doing this again, Angel. There was no way you could have known. Promise me you'll find a way to see that."

I hugged her against me, whispering I would and how much I loved her. How much I needed her and how much I had to make her my wife.

***

(Jay)

To say I wasn't pissed at my sister would be the biggest lie I had ever told. She hurt me. She made me feel like I did something where she couldn't come to me. We were sisters. Twins. We lived and breathed the other. I thought she knew more about me than anyone but I soon learned that I was wrong. Inviting her to live in my apartment was so I could keep her close and there was also no way I could go back. I knew Angel would never argue with me living with him. It appeased his inner Alpha to keep his woman safe and I was happy about that. I embraced his possessive hold on my body and my heart. I needed him to erase these nightmares that would no doubt threaten to destroy me. That would consume all of the light in my life.

Vice-One had been wracked to the core when they learned about their boss and his desires. His evil, sadistic ways. I was shocked that the man was who the agents said he was. It just proved you could never judge a book by their cover, no matter who they were.

After an hour or so, I met with the doctor. She was young, no more than a couple years older than I.

"How are you feeling?" she asked, putting my chart at the foot of the bed.

"I…"

"Be honest." He trailed a finger down the length of my jaw.

"I feel okay. A little stiff but…I feel better knowing those girls are okay," I told the doctor.

She nodded. "It's an amazing thing you did for them."

"I don't know what I did but I remember thinking that I couldn't let any more of them die. I had to know they were safe, that they would make it through even if I couldn't." I shrugged. "But I-I can't get him out of my mind."

"I understand." She stood up and handed me a card. "I want you to see a counselor. At least once," she added when I shook my head. "Even if you only see them the one time, you need to talk to someone."

"She's right, princess," Angel pressed. "You know you can always talk to me but there are things that even I can't help you with. An unbiased opinion might be better for you. Trust me. We can go together."

"You would do that for me?" I asked, knowing he had his own personal demons to work through. Being a Navy SEAL for so many years weighed on him. I could see the aging behind his eyes, the darkness he struggled with every day.

"Of course I would."

"All right," I told the doctor. "We'll make an appointment."

"Good." She smiled. "Now, I do need to tell you that we have to do a rape kit. Before you jump to conclusions, we do it in most cases as a precaution but because you were held captive by a male, we have to test to make sure you weren't a victim of abuse."

"Fuck," Angel mumbled under his breath.

"Okay," I agreed. I just wanted this shit over with.

The doctor performed the test with Angel standing by my side. There was no way I would allow him to leave. I needed all the strength I could get.

"Doctor?"

"You're fine, Genevieve." She patted my knee. "You weren't violated and you are healthy minus the bruises and scratches." Her gaze darkened. "Did you tell the Feds about the marks on your body?"

"Yes," I answered. "Can I please go home now?"

"Of course. I can't see why not." The doctor went to stand but hesitated. "I need to thank you."

"For what?" My heart started racing at the intensity in her gaze.

"For saving those girls. The world needs more women like you. Your strength and courage is inspiring and if you ever have daughters of your own, I hope you pass on those qualities."

My mouth fell open, my cheeks heating at the compliment.

Angel chuckled, pinching my chin. "She says thank you."

The doctor nodded, gave my hand a gentle tap, and left the room.

"She's right." Angel kissed my cheek.

I didn't do anything but I appreciated the acknowledgment. While Angel helped me get dressed, I kept thinking about how I needed to get out of the hospital and into his arms. I wanted to lay in his backyard, stare up at the stars, and have Buck between us. I didn't want to be afraid anymore, going through life thinking someone could be following me.

"Let's get you out of here, princess." Angel slid his fingers between mine, kissing the back of my knuckles.

"Take me to your home, baby,"

He captured my mouth in a tender kiss. "Our home."

My heart swelled. "Our home."

EPILOGUE

—jay

IT HAD been a month since I was taken. Every night for the past thirty-one days, I dreamt of him. Eric Vega. His face slid into my mind. Bloody and oozing, pieces of brain matter coating me. Every night I would wake up screaming, being comforted by Angel. When I didn't sleep, neither did he. Buck would lay at my side, sandwiching me between him and Angel. I had learned that when I stirred from my dark dreams, Buck would shove his head into the crook of my neck, wrapping his arm around me. Once he did that, I would fall back asleep.

"He loves you just like I do," Angel told me one night when we were in the back yard.

"And I love him," I brushed my hand through Buck's thick fur, smiling when he let out a heavy sigh. "What are we doing, Angel?"

"We are enjoying the here and now. We're taking one day at a time and not worrying about the future." He kissed me, his lips soft like the wings of a butterfly. "We are getting to know each other and taking this one step further each and every day."

We had talked about marriage when he unofficially proposed.

I was doing it. I was living my life and moving on.

Violet and I weren't the same. She apologized daily and I kept telling her that I knew she was sorry but a part of me didn't believe her. I couldn't just accept that she left to protect us. Call me selfish but if *I*

337

had to leave, I would tell her. I would feel the need to for fear that it would change our relationship. And it did. It would never be the same.

My father had lost his shit when she revealed herself to him. And finding out that she was addicted to drugs didn't help. After things had settled down, he cried, holding her close to him. It was a heartbreaking family moment but my dad and I were cautious. The fear of her leaving again would continue to poke at our minds.

Violet confessed to me her dark desires and how it was more than drugs she was addicted to. Sex. All kinds. And lots of it.

"I promised you I would help you through this," Angel said, interrupting my thoughts. "We will get through this together."

"But it just started, Angel. What if there are more people like Vega? What if Violet and I are never the same because she was gone for so many years?" My chest tightened. "What if I can't forgive her?"

"It takes time, Jay. You have been through a lot. You can't expect everything to go back to the way it was in a day."

"I don't want it to go back," I admitted. "I am stronger because of everything. Since meeting you. Since falling in love…with you. I am so sorry for what Vega did. I know Vice-One is having a hard time dealing with it." His jaw clenched when those words left my mouth but I continued, knowing he needed to hear what I had to say. "No matter what, you guys will get through this just like we will get through what happened to me. Those girls are safe. We brought down one person. We'll bring down the rest together."

"Not at your fucking expense again, though," he growled through clenched teeth.

"Of course not." I shivered. "I don't want to go through that again. I don't want to lose a piece of myself. I can't. I can't fall into that darkness."

"You won't. You're stronger than that," he reassured me. "Remember what your sisters told you?"

I sighed, curling onto my side.

"They told you they are proud of you." He brushed the hair off my nape, kissing my neck. "They said if anyone could make it through hell and back, it would be you." Another kiss. "You inspire them and you can see it every time you're around them. I know you and Meeka aren't talking right now."

"Well, she did that herself," I mumbled.

"Jay, how do you think I feel? Asher, my brother, a man I have known for years, suddenly tells me he's best friends with your girl and knew about your sister. I felt betrayed. I still feel it and yeah I punched Stone out, but I still love them. And *you* still love your sisters."

"I do." They were my life.

"We'll get through this, through whatever life throws at us; we'll continue getting through it together."

"I like the sound of that." I kissed him on the mouth, brushing my lips over his before I delved deeper. Into his mouth. Into his soul. We kissed, molding together as one.

This was how my life would be now. President of King's Harlots. Girlfriend to the squad leader of Vice-One. Scared but happy.

Angel and I had worked hard to be where we were now and we were one step closer to bringing these bastards down who threatened to destroy the innocence of these girls. We would make them suffer for the lives they took. And we would do it together.

Both of our worlds crashed together.

MC and Military.

From the first time he kissed me, I knew. I fell hard and fast. I never wanted to admit it, but even in the beginning, he dug his way into my soul and I was glad he stayed.

He was the ultimate desire—the sustenance to my cravings and the grit to my smooth.
He was my King.
And I was his Queen.

THE END

Be sure to add book two to your TBR list!
Stain (King's Harlots, #2)

Goodreads:
https://www.goodreads.com/book/show/28793866-stain

ABOUT

J.M. Walker is an Amazon bestselling author who loves all things books, pigs and lip gloss. She is happily married to the man who inspires all of her Heroes and continues to make her weak in the knees every single day.

"Above all, be the HEROINE of your own life..." ~ Nora Ephron

Facebook:
https://www.facebook.com/jm.walker.author

Twitter: https://twitter.com/jmwlkr

Website:
http://www.aboutjmwalker.com

CPSIA information can be obtained
at www.ICGtesting.com
Printed in the USA
LVOW11s0045110717
540827LV00002BB/357/P